The Aberhart Summer **reviewed . . .**

"By far the best piece of fiction that captures the period. . . ."
—*Bible Bill: A Biography of William Aberhart*

"By showing a community of Canadians at their best and worst, Powe has not only written a fine entertainment but he has revealed some of the complex subterranean forces that shape a common destiny."
—*Maclean's Magazine*

"The writing of Bruce Allen Powe is like the Great Depression itself: spare, lean and covered with a textured grit that owes much to the winds of imagination."
—*The Toronto Star*

"A compelling literary portrait of the people of the times."
—*Legacy Magazine*

The Ice Eaters **reviewed . . .**

"A novel of delicately phrased contrasts. . . . It is well worth your attention."
—*Calgary Herald*

"The novel . . . is thoroughly absorbing. The mythical dimensions are embodied in strong believable characters. The startling denouement convinces absolutely."
—*The Toronto Star*

GW00685752

ALDERSHOT
1945

ALDER SHOT 1945
The Novel

Bruce Allen Powe

NEWEST PRESS

Library and Archives Canada Cataloguing in Publication
Powe, Bruce, 1925-
Aldershot : the novel / Bruce Allen Powe.

ISBN 1-896300-77-4

I. Title.

PS8581.O88A74 2004   C813'.54   C2004-903603-3

Board editor: Harry Vandervlist
Cover and interior design: Ruth Linka
Cover image: T. R. MacDonald "Night Travellers" AN19710261-4361, Beaverbrook Collection of War Art, Canadian War Museum (CWM)
Author photograph: Rick Zolkower
The epigraph is quoted from *My Father's Son, Memories of War and Peace* by Farley Mowat, Key Porter Books, Toronto, 1992.

NeWest Press acknowledges the support of the Canada Council for the Arts and the Alberta Foundation for the Arts, and the Edmonton Arts Council for our publishing program. We also acknowledge the financial support of the Government of Canada through the Book Publishing Industry Development Program (BPIDP) for our activities.

NeWest Press
201–8540–109 Street
Edmonton, Alberta T6G 1E6
(780) 432-9427
www.newestpress.com

1 2 3 4 5 07 06 05 04

NeWest Press is committed to protecting the environment and to the responsible use of natural resources. This book is printed on 100% post-consumer recycled and ancient-forest-friendly paper. For more information please visit www.oldgrowthfree.com.

PRINTED AND BOUND IN CANADA

This one is for Katie,
T.C. and Jeremy

Table of Contents

"Nobody, in blunter terms, in my outfit is going to get rich off the black market. This may make us seem somewhat puritanical considering the black market deals in which Canadian Army equipment and supplies are traded for jewellery, precious metals, art objects, women, even cars and boats, on a scale you would not believe. The higher the rank, of course, the greater the opportunities."

—Farley Mowat, *My Father's Son, Memories of War and Peace*

Aldershot England: 6 July 1945

At first, she was to tell her interrogators, she thought he was taking a nap, his head down on the green desk blotter. Not too surprised at 2200 hours (ten PM to civilians) that the burdens of office, the endless struggle to round up shipping to move Canadian troops home after the war in Europe, finally had caught up to him.

Superhuman as he seemed—in other departments too, she didn't tell them, thinking of their times together in London—Lieutenant Colonel Ambrose Wellesley, Royal Canadian Army Service Corps, the transport arm of the forces, a veteran of Northwest Europe and onetime liaison to 21st Army Group in Brussels, must have realized that his efforts had been mocked, cheapened by the riots. Torrents of energy from this vigorous, spare man, who was called "The Duke," had not been enough to hold back Canadian soldiers from going berserk. Over two nights of the fourth and fifth of July 1945, thousands of them had broken out of the miserable nineteenth-century barracks where they had simmered, idle, resentful, short of pay, the food awful, waiting in vain to be sent to the ports and home. Was this their thanks for doing so much to defeat German Nazi oppression? And so they had trashed downtown Aldershot, that old garrison town thirty-five miles southwest of London, where the inhabitants had tolerated waves of scrubby soldiery since the Crimean War. The shopkeepers, those who tended the pubs and penny arcades, muttered among themselves that the rampage was worse than anything the Germans, had they landed in 1940, might have done.

That evening, she admitted, her feelings were of sympathy for the shame he must be going through; almost reluctant to disturb him, she stepped forward. And saw the blood. Drew back, tiptoed forward, as though someone might be behind the door. Glanced quickly; no one there. His forehead was slightly to one side where he had fallen or had been pulled forward. Between his jellied eyes, where flies now explored, she could make out the dark hole drilled just above his fine blade of a nose. Exact and final. Surely he couldn't have done it to himself; no weapon or spent cartridge in sight.

Her presence of mind at first impressed her interrogators. For it seems she had continued her careful shuffle across the room to the desk where she told them she had noticed the piece of paper. Pencil-printed, edges curling with blood, it had been placed outwards, that is, towards the front of the desk for all to see. The note, she gathered from a quick scan, seemed to be a warning, a badly worded threat to the effect that the commanding officer's demise was only the first if more wasn't done to speed up repatriation home.

Something else she couldn't very well miss, she said. On his desk to one side was a gas respirator, the face mask issued for protection against lethal poisons never released in that war's battles. The gas had found its uses elsewhere. Removed from its missing chest haversack, the mask was attached to its ringed hose leading to the filter, a yellow canister. It had been placed so that the round blank eyes appeared to gloat at the corpse.

She ran down the hall to the orderly room where the duty officer, a young lieutenant, wiped the smirk from his lips. Corporal Claire Evans, clerical worker, keeper of certain files, a member of the Canadian Women's Army Corps, her kepi with its diamond badge in her hand, her dark cropped hair shaking, a sheen on her usually reposed face, pointed back towards the office. The duty officer leaned forward, trying to understand the gabble.

PART ONE

1

Two sergeants. Both were to disappear from the scene of mayhem. One of them turned out to be the link to what happened after the riots. The other was fingered as a ringleader who had betrayed or reversed the time-honoured role of the non-commissioned officer, the NCO, as the glue that keeps an army together, the middleman between officers and footsloggers, their arbiter, their conscience. Perhaps in his own misguided way he felt he was fulfilling the latter duty to the men—the one of conscience—when he exhorted them to wreak damage upon the innocent shopkeepers of Aldershot who, for almost a century, had done nothing more criminal than to separate generations of soldiery from their meagre pay. While his motives to this day remain foggy, no further space needs to be given to that sergeant. He was cut out of the herd, duly sentenced to seven years penal servitude and presumably forgotten.

The other one was different. He didn't last long and nobody on the spot twigged to his significance in the events that were to follow. This sergeant, an agitator no less than the first one, was to escape the roundup net for another fate.

As to the riots, it must be admitted that damage was mostly to property, windows being the major targets. No pink-faced English ladies were raped. Looting was very selective. Injuries the result of push and shove. Anger and rage were no less, though, for those relatively sober depredations where the main intoxicants were the adrenalin and male hormones stored up in weeks of idle sloth.

Yet for this other sergeant, "the disturbances," as they came to be called in countless post-mortems, were an unexpected cover. It turned out he was nowhere nearby the evening of the sixth of July, with everyone on edge and armed for more violence, when somebody shot dead the lieutenant colonel, the commanding officer of repat transport, himself with sheathed pistol, while he sat and fretted at his desk in North Camp far from the turmoil. Apparently he did nothing more than juggle shipping manifests to send the boys home, his diligence seen as heroic under the stress of locating scarce hulls. Yet, when he looked up startled, he was plugged right between the eyes. A single shot; not even a safety to make sure. It wasn't the sergeant, but it came to pass there was a linkage that escaped everyone until much later.

The accepted version, enshrined today in reams of long mimeographed reports, pinpoints a group of Canadians who, for reasons unknown, were hanging out where Hospital Hill Road joins Wellington Avenue, the main drag of Aldershot. Exactly why they worked themselves into a lather remained a mystery, even after the courts of inquiry and courts martial had run their course and laid on punishment for a few. It seems that agitators, whoever they actually were, latched onto rumours of three blameless soldiers locked up in the local nick on High Street. Injustice was seen as the final insult for all they had been through or imagined they had. Off they went, yelling, across Princes Gardens and spilling onto the High Street to discover the joy of smashing windows. The military culture of collective violence had been turned onto itself in showers of glass. The only thing they lacked so far was direction, and so they milled around, conditioned as they were to the certainties of barked orders.

It, the leadership or one element of it, was to burst forth from the cinema down the street where a Sergeant Metro Timchuk with two buddies watched the end of a dreadful film.

Back in the two-shilling seats, the beam from the projector was just over their heads, a bluish ray cutting through the tobacco smoke that drifted up from the lower seats. No pay due until the end of July, they picked over coins until they had a small pool, enough to see something of distant home. The poster outside showed Errol Flynn in a fur hat. *Northern Pursuit*, with Flynn as a Mountie tracking down across Canada an improbably downed Nazi pilot, a saturnine Helmut Dantine. Given it was Hollywood back lot fakery, with stock footage of soaring mountains and white prairie, there wasn't much to bring on a yearning for winter back home. They were disappointed.

What set them off was the Movietone newsreel. A gigantic metal shape hove into view, the *Queen Mary*, its decks an organism of waving tentacles above grinning, pale faces. Out of Le Havre, the plummy voice informed them, Yanks on their way Stateside from France, the liberators of Europe, some of them about to go on across America to the Pacific to knock the Japs for six. A job well done, the announcer exulted as the troopship slid its delirious cargo out to sea. Before the lights came up in the theatre, a slide wobbled its way onto the screen. The stars and stripes. A few badly printed lines: "Independence Day America. Britain says its thanks. God bless!"

From between the other two, the sergeant was first onto his feet, crushed his smouldering cigarette under hobnailed boots, pointed as the ratty curtain squeaked across the screen. The necking soldiers and women around them gradually uncoiled, lips were dabbed with hankies, a rumble of boots and thudding seats returning upright as patrons shuffled into the aisles.

The sergeant turned to his two pals, privates with their Canada insignia and divisional rectangles below epaulets where they had stowed their rolled up berets. He wore a wine-dark Fifth Division patch; his beret was black for armoured corps. As they arose they pulled down the waistbands of their rough woolen battledress jackets in the style of lumpy windbreakers, laughingly called "blouses" by officialdom. Campaign ribbons newly issued showed the three were long service from Italy to Northwest Europe. They had snorted through the phony movie about their own country, but now anger and resentment, perhaps despair—built up over weeks of mind-numbing confinement in the dank barracks of Aldershot—simmered to the top.

"You see that? How come they get the ships? What about us, eh?"

The sergeant broke away, pushed ahead of the others through the departing crowd, muttering to himself, flapping his arms in a way that cleared a path to the exits. Out on the High Street his pals caught up to him. They lit Turrets and watched the departing crowd, many of them Canadians, a few lucky ones with girls, and shabby civilians, oblivious to soldiery, go into the soft July twilight of double daylight saving time.

"Come on, sarge. We got enough left for a beer."

As if they had stepped out of ranks, guilty of a transgression on the parade square, the sergeant scowled at them. Enough was enough, all right. Those grinning, well-fed fellas on the troopship, they were looked after, not us. Something had to be done to shake 'em up over there in the Pavilion or the Officers' Club—plenty of drink and liars' dice for them, good roast beef. They turned, curious, as civilians and soldiers streamed towards them. What? Yells, the ring and clatter of fallen glass, familiar uniforms dodging in and out of open doors, cigarette packs tossed like bread to the masses. Tall, rangy, his black beret clamped exactly one inch above the eyebrows, he waved his arms and spoke to the ragged edge of the mob, apparently from a Pioneer unit. Instinct brought them up short, three stripes still counting for something.

"What's up, boys? What's this all about?"

An odd manner, his stillness, brought others to heel as they somehow sensed that he was not there to try to force them back into line. The rasping voice called out again, "boys," now becoming his boys. The glittering dark eyes, the fury in them, this guy's got a bee in his bonnet, but he's not one of them for sure.

"What's with him?" From a Cape Breton Highlander. Wild guys, those.

"Oh, Metro, watch out. Got it in for officers. Says coupla them knocked off his brother in Holland. He got a fuse shorter than the dick onna new-born babe."

Someone shouted about the three captives at the police station.

"Okay, boys, let's go see."

On their way they kicked through the glass hailstones on the road. Giggling and jostling, a stream of them broke away, tempted by the fun fair arcade where its rigged machines gulped shillings and pence with dings and flashing globes to clean out their dwindled coin. Into the brightly lit arcade to smash the gobbling monsters. "Tilt," they cried. And wrecked the place until they tired of it and caught up with the sarge who had wrangled his crowd to the nearby police cells where the High Street and Wellington converge.

Chants of "let 'em out" brought a police officer to the door. In a thin voice he invited three to come in to see for themselves, who then emerged with sheepish grins, shaking their heads. Nobody there. A Jeep pushed through, a Canadian officer leaped up the steps to assure them their grievances would be seen to. Return to your quarters. By this time the crowd had grown to some five hundred. As they wheeled, unsure, away from the nick, a hoarse voice called out.

What exactly he urged them to do that soft evening, the blackout long ended and street lights flickering on, is not known. Afterwards, at the courts of inquiry, some witnesses said there was this tall NCO who swore at the officer as he tried to placate them, then he roused them up and laid on them the newsreel with the Yanks going home ahead of them, even those who had stayed on to fight the Japs. How many of you joined up for the Pacific? Khaki arms went up.

"Me too. We put our hides on the line again. Them bigshots don't give a damn. We're stuck here unless we show 'em."

The need for retribution, for destruction, was rekindled. This sergeant was different, as was another one working the crowds at the other end of the street. The two were anchors holding them back to infuse an untested level of courage. Those about to slink back to barracks were drawn up short by the fury of the two strange leaders of an uprising. Here, his eyes wild in the wavering light, the sarge pointed, and a march began to bring two ragged streams together to join in one procession along Wellington Avenue, back to the High Street where gaping windows beckoned, free for the taking. Tobacconists were favoured, stashes revealed under counters where they had held back cigarettes for privileged locals. Some began to slag one another over the tobacco loot. At a pub a gang roared in to demand free beer, duly served before they broke up the place. A few British Tommies uttered protest, but shrank back from the frantic spill of colonials.

On it went, now joined by more Canadians who had been wandering aimlessly or newly arrived from the train station, their faces glum at the prospect of endless time back at dismal barracks. Get back at them Limey shopkeepers, smug and indifferent, short-changing them, their standoffish blankness a provocation. Maybe somebody'd smarten up. Gone were the windows of Walker Jeweller (Engagement Rings), Naval Military Outfitters, Posner, Phillips, the works. Hated British red caps, military police, and Canadian provost, with a flurry of navy blue bobbies, began to show up to apply the manual of crowd control. Come on, lads, move along, said an elderly bobby with a white moustache. He was shoved through a broken window, his aging face newly seamed with jagged edges. Where would they stop? Women cringed and spat their hatred, but they were not touched. An odd decorum prevailed.

Now the crowd sniffed menace. From the verges three-ton lorries, gears down, whining, sifted carefully through gaps; firebreaks were cleared, clumps of rioters isolated by white-webbed provost and other suckholes with armbands. Many rioters slipped off to head back to the shelter of billets. Must have been rats among them, though, for the provost were precise to collar those who had kept the pot boiling or whose bulging jackets disgorged multi-hued cigarette packs, so desperate were they, even yellow Woodbines were worthy trophies.

The roundup closed in. Further along the High Street, Wellington, Station Road and side streets, the lorries crept forward, scooping them up with less discrimination as they went. Grabbed were stray British Tommies, a few American GIs (the final insult, red caps tossing them like sacks on Independence Day), a couple of sailors, and even some shopkeepers who had tussled with the intruders to protect their wares. A civilian, off the London train, was hoisted and shoved into a truck filled with soldiers.

But they missed Sergeant Timchuk and his two pals, for they, old campaigners who could sniff danger a mile off, ducked down a side street. It was there that the sarge leaned against a wall and muttered, "Jesus, boys, I'm sick." Propped up between the two private soldiers he was dragged along to Hospital Road where two military policemen in a Jeep cornered them, more fodder for the roundup, until persuaded that they were trying to find a medic for the sarge, who threw up on the shiny bonnet of the vehicle. Not drunk, it was agreed. One MP felt the man's slimy forehead. A quick decision and unexpected humanity from the "meatheads," as they were fondly dubbed. With no further ado they drove the three men to the Connaught hospital north of downtown. A nursing sister took one look at him and said, "I bet it's jaundice." The other two were spirited off for tests and confined.

Two nights later, while Sergeant Metro Timchuk and his friends languished in an isolation ward in the hospital, the colonel was shot.

As for the rioters, they stumbled off the lorries into a scene from a concentration camp—a paved compound, guards, tables set up with interrogators poised, headlights from circled vehicles. Some two hundred souls had been netted. At the side with seated officers, MPs and collaborators pointed out the apparent ringleaders or looters snatched at storefronts. Questions were barked in Nazi tones, the babble of voices echoing against the porticos of Maida barracks, a short hop from downtown. A few red tabs appeared to pace around, to scowl and whack their swagger sticks. By now it was near midnight. Most of the Canadians were detained overnight in makeshift cells. A bonus: several of the culprits were found to be AWL or deserters, apparently on the loose in the repat schemozzle anyway. Before they packed up for the night they culled a handful of ringleaders to be put on ice for another day, among them the one senior NCO, the sergeant, who was to be made an example of and, while some culprits spoke of another three-striper who had egged them on, he was never found. The brass went off to confer about setting up procedures to compensate irate shopkeepers for damages.

"As riots go, this one could have been worse," said a major.

Not so. The grapevine thrummed overnight along the lines as stragglers who escaped the dragnet regaled inmates about the fun to be had trashing this detested sinkhole. Sure, there were parades the next morning when severe warnings were issued to grinning troops. Satisfied, the officers and NCOs felt the wrath of discipline, combined with shame or the remnants of tarnished pride, would hold them fast. No order was issued or enforced to confine them to barracks. Nobody took the trouble to allay unrest with a statement, say, from the commander of Canadian troops, nice noises about imminent shipping to carry them off. Why this was not done remains a puzzle.

The next evening, around ten PM, a repeat mob filtered downtown to finish the job and show support for those arrested. Different ringleaders this time, not the sarge or his two buddies; others who were on the same wavelength of mischief and destruction—the trash-laden wake of war and the army itself, a residue of casual brutality, discomfort, and boredom. Time for a blowout at last. And Aldershot was the place. At least the French, the Belgians, and the Dutch had welcomed them.

By midnight on the fifth of July the downtown was ankle deep in broken glass in a more thorough harvest: two hundred shops wrecked, seven hundred windows smashed. Running wild, hundreds of soldiers ignored a brigadier, no less, whose shrill tones over a loudspeaker only brought hoots of derision. Somebody's idea of having officers patrol in pairs was equally useless; none of them from their own units, strangers to each other, they picked their way gingerly through the glittering slivers and made diffident cluckings to enraged merchants. Bobby reinforcements from the Hants constabulary tried to syphon off groups for lectures on decorum, to no avail.

The lorries came in again to circle and cut out small parties; other groups ran off into shadowy midnight. By this time, the General Officer Commanding Canadian troops in the area, Major General Daniel C. Spry, was called in by the civilian police to their headquarters. Spry counselled against sending in any more British MPs or troops, at the risk of provoking real carnage. By three in the morning, downtown Aldershot had fallen quiet except for the crunch of glass underfoot by patrols of mismatched officers. Of the hundreds pulled in to Maida barracks under the glare of headlights, eighty-five were singled out for detention and gathered for transport to the infamous

Reading Gaol. All told, the take was 115 from the two nights of mayhem.

Was it over? Nobody could say. Finally, they organized a Mob Control Centre in Ramillies barracks in the Marlborough Lines further north, away from the depredations. There they waited and planned, but there were no more outbreaks. Orders were cut to disperse troops to outlying depots far away from the wrecked town.

Winston Churchill was furious.

Field Marshall Alan Brooke, Chief of the Imperial General Staff, Britain's top military strategist, peered through his perfectly round dark-rimmed glasses and wrote "abusive," a reminder for his diary, to depict the prime minister's latest tirade. His small moustache and the rest of him immaculate, this aloof "brains of the outfit," as the US general George Patton called him, once again had to rein in his mercurial boss. This time it was the Aldershot riots.

Churchill, his jowls twitching, tore into his brass hats about those wild Canadians, the havoc they had wreaked upon the poor, inoffensive shopkeepers. He demanded to know why British troops or military police had not been ordered in to restore order. What was being done?

Brooke did not flinch. This iron soldier, who had threatened to shoot a stubborn French general during the 1940 evacuation of Dunkirk, could handle it.

In his quick way of clipped speech he warned Churchill he would not send in British troops. It would only make things worse. Matters were in hand, the troublemakers had been rounded up by the Canadians themselves with some assistance from the local constabulary. His cold annoyance got through. Or so he thought, as Churchill sat back, sighed in exasperation and scowled, the crisis over.

Until something happened that sent Churchill through the roof—again.

2

As it turned out, the colonel was the second Canadian to be shot that week. Churchill probably wouldn't have known about the first one, or cared. That killing took place in far-away Italy, east of Naples. There, on the morning of the fifth of July, the second day of the riots in Aldershot, a firing squad executed a private soldier who had been found guilty of murder and desertion. No announcement was made, records were sealed, but the news spread around Canadian Military Headquarters in London. For it was the top brass at CMHQ who had orchestrated the execution. The knowledge, or guilt of it, the killing of a poor, misguided youth, months after the war in Europe had ended, was to be a shadow over their response to the murder of Lieutenant Colonel Wellesley.

Churchill, too, through his rage, might have pondered the ironies of assassination in the vast encampment where barracks were named after his own ancestor, the Duke of Marlborough. Across Queen's Avenue, actually in Farnborough, were buildings to mark that Duke's long forgotten victories: Oudenarde, Malplaquet, Blenheim. Here, in some upper-level prank, Canadian soldiers were sent back from Holland, Belgium, or Germany to languish while awaiting ships from British ports. The locals were amazed and uneasy that hordes of Canadians were back among them again. The first ones had arrived long ago, in 1939, to mixed reviews and, as thousands of others followed, they had both charmed and infuriated the inhabitants. Most good burghers thought they had seen the last of them when the invasions of Europe began. The young soldiers had changed, too, many of them hardened and calloused from what they had seen over there. They were not about to tolerate their virtual imprisonment in the mouldering two- and three-storey barracks blocks, to be packed together in rooms of double wooden bunks with metal slats and paper-thin mattresses. The damp oozed from brick walls. There was never enough hot water to wash off the smells of strangers flung together.

Here, oddly enough, the ranking unit charged with the organization of transport from England was located in a low-lying, flimsy building of more recent vintage. Staffed by what were known as "odds and sods," the operation had been assigned to Lieutenant Colonel Wellesley since his arrival from the Continent in June. There it squatted, the object of scorn and abuse by the confined troops. But angry enough to pop him off?

That night, when word reached them over at the Mob Control Centre, faces turned ashen. Officers and non-commissioned officers, the NCOs, stood around shaking their heads at this aftershock of the riots, which God knows were scary enough. It had seemed to be over, the fingered looters and ringleaders hauled in under guard. Downtown Aldershot apparently was quiet now, except for the whoosh of brooms through glass shards and the muffled curses of the citizenry.

But this was different. What on earth could it mean? The words "conspiracy" and "revolt" were heard from pale lips. And a shudder came over them.

As it did in Whitehall, in London.

Brooke's diary entry for 7 July 1945:

"Midnight call from Winston, had hoped he had given up his wartime nocturnal habits. Highly agitated, informed of foul murder of a Canadian senior officer in Aldershot. 'They cannot control their own troops, now this outrage. This slaying may have far-reaching implications for order and discipline throughout our armies. We must stiffen resolve for the assault on Japan. Do we not have laws that bring capital crimes committed by Empire troops on English soil under the purview of our justice? With demonstrated incompetence of the Canadians we must insist on Scotland Yard involvement, probably Special Branch and MI5 if this presages mass disobedience or even insurrection. The prospect of subversion must not be overlooked. Pray take the necessary steps with your counterparts. I shall speak to Home Secretary.'"

Brooke notes: "To keep Winston out of it I made most calls, following which contacts made through channels to emphasize the seriousness of the situation to Canadian authorities."

Who jumped.

3

Four hours had passed. As the remains of Lieutenant Colonel Ambrose Wellesley congealed, so did the investigative machinery. Eyes blackened, face a bright red, his fine nose blade resting on a file folder partly covered with mouth blood under his drilled forehead, the colonel, in effect, was on ice. Another infestation of bluebottles had arrived to mingle with the two-legged variety, the July crop of ecstatic flies to indulge in their orgies and spew out eggs.

"Bloody marvel," were the first words of Detective Chief Inspector Timothy ("Tiny Tim") Bollock, age 45, in a grating East End accent, and member of the storied Murder Squad, Criminal Investigation Department (CID), Scotland Yard. "Nobody's been in?"

He stood outside the closed door of the colonel's office guarded by a white-webbed Canadian military policeman and a Hampshire (Hants) constable in vizored hat with checkered band. Beside him stood one Major Richard ("Spotted Dick") Clancy, assistant provost marshal for the Canadian area command, until now preoccupied with culling the rioters at the Mob Control Centre. He had been phoned personally by Colonel A.D. Cameron, senior provost officer at head office in London, to get over there pronto, seal it, and alert the local constabulary for backup. A Hants detective hovered diffidently.

"Only two, far as I know. Our unit was alerted by the duty officer here. The colonel's body was found about 2200 hours by a Corporal Evans, CWAC, who came to his office for some reason she has not revealed to us yet. She ran to the orderly room where she still awaits questioning. I ordered detachments from my own Nine, Fourteen, and Seventeen provost companies to cordon off the area. Hants police were quick to respond. I made a decision to summon our medical officer, standing by over at Ramillies."

"In the event some of your charges might need medical attention?" grinned Bollock, evoking images of truncheons. Risking a crick in his neck, he peered up at the cold eyes and pocked face—as if the major had been blasted by a shotgun, actually nothing more than lingering acne pits. The uniform was spotless, with knife-edge pleats, a dandyism carried over from the days when Clancy, a flower in his lapel, was a floorwalker at Woodwards department store in Vancouver. At the outbreak of war, management was relieved when he joined up to scare off the enemy instead of customers.

"A precaution, okay? Major Kinmont, the MO, awaits in the orderly room. He entered the office, confirmed the colonel was deceased. Corporal Evans is quite sure of the victim's identity. She's badly shaken up. After the doc left the room I did a visual check to ensure all windows were closed. There are pickets outside, but I've kept them at a distance. We don't want the ground outside the windows disturbed."

"Good, major. Are you the investigating officer?"

"No, sir. He's on his way from London."

"And who might he be?"

"Captain Horobbins, officer commanding Six Company, Canadian Provost—our military police, in case you didn't know. Before Normandy, it was some 350 bods charged with roping in our lads guilty of many sins in these blessed isles. Now much reduced. Horobbins also commands our Special Investigations Unit, SIU, located at Canadian Military Headquarters, CMHQ—you know, off Trafalgar Square. Former copper, very smart fella; has handled some hard cases. Be here in a jiff."

"Well, let's take a dekko. I want you to confirm his identity. Did you know him?"

"Not well. Attended meetings with him on repatriation problems. Never socialized. My mess isn't here."

"You any idea why anyone would want to pop him off? No? Come on then."

Bollock had lost out on the night's lottery. There, in the "murder room" in the Yard's nerve centre near the Embankment, his number came up. Three officers—usually of detective chief inspector rank—were on call, their names pinned inside a wooden frame, the first name on an hour's notice, the second for eight hours, the third for twenty-four hours. He was number one in the frame when word came down from the assistant commissioner.

"Seems a colonial senior officer has been topped in Aldershot. Suicide not likely from a preliminary assessment by the senior Canadian provost officer on the scene, a Major Clancy. You shall work with them, you know, their red caps."

"Love a duck. Why?"

Complications were revealed with distaste. "Home Secretary rousted by PM, now professes keen interest. Canadian High Commissioner Massey awakened, has rung up General Montague, chief pooh-bah at their headquarters, who's ordered Colonel Cameron, their head policeman, to liaise with us, which he's done. Your counterpart, their man, is about to be despatched to Aldershot."

"Who'll be in charge, sir?"

"They've reluctantly agreed they can use our expertise and technical help, if indeed it is murder. You'll need the Canadians to open doors."

"Sir, aren't we jumping a bit too quickly?"

"We are ordered to be on the scene. Everyone seems to assume it's a killing, without any evidence to verify. That's your job. If it is, you carry on from there with full authority from us."

"If an arrest is to be made, who does it and under what jurisdiction?"

Assistant Commissioner Rossiter was prompted to display his origins and steeltrap memory as a solicitor from the Inns before he went over to the other side.

"You're well aware of the Visiting Forces, British Commonwealth Act. We made sure their miscreants—Aussies, Kiwis, South Africans, Canadians, the lot—would not escape our own courts of justice for major crimes perpetrated upon our innocent population. Notably Section 41: 'A person subject to military law may be tried by any competent civil court for any offence for which he may be triable if he were not subject to military law.' That do for a refresher, Bollock? Regrettably, the Act was invoked far more often than we had ever anticipated."

"Pity, sir, we had to hang six Canadians for murder. And?"

"Whether the Act will apply to this case, we can't tell yet. Some chaps at Whitehall seem to think it's a cert. Higher levels will have to thrash it out. If a British, or say, an Irish civilian is the prime suspect, it's likely ours. If a Canadian soldier, possibly theirs. For now, carry on as if it is your case, cooperate with the Canadians, call on any support you need."

Which Bollock did before departing his Chiswick house, still under snail-like repairs after last September's first V-2 rocket had plunged into a street nearby. He called on a neighbour to look in on his wife, who had not completely healed from last autumn's shock. Then he made three quick calls: to Chief Constable Hants for assurance the death scene was preserved and guarded, to Hendon for a forensic team, and to one of the dozen or so pathologists who were supposed to be on tap. His boss had released a Wolseley saloon car and driver to speed him on his way, a nice change from usually having to take the train.

Even with his black suit and vest, white shirt, wrinkled collar, and peculiar tie, Bollock struck Captain Hugh Kirkpatrick Horobbins as a dockworker decked out for chapel; wide as a house, mashed nose slightly askew, droopy eyelids, and crooked teeth exuding tobacco fumes, the source of which was a Senior

Service fag lifted by lumpy fingers from fleshy lips. Were his intonations Cockney, or what?

"You're it, I gather?"

When the provost captain nodded, Bollock grasped his arm, led him into the hallway where guards preserved the death scene.

"We're both up the river without an oar," Bollock said, a first try at building mateship. "Fair to say we'll need each other."

"I suppose."

"You suppose? What are your orders?"

Over the dedicated phone line at his subsistence digs on Inverness Terrace off Bayswater Road, Horobbins was awakened by the barks of his commander, Colonel A.D. Cameron, as if they were still in barracks. Except for the Quacks (CWAC), the headquarter's penpushers and chairwarmers were farmed out to assorted homes or flats at scandalous rents, paid for by Victory Bonds back home. Hints of a slur in the old-time disciplinarian's voice revealed the lateness of the hour or brandy and, with it, an unusual candour that may have reflected a contagious winding down of wartime rigour. A veteran of the Great War, then service with the British on the Gold Coast, later Ghana, West Africa, he had to concede Horobbins was one of his best investigators, the one who came to mind when the problem of the dead colonel and the prospect of British meddling was dumped onto his lap in the wee small hours.

"You heard about the disturbances in Aldershot?"

"Yes, sir, but no details. Just in from Liverpool, you know—that gang working the docks."

"Right. The execution of that poor sod in Italy?"

"No, sir. So they finally did it?"

"Nobody's supposed to know. Final order came here from Ottawa, then on to Italy; our esteemed master bloody-minded about it. Everyone in an uproar about the riots—you should hear Matthews going on. Now there's something else. One of our colonels has been popped off in Aldershot. That's where you come in." Cameron outlined what he knew.

"If it turns out to be what we think it is, everybody and his dog is going to try and horn in," Cameron said in an unexpectedly fatherly tone. "Had to alert our Aldershot area commander, General Spry—guaranteed to interfere. The

Honourable Percy"—that was going over the line: Lieutenant General P. J. Montague, chief of staff, was a former Manitoba judge—"best legal minds around the shop will ensure our interests are protected. Just the same, he's concerned you'll be inundated with shadowy types from MI5, Army Intelligence, and Special Branch. Churchill and company in knots about mass revolt, mutiny or conspiracies, maybe even the IRA. Must pump up the troops for assault on Japan. The reason for such precipitate action is Dick Clancy's info that he found a threatening note left at the scene. Suicide seems most unlikely."

"A note, sir?"

"Something about this one being merely the first. More assassinations hinted. Coming after the disturbances, it puts a whole new complexion on the troubles. I'll send my car. Every resource at your beck and call."

"With everybody but George Six in on the act, who's in charge?"

"As much as you can, make it goddam plain it's us, yourself. Don't let 'em push you around. First, there's the small matter of a prime suspect."

"The victim is Lieutenant Colonel Wellesley? Sir, I think the name rings a bell. I'm sure I noticed something about him, a file that crossed my desk earlier this year."

"What was it about?"

"One of our SIU investigations on the Continent, I seem to recall. No action taken, as far as I know. Something about diversion of supplies during the Dutch famine relief exercise in April and May. Sir, could you—"

"I'll bring in staff today and have it sent to you, if we can find it. I shall ask around, see if anyone here took a closer look. Must say I only have a hazy recollection. Struck me at the time, no doubt, that it was rather farfetched."

"After all, he was in the Service Corps."

"Enough, Horobbins. Get cracking."

"I suspect," Horobbins relented, "we've shared the same concerns with our masters."

"Not the least of which are high-priced fingers up the wrong flues."

Horobbins allowed a faint smile and extended his hand for the first time. "Then, Mr. Bollock, let's get on with it."

"The lads from Hendon have arrived; still awaiting the medical examiner before the flies muck up the evidence. Had a quick recce to make sure nothing has been disturbed. You have gloves? One other thing. Some woeful sods, your people, are in the orderly room, the ones who were first on the scene. One of your uniformed bints actually found him."

"Have you seen them?"

"Your bailiwick. He'll keep. Want to take a look?"

Horobbins went in to stare at the bent figure. Olive-smocked forensics stood waiting for the inspector to turn them loose. As he turned away he felt a cold fist in his stomach, a sense that the war had never ended, indeed it hadn't, and now a backwash of what could be another form of organized violence merging into something beyond their grasp. Could it be suicide, after all? He blinked as circling police cameras flashed.

The orderly room was in the middle of the single-storey, green-shingled wartime temp thrown up on concrete slabs, discreetly apart from the three-tier barracks blocks. Like such places from time immemorial, it was a clutter of desks, rows of filing cabinets dedicated to the production of part one, part two orders, memos, admonitions, syllabi, orders, anything to make life difficult for the troops. Now it was occupied by dozing, slumped bodies resting heads on desks, eerily an extension of the corpse down the hall. A massacre? No, the forms stirred.

He was relieved to find one of his own men minding the flock. One Sergeant James ("Pearly") Gates from his Six Company SIU, sent down with others to help quell the riots. It seemed Major Clancy, who had since been called back to deal with more unrest at the Mob Control Centre, had pried him loose and placed him in charge of witnesses, finders, or anyone else who had been around at the time. "Pearly" referred not to oyster sands but the heavenly gates, for which he seemed a least likely candidate. Rather, his visage resembled an outer oyster shell—hard ridged, lumpy, a rough engine for intimidation; yet underneath he had such keen sensitivities to the undercurrents of imminent trouble, skills or aptitudes honed as a guard at the federal penitentiary in Kingston, Ontario, his value to the Special Investigation Unit was never in doubt.

"She found him," Gates pointed. "I've taken statements. Major Kinmont is here, the MO. The lieutenant over there is the duty officer who alerted the authorities."

"Anybody hear the shot?"

"They say no. Convoys passing to move the boys out, motorbikes, lorries, possibly backfires. His office is at the far end of the building."

Horobbins drifted over to the stricken woman who stood to trembling attention.

"I gave her a sedative," said Major Kinmont, squat, florid, with glasses. "She's in shock; should be under observation and care."

"Sergeant Gates, will you see to this lady? We'll interview her later."

Corporal Claire Evans, pale, dark cropped hair, large brown eyes, managed a nod to the unexpected courtliness. Lady? When had anyone ever? Horobbins picked up real grief, not merely the jolt of grisly discovery. Why had she been in the colonel's office at 2200 hours when the camp, supposedly, was shut down?

"Major Kinmont, you've verified the death of the victim?"

"Yes. I gather I'm to follow through. Have contacted Cambridge hospital, arranged for their morgue and autopsy facilities."

"Fine, sir. If you'd come with me to the scene. We await a pathologist from London. Presumably the two of you can see to the removal of the body and autopsy report soonest. I'm afraid you'll have to work right through."

As they headed for the door, in blew a presence—someone with stature enough to break through the cordon, every inch the British officer of Sandhurst vintage: a major complete with bushy moustache, leather-sheathed swagger stick, immaculate tailored battledress, probably from Thomas and Stones or suchlike in London. Until Horobbins took in the Northwest Europe ribbons, blue and yellow Service Corps flashes, then winced at an Upper Canada College honk, its rebuke to the classless society of the New World.

"Todder, Two IC." Wellesley's second-in-command. "Just in from London."

"Sir, isn't everyone confined to base?"

"Oh, come on, captain."

"The trains run this late?"

"Have me own little puddle jumper. Is it true? Ambrose, Colonel Wellesley's been shot?"

Horobbins sized him up, made a decision. The donkey could well be useful. "Come with me, sir. We have to confirm the identity of the victim."

Pearly Gates muttered to him. "Already done, sir. Corporal Evans and Major Clancy when he was here."

"Never mind. This way, sir."

4

When Bollock opened his black murder bag, a cavernous briefcase, the first thing Horobbins noticed was a bottle of Bell's Scotch. Around it were crammed a container of plaster of paris, an oil bottle with nozzle to preserve shoe and other imprints, a camel hair brush, plasticine or putty to make casts, a spool of adhesive tape to lift fibres, a roll-up steel measure, assorted vials, scrapers, a scalpel, paper bags, scissors, twine, sticky labels, fountain pen, pencils, cotton gloves, and handcuffs.

"My sergeant usually totes it about. Manpower shortages, and it is the weekend. He'll be down later. Who's this? I thought I made it plain—no tourists."

"Major Todder, second-in-command. Just in from London."

"What were you doing there, sir? Isn't everyone on standby to keep your mutineers in line?"

"My business. Who's he?"

"The major may shed some light. Sir, is that Lieutenant Colonel Wellesley?"

"My God, I can't believe it. Who'd? No question it's him."

"Now, sir, if you'll step carefully to the front of the desk."

"Can't you do something about those flies? Place stinks to high heaven."

"The battlefield smell, sir?"

Todder turned. He caught the aspersion he didn't seem like someone who had been anywhere near a slit trench. Bollock lit a Senior Service fag, making it worse. "On the edge of the desk you see a note? Don't touch."

They craned over a rectangle of paper, red-edged from creeping mouth blood, the back of a mimeographed orders sheet with the message scrawled in pencil, the use of shaky caps as if a left-hander had decided to use the right hand to throw off any clues to its origin. "*We bin too long. Get us outa here. Yer the first if nobody moves ass. More to come.*"

"Awkward syntax," said Todder. "Illiterate clods."

"You can appreciate, sir, the upper echelons have the wind up over what appears to be a threat. Did you ever come across anything that would indicate a cabal of rioters or rumours of an uprising?"

"Not a clue."

"Clueless, all right," Bollock muttered as he copied the note, took tweezers from the murder bag, lifted it, placed it in a paper bag he handed to a forensic in olive smock, told him to have it dusted back at the lab.

"And there it is, Horobbins, the source of our woes. If your Major Clancy hadn't mentioned the note and the gas mask to our Hants Chief Constable, and expressed doubts of suicide, we shouldn't be in this flap. London was duly alerted with the dire consequences you and I must face. Major Todder, the colonel's sidearm is still in its holster on his right hip. Why was he wearing it?"

"We did the past couple of days. We had no idea what might happen."

"Nor do we if that note means anything. Next I direct your attention to the gas mask. Note that it's only the face mask, hose and canister. No haversack. Do you suppose it's part of the message that this group, or whoever, is about to release poison gas upon the good citizens and soldiery of Aldershot?"

"Gas? Where'd they find it? Doubt if any is stored around here."

"Could you find out if there's gas storage on the base and how well it's secured?"

"I'll lay that on downtown," referring to area headquarters.

Bollock continued with extreme dislike. "Now, sir, where do you store your gas masks?"

"Haven't the foggiest. Nobody's used them for years except for training. I'll find out."

Bollock beckoned to the forensic to bag the respirator. "If there're fingerprints anywhere you'll find them on or in the gas mask, maybe hairs or skin residue. Major, can they be traced, signed out, or assigned for a soldier's kit?"

"Not these days; no longer an item of issue."

"You have any questions, Horobbins? Very well, sir, we won't need you for the moment. No more jaunts to London if you don't mind."

"Wait a minute." Todder's blonde moustache seemed to slip its moorings. "When can we move him, give him a decent burial?"

"My sawbones will take him for medical examination. Your own MO is here. The autopsy will be performed immediately. Then we'll see."

Horobbins moved to the door with Todder. "Sir, could you see that we have a muster parade and rosters for staff working in this area. Also a summary of the colonel's movements over the past week, your own too. I suggest 0700 hours for the muster parade."

"On a Saturday?"

"Sir, we need to know if all personnel are accounted for. No day passes are to be issued. We want everyone here. I'll brief them on the procedures we'll follow to interview them, one by one. Handwriting or printing samples and fingerprints will be taken, including officers, NCOs, and other ranks. How many are we looking at?"

"Last count, forty-eight."

Horobbins whistled. Bollock rolled his eyes.

"Are any away on leave or off base?"

"We have one captain, two lieutenants, four NCOs, and seven other ranks on transport duty in Liverpool, Greenock, and Southampton. I'll have to get a count on leave passes. Anyway, they couldn't have been here."

"We'll see. Now, sir, immediately after the muster parade, I want an 'O' group of your officers and NCOs to fill them in on search procedures in Blenheim and Malplaquet barracks for the repats confined to base. The entire area will be searched. Can you see to it?"

"At this hour?"

A staff sergeant appearing from the orderly room was allowed to poke his head inside the doorway to hand Todder a manilla envelope. "Runner just dropped this off, sir. Urgent attention from downtown."

At least this time he wasn't being pushed around by a lowly military cop. The major read out a summons from General Spry's staff to attend at Canadian area military headquarters on Cavan's Road at 0900 hours Saturday; handed duly ticked copies to the provost captain and the Scotland Yard inspector, also on the invitation list.

"A galaxy of stars for the general. Who're these misters? Civilians?"

"Not exactly, sir. Other government services, shall we say?"

Todder glared at Bollock, despaired of Horobbins, turned on polished heel and clumped out, followed by the cringing staff sergeant faced with a sleepless night.

"Wotta prat." Bollock turned. "Ah, here's my Mr. Parlow, our medical examiner. About bloody time."

A florid face contest, Horobbins noted. The London pathologist, a tweedy Mr. Parlow, was from the same evolutionary path as Major Kinmont; both men—stocky, with bright chipmunk cheeks marked by faint blue fault lines—paused to size up each other with arcane lodge signs of recognition. True to form, they sidled off to a corner of the large office to consult beyond the hearing of patients.

Horobbins didn't dare move closer to the desk or beyond, where spattered fragments of skull, some hairy, mashed potato blobs of shattered brain, raindrops of blood, decorated the brown linoleum floor. The colonel's office was spacious but bare of the usual personal touches, a makeshift command centre of metal filing cabinets under faded green walls, a bare conference table at the far end. Any regimental group photos, carpet, or looted antiques had long since been spirited off by the previous occupant, whoever he might be. Bollock waved a magnifying glass and mirror at the returning medics.

"Mind if I take a look?" He jiggled the mirror and glass without touching the downed head. The doctors peered with him to make noises in some primitive click tongue. Bollock focused on the file folder held in place by the patrician nose. Streaked with dark blood, the file tab was still readable. "Report on shipping schedules, it appears. We'll have forensic examine the contents. Now, sirs, would you step very carefully around the litter behind the desk and give us your preliminary opinion. First question: is it suicide?"

While the doctors prowled gingerly, whispering to each other, Bollock took Horobbins very slowly, on tiptoe in places, to the bank of filing cabinets about five feet behind the desk. He located what he was trying to find—a starred dent in a filing cabinet drawer.

"Went through him and bounced off here."

"It'd have to be very low velocity."

"Right. Charlie, you see it?"

A forensic in heavy-framed glasses circled warily, squatted in a clearing, studied the reeking shreds on the floor, followed the trajectory backwards from the cabinet towards the chair, sat for a while in contemplation, then pointed to a coppery gleam amid the blobs.

"Sir, I believe that's a projectile on the floor. Permission to lift it."

Primly, he skipped around the sludge in a kind of duck walk. Bollock sought approval of the doctors, who nodded. Teetering, his long legs wavering, the olive smock reached forward with tweezers, held up to the light a blood-smeared tapered object no longer than three-quarters of an inch. "Full metal copper jacket. I'd say nine millimetre, possibly German. I'll bag it now for ballistics."

"Any sign of an ejected cartridge casing? It'd be back there in front of him or thereabouts, unless it was kicked aside. Have you searched the corners?"

"We've looked everywhere, sir. It would've shown up somewhere, even in the remains on the floor, after the shot. Seems to indicate he didn't do it himself. The casing would be nearby as it ejected from the breech, assuming it's an automatic pistol. And obviously no weapon about."

"Gentlemen, we have to consider or eliminate suicide. The missing weapon may not be definitive. Someone could have popped in and picked it up from the floor, a valuable souvenir pistol possibly."

"Not likely, is it?" snarled Mr. Parlow, fighting drowsiness while he brushed at flies in the sultry closed up room. "Whoever did it must have had the foresight to collect the spent casing."

The forensic agreed. "If we had that, sir, we could establish the weapon. A Luger, for instance, has a triangular ejector mark on the base of the casing."

"What are the odds of suicide, then?"

Having circumnavigated the corpse, pointed and made notes, the doctors fed each other lines.

"First off, why wouldn't he have used his own sidearm? Still in his holster."

"Issue revolver, probably a Smith and Wesson," offered Horobbins.

"Second, we cannot detect any close-range firearms discharge residues." Aiming with a fountain pen. "There is no sooty deposit around the entry point, nor any stippling, the tiny wounds caused by unburnt or partially burnt grains of powder. It was not a contact shot. Third, our conjecture is that he was shot face on from a few feet in front of the desk, just one clear shot leaving a single entrance hole in his forehead. The projectile, slowed down by layers of skin and bone, exited the back of his skull spraying contents around as we and the flies have noted. Death instantaneous. Heart stopped at once, shown by redness of visage. Hydrostatic pressure forced blood and fluids from his mouth. Note there is not much blood elsewhere."

"Time of death?"

"We see the beginnings of *rigor mortis*. But with this ungodly heat we can't establish an exact time. Major, is the ambulance here?" Kinmont nodded.

"Then we shall remove the body to the Cambridge and proceed with our examination. I assume there's some urgency. We'll take him clothed as he is. Presumably your chaps will be on hand to collect his clothing for their tests. However, you may remove his personal effects, his valuables, identification, and his pistol. Careful. Do not disturb. Who's responsible?"

Horobbins was about to speak, then caught Bollock's gesture to the smocked ones.

"My lads will go through his effects first at the lab. Then we'll go over their report and have a look-see ourselves. That all right with you, captain?"

"How soon?"

"It'd better be yesterday."

Horobbins gave in, watched grimly—sickened but not nauseated, for he had seen worse—as gloved pickpockets dived, then placed each item into paper sacks. Two British medical orderlies arrived, scrawny and pale as if awaiting their own blood transfusions, they displayed unexpected strength to unwind the six foot frame of the bent figure and push him down prone, face up, onto the stretcher with its own faded bodily stains.

One of them, a sensitive soul, closed the colonel's eyes.

5

The paper bags rattled with his belongings: a gold, plated Bulova wristwatch, not army issue, two blue tissue V-mail letters from Montreal, a Parker fountain pen, a lambskin wallet, English coins, railway ticket stub, a steel cigarette case, but no key ring. Odd. So who was he? What had compelled someone, obviously an expert pistol shot (professional assassin?) to loom before him, probably a familiar or known face, and fire a single shot into the patrician forehead above the long sharp nose, his primped sandy hair eerily intact on top of his shattered skull? The medics guessed that the colonel, seeing the gun, had started to rise, was hit and fell forward onto the desk.

What had he done, or what did he symbolize, to attract a killer in an obscure office far from the area headquarters, isolated from the violence downtown, merely a juggler of schedules, troop trains, and ships; nothing lethal involved except the simmering impatience of the troops awaiting passage.

Surely his task or even his autocratic disdain for the proles, a common affliction of those festooned with red tabs and uniforms that were never soiled, couldn't merit such a dire fate. Like Todder, he affected a tailored uniform, highly polished handmade brown oxfords, even brass pips and crowns on his epaulets instead of issue cloth. Would his personnel file give any clue? Not likely. Other sources would have to be scoured.

The two signals or messages, the note and respirator, meant something to somebody or a group, but what? Were Bollock's first assumptions right, they were red herrings of some sort? Horobbins wasn't so sure. They were put there for recognition or confirmation to others who might rejoice silently at his death. Conspiracy theories with political overtones seemed farfetched, but obviously attractive to certain elements and agencies that needed them.

What was in that siu file buried somewhere at Cockspur Street? Vaguely one of many, flagged for info only, not action. Was it yet another tale of venal dealings in precious supplies? Holland, was it? God knows they had all seen enough of them, little and not so little epidemics of corruption springing up where temptation was almost irresistible. That his finely tuned retrieval system was faltering notched up his frustration level. Horobbins felt a jab in his chest, a kind of pang or warning to step back and restore focus. Was this handsome, dapper colonel the final casualty in the backwash of a long war? Or merely the first in a new one?

Exhausted, they inhaled fetid air, swatted at flies, stared at the now empty chair, and sighed at the task ahead of them.

"You any idea where the colonel parked his weary bones after a hard day's paper pushing?"

Caught out, Horobbins woke up and summoned Pearly Gates to locate the colonel's living quarters. In a spider hut down the way, the sergeant reported back, then was sent off with pickets to apply the three "S" bible: search, seal, and secure. Bollock growled at two Hants detectives; ordered a search at dawn's early light, toe to toe, every blade of grass in the cordoned zone, dust bins, drains, cookhouses, the barracks blocks. Objectives: a sidearm, possibly Luger or Walther, a rimless spent cartridge casing, pouch or haversack for a gas respirator.

"And gloves, maybe rubber," Horobbins called out.

White cotton gloves on, the detective chief inspector started off on his own search, opened file drawers, peered under tables piled high with papers, into corners, to satisfy himself that the weapon or casing was nowhere to be found, or was seeking something else entirely. Then Bollock suddenly turned to study the captain as if sizing him up for the first time. A silent third degree as Bollock took one of his "quick dekkos" over his newfound partner: sharply-creased battledress, beret rolled into an epaulet under three pips, black and red provost shoulder flashes, a lone white web belt, no sidearm, no other unit markings or medal ribbons, as if the man had just picked up the uniform from his batman. Was his anonymity an affectation? Bollock could not know, nor was Horobbins about to tell him that in a rare moment of rebellion he would not wear the CMHQ shoulder patch, a circle in black with a yellow maple leaf. Yellow, all right, sneered troops back from the Continent, even if they had been nowhere near real action. He didn't want to sport what they called the "flying asshole." Enough of those around.

It was a sartorial quirk much bruited about among the military and British civilian staff on the floor shared by the provost officers and uniformed lawyers in the Judge Advocate General branch. Under dire threats from Colonel Cameron he wore the yellow patch to the office, but when he was out and beyond he put on another jacket without the insignia. Moreover, his prominent hooked nose and olive hue created another dilemma, or diversion, for the deskbound idlers. He seemed older, somehow, difficult to place.

Common to gangs and armies is an apparent need to hang a nickname on anyone who is associated with them in some way, as friend, member, or enemy. The military tends to standard usage: anyone named Rhodes automatically becomes "Dusty"; a Bates, of course, is called "Master," and so on. So what to do about the elusive Horobbins? They didn't really have a fix on him. On those rare occasions when he joined a group at the pub across the street, he was amiable enough and, after several pints, could spin tales that hinted of his Irish origins; but most evenings in town he was off to his "someone" out in Putney, name of Mavis, he once mentioned as he got up to leave. Otherwise, he was a hands-on officer busily putting out fires by misbehaving Canadians from Aberdeen to Southampton. Even when he was absent, the office crew continued to struggle with sobriquets, including "Eaglebeak,"

"Hawk," or "Shylock," the last one deemed inappropriate for someone of declared Irish origin and who, after all, did stand rounds when he showed up at the pub. "Paddy" or "Stringbean" somehow missed. "Good egg, anyway," they agreed, to excuse their lack of creativity.

On the night of the fourth of July, Horobbins had not been available for Aldershot duty. Instead, he was up in Liverpool tending to a messy situation where a Canadian soldier had shot up a pub in the old walled town of Chester—much damage, no casualties. Managed to extract him from the clutches of the local constabulary who wanted to invoke the Visiting Forces Act. Found the perp was a deserter and, with good work by his Six Company detachment in Liverpool, opened up a Merseyside gang that pilfered God-knows-what from the docks. The thieves, as it turned out, were headed by a US Army topkick, also a deserter, who, of course, was exempt from the Act. When their thousands had arrived in Britain in 1942, the Americans had vowed they would not be "treated like the Canadians." They insisted on their own justice system, more secretive than the public exposure wreaked upon many Canadians by the British courts. No sooner had he returned to London than he was awakened at his rooms by Colonel Cameron's phone call.

Now stifling yawns, Horobbins was startled to be on the receiving end of a mumbled commentary that on Bollock's home turf would be termed a "billingsgate." The Yard man resumed his pawing of file drawers and table tops while, over his shoulder, he probed the fibre of the collaborator who had been foisted upon him.

"Horobbins. What kind of name is that? Hebrew?"

"My parents are Irish."

"So's De Valera," referring to the president of Eire.

"He had a Spanish father, Irish mother, was born in New York. Hardly the same."

"Still, it's a bit odd."

The ploy was only too familiar to Horobbins: the suspect drill, the deeply ingrained skepticism of constantly sorting through lies and evasions, in a way a mirror reflection of himself; one he might well have initiated first to establish a working relationship. Clearly, Bollock was trying to immerse himself in the barmy traits of these Dominion warriors, of which his new colleague was the first enigma. Who was he: swarthy complected, hook-nosed, marble dark eyes? Not one of those Irish blondes with black hair, white skin, and blue eyes. Horobbins, for the sake of the larger cause, decided to meet him halfway.

"Okay, but long before De Valera. Most likely Spanish blood from some castaway off the Armada. Maybe a survivor who wasn't turned over to be boiled alive. Became a Robbins. Some ancestor had an ironmonger's shop in Sligo, H.O. Robbins over the door. Came to be called 'Horobbins.' At some point, in the dim past, the name was changed to what everyone actually called them. It's pronounced Horro-bins, not Ho-robins."

"What's this Special Investigation Unit you're from?"

"As advertised. After D-Day I also inherited Six Company. I'm down to an overstretched SIU—criminal investigations of our boys who commit fraud, robbery, assault, or worse. Most of us are former policemen."

"I can tell you were a copper."

"Correct. Did a short spell with the Toronto city police. Someone took a pot shot at me, fortunately missed, and I did run him down. So I finally joined the army. Better odds, maybe."

"Bloody America. Who shot at you?"

"Not many guns up our way. A bank robber I ran into."

"Still, a violent society, innit? You must have your hands full with your lads."

"Hands full?"

"Some lot you have. My chum Greeno ran in one of yours, a Red Indian, by Hankley Common, near your Jasper Camp, in '42. He'd done in a gal he was bonking. We hanged him. Your blokes shag our women then dispose of 'em like a French letter. Aside from assorted civil crimes, we hanged six of your fine chaps, murderers all, and I wager we have another one coming up. Then that luverly mass breakout at your detention barracks in March, over in Grayshott-Headley, wrecked the place—broke out, hundreds rampaging over the countryside, terrorizing the locals. You had to send in a company of infantry to round 'em up. And guns, the Wild West brought across the pond. Those two of yours who held up the cinema in London, smashed the face of the poor old chap at the door; another shot dead a pub barman, avoided the noose when they found the victim had a rotten ticker and was about to pack it in any moment. Guns, your lads are crackers about 'em, picked up as souvenirs they'll take home to wreak more mischief on your hapless civilians, aside from knocking off the odd colonel here and there. Then they turn their beady little eyes onto Aldershot and take it apart. A fine body of men."

"Don't tell Noah about the flood, Mr. Bollock. The past two years I've been in on a lot of them." But for the moment self-discipline prevailed. Instead of opening up about the firing squad in Italy, the goadee pointed easterly. "Bodies? How about some twenty thousand buried over there, not counting air force or navy?"

Bollock's grin was marred by a missing front incisor that seemed like a small entry into a coal mine. "Right. No aggro about that. But you do seem to have more than a few pushcarts of bad apples. Even so, I don't cotton on to any idea of some revolutionary cell. It's personal, Horobbins, I feel it here." Tapped his black vest.

"Maybe not entirely. I'm expecting a file on him from London."

"Doesn't everybody have a file?"

"Not in our section. I seem to remember it crossing my desk. Something to do with black markets in Holland. Obviously he was cleared, but still."

"There we go again," smirked Bollock.

Pearly Gates back from the colonel's billet reported it was sealed up tighter than a drum, had a quick walkabout, but no sign of weapon or disturbance. He showed alarm at his captain who held onto his left side and leaned against a table.

"Touch of indigestion, I guess."

"You better get some rest, sir. I spoke to the duty officer at the Mob Control Centre. He's lined up a temporary billet for you across the way. Not much, I'm afraid."

"You look ghastly," Bollock said. "Go take some shuteye. My driver's found a spot for me in town. Me and my lads, we'll drop in on the autopsy. I'll report back to you. See you here at dawn's early." He lit another Senior Service fag, driving the pale Horobbins to the door. "You chaps finished?" Waved to the olive smocks busily dusting for fingerprints—everything in sight including flies—to pack it in for now and meet him outside. Last out of the office, Bollock turned. "Be a while before they can hose it down."

Then flipped off the lights.

6

On a July morn, the cracks in the beige wall led the eye to high tide marks on an oaken floor where contours of spilled gin or port, possibly vomit, mixed with craters from dropped cigars, the souvenirs left by generations of subalterns who had passed out or slept in Ramillies barracks overlooking Queen's Avenue. In the brief dark between dusk and dawn, Horobbins had been driven here to sprawl on a narrow cot with crackling sheets and itchy blankets. A dim lamp showed a charred fireplace, a bureau of drawers, a washstand, and a print of the Thin Red Line in the Crimea, about to get thinner judging from the fallen bodies. The everlasting lot of infantry. Across the parade square the Mob Control Centre had settled into prison floodlight. Hants police bunked in one of the blocks.

Was there an ablution room anywhere? At 0600 hours he arose from fitful tossing, his chest pains gone, found the washroom where the water was tepid. Alone at a dirty zinc basin he swabbed himself, hacked off facial stubble, found a clean shirt and socks in his kitbag, and went out.

It was Saturday. Crossing the treed avenue was without peril, the convoys to move out Canadians not yet cranked up. A Jeep with two British red caps slowed down to look him over. He walked towards Malplaquet past pacing bobbies and provost trying to stay awake. At Blenheim he came upon a stirring of life, or what passed for same.

On the parade square a facsimile of military ritual took the form of stragglers emerging from various barracks blocks, the available admin staff about to assemble for muster. Bollock showed up in his black saloon. A company sergeant major bullied the ragtag clerks and drivers into a semblance of ranks. Half of the thirty or so troops were women, healthier specimens than the mixed bag of males; most of the latter wearing rakish wedge caps and no unit markings, sure signs they had never been outside Britain. He watched Claire Evans, face white with determination, her arms swinging defiantly.

Major Todder, showing traces of hasty grooming, his khaki tie askew, brought the parade to order. Said a few words about the sudden death of their beloved CO, turned it over to Captain Horobbins who, to Bollock's surprise, found deep inside him a parade-ground voice that rang off the silent buildings.

The recipients goggled at what was expected of them: more than the usual hurry up and wait routine; a virtual imprisonment in the rooms and offices of the admin building for God knows how long, to be badgered by looming provost and civilian police. Once they had been hustled off under escort to their mess for a quick breakfast, Horobbins held his Orders group with the officers and senior sergeants.

Severe instructions about how to deal with the seething repats. Too many to haul out on a mass roll call; could lead to more unrest or active disobedience. Break it down. Take attendance in each billet, floor by floor. Tumble the whole goddam works and don't let anybody refuse a search. We have support standing by. Confiscate weapons. As to the admin staff, we'll begin with those who came directly under the colonel's purview—clerks, secretary, driver, batman, anyone else who had daily contact with him. Questions?

"Smartly done, Horobbins. You seem a bit peaked around the gills."

"Starving. Maybe I'll go over and beg at the other ranks' mess."

"No need. We have time before the inquisition with your general. My hotel offers a modest feast of rock buns and tea in the lounge. Come on, hop in and I'll bring you up to snuff on the autopsy and first go-round by forensics. Good lads, worked right through."

Down Queen's Avenue "The Camp," as it was known, intruded into the town out of Dickens—with brick chimneys and slate roofs atop the dank barracks, flues that led down to tiny charcoal fuelled stoves that, in winter, heated nothing except the hands of shivering troops clustered around. The summer air still had a lingering drift of smoking chimney pots, the rich smells of petrol and oil that never left one of the largest military bases anywhere.

Along the empty avenue, shakoed cavalry in tarnished braid once had clopped, redcoats in pillbox hats, or the tan-garbed marched on their way to the Boer War, or the first volunteers in two global wars, out of step in their flat caps and civvies. On their right the green expanse of the Queen's Parade, site of many. Through the Stanhope lines, then on their left a gleam of white webbing as MPs stood guard at Maida barracks where the rioters had been rounded up.

Down Hospital Hill Road they crossed Wellington past some early carpenters who, defying the usual work ethic, lifted wooden panels to darken the shops. Short Italian prisoners in dyed green battledress listlessly swept the pavement. A few locals, likely shopkeepers, watched the repairs. An adaptive species, the Aldershot civilians. Swamped by tides of soldiery from one war to the next, they had evolved into the wary, reserved mannerisms of the occupied: quick to earn a pound from their visitors, maybe shortchange new arrivals from the colonies, at times making gestures to entertain them, but not go overboard to be too effusive or matey. You never knew. Like when that Canadian mob turned on us. After all we had done for them since 1939. This time they had overstayed their welcome, to put it mildly.

"How come the Germans never flattened this place? Here it is, a huge sitting duck, thousands of troops jammed into dismal hovels."

"Never got around to it, did they?" Bollock threw a cigarette butt out the window. "Perhaps they thought we'd never be so stupid as to concentrate soldiery in our famed garrison. On that score they may've been right. The bulk of the army was massing along the coasts to repel invasion. Yet, there were still lots of 'em here, no question. Possibly they had other fish to fry: factories, airfields, terror bombing of London. One story around in 1940 was they wanted the camp for their own army of occupation. Surprisingly, not much of a Blitz here. Only a few raids, some of your chaps killed in barracks. The Aldershot Fire Services actually sent crews to the bombed areas, including London. No one dead from the missiles. Bomb alley missed this place. I suppose we'll never know."

In the small lounge of the hotel on a side street south of Wellington, Bollock led the way through a jungle of potted ferns to a table set with napkin covered buns. A kettle steamed over a gas ring.

"Custom of the house. Goes on all day. Tuck in."

They settled in cracked leather chairs to take tea from Minton cups and, from delicate plates, ugly sawdust buns to be slathered in margarine and powdery jam. Bollock placed his ration coupons in a saucer on the table.

"Your call on gloves was dead on. The Hendon boffins found no fingerprints on the note or gas mask. We'll have to organize handwriting samples from the staff. The gas mask has never been used. Must've been taken straight out of a stockpile. As to the projectile, it's as we thought: full copper jacket, six grooves, right hand twist, rifled barrel. Nine millimetre confirmed. Suspect firearm could be a P08 Luger or Walther P38, among others. We need that casing. I attended the autopsy. Exactly as predicted. Single shot from a steady hand. Nothing more complicated than that."

"You any idea how many souvenir pistols are out there? We can't search the whole goddam camp. Suspects in droves are being shipped out to other depots. Those in the blocks we've cordoned off—if they miss more drafts home we'll have another uprising."

"I don't care if you have to bring in tanks."

"You seem to be assuming it's close to home. But someone could've slipped in and out from afar, even the Continent."

"You'll have to convince me on that score. We'd better be off. What can you tell me about your General Spry?"

"Turned out to be one of our brighter lights, I believe. A rare permanent force type who shaped up. Came up from Italy to take over Third Div. in France last August from the unfortunate Keller. When the Canadians were diverted to medieval sieges of the Channel Ports, he is said to have pulled off a smart one at Calais. Agreed to a forty-eight hour truce to let the civilians out. By the time we opened up the attack again the Jerries had enjoyed the break so much they ran up the white flag. Rebuilt the division into the famed 'Water Rats,' known for their amphibious skills on the Scheldt, the flooded polder, and the Rhine. This year posted here to oversee repatriation. I hope he doesn't take the fall for the riots."

"Someone will. He's probably a prime candidate. You had gone to your digs. I was about to depart for the Cambridge when one of ours appears, a staff major from our General Curtis, district commander. They're much upset by your chaps, then this murder. Seems our general felt that yours could've done a better job to inform and coddle the disaffected soldiery; a true cockup, now this. I was ordered in no uncertain terms to keep our own headquarters informed. You can't remember anything more about the colonel?"

"I wasn't involved in the investigation on the Continent. Stacks of files pass over my desk. My CO's supposed to be digging it up. Here we are."

Near the corner of Queen's and Cavan's Road, the Canadian area headquarters buildings were marked by an ordinary house with pointed roof, then a low structure that could pass locally for art deco. Built in the 1930s, in expectation of war, it had housed the British Second Division before the Canadians took it over. Later it was to be named "Wavell House," after the then commander of the British unit, who went on to a stellar career as the general who presided over the loss of Greece, Crete, a cluster of smaller islands and most of North Africa, then to India for an encore.

Lines of provost trampled the lawns. High-priced help in the form of a staff major led them to a stark conference room, the place eerily still on a Saturday morning except for a rumble of voices through the open door.

"Cast of thousands," muttered Bollock.

Khaki mostly, a blizzard of pips, crowns, and red collar tabs, two Hants senior officers, ruddy British liaison officers, and several pokerfaced civilians placed far down in the seating order. Bollock thumped his murder bag onto the long table, opened his notebook on top. Two of the civilians nodded to him.

"Milne from Special Branch. That one's Nigel, a spook," Bollock whispered.

Horobbins waved to a couple of officers, including Major Clancy, head of area provost, and Todder, who had restored his spotless garb. Their arrival, completing the invitation list, now brought forth the General Officer Commanding—"Dan," to his peers. Sleepless minions scraped to their feet, followed by reluctant civilians who seemed to be at the wrong funeral. Heavy set, blondish eyebrows and moustache, baggy-eyed from exerting decisive leadership, the general could not conceal the plaintive bitterness of a loyal officer whose final crowning glory was to preside over riots and murder. To imply Montgomery steel he had banned smoking. Horobbins didn't mind, but Bollock became twitchy and irritable. The general began, as if reminiscing in some club back home.

"I can't sit here today without recalling how uplifting VE-Day was in May. Thousands of good citizens at the recreation ground, troops on their best behaviour. Thanksgiving service. Nothing like the shameful disorders in Halifax. Now, I am convinced there would have been no such outbreak here if racketeers hadn't stirred up the mob. It has all the signs of trained agitators at work. That is why the murder of Lieutenant Colonel Wellesley potentially assumes significance beyond the foul deed itself. Is it possible it could be a planned assassination? That higher places are deeply concerned is shown by the presence today of certain gentlemen from various security agencies. We also welcome the expertise of the Hants police and Scotland Yard. Let us all dedicate our energies to the one goal, to find out who is responsible for this heinous crime and bring the perpetrators to justice. Very well, first we should hear the autopsy results from the two medical examiners who worked through the night. Our gratitude, gentlemen. Then we shall have situation reports from the two lead investigators from our own provost and Scotland Yard. Following which I will entertain your appreciations and proposals for action."

The Parlow–Kinmont duet relayed findings that contained no last minute surprises for Bollock or Horobbins. Immediately, the medics dismissed suicide. Their elaborate description of the entrance wound in the midfrontal region of the skull, how the projectile traversed his brain and exited at the back of the skull, tested the general's patience.

"We get the picture, gentlemen. Was there only one shot?"

"Yes, sir, standard pattern, nothing unusual."

"The whole bloody thing is unusual, doctor. What happens next?"

"The remains may now be released with proper authorization of the coroner."

"Coroner? Stuff the coroner. We'll do our own court of inquiry. We'll see to authorization." The Hants constabulary were stricken. "You tell us it is definitely not suicide. More than that, not a close range shot?"

"Well over three feet away, sir. We estimate it could be as far as eight feet. The individual was standing, held the weapon steady, discharged a single round. Either lucky or an expert marksman. We would hazard the latter because whoever it was didn't even bother with the *coup de grace*—a final shot to make sure."

"I know what it means, doctor. Then do we assume the killer came forward, placed the threatening note and respirator on the desk?"

"It would seem so, sir."

"All the marks of the professional. No weapon, no cartridge casing. What have you found out about the round itself, inspector? Our thanks to you and your colleagues for toiling through the night."

Bollock repeated the findings from Hendon, including the dearth of fingerprints. In the awed silence that followed, Horobbins cleared his throat to put in his oar for full logistic support to organize an operations centre on site. Bleak smile from Spry.

"Despite the weekend, we shall demonstrate the army hasn't fallen into complete disrepair. Major Todder, you'll see to it. My staff is at your beck and call. Now, gentlemen, let us not forget the war is not over. The invasion of Japan will be on a scale vaster than D-Day. Casualties will be high. We cannot allow slackness or rebellion. Let me summarize four main questions the senior levels of government and the military, British and Canadian, direct to us to resolve. First, is the IRA or other revolutionary cells the instigator? Two, is there evidence of a widespread revolt organized by Reds, or extreme elements of Labour, to cause massive disruption before the British election? Three, is it a Japanese espionage operation, possibly using the pro-Japanese Indian independence movement? Four, what steps are being taken to protect other senior officers and public officials from assassination?"

Including himself, thought Horobbins. No wonder he's careworn. Bollock rested his elbows on the murder bag, clamped his bowed head, his dark hair greasy with neglect—the body language of one who didn't buy the dire scenarios. Including a footnote from the general.

"To which I add number five: the threat of a lethal gas attack. Jimmy," to an Ordnance half-colonel, "thorough inventory and security of gas storage in the entire district. Work with our British friends." He turned to the spooks. "Undoubtedly it is beyond our capacity, as humble soldiers, to carry out the kind of investigations needed to resolve the questions raised at higher levels. I assure you of our cooperation, but I do expect you to keep me informed if any of your findings involve any member under my command. You have already requested permission to interrogate the hoodlums we now have in custody here and in Reading, notably the ringleaders. You will arrange that, Major Clancy." Spotted Dick's visage erupted in livid acne, confirming his nickname. The general settled on the civilian Bollock had identified as "Nigel" who, with his flecked sandy hair and moustache, appeared to be the most substantial of the shadowy delegation. "Do you gentlemen have any wisdom to impart to us at this early stage?"

"My colleagues and I are grateful for your support, sir. A difficult task lies ahead for all of us. However, there is one reference to outside influences that has come to our attention. It appears that some of your troops involved in the disturbances made republican utterances that could be attributed to extremist Irish factions. It was noted some of them shouted: 'Down with King.'"

General Spry and the other Canadians around the table struggled to remain earnest.

"Not likely the monarchy. They were no doubt invoking the name of Mr. Mackenzie King, our prime minister, who is not too popular with the common soldier."

"Then, sir, perhaps certain parties in Canada should be alerted."

"Why bother?" someone muttered.

Spry leaned forward in the mode of one about to make a command decision. "Gentlemen, this is indeed a sad time for our army. For your ears only, not to go beyond this room, on 5 July in Italy a private soldier was executed for murder. To my great regret, before he deserted to lead a life of crime in the cesspool of Rome, he was a member of one of my fine regiments in First Brigade. I mention this to emphasize that we shall carry out our duty, whoever is guilty of the crime—no ifs, ands or buts about it."

Then leaving others to haggle over details, such as keeping the Press at bay, he beckoned to the two lead investigators to follow him into the hallway where they gathered under framed Canadian Pacific Railway posters of resorts at home, including Banff and Lake Louise, the idyllic displays hardly conducive to improved morale.

"I fully realize it's far too soon for any conclusions, but off the record, what are your hunches, ideas, assumptions? Do you have any?"

Bollock took up the nod from Horobbins who needed two more seconds to think.

"Without committing myself, sir, it seems likely that someone held a grudge against the colonel, overpowering dislike or hatred."

"You're implying you don't buy the larger conspiracy theories?"

"Impossible to say, sir. We shall, of course, proceed to collect evidence and duly evaluate it."

"Knowing Lieutenant Colonel Wellesley as I do—did—of all my officers he's the least likely candidate for assassination. Fine management skills, efficient, of exemplary character. There must be something else. Captain?"

"Sir, why did he insist his repatriation admin unit be set up in the far reaches of North Camp?"

"Nothing more than shortage of space, as far as I'm aware. Until we started moving troops out after the disturbances, the base was jammed to the rafters. What're you implying?"

"We're exploring every avenue, sir. We have to look into any aspect of his activities that might have inadvertently triggered his own death. We will be thoroughly interrogating every member of staff."

"Including senior officers?"

"Officers, sir?"

"Fellows like us with funny little bits on their shoulder straps."

"Yes, sir, rank will not be spared. I may have to refer any complaints to you and hope you will back us up. The sanitation zone we've set up comprises several blocks of other ranks in Blenheim and Malplaquet. Until we've completed a thorough search and the interviews, we can't release them for shipment home. I have to warn you there may be more trouble, certainly unrest."

"You call my office the minute you need reinforcements. We shall not tolerate any more of that nonsense. I want daily progress reports directly from you, the same information you pass along to Colonel Cameron and his superiors. Do I make myself clear, Captain Horobbins?"

On their way back to the car under the protection of meandering provost, Bollock grinned through gapped incisors. "Clever chap, your general. Actually wanted the word out, dint he? You hadn't told me."

"Not supposed to. Yes, it'll be all over; I see it a gamble to flush out the killer or informants. Might work, might not."

"Nor did you tell him you have a file on the colonel."

"He'll find out soon enough. Didn't want to spoil his day."

7

A wavering line of geese, a provost sergeant at the wedge point: the gaggle stretched out in ragged formation, the searchers peering down for a German pistol, a shiny brass casing, a gas mask bag, rubber gloves. Blue constabulary mixed with dun MPs, plus a contingent of bespectacled weeds from the Pay Corps, presumably dragooned for their keen eye for the bottom line. Others in denim coveralls poked long sticks into drains. Two sappers with metal mine detectors had been unearthed; earphones clamped, they swept their pancake sensors, swathing in rhythm. From doorways, confined soldiery hooted. In Bollock's saloon car the two investigators took in the scuffed tarmac, trampled sward, and the undulating line of odds and sods.

"Look at that lot. A wonder we won the war."

"We didn't. It was the Americans and Russians. Remember?"

The first bit of pay dirt arrived from two coveralls who loped across from the nearby cookhouse serving the other ranks' mess, a low brick structure with a sheen of grease from the ages. They brandished Robin Hood flour sacks at Horobbins. Revolt over breakfast, they reported; found in oatmeal porridge, bits of shredded rubber—probably the gloves, showing signs of passage through a meat grinder. In triumph, from a waste bin, a soggy respirator bag. The exhibits were handed over to the forensics, the kitchen and mess surrounded and closed off, the chefs and their bottle washers subjected to a different type of grilling. Results disappointing: nobody had any memory of unauthorized use of the meat grinder and, as to strangers, the place was a heavy traffic area, yes, rosters of those sentenced to kitchen fatigues, but more likely someone had crept in overnight. At any rate, two items down, two to go.

Ribald comments about improved quality of the food featured at the next Orders group around a trestle table in a room where the occupants had been ejected by the "can-do" work parties promised by the general, a weekend marvel of activity. Scraping boots, confused orders, a milling about of sweaty pen-pushers, CWAC, provost, signalers, plainclothes detectives, to set up tables, chairs, Gestetners, typewriters, phone lines. Most vital: coffee and tea urns.

Sergeant Gates produced his clipboard of the repat unit's staff. "We've started with those closest to the colonel: his batman, driver, clerk, anyone who reported to him directly. What about Major Todder, sir?"

"I'll see to him. You flag the ones we should follow up on. Now, could you extract Corporal Evans and bring her here?"

Two dames for the price of one, it seemed. Corporal Evans was ushered in by a dumpy, square-faced CWAC officer, black shoulder tabs with three pips: Captain Karen Williams, officer commanding the Quack detachment—the queen bee who protected her charges from the groping forays of the chair warming drones. Her deep voice echoed in the bare office, startled the two investigators and reminded Horobbins of a school teacher's scold, uttered with East Coast inflections that only a denizen of the North American attic would detect.

"What's this about kit inspection? I won't have your men pawing through my girls' belongings. I want to conduct the search with my own."

Horobbins hadn't thought of it. Careless. Quickly surrendered, tried to mollify the captain by bringing her up to speed on what they knew so far, including the items they were seeking.

"My gals don't have weapons, let alone souvenir pistols."

"You sure? Who around here might be motivated to do him in? Did he ever pester or harass any of them?"

"I have received no complaints. Haven't noticed any such behaviour on his part; maybe others, but not him."

"There has to be something."

"One thing I'll say to you now, Captain—ah, I bet it wasn't anyone on our staff. You realize who we have here? Rejects—category types unfit for active service or much else. None of them proficient in anything, if that, except typing, filing, and forms. The weak, halt, and lame. My girls are in better shape."

"Spot on," said Bollock, who provoked a death stare.

"Who's he? I'll bet my bottom dollar there isn't a marksman among them. Are you considering an outside hit?"

"Others certainly have, madam," said Bollock.

"Why is he here? Isn't this a military matter?"

"For the reason you just mentioned, we have to investigate every possibility. There could be civilians from various subversive or criminal groups involved. You are not to speak to anyone else about this. I've taken you into our confidence. You've brought Corporal Evans. Is she fit to be interviewed?"

"Why don't you ask her?"

"Fine. You may go now."

"I'm here to see to her needs."

Through the wringer, blotched patches on high cheekbones, kepi on her lap, Evans had swimming brown eyes, rather thick eyebrows, straight dark hair lank from a sedated night on a cot in sick bay, a fine nose, bleached full lips;

her upper torso erect in the chair was full breasted, shaping her tunic. Aware enough to allow a slight nod. Not that fragile, perhaps; she had managed to haul herself out for the early morning roll call.

"You found him. What were you doing in his office at 2200 hours when everyone was confined to barracks?"

"I dropped in to pick up something from my desk."

Corporal Evans blew into a well-washed tan handkerchief. Her boss patted her on the shoulder.

"Take your time. What was so urgent at that hour? Did you find the colonel's door open?"

"Yes, sir. There he was, head down."

"Did you touch anything?"

"No. When I saw the blood, I knew. I went over, saw the note and the respirator."

"You have a copy of the note?" Williams interrupted. Horobbins read out his scribbled copy. "Nobody around here could write that."

"What went on here the two nights of the riots? Any disturbances?"

"Heavens, no. Officers and NCOs were issued sidearms. Sentries posted, including guards at the CWAC quarters in case any hooligans got this far with you-know-what on their little minds. It was tense, but quiet. Lieutenant Colonel Wellesley was on duty in his office throughout, I believe."

"Corporal Evans, you slipped out of your billet without anyone stopping you?"

"It was the day after; everything had quietened down."

"Are you her lawyer, or something? Corporal."

"Yes, sir. I recognized the guards, of course, our own staff, they let me pass."

"We have to take your fingerprints. The police are setting up in the next room."

"I didn't touch anything."

"Did you hear the shot, see anyone lurking about?" Bollock's antennae were up.

"No. I walked over from the spider hut where we're billeted, those nice ones built for the Canadians on base. There were lorries and motor bikes going by."

"Nor did anyone else, apparently. You think it must have happened shortly before you arrived at the orderly room?"

"That's my impression. The, um, blood was wet."

"Did you see anyone leave the building?"

"Not a soul. The lights were on. I went straight to the duty officer to report it."

"You say you walked over from your billet for something you had to retrieve from your desk. What would that be?"

"Actually I'd run out of sanitary napkins and remembered I had some in my desk."

"Show me."

"Really, sir."

"I don't mean if you're wearing one. Your desk."

"It's two doors along the hall in the filing room." She implored her captain. "There aren't any there now, I took them."

"You came in the front door of the orderly room, walked along the corridor to your desk, removed the, ah, items. Why did you not return the same way, back through the orderly room? The colonel's office is at the far end of the building. Was there another reason for your visit at that hour? Was he expecting you?"

"What on earth?"

Horobbins glanced at Sergeant Gates, who became a threatening presence in the doorway as if to prevent escape. Some kind of signal had passed between them. "Sir, I have information his staff car was outside the building, down at the end. He'd dismissed his driver, a Private Nolan."

"The two of you about to take a nice little spin somewhere?"

"Sir, I resent . . ."

"Answer the question. We'll find out sooner or later."

Swaying on her chair, Claire Evans slipped off at an angle to lean on the ample shoulder of her protector.

"Put a sock in it. She's had enough for now."

Horobbins sized up the corporal's shiny forehead, her jumpy eyelids.

"Can you make it back to your hut? You better get some rest. No, captain, I want a word."

Gates took her arm, but was brushed off. The corporal straightened up, put her kepi low on her forehead, saluted, made an effort to march, rather than stagger from the room.

"Captain Williams, wouldn't you agree that's kind of an over-reaction? I mean, almost personal?"

"What're you getting at? You have a dirty mind, captain. The poor thing walked in on a horrible sight. No wonder she's shook up."

"Granted, but I have to wonder how come she went on down the hall to the colonel's office. Her story doesn't hold water. You aware of any connection or relationship there? Surely you've heard something."

"No I haven't, Captain Ho-robbins, is it? She's a fine girl."

"Maybe so. Look, you appreciate we have to explore every possible avenue. I can't emphasize too strongly the pressure we're under. Upper levels are having a fit about the note—visions of conspiracies, revolution, espionage, you name it."

"I had no idea." Williams revealed unusual twitches of doubt and a certain awe at being let into the inner leagues of statecraft.

"You will appreciate we need the cooperation of everyone to arrive at a speedy and just conclusion. Now, you seem to have developed a good rapport with Corporal Evans. She trusts you."

"I take care of my kids, unlike some others I could mention."

"And who'd that be?" Sly Bollock.

"Never mind. What're you leading up to?"

"I'm asking if you would agree to follow up with Corporal Evans, delve a bit more into any possible personal relationship with Lieutenant Colonel Wellesley."

Her face hardened. "You want me to be an informer?"

"I may have to hold her as a material witness. And I can always order some of my rougher elements to search your quarters, they'd enjoy that. You have to decide, right now. I'm sure you're as eager as we are to clear her of any suspect activity, or even indirect knowledge that could help us."

"She isn't capable of."

"I didn't say she was. What I'm suggesting is for you to take her off for a quiet drink or something and have a heart-to-heart, as her mentor and friend."

"Just us gals, eh?"

"I leave it to your good judgment. This sector is locked up tight, but I'll issue you with passes now. You fill in the date and time. Take it as an opportunity to escape this foul place and just maybe put your own mind to rest. Anyway, the poor girl needs support, and you're the best one to give it to her."

The chief of the local Quacks picked up the inscribed rite of passage, gave him a shriveling stare that probably would have terrified her girls, and left.

"Not bad, Horobbins," said Bollock. "Couldn't have done better meself."

8

Off to one side, lethargic disarmament went on at a chain link compound. They stopped to watch. Helmets—traditional dishpan, streamlined invasion models, buckets worn by despatch riders or paratroops—were tossed, skimmed clanking to become a mound of scrap metal to be sold for never-ending war somewhere. Repats, newly arrived from the Continent and destined for billets outside of Aldershot, lined up to shuck off heavy lids, no taking them home as mementos; German helmets, maybe, but not their own. At the compound gate where a fifteen-hundred weight lorry waited for clearance, Horobbins peeked over the tailgate at stacks of Lee-Enfield .303 rifles.

His murder bag pulling down an arm, Bollock shook his head. "Won't you need them for the Japs?"

"Not me. I haven't signed up. Unfinished business here. Our Pacific Force is fated to come under Yank command. For once they'll have the best equipment and awesome backing."

"They'll miss us."

"You kidding? Ice cream instead of British slop. Still, I don't envy them. The Japs'll fight to the last chopstick. Europe will seem like a picnic."

"Don't count on it. The fire-bombing is one massive fry-up. They can't last."

"What about Okinawa? Dress rehearsal for millions of fanatics on home turf. You should know—like 1940, to the last man on the beaches."

"Plucky Britain standing alone, what? You weren't here, right? One day it may come out, but let me tell you now in full breach of the Official Secrets Act and the like, that it was a near-run thing. I'm not speaking of the air war, the first major setback for the Nazis. That was later. Just how dicey our situation was first came home to me in May 1940 when we were called in for a special briefing. I had just been promoted to CID. Very hush-hush, we were warned of a move afoot to dump Churchill and seek an accommodation with

Hitler; nothing on paper, but we were briefed on a contingency plan to restore order in the event of disturbances. Instructions were issued about how to cooperate with the German authorities when they arrived, an inevitability it seemed. There was the possibility of that walking cadaver Halifax as a tame PM, supported by your man Beaverbrook, Hoare, Rothermere, even Lloyd George among that lot, aided and abetted by Mosley, Diana Mitford—not the one who shot herself over her love for Hitler—the Astors, others in the old pro-Nazi gang. If ever a police force rumbled mutiny, that was the day."

"I never heard that before."

"Small wonder. The public was kept in a dream world, no one could imagine the possibility. But the realities were brought home to some of us privileged to be given the inside dope, because we would be forced to take on unspeakable duties, such as rounding up dissidents and Jews, when the takeover happened, and there was little doubt it would. Nothing to stop them on the ground, just a gutted BEF evacuated from Dunkirk without a pot to piss in, only five rounds per man in some units. Your two divisions might have put up a fight if they'd sobered up enough. How we got through it is nothing short of a miracle. Churchill, Winnie the Pooh, blustered on with nothing, until somehow a few politicians with more backbone than the others supported him in his folly of continuing to resist. We were summoned again and, under penalty of treason, ordered to forget about the previous briefing.

"Then that summer RAF came through. Even that was sheer luck. A few of our Wellingtons dropped some bombs on Berlin. Up to that point the Germans were winning the air war, knocking out our airfields and radar stations, one by one. It seems Hitler had one of his fits and switched the Luftwaffe over to terror bombing our cities. Gave our lads a breather to recover and create one of those legends that will live on because they work. It's not the same for the Japs. They're being bombed into the Stone Age." Bollock pointed to the lorry. "No, we'll need those guns to take on the Russkis. Want to wager on it? On our way, why don't we do a walkabout through that block, see how your blokes are doing in confinement?"

Their retinue moved on. Dragging anchor between a CID man and a provost corporal was a hulking, muscular soldier, a weight lifter slumming. Extracted from the staff table of establishment, he was the batman, or valet, to the late colonel.

"Private Montgomery?" Horobbins read off the interview notes when the man was escorted to his door.

"Sapper, sir. No relation." Meaning the famed field-marshal.

True enough, the giant wearing Royal Canadian Engineers and First Div patches, Italy to Northwest Europe campaign ribbons and two gold wound stripes on his sleeve, was an unlikely pants presser for fussy officers. I bet he's someone who can handle small arms, Horbbins appraised, as he ordered him to join their search of the colonel's quarters in the cluster of luxurious spider huts down the way near the Lynchford Road beyond the Blenheim lines.

Could anyone be closer, more familiar with his habits and quirks than the colonel's own manservant?

They entered the ground floor of the barracks where the stacked bunks, designed for Crimean war midgets, remained unchanged, with thin mattresses over boards. Confined troops sprawled amid a fug of tobacco smoke, stale sweat, reeking woolen socks, greasy dubbin on boots, the foul bodily fluids of countless soldiery since the 1850s.

"Kit inspection," yapped a sergeant, running advance guard with two MPs. With a low rumble of obscenities the men lugged out duffel bags and took down jackets and greatcoats from nails driven into crumbling brick walls. Hopes fading they would ever get home, the underclass stood more or less at attention to size up the intruders. The provost captain, swarthy as a desert nomad, hooked nose, protruding eyes, conveyed a sense of watchful sympathy for their plight. With curiosity they tried to figure out the civilian in black suit and vest, stained fedora like a relic from the Blitz, the usual shoddy British dental work revealing itself in a mouth of crooked teeth and one gap, the impression of a derelict fence. He carried a square black case. Plainclothes dick written all over him. The tour perked up when an MP pulled a Luger and a Walther from kitbags. He held them with two fingers on the trigger guards, checked the safeties before demanding the owner's name and number, wrote them on tags, dropped the pistols into a canvas bag.

"Leave the clips in," Bollock ordered. "We'll be doing ballistics."

"When do we get 'em back, corp?" The owner was in post-war mode, bordering on protest.

"Tough tit, you shouldna have them anyways."

"How long'll we be cooped up here?" the brave soul went on.

Another inmate goaded him on. "You tell him cactus, you got the prick."

At closer range the provost captain showed half moon smudges under his eyes. Must be under thirty, but seemed closer to fifty. His voice hoarse with fatigue, he had read the mood of the troops and went out of his way to avoid further provocation. "Sorry, I can't say. You'll stay here pending investigation into the death of Lieutenant Colonel Wellesley. If any of you have information that can help us, come and see me at the orderly room. Confidentiality guaranteed. The sooner we find the culprit the sooner you're on your way home. Understood?"

With no followup questions, the captain was attracted to a bunk where, on a blanket, the glittering contents from a kitbag seemed like a store display. A private with North Shore Regiment patches stood by his stack of Nazi naval badges, hats, even a tunic with gold braid.

"What're these?"

"Naval stores, Kriegsmarine from Emden, sir."

The captain pointed. "Those submarine badges, they're really keen. How much?"

The corporal behind him clucked. "I don't think so, sir."

Horobbins tried to assume kit inspection severity. "Did you amass this hoard by yourself?"

"No, sir. Added to my collection, got lucky in the games."

"What games?"

"Poker and craps every night in the ablution rooms."

"You ante up souvenirs and the like? That include pistols?"

"Anything you wanna name on the table, sir. Big turnover of stuff. Yeah, pistols too."

"My God, they're trading weapons like candy. You any idea how many are floating around?"

"We only need to find one," Bollock said.

Raucous horselaughs followed the visitors on their way out of the fetid place. Anarchy was catching.

"Blimey." Bollock parodied his East End roots. "No bleeding chimney pots."

He stopped to admire the Canadian-built wooden barracks, a discreet lumber camp in the midst of Crimean ruins.

"Much prized. Most of them down the road at Cove. Central steam heating. Called 'spider' huts: the ablution rooms and boilers at the core, the wings offshoots, hence spiders. Only the most fortunate end up here. That one, I believe, is for the women where our Corporal Evans hangs her hat; this one with cubicles is for officers." Along the corridor he peered into an open door. "This one's empty. I'll see if they can move me over. I think we'll be here for a while." The cubicle was under lockdown, a guard at the door. A passing through place, a transient cell bare of decoration except for a photo of a pretty woman and two small boys. Bollock opened his murder bag on the desk, put on cotton gloves.

"None of you touch anything, just point when I ask." In a stately shuffle the policeman circled clockwise to poke through the furniture, overturning the armchair to grope underneath, peeled back the bed mattress, crawled under with an electric torch. The closet had three uniforms, two navy blue lounge suits, khaki shirts, three white ones, a leather suitcase, and a metal trunk.

"When did you last see him, Montgomery?"

"About 1700 hours, sir. I had done brass and boots, pressed uniforms and one of his suits. Told me didn't need me the rest of the day."

"How did he seem at the time? Wearing his sidearm?"

"Everybody had the wind up."

"What were your own movements the past three days?"

"A bit constipated, sir."

"Montgomery," said Horobbins under tight rein, "I will see you later. Now we're talking about the sixth, the disturbances pretty well under control. Why'd he continue wearing his pistol? Was he expecting someone or more trouble?"

"Didn't tell me, sir."

"Come and see this, Horobbins." Bollock had used a screwdriver to pry off the lock on the tin trunk. "A cornucopia. Why didn't you inform us, private?"

"Sapper, sir. I figure you'd get around to it."

From the trunk Bollock lifted bottles of whisky, Dutch gin, French cognac, and cartons of American and Canadian cigarettes, tore open a carton and spilt the cellophane-wrapped red, black, and white packs onto the linoleum floor.

51

He peeled open a pack and lit a cigarette. "Odd names for your fags. You sure it isn't Sweet Corporals? No traces of narcotics, but I'll have Hendon go over everything." He tapped around the trunk for hidden compartments. "I suppose this treasure has to be put into bond. A shame this one's broken." Bollock swept the loose packs into his murder bag. "Won't miss these, I daresay." The Canadians smirked. "What was he doing with this stuff? Everyone around here keep a hoard like this? Don't have a clue, do we, Montgomery?"

"Give you two guesses," said Horobbins from the small desk where he emptied its two drawers of flimsy blue V-mail letters not important enough to be locked away, seemingly personal stuff to pore over later. "There's no daily calendar here. We didn't find one at his office. How did he schedule himself, keep track?"

"I seen him writing in two little notebooks—you know, pocket size. Kept them on his person far as I know."

"We didn't find them in his personal effects, and he must've had a key ring. Inspector, if, like most of us, he kept keys in his trousers pocket, the killer would've had to fish them out. There weren't any footprints or anything, say, to show somebody knelt to pull out the keys?"

"Not that I could see. It could mean our assassin made the colonel hand them over before he was shot. Somebody wanted the keys and the notebooks, or it's always possible they're more red herrings to entertain us, like the note and the gas mask. Long way to go yet, captain. Sapper, when did he swan around in those Saville Row tatters?"

"Only when he went up to London, sir, most weekends. He had a flat there."

"God almighty, you say a flat. You have an address? Where's the key?"

"Don't have no address. I expect the key's on the ring you're looking for. His driver, Stan Nolan, might be able to tell you more. He'd take him to the station for the up train to Waterloo. Stan told me the colonel shared the flat with some other officers, seems he had it before he was posted here; maybe they kept it for when they were on leave. One thing you might look for is the phone number he'd leave at the orderly room if he had to be reached."

A gradual thaw came over his tormentors. "More like it, Montgomery. Did he entertain visitors here?"

"Not that I recollect." Crafty again. "Nights I couldn't say."

"Did he ever take anyone with him? I mean to London from here?"

"Always a possibility, sir."

"Do you know or don't you?"

"Can't really say, sir."

Horobbins took on the hues of red oak. Bollock snorted at yet another breakdown of discipline in this dissolving, ragtag army.

9

Until the messenger from London handed him the envelope, its flimsy heft a bad omen, Horobbins had with some difficulty managed to keep the well-honed "been there, done that" cool of the professional. But this was one beaut of a case with its infinite pool of hundreds, perhaps thousands of suspects, some of them likely on their way out of the country. Turn over one stone at a time. Narrow it down. Sift evidence over and over. Search for nuggets in the stacks of interviews piling up in the scrawled notes of the military and civilian interrogators. Keep calm, stick to your own assumptions of a connection to nefarious doings on the Continent, hold onto your skepticism about political or revolutionary conspiracies at one end and, at the other, Bollock's murder squad mindset leaning to personal motive. Stay the course.

What he now had on his trestle table in the makeshift office was the dossier ordered from London. Not at all what he expected. Instead of a wad of reports he found one long sheet in a legal-sized folder, a message (Army Form C2136) a carbon copy typed in caps, date blurred, early May 1945. From Assistant Deputy Provost Marshal (ADPM) Headquarters First Canadian Army, Holland, to many other acronyms, including his boss Colonel Cameron.

Thoughtfully, for once, the latter had attached a handwritten tab: "This must be a disappointment for you. I shall be at my desk after 1300 hours today."

Swell.

Para I referred to instructions from First Echelon, Canadian Section HQ in Brussels, a lieutenant colonel identified as an ADJAG, Assistant Deputy Judge

Advocate General, legal boffin, apparently relaying the views of his commander, Major General E. L. M. Burns. No further action or inquiries to be pursued re the allegations by SIU against Lt. Col. A. Wellesley and Maj. P. Todder. (So, Todder was mixed up in whatever it was).

Para II: Allegations of SIU investigating officers remain unproven and strongly denied by subjects. The latter have accounted for their movements on the dates in question to satisfaction of senior staff here. Relevant work orders and transport requisitions were produced and verified.

Para III: The death by drowning of one Cpl. Orest Timchuk, RCASC driver to Lt. Col. A. Wellesley, is assessed by medical examiner who performed autopsy as a vehicle accident, possibly suicide, and in no way attributable to the abovementioned officers or alleged activities during the famine and medical relief operations in Holland.

Para IV: The situation for First Canadian Army is highly fluid with all personnel engaged in arduous duties. To continue the inquiries instigated by SIU would be detrimental to efficient allocation of resources at this crucial stage in concluding actions against the enemy, the control and evacuation of enemy POWs, implementation of reconstruction and aid programs for the civilian population.

"Sir, what in God's name happened to the rest of the file?"

"Beats me, Horobbins. Seems the supporting reports and attachments from SIU have been removed. I'm trying to find out who and why."

"Do any of the details come back to you, sir?"

"Only in general terms. It had to do with a shipment of medicines and drugs that allegedly went astray during the Dutch relief exercise. See here, I'm as disappointed as you are. I've sent signals to my counterpart in Germany to track down our investigating officers, if they're still around. We need to know their side of the story and what went wrong. If I can locate them I'll put you in touch. You still believe it's relevant?"

"Somebody thought so if the file was stripped. Thanks for following up, sir. We attended a conference with General Spry this morning."

"So I heard. Work closely with him, he has resources at his beck and call. How're you getting along with the Scotland Yard inspector?"

"Fair enough, sir. Our teams are interviewing every member of the colonel's staff. Barracks and grounds are being searched for the weapon and other items. Some of the key interviews I'll follow up on myself. We have found out from his batman that the colonel kept a flat in London. We'll get a handle on that before the day is out. The file refers to Major Todder. He's still here as acting CO, but it seems he was off base the night of the murder. He's first on my list."

"He's been with the colonel right through, hasn't he? From their days in Alberta. Well, let me pass along an anecdotal bit I picked up just before you phoned. I was discussing the case with George" (Cameron's second-in-command) "who was IC Military District Thirteen provost out of Calgary, Alberta, before his posting here. Seems there were some ruckuses about our colonel when he commanded the Service Corps training centre at Red Deer, to the north of Calgary. In September '43 he rousted out the Quacks for a revel to celebrate the surrender of Italy. Complaints lodged. Also accused of purloining an ambulance as a personal joy caravan for himself and chosen gals. None of it stuck."

"Never does with him, does it?"

"Not until now, Horobbins. Somebody or something caught up with him."

Outside his door he amused an idle typist with a request for a stack of old mimeographed part two orders and to punch two holes in each sheet, the scrap paper to thicken up the sparse file folder with bogus reports he would try out on Todder. Then he called in Bollock and Sergeant Gates from heavy duty supervising the "weak, halt, and the lame," in Captain Williams's parlance, as they were interviewed, fingerprinted, and subjected to penmanship samples. Every member of staff, no matter how unlikely a suspect, had to copy out the threatening note left on the colonel's desk.

The three men ate a late lunch of sandwiches, fingering them carefully for traces of rubber gloves amid the pink Spam, while they listened to Pearly Gates report on his foray into the orderly room.

"Craziest setup I've ever seen." Gates waved his notes. "Orderly room sergeant says this is their only contact phone number, but not the colonel's flat, it's Major Todder's in London; not even his, the girlfriend's. The drill was— say the colonel was in London and Major Todder, too; the instruction was to phone the major in case of emergency. If needed, he would then reach the colonel at his flat. The only one around here who has the number is Major Todder, unless, of course, Corporal Evans or someone else we don't know about."

Horobbins choked.

"Take a deep breath, sir."

Bollock shook his head. "Rather casual approach to command, innit? Seems based on the assumption that the major never would be in the colonel's flat with him at the same time. Doesn't make sense. Right, if you can extract the number from this Todder chap, I'll post a man outside the door. You hand him the number and he'll see it's transmitted to the Met. They will trace the address and have a looksee."

10

Disarming, quick to size up the glowering interloper, Major Philip Todder, in an attempt to put off or mollify the inevitable, became the amiable host. Now in charge after the demise of his mentor, he was swamped with papered complexities as the repats were scattered to far flung outposts, his staff available only in short stints between third degree ordeals. In his creaking swivel chair in the cluttered office across the hall from the sealed crime scene, he lolled back and drummed a leather-covered swagger stick on his knee, his pose of relaxed authority marred by acquired British mannerisms and an Upper Canada College honk, not a good start to build rapport with the seething provost captain. Worth a try, though.

"How're you settling in, Horobbins?"

His adversary relented slightly, went for the bait, allowed he was not settled at all. Todder dinged a bell on his desk, bringing forth a grey-haired staff sergeant.

"Staff, see that Captain Horobbins is signed in for mess privileges. Food's quite good over there. And find him a billet in our wing of the spider huts." He pointed his stick at Horobbins's midsection. "Your belt could do with touching up. Bring your batman with you?"

Horobbins glanced at his grubby web belt in need of white blanco. "In London three of us share a batman part-time. Yes, I suppose."

"Consider it done. Staff, is Bremner still up in Greenock? Right. Assign his batman to Captain Horobbins here, see that his kit is moved. Let me speak to him first." Todder lifted a handwritten sheet. "Was writing to the bereaved widow, follow-up to General Spry's letter. His wife, widow, cables she wants the remains returned to Canada. Not the usual drill. We'll see. If he's hacked up by your sawbones I don't see the point, casket would have to be sealed. General Spry has laid on a memorial service here, tomorrow. You received the invite yet?"

"I'll check when I get back."

In another attempt to moderate the frosty climate, Todder brought up the question of the execution. "If it's so hush-hush, why did the general blab it to a cast of thousands?"

"You figure it out, sir."

"How'd they do it? Didn't think we had anybody left in Italy."

"I gather they kept a small contingent of odds and sods there expressly for that purpose. The British, having already shot two of their own from the same gang, put on the pressure for us to act. Ours was delayed until our Mr. King got through his June election. Make no mistake; General Spry is deadly serious about what'll happen to Wellesley's killer. Now, sir, I need something from you: the phone number, address, and key for Colonel Wellesley's flat in London. Some set-up you two had. Why didn't he leave his contact number with the orderly room?"

"Had his own reasons, I daresay. Didn't want the unwashed snooping about."

"Come on, sir, it's ridiculous. Your lady friend's number the only link in an emergency? How was it supposed to work if you were at the colonel's flat?"

"Simple. Was never there. Not in his social circle."

"You were with him in Canada, Northwest Europe, and here, all the way through, and he cut you out. Why?"

"His business, not mine."

"What business?"

"Look, I don't have a key or the address." Todder consulted a small notebook from which he wrote a number. "There. Are we finished?"

Horobbins gave him the pitying smile of interrogators anywhere. "While you're at it, your lady's address." Copied the information, handed it to the waiting CID man outside the door, then returned to open the improvised file folder across his knees beyond Todder's angle of vision.

"You haven't answered anything yet. You knew him better than anyone around here, so tell me more. He's not what he seems, Major Todder, maybe you aren't either. Somebody felt strongly enough about it to kill him. When we were in his quarters I noticed a photo of his family, two young sons, pretty lady. Let's start there."

"Oh, Ambrose came from a fine Montreal family—Westmount. Father a big-time bond dealer on St. James. Ambrose was taken into the firm, nicely survived the Depression. Unlike so many in that Anglo enclave, he made himself bilingual; went out of his way to seek out Peasoups to yammer in their own lingo. Very popular."

"Not with everyone, for sure. Why was he called 'the Duke'?"

"Rather obvious, isn't it? Ambrose Wellesley. Wellington, the Iron Duke, whose statue glares over Aldershot. Suited his style—very imposing, over six feet, lordly jaw and deportment."

"Wasn't the real one an Arthur?"

"Close enough."

"What do you mean his style?"

If Todder resented the note-taking, his suspicions were aroused by the thick file folder draped on the other's lap.

"What's that you've got there?"

"You should know, sir, the Special Investigation Unit reports on the late colonel's activities in Canada and on the Continent. You seem to have a supporting role throughout."

Todder inhaled an unfiltered Buckingham, considered strong even in those days. "Hand it over. It's garbage, you know. I'm surprised you have it. I thought it . . ."

"Thought what, sir? I can't let you see it, but I can tell you we're taking another look at the entire file for any connection to the colonel's murder."

"Nothing there worth a fart in a windstorm. Tell me what this is leading up to. Be careful. There's no proof of anything."

"We'll see. I'm counting on your full and frank cooperation. So let's go back and start with you. Your service book shows you were with him when he commanded the base at Red Deer. How'd you end up there?"

"You want the straight goods."

"It'd help."

Todder sized up the implacable skeptic across the desk, pondered, then changed gears to startle this odd duck military cop who wore a soiled web belt. The mannerisms that were clearly an irritation, seemingly in the way of convincing him of his innocence, were shucked off for a moment of candour that might buy some time or a bit of goodwill. The voice shifted into a register Horobbins identified from his days on the beat in Toronto; not an accent or argot, rather a slur, a throaty growl to guard the pack against yet another menace coming out of the dark. A flash of recognition when Todder asked if he knew Toronto and Horobbins owned up he had been with the city police. Instincts right: this was the card to play.

"Cabbagetown, Riverdale, you know 'em. Orphan raised in vile foster homes; in it for the money they were, till I ran off at sixteen to work heaving furniture for a moving van outfit. McClintock's. Remember them? Very classy navy blue vans with silver lettering to try and entice the carriage trade. A cutthroat business in hard times. We'd have pitched battles on the doorstep when another van came up to give a lower rate, right on the spot when we had the contract. When I got a reputation for management skills, with my fists and proven salesmanship, old man McClintock took a shine to me, saw that I was trained as a mechanic in their garage, and staked me to night courses in accounting. Then at nineteen, assistant manager of northern district—always acted and looked older, right? West of Yonge, north of St. Clair, it took in Forest Hill Village, a place apparently immune to the Great Depression, a mixture of old money and nouveau riche, you know. We moved some of your breed in and out; they were more restless or forever going in and out of bankruptcy. Hung around Upper Canada College, watched the rich kids in their flannels and how they played at leadership on the soccer field. I listened to the voices of upper crust clients, the women impossible to deal with, their hectoring stuck until I started aping them to amuse the guys. Got it right, didn't I? With that under my belt, the army was quick to post me to motor transport. Even with little schooling to speak of, they moved me up fast and sent me on for my commission. Not bad, eh? It's like acting, the Duke used to say; you put on the kind of show the men expect. How's that for full and frank?"

"It's a start. You must have envied the privileged like the Wellesleys."

"Not enough to knock him off, if that's what you're getting at."

"And on the Continent, the main chance to make a pile of dough so you could come out of the war and live like them."

Todder stood up, banged his knee on the desk. "Out, Horobbins. No more. I'm calling General Spry."

"You want to check that out downtown, be my guest. So why don't you settle down and we'll go on? I'd like to hear your version of certain events that happened back in Red Deer. A bit strange, wasn't it?"

Todder, craning to peek at the page Horobbins had opened, actually a directive on the washing and storage of mess tins, seemed to realize his heartfelt life story had made little or no impression, abandoned the moving van epic to revert to the character he had so painstakingly created.

"I haven't a clue what you've got there or what you're looking for. Okay, the base, known as A-20, is on the flats by the river—quite scenic in the fall, the birches on the surrounding hills masses of yellow. Up on the hill is the local loony bin, A-21 we called it, where Alberta sterilizes its unwanted. The Duke ran a tight ship, much admired by the front office. Object of the exercise was to train lorry drivers, driver-mechs, and despatch riders, hence a mix of odds and sods in lower categories cheek by jowl, quite a contingent of CWACs, some of them very adept with the trucks. Decked out in their winter sheepskins they were massive and dangerous teddy bears. I was captain then, over lorry training. We had mainly sixty-hundred weights with righthand drive, Fords and Chevs, the latter easier to double clutch. The Fords had quirky transmissions if you didn't shift within a narrow speed band—lot of stripped gears. But the farm kids are great drivers and know how to fix things, have earned the king's shilling hauling stuff through God knows what to the frontline needy. We trained 'em well. The problem with that kind of operation is it can get sloppy, non-combatants immune to discipline, like it is here. The Duke'd have none of it. All ranks on parade every morning, complete with band—a very good one, as was our hockey team. Inspection and marchpast, full kit. Thursdays were gas days."

"Surely nobody was going to use gas at that stage."

"Didn't matter. Tear gas let loose. We ran around twirling alarm rattles and shouting like idiots while the troops remained in line and donned their respirators smartly, or else. I admit it was a trifle overdone."

"Then, sir, what do you make of the respirator left at the scene?"

"As ordered, I've had the storage area searched. One of your men and a flatfoot were there. There's a section in the quartermaster stores where respirators are kept, most of them unused; appears one could be missing. I'm afraid in the lax period we're in, the keys are hung on nails by the sergeant's desk; bods come and go, not all of them take the trouble to sign in or out."

"Rather slack, isn't it, even given the times? At the meeting this morning you must've picked up on the flap about possible use of lethal gas to wipe out the area, stores to be tracked down and secured."

"I thought it farfetched. No, I'm as much puzzled as you are by that item. Why leave it on his desk when presumably he was already dead? Then, too, the note. An uprising of sorts seems rather remote. The racketeers are in the jug, most others dispersed. Who's left to rise up? Most of them only want to get home. Shall I go on?"

"What I'm saying about him—he was always prepared, thinking ahead. Even back in '43 he foresaw the reinforcement crisis, predicting that those of his flock who were fit enough to go overseas would end up as infantry, he saved future lives; turned A-20 into an infantry school of sorts. The boys spent as much time on the rifle or grenade ranges as in their lorries. One winter he found white parkas and sent us off on ski and snowshoe exercises. Why wouldn't the Canadians be sent to Norway? Turned out to be a shambles he never tried again. The problem was the skis were secured only by a single strap over army issue boots with hobnails, hardly conducive to imparting alpine skills. We found most of the men, except for a few from BC, Ontario, and Quebec, had never been on skis; nobody could afford 'em during the Depression. After too many sprains we gave up, but he made sure everyone was in tiptop shape—route marches and battle drill up and down the Red Deer River valley. I'd protest the time lost on vehicles, but he wouldn't listen."

"The perfect commandant. So why was he removed?"

"What bumf you have there? He wasn't removed. He'd been salivating for an overseas posting."

"It says here" (a page concerning the need to conserve mimeograph ink rollers) "there was a complaint about an orgy the night Italy surrendered."

"Oh, that was just Ambrose doing his tribal chieftain thing. Granted, that night in September '43 he turned the Quacks out of their beds, in nightgowns or such like, made them join a conga line while the sleepy band played off tune; harmless fun, really. That what you have there? Don't you have better things to do? All right, the queen bee lodged some sort of complaint. Nothing came of it. The brass dismissed it as high jinks, no big deal."

"You recall her name?"

"You know, don't you? Captain Williams. Do I pass?"

"The same officer commanding the women here."

"Correct."

"You running a kind of Red Deer graduate school? Wasn't there something else, the matter of the ambulance? He was shipped off right after."

"Oh, that. I suppose it doesn't matter now. I have every confidence his reputation will emerge intact."

"Even if himself didn't."

"Okay, some service clubs had raised funds for an ambulance they donated in the expectation it'd be sent overseas to trundle around our wounded boys. I'm afraid it never left the base."

"Why not?"

"The fact is the Duke had it converted into a caravan for his personal use, complete with cots, bar, and a small galley. His detractors claimed he tootled around the countryside entertaining Quacks or local talent, as the case may be."

"Did you ever join him on his little excursions?"

Long pause. Stroking of blonde moustache, whacking of thigh with swagger stick. "Might have. Bit of a lark, actually. A minor blot on such a fine officer."

"You mean he ran around the countryside with the red cross on the ambulance? Wouldn't the donors wonder?"

"He had it painted over, made it look like some sort of command vehicle."

"Who blew the whistle on him?"

"Don't know. Not me."

"He must've had drivers."

"Only one, also his trusted servant. He wouldn't spill the beans. A corporal something, yes, Timchuk."

"You knew him better than that. Didn't he go with him overseas?"

"Why're you asking me this? You seem to have it all there."

Horobbins decided to embellish his empty dossier. "The fact is you were with Lieutenant Colonel Wellesley when he was posted to General Burns's staff at 21 Group headquarters in Brussels, including transport liaison for the Dutch relief show earlier this year. Evidently one convoy never reached its destination, went astray somewhere; drugs and medicines ended up on the black market. Then your Corporal Timchuk was found drowned in the Maas, apparently a Jeep mishap. It wouldn't be too difficult for someone who repaired moving vans to rig an accident."

"Let me see that file. Yes, your people did some snooping around. We were cleared: no proof, no charges. Our, his, record is unblemished. When he was posted back here for his superb organizing abilities he asked for me as his Two IC. We were a good team; had this place cracking in no time. We've been just as ticked off as the troops at our inability to round up shipping. The first night of the riots downtown he turned to me ruefully, says: 'Can't really blame them, eh, Phil?' He understood the men. I don't believe our fellows were part of any large-scale conspiracy."

"Then who'd be angry enough to pop him off?"

"Not the foggiest. Obviously, you haven't come up with a clue."

"Don't be too sure. We're just starting. The episode with the ambulance— did he embark on any like forays around here?"

"For God's sake, he was too busy. We all are."

"Not too swamped to take time off for jaunts to a flat in London. If not you, did he ever take anyone with him? Why would he have his staff car standing by the night he was killed?"

"He didn't share personal matters with me."

"I bet. You have a souvenir pistol?"

"No. Your men have already searched this office and my quarters. Don't they keep you informed?" A minor recovery for the grillee.

"The night after the disturbances, the colonel in his office is slain by someone with a souvenir pistol, probably a Luger, a marksman who neatly drills him between the eyes. Leaves the note and the respirator. Nobody hears the report or apparently sees anyone come or go. He was found by Corporal Evans, who, despite the crackdown, left her billet to come here. You any idea why she'd be in his office at that hour, his staff car parked outside?"

"None at all. What're you getting at?"

"And you had gone off to London. Most irregular, in view of the unsettled conditions here. Did you have his permission?"

"Yes, he was very understanding. Confession time again. I had an urgent personal matter to attend to—involves a lady whose hubby is about to return from the wars, that's the address I gave you. For God's sake don't harass her. Anyway, we still have decisions to make."

"Are you married?"

"No. You must run across these situations. Not pleasant."

"All too common, I'm afraid; our dubious legacy to the long-suffering Brits. However, I need verification of your whereabouts, exactly where you went and at what times. Forensics will go over your car in the vehicle park. Please write out an hour-by-hour account and leave it with my sergeant."

"Oh, come on, Horobbins, I wasn't here, couldn't be a suspect."

"Do you consider yourself a good pistol shot?"

"Christ, can't you lay off? I did the usual range practice. I assure you it'd take me more than one round to do him in, even at close range."

"Sir, in view of the information in this file, I am instructing my sergeant to bring in his team to search your office and quarters again. That notebook you just wrote in, please hand it over. We'll return it soonest. Now, I want you to appreciate your situation. You are to remain on base. I'm assigning shifts to keep a watch on you. If anyone complains to General Spry it's me. You've tried everything in the book to avoid telling the truth, and I'm not about to let you get away with it. That clear?"

"Captain, you got a screw loose somewhere. Nothing more to tell."

Horobbins consulted the dossier and paused at a directive about the correct number of buttons to undo on a tunic when wearing a black tie as walking-out kit.

"If there's any glimmer of truth to the allegations in this file about your activities on the Continent, isn't it likely he, or you, crossed some bad elements who wanted him out of the way?"

"In that case, why wouldn't they come after me as well?"

"The thought had occurred to me, sir."

"Oh."

Horobbins got up and left an ashen Todder to ponder his own fate.

11

If Sapper Montgomery had decided to do in the colonel his best weapons of choice were attached to his arms—gnarled, scaled hands probably capable of crumpling hardrock ore. Now, after an earlier grilling as to his whereabouts the night of the colonel's murder, there was a shudder, a dormant volcano about to erupt when he was brought in for an encore in front of the provost captain.

"You have breakfast today, Montgomery? Enjoy your porridge?"

"Naw, don't eat that stuff."

"Or you knew what was in it."

For a moment Horobbins wondered if he was about to be throttled on the spot. He became transfixed by the mighty instruments aflail while the unlikely ironer of uniforms and shirts vented his contempt—not specifically at him apparently, but everything he represented, this chairwarmer with no validating campaign ribbons or unit badges. The dusty voice shook the walls of the cubicle, as if to bring down falling debris in the depths of the Sudbury nickel mine where he had bulled an eighty-pound drill before giving up his exempt status for the surface perils of army service. The stonewalled *versus* the rockface.

After the confrontation with Todder, Horobbins, finding himself in another struggle for composure, swallowed and remembered why the image of Montgomery so unhinged him. The ex-miner reminded him of Randall, the bully, a dogged tormentor who was the bane of his life through grade school to high school when the big clunk thankfully dropped out. There had been no final scene when a skinny Horobbins, jeered at for being a dirty "foreigner," punched out his lights. Now he recognized another, at least in memory, and was prompted to remind him who had the upper hand.

"It doesn't fit. You end up as the colonel's batman. How come?"

"I applied, eh? He seen me personally. Seemed to get a kick out of the idea."

"Maybe he saw you more as a bodyguard."

"Sir, why'd the colonel need one?"

"Somebody got through to him, didn't they? You tell me."

When the giant clammed up again, tight as an ore crusher, Horobbins searched for a way of leading Montgomery to what his intuition told him was a nugget somewhere in the drift. An entry in the man's brown service book, dating back to 1940, caught his attention. It was clipped to the interview sheet from his early morning go-round with an interrogator.

"Gibraltar?"

"March '41, us miners in Number Two Tunnelling Company sent to the Rock. Cut galleries for a bombproof hospital and storage. We must've pulled out a hundred thousand ton."

"Gateway to the Med, yet they never went for it."

"We used to wonder. That little fat fella with the tassel on his cap."

"Franco." A name only too familiar to Horobbins back in Ontario where his communist-leaning father had raged at the fascist dictator who won the Spanish Civil War, taking over the country in 1939 just before the big one broke out.

"They could of taken it. We had it doped out if they'd ask us. Call in the Jerries, you air drop expert teams, clean 'em out from the top with amatol, shaped charges, flamethrowers, and gas, like they done with them Belgian forts. We'd been bottled up in the Med. Rommel would of taken Cairo, gone on to the oilfields."

The desk jockey allowed a grudging nod to the strategic insights of the working stiff, the field smarts of the benighted footsloggers. Too bad nobody ever listened to them.

"Didn't the Brits have that figured out?"

"Sure. Like Singapore, eh?"

"Then in '43 with First Div into Sicily and on up Italy. The soft underbelly of Europe, Churchill said in one of his drunken moments. And you guys, the engineers, were up front clearing mines, booby traps, building Baileys, bull-dozing the way. You did a great job."

"Well, thanks, sir. They shoulda called us 'saps', not 'sappers.' You know, I can't recollect anything sunny about Italy. More like being back down in the mines—always night and raining, a drift with no end where we lugged our gear over scree and rock with unfriendly fire slicing at us, never seen such a black hole till the star shells went up and we were caught out in the open. Now I see it as a time of soaking cold, shaking from nerves and that chill worse than winter in Sudbury. Never got it out of my bones; lucky I never got malaria. We'd come to a smashed up town, find shelter in a church, lotta them still standing. Whole village there, scared shitless we're Tedesci. They see us, out comes the vino. We give 'em smokes, vittles. Warmed us up every time, them poor Eyeties.

"How those infantry guys went on, I dunno; shortchanged by Ottawa on replacements and equipment. Crying shame, sir. Up there near the end when we finally stalled at the Senio north of Ravenna, this Limey Eighth Army general, he says, give me Canadian troops but without their dumbass red tabs. In fact, they tried to remove our corps commander. Up there, you know, they conned us: one more shot, boys, you'll be in Vienna in three weeks. Nobody took the trouble to find out that the area north of the Appenines was a flood plain. Last fall, when the rains came, our guys crawled from one river to the next canal through stinking swamp, and the Jerries as usual made us pay for every yard. That's what they did to us, and we ain't about to forget."

"If we had in this room Yanks, Brits, Kiwis, Indians, Poles, say the Cassino vets, you think they'd be any different? You take survivors of the 36th Texas Division, what would they say about their General Mark Clark after the Rapido fiasco?"

"We know about him, for sure. By June '44, way after the meat grinders Ortona and Liri Valley and the rest of it, we'd moved west, could of taken Rome. But this General Clark, he says if the Limeys and Canucks go in first he'll fire on us. So we had to sit it out while he took all the glory parading into Rome. Them mucky-mucks, all the same."

"You've got problems with officers."

"Don't exactly care for where this may be heading, sir. Well, them on the line with us were mostly okay, tried to do their best for us. I felt sorry for the kids, two-pip wonders who only lasted coupla weeks; but those higher ups in the rear, they was something else. Didn't give a damn about the troops, sent them in over and over again while back in Rome, or wherever, they ran their rackets. Lotta guys took off. I don't blame 'em."

Horobbins resisted an impulse to tell him about the execution. "You ever take off, yourself?"

"Nah, a sucker I guess, but I didn't wanna leave the guys after all we'd been through. Came awful close. I tell ya, by last December some of our best units were so worn out they just laid up in front of Jerry lines to wait for the end, run out of what little poop they had left." Touched his two gold wound stripes.

"Got scratched up myself, but I guess I'm tougher than a lot of them. No, the fact is, sir, they was bled dry by the D-Day invasion and Ottawa holding back them deadbeats drafted for home defence. Big joke on us. So staff officers, they'd come up and lay it on the troops for having muddy boots. Damn near got charged once for letting off a 69 grenade—you know the bakelite ones with the ribbon—when we had this brigadier up for a look-see he flops face down in the mud while the rest of us stand round and have a big yuck. When we were pulled out and got to Holland we couldn't believe the bellyaching. They had gear, vittles, and air support. A candy store. Got into a few fights when we ragged 'em about taking so long to get there."

"The Dutch relief operation, you in on it?"

"For sure. Us engineers, we were up front to sweep for mines and booby traps. We couldn't believe it when some Jerries came out to show us so the food convoys wouldn't run into them. We knew then the war was almost over."

"You ever hear about diversions of supplies that were supposed to go to the Dutch, like a shipment of medicines and drugs ending up on the black market?"

"Same old story, eh? Picked up word here and there. That's your job, right? You trying to tie it into what happened here?"

"Look, you had access to Colonel Wellesley, you know every inch of his room and what he did for kicks. You're a mine of information, if that's the right way to put it."

"Just saw to his duds and kept the place clean. I dunno what you're after, sir, but I can't recollect anything that'd help you."

"When we did the search you gave us the tipoff on his phone contact in London. I need a few more of those. Montgomery, it doesn't add up. With your points you want to stay around here. What's the big attraction?"

"No hurry, sir. I don't want Occupation or the Pacific. And I'm not looking to go back underground. Fact is, I don't know what to do."

"You could take up dentistry."

For the first time there came a softening of the granite visage into a semblance of a grin. Horobbins sat back waiting.

"Well, sir, like a lot of the fellas I guess I have someone here. We're kind of in a pickle as to what to do. She's over in Guildford, been tough cooped up here. When'll we be sprung? Any day now her bloke's coming back from over there."

Yet another one, but there was only so far you could go to open up rapport or confession. Horobbins almost let it out: "join the club;" for like so many arrivals on that crowded isle, where the local males mostly were off in distant climes, he too "had someone," as it was so quaintly termed. Mavis from Putney, westerly London, her spouse mired somewhere in Burma. He pondered Montgomery's vulnerability on that score.

"Your problem isn't that unusual. A lot of our boys are taking war brides home."

"Not if they're still hitched."

"We hope."

With that settled, back to business.

"The colonel's flat in London—we're tracking it down. Who else would know about it?"

"Maybe your best bet is Stan Nolan, his driver, or that fat fella Glen Helmers, his clerk, maybe others."

"We'll get to them. Others? Like who?"

Another shrug. "Sir, I didn't plug him, I swear."

"Swear on a stack of Bibles all you want, the fact is, Montgomery, you're one of the few among the misfits around here who can probably handle a pistol. My men didn't find a souvenir weapon in your kit. You ditch the gun that shot the colonel?"

"Sure I had a PPK, but I lost it on a side bet at the craps game in Malplaquet. That was before the riots, probably changed hands several times. You'll have a helluva time finding the one that done in the colonel."

Horobbins didn't tell him it was likely a Luger, not a Walther, tried another tack. "You told us about the colonel's pocket notebooks. We haven't found them yet. Probably the killer took them. Are they worth a man's life?"

"Depends what's in 'em, I guess. I bet they turn up."

"Smart. That's really smart. Tell you what. I'll make a deal with you. It'd be a big help if you'd mosey around, see if anyone's ready to cough up the notebooks. They'd listen to you, or else, eh? And we'd sure like to find out if something's in the works over there in the blocks. We're concerned about that note left on his desk. You had to copy it out. It's a threat of mass action or more killings. 'More to come,' it says. If that isn't a threat I don't know what is. So how about it?"

"No stoolie, sir. Those fellas over there? That's a stretch."

"Jesus, Montgomery, how do I spell it out for you? You realize you're now unemployed? There's no reason to keep you here. Once this is over I can put you on the next boat home, assuming, that is, you aren't in the cooler. Or I can put in a word with whoever takes command here to help you stay on and sort out your situation with that lady in Guildford. What do you say?"

"You done with me now, sir?"

"Stick around. There's something else." Somehow Horobbins managed to summon up his relentless calm, fraying at the edges as the hours slipped away.

"As an engineer, do you have any thoughts on why the respirator was left on his desk? If our side had decided to use gas, you guys would've been in on it. You've probably heard there's a big flap on downtown that the note and the respirator may threaten a mass gas attack on this area. Nothing to laugh at. Who around here, besides yourself, would have the expertise to do it?"

"Gas attacks this time would of come from the air force, not likely us. I never took launch training; no more'n the rest of you, like those goddam gas shacks. They pump in the tear gas and you have to peel off your respirator, then the other one that makes you puke, then chlorine, and the one that smells of pretty flowers. You put two fingers in the side of your facepiece, take a sniff, then dabs of liquid mustard gas on your arm. Ever figure what'd it be like fighting a war in a respirator, gas cape, rubber boots, and safes covering your rifle? We would of waddled round like ducks in molasses. No, the problem is once you start jackin' round with gas you can't control it. Our training, at least in the field companies I was in, was for defence, but I have a pretty good idea who does have the know-how."

"You do?"

"The ones we just cleaned up on, sir. The Nazis. They was the only ones to use gas in the war, the camps where they wiped out all them Jews. Sorry, sir, you must feel badly about that. Hope you didn't lose any family. Now, just supposing what I pick up from some of the boys passing through here, fellas who were in on the inside track in Brussels and Antwerp, and they knew quite a lot about the colonel and some of his pals—no, sir, those guys are all gone home, you'd never find 'em now, and I don't remember their names—they tell us stories you wouldn't believe, how he was up to his eyeballs in heavy deals

70

in Belgium and Holland. Exactly what else he was into around here wasn't spelled out; those guys didn't want word getting back to him, all they wanted was to get out of here and go home. Okay, you ast me. There's one thing I did pick up in the wet canteen when we were putting back the bullshots with booze they brought over, a Dutch relief convoy that went to hell in a hand-basket, thanks to him and Todder. And since, I been thinking about some of the stuff floating around, and suppose they's true? If he was the big time oper-ator they say he was, and I had no way of proving it—he made sure I didn't snoop round in his room—it could be possible he crossed some wheels in the rackets over there and they come after him over here. Then what if he got mixed up with some of the top business guys, the armaments and chemical mucky-mucks who sold gas to the Nazis so they could wipe out your kinfolk? Yes, sir, the respirator meant something, and maybe that was the message left when they arranged to rub him out."

Horobbins couldn't hold back his slack-jawed disbelief. First Todder, and now this sapper, had made assumptions about his origins that may have had a kernel of truth in them, if indeed his long distant Spanish castaway ances-tor had been a *converso,* a convert to Christianity. But had they been allowed on the Armada galleons? In that stifling cubicle in Aldershot, he remained silent; to attempt to clarify his own ancestry, murky as it was, would only show disrespect to those who had actually perished in the camps in the 1940s, not the sixteenth century. The schoolyard bully on the other side of his desk had pushed him into a corner once again by a fantasy with a purpose he couldn't fathom and without question delivered with the cunning of those who had survived against the odds and were equally dedicated to outwitting their officers as they once had been with their wartime enemy.

The mountain shifted again and his chair creaked.

12

The body of the driver Nolan was face down under the colonel's staff car. Horseshoe clamps on the heels, studded soles stuck out in the gravel. The boots twitched. Horobbins waved to the guardian MP who kicked at the footwear, then grasped gaitered ankles to haul the dusty victim out from under. Very much alive, the man dabbed at his battledress and leaned against the tapes sealing the car door. Overhead the offbeat throb of a Heinkel 111 bomber, its crosses and swastikas painted over, faded as it wheeled towards the Royal Aircraft Establishment across the Farnborough Road.

"Circuits and bumps," said Horobbins. "Testing captured aircraft. The Japs can't reach us yet. That was some dive."

"It'd been Jerries wiped us out we wouldn't have minded so much. Our own did it."

Nice bit of theatre, but it wouldn't get Nolan off the hook. Horobbins pointed for the MP to remove the tape on the doors of the khaki Chev with its righthand drive, secured in the vehicle park where he had led the colonel's driver for a followup grilling.

"Get in, behind the wheel." Horobbins, seated beside him, emptied the contents of the glove compartment into a paper bag. Apparently the vehicle had not yet been searched, an oversight by someone. Maps of the area, maintenance manual, tire gauge, log book. "Wait here." As if Nolan, head bent, was going anywhere. Horobbins went around to open the trunk, not "boot" to Canadians. Only a tire jack and some tools; he glanced under the floor cover, found nothing. In the front seat he studied the soldier whose knuckles were white around the steering wheel. Still wearing Royal Regiment shoulder flashes with three-year red chevrons on his sleeve, his soiled beret on the dashboard, Nolan sweated—a slick on his creased forehead, his jowls saggy, his sparse hair showing silver highlights.

"How old are you anyway?"

"Thirty-one, sir."

"You look as if you should be home on pension."

"Hope so, soon, sir."

"What brought this on, Nolan? We've got one person badly shook up by the colonel's death. Now another? A bit overdone, I'd say."

"Nothing to do with that, sir."

Horobbins noticed traces of education, the "g's" intact at word endings. "What'd you do before?"

"Teacher in Brampton, sir. I'd like to go back, take my degree."

"Only if you get your veterans' credits. If you nailed the good colonel you'll be in another kind of school."

"I didn't plug him, for sure. See." He held out shaking hands, clearly not suitable for one exact shot, but tremors can be faked.

Horobbins glanced at the clipboard with its notes of Nolan's first interview. "Says here you brought his car around to the back of the admin building, then waited for him in the orderly room; were there when Corporal Evans came rushing in. Correct? You're one of those closest to the colonel, drove him everywhere. What was he up to? Who else knew about it? How long were you with him?"

"Since he arrived in June. Assigned out of the motor pool. I have no idea what he intended to do with the car that night; he'd often order it for his private spins in the evening. On day shifts I'd mostly drive him around the area to inspect camp conditions and other business."

"What other business?"

"Not for me to say, sir. He'd have me stop off at phone boxes in towns around, order me to drive on ahead a short spell and wait. Sometimes he'd mention the bellyaching about the delays and conditions, could sense trouble was brewing. Hinted the higher-ups weren't paying heed. So maybe somebody blamed him and did him in."

"Seems a bit extreme. Why him?"

"My thoughts too, sir. It's strange, all right."

"You copied out the note found on his desk and no doubt heard about the respirator. You have any idea who'd do that or what they mean?"

"Doesn't make sense, does it? Unless there really is some kind of scheme. Somebody cooks up the riots, then they start knocking off officers. We hear around the higher-ups are in a kind of panic. I just don't see our fellas doing it."

"We're not ruling out a lot of things. You have a souvenir pistol? None was found in your kit."

"Not me. I was out of it last year, invalided out of Normandy in August."

"Wounded?"

"Not exactly, sir."

Horobbins began to realize he could be dealing with a severe case of battle exhaustion, prone to unpredictable behaviour, like diving under staff cars. "So when the colonel took his car out on his solo jaunts, you don't have a clue where he went or why?"

"He never stayed out all night or anything. I'd always wait in the orderly

73

room till he came back. There're witnesses I never left the night he was shot. You'll find the daily mileage in the log book."

"What about his London travels? You ever drive him? What about his flat?"

"Only to the station. He'd take a cab back. Wore his civvies. No, I don't know where he went up there."

"Did anyone else go with him?" Nolan produced a cheek flutter. "What's it take to get through to you guys? You keep stalling, I'll have no choice but to turn you over to the tender mercies of some of my fellows. Better still, how about a stint in the Glass House?"

He meant the notorious Aldershot military detention barracks across Queen's Avenue on North Road, its high masonry walls topped with broken glass and wire to conceal a terrible brutality within. Nolan banged his furrowed brow on the steering wheel, a tear managed to find its way down a facial seam. Horobbins relented, opted for a more circuitous route.

"Simmer down, Nolan. Okay, how about you tell me what brought you here to become an unlikely chauffeur for the commanding officer? For one thing, you seem too goddam nervous to drive a car, let alone a push cart."

"Sir, you sound like those head doctors at Number One Nuts before I came here. No, the colonel never complained about my driving. I know how to drive in the blackout on the wrong side of the road."

"The blackout's long gone. You mean another kind?"

Just how damaged was this graduate of Number One Neurological in Basingstoke down the road, a haven for the maimed and those too far gone to be turned around and sent back into action? Seemed that Nolan was one of the latter. The place was closed up now, he didn't have any idea where to find anyone who might have treated him; his amateur status would have to do, if it led anywhere.

"You could say that, sir. You have time for this?"

By the English clock it was almost teatime. "My luck so far. Confessions of the innocent." Horobbins sighed. "Your nickel."

The innocent, Nolan said, the first time I came across the term "loss of innocence" was at group sessions some of the head docs at the nuthouse tried out on us. Guinea pigs we were. Ben Couteau, he's Objiwa from around Kenora, we call him "Chief Two-Tooth" for those he had left. Got hit on the head—they rebuilt his face with skin grafts, gave him a kind of zebra look, the skin from his back was a lighter colour. Anyway, Two-Tooth says they're trying out healing circles, but you got to have sweet grass and smudges for the real thing.

Loss of innocence? We laughed at them. We were never innocent. Those years in England, we were fit and lean, learned how to move, use ground, handle our weapons. Exercises like Spartan helped some. In October '42 I was posted to the Royal Regiment, rebuilding after the Dieppe massacre in August where not many came back from the bloodbath at Puys. Those who did told us what it was like. When we landed in France in July '44 our few Dieppe survivors looked around in disbelief, piece of cake, they said, maybe they did learn something; until Second Div moved inland and was shot up at the Verrieres Ridge screwup outside Caen. Same old story, after all.

The real bull sessions at Number One Nuts took place at night when the lights were out and those of us who still had a few marbles left speculated about what happened to us and why. We tried to work our own way out of it, going over stuff we'd never own up to the docs. They were officers, anyway.

The way I see it, sir, we came up against situations nobody had predicted or expected. With the Russians smashing through in the east I guess our big brains reckoned the Germans would be on their last legs in France, maybe even let us in to avoid being over-run by the Russians. I give them some credit; they pulled off a smart deception by fooling the Jerries into holding back for our major landings across the Channel at Calais, instead of the end run into Normandy. But nobody counted on their ability to bounce back.

There in the darkened ward we worked our way through the shocks and surprises that threw us off, we who thought we were seasoned and ready, to end up unfit for anything but the loony bin. Sometimes the memories shut us up until we could face them again another night. Maybe we'd stumbled across our own road to recovery. Like we kept no notes, it wasn't a clinic, but near the end we reached a kind of consensus on four things that stood out as turning points that had rocked our socks, set us back, shook our confidence until one final insult sent some of us off the rails. Each one of us owned up to a specific event or happening that became the final straw we wouldn't dare admit to in front of the officers who ran the place. We were still edgy about being accused of cowardice, which some had been stained with by their own commanders. If you want me to go on I'll tell you how we arrived at the "four big ones," as we came to name them.

Only a few days after the landings in June, Nolan went on, the Canadians found what we were up against. Sent back on their heels by a bunch of pimply-faced teenagers, Hitler Jugend, Twelve ss Panzer. No one had imagined such fanatics existed. Howling like banshees, over and over again they took over the fight, shot Canadian prisoners, kept coming, spat out their hate. If you did take any of them, you had to put them out of their misery. They weren't the only ones, but their almost religious belief in the Fuhrer mystified everyone and planted the first doubts. What can you do with people like that?

This underlying disbelief began to take hold when more of their vets from the Russian front showed up. Their inhumanity, their at-all-costs disregard for life or safety, made us realize just how brutal the war had been in the east. They dug in, counterattacked, sighted their weapons dead on, and, worst of all, regarded us with sneering contempt. Bunch of sissies compared to the Russkis.

As the whole British and Canadian effort bogged down around Caen, it began to dawn on a lot of us that we couldn't win it, man for man, on the ground. Frankly, we were outclassed, not only by their superior leadership at the unit level, but by their weaponry. Our armament was crap. We'd been equipped for the last war. Heavy battledress in summer heat. Old Lee Enfields, nothing more than muskets. Tanks undergunned, gasoline that blew up, Ronson lighters, wiped out in that crazy Operation Goodwood near Caen. Outside of Falaise the Fourth Armoured lost so many tanks and crews, fifty in one day, they didn't know which way was up.

Now the Sten gun was bad enough—shoot off your foot if you didn't cock it right—but the worst piece of hardware they dumped on us was the goddam PIAT, you know, the projector infantry anti-tank. You ever tried to use one, sir? Has a big coiled spring in a tube. You cock it by placing both feet on the butt pad; maybe lie down and double up your legs. Starving, thirsty, scared, you had to summon up the poop to wind it up like some kid's toy while the shit flew and you tried to steady your hand to arm the bomb with the twenty-two detonator, then stand up in the slit—the recoil sends you backwards and God knows where the bomb ends up. Craziest thing ever invented. Yanks had their bazooka, the Jerries their *panzerfaust*—good shoulder weapons. Some guys cried in frustration at what was expected of them. Only two things saved our bacon, over and over again. One was the twenty-five pounder gun and the way our artillery could drop in a stonk when and where needed. And I grant you, none of it could've been done without the air forces. They shot up anything that moved; knocked out tanks, bridges, pillboxes and rail lines, those Typhoons, they worked close in with us ground troops. The USAF had unloaded on a bunch of our guys by mistake, but, as it turned out, it was our own air force, the RAF, that truly did us in. Finished off a lot of us for anything useful, the last straw, at least for me.

By this time, by default mainly and high casualties, I was a platoon sergeant with the Royals. On the fourteenth of August it happened. A few days before our night attack with searchlights and the works was stopped cold in the dust and confusion as our tanks brewed up, on fire. We regrouped, tried again, this time in daylight. When the bombers came in we thought at last we got it made. Then, as we sat there, vehicles ticking over, us weighed down with gear, we were buried. Some mixup in the flares, the yellow smoke markers for the Pathfinders. We heard after the Jerries had nabbed an officer with a map showing the layout, and sent off their own flares. "Falling short," it was called. The RAF carpet-bombed us into hell. We couldn't believe it. Our men were smashed into shreds, sent crazy; not by what'd been done, but the knowledge it was our own doing it to us. Guns, trucks, flew in the air, the ammo dumps blew, craters deep as a two-storey house. Most of my platoon was wiped out—I could see when I dug out of a crater to watch them stumbling around, blind. Those still in the slit trenches were paralyzed. They say I was hollering at the sky, some boys pinned me down, laid me out on the ground, sat on me. We were rounded up, a quaking bunch of nut cases you ever saw. Got us back to the exhaustion unit in ambulances and on carriers, shot us up with sodium amytal, sweet tea—while through the roar in my ears I heard a guy cursing the Mustangs that had strafed them. Things quieted down a spell, what with the shots and so on.

"Give 'em a coupla days, they can go back," somebody says.

Then all hell breaks loose again. The Luftwaffe wasn't the gone goose we'd been led to believe, a stick of bombs came down right outside the dressing station, those two-beat engines that set me off again today, I guess. Next thing, every last bugger off his cot out into the fields, me included. By night they'd corralled most of us, though I heard later they never found sixteen of them. Maybe their bones are still there in the wheat grass till some Frenchie decides the hell with the mines and unexploded bombs and starts to plough again. So we were a sorry bunch, churning with panic and shame, me among the worst, and not sent back right away. Those of us tagged as bad cases were taken through the jumps, too doped to figure where I was till I ended up in Basingstoke back here. Came around to see this mansion with Nissan huts on the lawn. Went through treatment and reboards until they decide to give me an S-3, not enough for discharge. Light duties. I end up here, a driver. Others at Basingstoke were declared cured, sent back in time for the Rhine crossing. First big barrage they go to pieces again. Thank God they never sent me back.

If there're still some who slag the Brits, the Canadians, and the Poles for not closing the gap at Falaise, let too many Jerries slip out of the pocket, I don't buy it. Fact is, the Yanks didn't move up from the south to close the gap. Whoever's to blame, too many Jerries got away to regroup and fight again, over and over, hard customers all the way. We underestimated them right up to the end. How our guys hung in the way they did, I'll never know, given that the home front let us down. That ate at a lot of us—those useless turds, the Zombies, in their thousands sitting around in Canada while our boys died, an injustice behind their backs they'll never get over. If back home they didn't have the guts to send them over, there was one obvious answer. Pay the poor bloody infantry like they do the fly-boys; they could've cracked the reinforcement problem, or at least eased it up a lot. Instead, they treated us like dumb clods, pack mules, while they sat up there and toted up kill ratios—the worst being some of our generals who ranted on about our lack of drive and offensive spirit. Now, look, there's no question the army recovered after the Normandy bloodbath—and I'm sorry I wasn't there when they actually went into the business of liberating towns and villages that were still standing and where the welcome they got made it worthwhile and made them realize just how much the Nazis were hated. And also to see that there was a civilization of sorts beyond the killing grounds, for our only sense of France was field after field ripped by explosives and fire in heat and dust. No, I'm sorry I missed that.

So, if you're trying to find out what led to the Aldershot riots, there's your answer. The guys just boiled over. But I can't say, any more than anyone else, that there's any connection to the shooting of the colonel, useless as tits on a bull as he was. You got some job ahead of you, sir.

Horobbins did nothing more than nod, then extracted Nolan from the car, took him back to his cubicle, ordered tea, sat him down and tried again.

"What the hell's that supposed to mean?"

"I guess what I'm trying to get across, sir, is you can never tell when an ordinary soldier can go off the rails. Everybody has a breaking point when they can't cope any more. Anything can trigger it. It wasn't me, sir, but you have to understand how some of them became unstable, I guess you'd call it, through nothing of their own doing or fault."

"It's a big jump from that to commit murder."

"Maybe not if you've seen too much, yeah, the innocent dead, and you decide to do something in their memory by making a hit against someone who sure as hell isn't any goddam angel."

"Jesus, Nolan, is that what you think happened? If that's the case, you must have a pretty good idea who'd be in that state of mind. Speaking of which, have any of your pals from Basingstoke been posted here?"

"Not that I know of, sir. You think maybe there's a nut case loose that did it?"

"You tell me." He made a note to check the personnel records again.

"I don't have anybody in particular in mind. I was just thinking out loud; maybe give you some idea what you might be dealing with."

"You've come awful damn close to giving us a suspect profile. You think about that some more and your own situation. I'll be back and I'll expect something a helluva lot more specific. For now, you're not accused of anything, yet. But one thing you've got to tell me. Did you ever, on the colonel's orders, take someone else to the station? You don't tell me now, I have no choice but to place you in custody for withholding evidence until you own up. That clear?"

Nolan seemed to ponder what fate might await him at the Glass House, or Reading, or Headley Downs to send him over the edge again before he even left here. He wasted a few gulps of his tea, met his interrogator's strangely still large brown eyes, couldn't read them, came to a decision.

"Long as it doesn't get back, sir. I was told to take her to the station to make sure she got a seat on the Waterloo train. He always went on ahead. And

I'm afraid it was Corporal Evans. I don't want to make trouble for her. She's a nice girl."

"So she was going to meet him in his office the night of the sixth, maybe for a little spin in his car, but not to London that night. What do you know about the flat he had there?"

"Not much, sir. I gather he had digs he shared with some other officers, but who they were I have no idea. Corporal Evans never discussed it with me. She always gave the impression she was off to London on her own, but I knew better because the colonel had asked me to look out for her and see she got a seat on the train. He must've trusted me not to blab it around."

"Good for him. So Corporal Evans has the address and probably a key. So they had something going, right?"

"Not for me to say. You haven't asked her, yet?"

Horobbins caught the quiet amusement. "There must be other records around the office—payment of rent, correspondence with a landlord, or such like. Corporal Evans wasn't his secretary?"

"No, sir. She's files and personnel records. His secretary or personal clerk is Private Glen Helmers."

"With all the Quacks around, he had a male secretary?"

"Yes, sir. Helmers is low-point, categoried, never been out of England. A whiz typist and steno." Nolan allowed a rare sneer. "One of them who never got overseas." Overseas meaning the Continent.

"Thanks, Nolan, we'll talk to him."

"You mean I don't have to go to the Glass House?"

"Not for now. It's still on the books if you don't work on your memory some more. Not about Normandy. About here. You help me, I'll do my best to get your ticket home, assuming you're just another one of the innocents with which this place seems to be overpopulated. You can go, but not off the base. Understood?"

13

"Do them up, your buttons."

The hulk who had barely made it through the doorway designed for scrawny British national service types ran his fingers over his fly.

"Your blouse."

Thick fingers fumbled at the rear buttons that were supposed to attach the battledress jacket to trousers, gave up, and allowed his shirt to spill out. Horobbins hadn't known what to expect, perhaps a skinny little fellow who crouched in a chair while the imperious colonel dictated at lightning speed, then the clerk off down the hall to clack away at an Underwood typewriter. Instead, here was this khaki blob, a slug-hued moon face topping a six-foot frame of Guards stature—if he didn't have bottle-gauge glasses in steel frames and immense flab straining his wrinkled uniform. Straw tinged tresses needing a trim, blinking grey eyes under piggy eyelashes, an aura of sweat and cologne reaching across the desk to the sensitive nose of the non-smoker: Private Glen Helmers, clerk-typist in the same shark pool as the CWAC. With rising distaste Horobbins summoned up vestiges of Irish charm, sorely tried that day.

"What's that thing?" Pointing to a blue and white ribbon next to the man's Canadian Volunteer Service Medal and clasp, his only other validation of service.

"I realize, sir, it's unofficial. Got it from a Yank on Kiska."

A quick flip into his paybook, attached to the clipboard, showed that was indeed so: the tub of lard, it appeared, had actually been in on the Aleutian Islands landings off Alaska, when in 1943 a combined American–Canadian force had set out to eject the Japs from their only toehold in North America. It was, Horobbins recalled, a sideshow that began in that deciding battle of aircraft carriers near Midway Island in June 1942, when the Nips had hoped to divert the American fleet and panic them into withdrawing forces to defend home turf. In May 1943 the Americans had retaken Attu island after a bloody struggle in which only some twenty enemy had survived of a force of 2,500. A larger garrison of over five thousand remained on Kiska, part of the island chain—a terrifying prospect. From the West Coast the Canadian contingent had been made up of conscripts, on the grounds that the campaign was "home defence." They had formed the hedged bet of Prime Minister Mackenzie King, a huge reserve army allegedly to protect Canada's shores, uniforms aplenty to convince the public of a major war effort. At that time, only volunteers were sent overseas. The much reviled conscripts became known as "Zombies," the walking dead, an unthinkable fate that now faced them on Kiska.

"You went with the Zombie force?"

"Yes, sir. Four battalions of them, a big shock for a bunch of slackers who never expected combat. Hundreds jumped ship, took off before we left port on Vancouver Island, from Nanaimo and Chemainus."

"Surely you weren't in a combat capacity."

"Not likely, is it, sir? I was aide to Brigadier Foster; his secretary. No Zombie, me, I asked to go. Wanted to see for myself how those bastards would shape up after their bellyaching while our boys died over here. You know, sir, there was a kind of backass way of holding up morale among them, faced as they were day after day with heavy duty pressure to go active and sign up for overseas service. How they handled it was to make it a point of honour *not* to volunteer. Any who did were jeered at, made fun of; so to keep in with the group in barracks you had to show how tough and stubborn you were to resist the parades and lectures on joining the real army. With my General Service badge I stood out like a sore thumb; they razzed me a lot about how the army overseas was in real trouble if a fat slob like me was the best they could scrape up from the barrel."

"So what was it like working with the Americans?"

"Conscripts no big deal with them. Most were draftees, anyway. We were set up along American lines, helmets, everything except some of our weapons. Instead of M1 Garands we kept those old Lee Enfields. The officers were issued Winchester carbines instead of Stens. The Yanks transported us in four ships to Adak for more training. Food was better'n ours. I didn't take part in the exercises; I was busy with the brigadier. Then on August fifteenth they went in."

"And found the Japs had absconded."

"Correct, sir. We were thankful the Yanks had screwed up."

"How was that?"

"Far as I could pick up from the signals coming into brigade, the Japs had sent in a task force under fog cover while the US Navy was off somewhere being refueled. In a matter of a few hours the Japs took off every one of their five thousand and, hard to believe, slipped clean away. When our fellas went in after a big bombardment and found nothing, except maybe a few booby traps, they combed the island, about twenty-five miles long, mostly rock and moss. Some Yanks shot their own in the fog, real scary. Then the worst part began, our brigade was stuck there under canvas for over three months in the fog, rain, and howling winds that made noises like Eskimo demons trying to do what the Japs hadn't—drive us off their sacred rock, or whatever it was. For me, I stayed with the brigadier and went back to our base on Vancouver Island. One big snafu, but I suppose we oughta be grateful lives were saved, even if it was the worthless hides of them Zombies. I think all of us who were there will keep on wondering how come the Yanks missed the whole thing and let them sneak away. One of our intelligence officers had the view it was deliberate; they knew from code intercepts the enemy was about to evacuate, so they let them go, it being the sensible way out, especially after the blood-bath on Attu. I guess we'll never know."

"How do you think our fine body of conscripts would've done?" Instead of getting on with the business at hand, Horobbins seemed to be unusually interested in the subject.

"Hard to say, sir. The training under the Yanks was good, but most of our officers, except for the younger, junior ones, were unfit for active service. As to the men, I never saw such a scared bunch. Remember, there they were on the West Coast, putting in time, under no danger or attack, resisting all attempts to send them into action over here, and suddenly out of the blue they find themselves tabbed to take on the fearsome Japs—worse than the Nazis, suicidal maniacs unbeatable anywhere in the Pacific, except maybe Guadalcanal. As I said, a lot of Zombies jumped ship and disappeared. Now there're thousands of them out there running loose, or sneaking into good-paying jobs in the war plants, or hiding out on the farms where no Mountie or MP is going to take the trouble of facing down dogs and shotguns. They'll never be picked up; too late for that, and they know it. You've heard about the mutinies last November when the government reached down deep and found its balls because the army in Europe was a mere shadow of its former self and some kind of national pride had to be maintained, so they changed the rules and decided to send a limited number of conscripts overseas as replacements. When this news reached the West Coast there were outbreaks all over the place. It was rebellion, just as surely as the one here in Aldershot, with one big difference, the one here at least had good reasons behind it. But I wouldn't be surprised if some of them, a few who actually got to the Continent near the end of it, took their cue from what had happened on the West Coast, stirred 'em up here. No wonder the bigwigs have their shorts in a knot."

"Then is it possible there actually is a movement to take it up a notch and start rubbing out officers like Lieutenant Colonel Wellesley?"

"Doesn't seem likely, does it sir? But I keep thinking about them mutineers out west. Nobody knows how close we came to a shooting war on our home turf, let alone the troubles in Quebec. And I can tell you the officers were spooked shitless by the fact that those guys in barracks had the weapons and nobody could've stood up against them unless you brought troops home from overseas. They'd have cleaned 'em out in a hurry. Anything's possible, I guess, but it was a damn close call."

"Were you there during the mutinies?"

"No, sir, I actually came over here in October. What I've told you is from letters I got from a few of my pals who were also general service. Even though I'm low category, physique P-2 for my weight." A thin smile if that's the way to describe a vast moon face. "And eyesight, an E-3 bordering on E-4. Got in to begin with by memorizing eye charts, you know, while standing in line in the buff with the guys. Managed to pass basic till they sent in a what-d'you-call-it in a dark room with a lantern slide eye chart."

"Optician."

"That's it. He takes off my glasses and says read the letters from the top. I say, what letters? They sent me to Red Deer to train as a driver. But my eyesight and coordination aren't any hell, so I was posted to Number Eleven Vocational Training School in Vancouver as a clerk-typist, then to Pacific Command HQ. After Kiska I persuaded them to put me on overseas draft, and I've been stuck here in Aldershot ever since."

From the front of his paybook. "You're a westerner."

"From Saskatoon, sir. Really Sutherland, CPR railhead east of the city. My dad's a brakeman with the railway. We managed in the Depression except our house started to fill up with cousins and relatives driven off their farms. Our place wasn't much different from the huts around here, the way they razzed me about my weight and eyesight, 'Cousin Four-eyes,' they called me among other things, so by the time I got to grade twelve I'd turned eighteen and joined up to get some privacy."

Horobbins caught the sarcasm. "Then did you know Lieutenant Colonel Wellesley when you were at Red Deer?"

"Course not, sir. He was the commandant."

"What was he like to work for here?"

"No worse than any others. I had a good reference from Brigadier Foster. He had a machine gun mouth, but I kept up. They taught us Gregg at VTS and I'm pretty fast. He'd call me in at any hour. Very busy with the big job ahead and, if I may say so, pissed off that he couldn't move the men out as fast as he wanted. Couldn't line up ships."

"He didn't call you in the night he was killed?"

"No, sir, I was confined to barracks with some others who weren't out on patrol. You can ask around."

"You have a weapon of any kind stashed away? Nothing found in your kit."

"Course not, sir. All I can do to handle a typewriter."

"Why I want to talk to you, Helmers, we're tracing the colonel's activities in London, the flat he had, but we need to know more. He must have given you dictation, say, notes to the landlord or contacts with pals who shared the flat. Did he ever give you letters that we'd call unofficial to anyone other than his family?"

"Sir, a lot of stuff went through my hands. I can't remember anything like that. Anything unofficial, there wouldn't be any carbons on file."

"You do keep your steno notebooks."

"In my desk drawer; your guys've seen them."

"They can't read shorthand. I want you to retrieve them and transcribe anything that might give us a clue about that flat—who went there, anything else about his off-base activities. Are you aware of a couple of small notebooks he kept and a set of keys?"

"I've seen them. Sometimes he'd stop as if something occurred to him and he'd crook his arm out in front so I couldn't make out what he was writing. Never left them sitting around, he'd write away like a kid in school, his nose almost on the page, then he'd lift his head and give me a warning stare not to snoop. He kept them on his person at all times, in the front pockets of his jacket. Even in the heat he never took his jacket off. Joe Montgomery, he got a big kick out of the way the colonel'd take the notebooks and keys with him into the shower in a sealskin pouch, they must've meant a lot to him, all right. Never saw much of the keys. He didn't use them here; classified documents are kept in a special safe and the other file cabinets are open."

"Well, they weren't on his person that night. Somebody must've taken them before he was shot. Any thoughts on why? No? Your statement says you weren't summoned the night of the sixth when he worked late. Yet it seems Corporal Evans was. You any thoughts on why she was called in and you weren't?"

"I'd think you'd have found that out by now."

The insolence of the soft voice infuriated his interrogator, who tried not to show it. "Found out what?"

The hulk moved on the shaky chair, already weakened by Sapper Montgomery. The grey eyes did not blink.

"I'd have thought you'd have spoken to Corporal Evans herself by now. Nothing to do with me."

Same line as Nolan, as if they had rehearsed.

"Helmers, don't you ever try to tell me how to do my job. What I'm going to do is bring in a couple of stenos who can read Gregg, and they'll sit down with you at your desk and watch you go through those notebooks and you'll transcribe any items that have any bearing on the colonel's extra-curricular dealings. You'll keep at it till you've been through every notebook. If any are found missing, by God, I'll see you on pack drill till you're down to a bean-pole. And take that goddam Yankee ribbon off your uniform. Smarten up."

Where had he heard that before? The colonel, he'd bark at him, sniff in disgust, and rattle off dictation at a speed to hurry him along out of his sight. He, too, had given up on the Kiska Kid.

14

The buildup for the invasion of Japan gradually enveloped the camp. After victory in Europe, or what passed for same, a strange silence had befallen—a drawing of breath, a climate of relief as the repat traffic flowed. Lucky British vets were hustled through dispersal centres at Talavera and Waterloo barracks, then packed off to Woking or the Olympia in London to choose sartorial splendour from miles of racks hung with boxy civvies, nothing remotely akin to the late Lieutenant Colonel Wellesley's Saville Row lounge suits. The Canadians, isolated in their compound after their little outbreak, were sent off into smaller hovels to be contained until the slow boats arrived. Their empty barracks began to fill again with British troops mustered for the Far East. Once again, gunfire echoed from the ranges outside Ash Vale and Caesar's Camp; base plugs from Number 36 grenades whizzed overhead, denting vehicles, bouncing off rooftops, onlookers sent diving for cover, convoys of lorries polluted the Long Valley and Laffan's Plain with a smog of fumes and dust, flares streaked up into the sky, as if to mark a national holiday. But not on a Saturday evening.

Horobbins, sipping tea from an enamel mug, stood at the window to contemplate a relic on the parade square, a silvery wooden replica of a Landing Craft Tank. Complete with ramp, it had once trained lorry drivers for last summer's invasion of Normandy. They would back their vehicles up the ramp, juggle around to face the bow—ready for touchdown on Mulberry, the artificial port towed across the Channel. He imagined the real ones about to scrape onto the cold shores of Nippon to be met by millions of banzai fanatics and, from the skies, hundreds of plunging kamikaze suicide bombers off to celestial sushi.

Behind him, personnel files and scrawled notes of interviews were piled on his table where he had flagged those for his own interrogation. He stared at the scribbled draft of his first report. Day One. What did he have to show? Paperwork was second nature to him now, and usually his facility for offical-dom, if not glibness, carried him through the jumps where his masters nodded at an unaccustomed literacy from a military cop. No problem outlining the bare bones of what they had found out so far, including his neat diagrams of the murder scene, his annotated and self-censored summaries of the unsatisfactory clashes with "Lt. Col. Wellesley's 2-IC, batman, driver, and clerk." Until he found himself coming to a snag, more like a screeching halt, at the matter of Corporal Claire Evans. How to explain his indirect approach through Captain Williams to find out her true feelings about her dearly departed commanding officer and—what? His drafting stopped at this item:

"9. A key witness to be re-interviewed when her physical and mental condition warrant is Cpl. Claire Evans, CWAC, as noted above, a file and registry clerk who discovered the body about 2200 hours. She had entered via the orderly room, as stated in her first interview, to retrieve an item of personal hygiene from her desk (see diagram of office layout). Lt. Mason, the duty officer, reports shortly afterwards she ran down the hall to report finding the deceased. We are convinced subject has information about Lt. Col. W.'s movements and activities of an unofficial nature. As well, we are certain subject has visited the deceased's flat in London and probably has an entry key. Location of the flat itself is being traced by the Metropolitan Police and will be sealed once found. Preliminary interviews with her have produced little information, for health reasons as stated above, but we will duly proceed as soon as circumstances warrant, to explore subject's likely unofficial personal relationship with the deceased. . . ."

Her hands, long white fingers enlaced as if mating, her head lowered, not daring to meet his stare, she had been beyond distress: she was in mourning. Then what was she: mistress, quick lay, a courier or a party to his foggy deals, whatever they might turn out to be?

The smell of Bollock wafted ahead of him into the room: cigarettes, sweat from the heavy wool suit, and a whiff of Scotch, no doubt taken from the bottle in the murder bag. The bag was now in the hands of another man introduced as Detective Sergeant Fisher. "Finally arrived to tote it about."

"Where've you been?"

"Eliminating suspects. We're narrowing them down to a few thousand, give or take. Reading Gaol, worst nick I've ever seen. Thought I'd pop in on our associates who're getting a trifle stroppy with your so-called ringleaders. Sad lot—not capable of organizing themselves to place one leg at a time in their trousers, let alone assassination. Special Branch, MI5 or what-have-you, somewhat ticked off as grand theories fly out the window. They mutter darkly about sabotage in the cookhouse, but don't really believe it. They're about to cast a wider net, winkle out stray Paddies, Wogs, Reds, other agitators who they've been itching to round up. They have to do something to justify lavish expense accounts."

Horobbins rattled his papers. "I have a lot to go over with you."

"Good God, man, you need a breather. Long past tea time; allow me to take you into town for sustenance."

"They gave me a mess card here somewhere."

"Bugger that. Fisher, with the captain's permission, you start on those files over there. You know what to look for."

Horobbins nodded to the murder bag custodian who removed his hat to reveal a peeling sunburnt pate framed by white puffs of sideburns; grumbled something about being hauled away from his garden. The murder squad was a wartime throwback of geriatrics. Fisher's knees clicked as he hobbled over to the stacked table.

Their table at the Lord Cardigan pub, its tabard a worn painting of the ferocious old duffer from the Crimea, was in an alcove off the saloon bar where the safest fare seemed to be the ploughman's lunch with Stilton, Gloucester, and two pints of genuine Guinness, a miracle of some sort. Undamaged by the rampages of the previous nights, the place was spotted by a few hardy locals who snarled at the Canadian uniform. In the beery heat, Horobbins draped his jacket on the back of the chair and watched in silence while Bollock, who didn't divest himself, scanned the draft report and interview notes.

"That's as far as I got when you came in. You'll see I've concentrated my own interviews on the four men closest to the colonel in some capacity: Todder, Montgomery, Nolan, and Helmers. Every one of them must have a piece of vital information. We'll have to lean on them, for sure."

"And the fifth intimate, the crumpet Evans. Is she the connection we need? What was she getting into with him?"

"More likely *vice versa*. I'm not going to bring her back until Captain Williams has her chat. A gamble, I know. What do you think?"

"Under duress, not reliable or won't press her in the state she's in. Williams herself, she lodges a complaint against the colonel back in Canada, ends up here in the same unit. Do we have a thread running through this?"

"More like a torn net."

"Motive, opportunity. Where do we find them?"

"Unless it does go back to the Continent."

"Until your mates over there come through, Todder's our only link. Seems to have an alibi for that night, but he as much admits or claims he no longer was pally with the colonel. Why not? Must tighten the screws on that braying ass."

"I intend to. Not such a twit, I found. His mannerisms are a front."

"As are those other three, having great fun leading you up the garden path. That sapper blighter is the worst. What the hell'd they think they were doing? Diversions to what end? And their endless whingeing. Same old story from the ranks, innit?"

"Not quite. You combine resentment at the Wellesleys and Todders of their world with a sense of betrayal, you've got a powerful mix. Why they'd pick specifically on the colonel, I have no idea, but someone cottoned onto the sentiment brewing out there and left that note. It may not mean anything, but it does express the sense that the home front let them down. Appeasement didn't end with your Chamberlain. We had our own PM, Mr. King, who vowed he'd never risk the open rebellion of Quebec that blew up in 1917. He wanted a war without disunity and the fewest possible casualties, yet he let the military planners talk him into an army of five divisions that couldn't be sustained by volunteers. As a sop to a more militant English Canada he injected compulsory service in small doses for home defence only. It was a disaster."

"No doubt the voters will take their vengeance on your Mr. King."

"You won't believe this. Last month, an election. King lost his own seat but hung on with a reduced majority. What's more, he did better than anyone expected with the service vote. Perhaps he was seen as someone who had kept a divided country together. It wasn't only the English–French problem, not all the draftees were from Quebec. Many were from the west: Ukrainians who weren't about to go to war to save the hated Soviet Union, sons of other European immigrants who wanted no sacrifice for the rotten homelands they'd left behind, holdovers from the Depression, radicals if you like, disgusted with a system not worth defending, and a good number of garden variety slackers. Then there's me."

"You're handing me a line, Horobbins. You weren't a whatsit—Voodoo material—surely?"

"Zombie. Afraid so. Family reasons more than anything else."

"There you are, no different from the others, but you must have changed your mind at some point. Perhaps this isn't for me to say—stop me if I cause offense—but frankly I'm not surprised your Mr. King was re-elected. There's no question Britain will always be grateful for your prompt entry into the war in '39, the way you kept us going with food, supplies, and manpower before the Yanks were forced to come in. My question is this: why come in at all? There you are, far removed from peril under the American umbrella. The fight against the Nazi tyranny was a worthy goal, but you could have done your bit without plunging in the way you did. For a decayed Empire? The fact is you had the luxury of choice, not the struggle for survival we had to face. Your Mr. King, I'd hazard, correctly read the public's mixed feelings about the whole exercise. As to your conscripts, who can blame 'em? The rules were clear enough: you volunteer at your own risk for the dangers and earn the respect of the community, or you can sit back and wait for them to overcome the internal divisions of the country and send you. By so doing, as a draftee, you then proceed to create your own code of honour to earn the approval of your mates, by never volunteering for anything. Isn't that the private soldier's credo from time immemorial? Sorry, Horobbins, I'm putting you off. Why don't you tell me about your stint, a short one I gather, as a copper. Someone actually took a shot at you? What was that about? We need another pint." Bollock went to the bar, came back with two mugs and an amused grin. "Three of your fine chaps just showed up."

Horobbins swore, got up to peer around the alcove. They wore Second Division blue patches, floppy balmoral lids, Essex Scottish, named after the south Ontario county. The locals sidled away from the infection.

"They're out of bounds." But wearily did nothing.

"Done a bunk from their cage? Seem to be quiet enough. Is there such a thing as a Zombie copper?"

"No such animal." Horobbins let his eyes stray in the direction of the bar. Were voices rising? "By the time I was drafted in the spring of '41 they'd extended service from thirty days to four months, then indefinitely, but for home defence only. Your point taken on conflicting attitudes about Canada's role in the war. But what offended the majority, mostly in English Canada to be sure, was that the system rewarded inequality of sacrifice. Parents who got the telegrams were in no mood to coddle the shirkers. Disgusted by the whole setup, I still listened to my mother's fears about signing up for active service. One of those messengers at the door would have been more than she could bear, for, you see, I am their only son in a family with three girls. So, yes, I pulled strings to get out and was released from the army for the Toronto police force. My father, despite his communist leanings, remained active in the Orange Lodge, a powerful underground network in our neck of the woods."

"Odd colour combination that: Orange Lodge and a Red."

"If, as you say, the Russkis are next, my father'd be out there rooting for the Soviets. He truly believes Uncle Joe Stalin won the war to bring socialist justice to Europe."

"Good God, on top of everything else you're a commie?"

"Far from it. At the time of my first army stint in '41, Russia wasn't in the war. To my dad it was a struggle for markets among imperialists to be avoided like the plague. He had already turned on my mother when, in '39, she stood out in the cold with a coin box to collect for the brave Finns holding out against the Soviet invaders. My father had mixed feelings about activating the Orange network to extract his son from the imperialist stooges in the army to join the crypto-fascist oppressors in the police. To make amends for the fears of my mother, he went along. Actually, he was an unlikely communist; never joined the party, thank goodness, for they were rounded up in '39 on the outbreak of war. At that time, as you know, the Nazis and the Soviets were in the same bed."

"While I'm not one myself, I'm quite aware of the Masonic network. But the Orange Lodge's out of Ulster, innit?"

"Correct. My father's Protestant from Sligo, now in the Republic, who migrated to Belfast to work in the shipyards—claims to have worked on the *Titanic*, hardly a monument to his welding skills; then through Orange Lodge connections to Colonel McLaughlin's automotive plant, later General Motors, in Oshawa."

"Your capital," said Bollock, showing off.

"That's Ottawa. Oshawa's on Lake Ontario east of Toronto. There, in the midst of the devastation of the Dirty Thirties, was this vast palace belching forth metallic plumes that, when the wind was off the lake, left a fine coating on our little bungalow in the north end of town. On those days we'd close the windows tight and suffocate because mother wouldn't let us play outside. The plant itself, with its mass of sheds and production lines, was not a dark satanic mill, but one where it shone brightly at all hours. At one point father had the idea of getting me released from the army as an essential war worker; spoke to the foreman who was amenable, then took me on a tour on his day off. Until then I had never been inside the mill. The noise of machinery was so familiar to us we never noticed, but inside, under those lights day and night, it was a clanking, screeching hell while men scrambled and sweated to keep up with the conveyor belts—Henry Ford's devilish invention adapted by every carmaker. Where the welders sprayed their blue arcs in showers, the men had the appearance of World War One flyers in smoked goggles and scarves around their necks. I understood then why father would never allow us to have firecrackers and pin wheels on the Queen's birthday, May 24, Victoria, that is. And when I reeled from that inferno of noise and heat, I felt a new respect for my father's daily pain to earn a living for his family in such hard times. I pressed him again about the police force idea.

"And I came to appreciate why, four years before, the assembly line workers had gone on a wildcat strike—in the depths of the Depression in 1937, for God's sake—a quixotic fling when jobless men were hawking apples on the streets. Its nerve, its folly divided and stupefied the community. Then came the spectre of Red infection. Maybe there were Reds among the United Auto Workers out of Detroit who came in to organize. Who knows? What sent dad off the deep end was the drastic reaction of the Liberal premier of the province of Ontario, one Mitch Hepburn, a wild man himself who kept a harem in the King Edward hotel in Toronto. Ranting on about communist plots, he raised an army of some four hundred sworn constables to put down the uprising, to be dubbed 'Hepburn's Hussars.' Fortunately they were never used, the strike ended quietly enough with a compromise, as usual, when the union was recognized as a local affiliate or some such. Father says: 'If we're supposed to be Reds, that's where I'll be. It's the future.' Now he wasn't drunken Irish, far from it, never touched a drop; but he became a convert, a hardliner outside the party, never joined the local cell because he couldn't stand 'em, a raging individualist hankering for a collectivist utopia. After the Hitler–Stalin pact, when he railed against the war, I prayed he wasn't a saboteur in the plant now turning out military vehicles. When I made it plain I could never work on the assembly line, and went back to languish with the draftees, my father, under more prodding from mother, with great reluctance, sought out his cousin 'Short Strokes Stokes,' a luminary in the Loyal Orange Order—once rode as King Billy in the annual parade—who was a sergeant in the Toronto police. Got me released, wartime shortages taking their toll."

"That's when you were shot at? You actually carried sidearms?" Bollock turned. "Yes, my man?"

The publican, as befitting the trade, was portly with a scarlet face and bald head to match as he kneaded his hands within a stained bar cloth. He had ventured into the alcove for advice or perhaps the authority he had divined in the two men. His eyes sought out Horobbins whose absence of jacket left a note of uncertainty.

"Sir, your lads out there. . . ."

"They making trouble for you?"

"Not yet, sir, let us say the temperature is beginning to rise somewhat."

"About what?"

"I heard one of them say my establishment evidently had been overlooked in the disturbances. They are currently debating whether to remedy the situation."

"But they haven't done anything?"

"Not yet, sir."

"Then clear off for now. We're busy."

"The first sign of anything you let me know," said Horobbins.

"Back to your own Wild West."

"We packed a Webley on the left hip. September '41, at a call box at Yonge and St. Clair in north Toronto, normally a low crime area. Fellow in a cloth cap comes running out of the Imperial Bank branch right under my nose. Gun in hand, paper bag of loot in hand. I yell for reinforcements into the phone, leave the key in the lock, go after him, doesn't have a getaway plan beyond a passing streetcar. When he turns, startled, and fires, I fumble with my holster, can't unclip it, then tackle him, snap on the cuffs. That was it. My picture was in the papers. Afterward, when I had delayed shakes, I concluded that if I was going to be shot at I might as well improve the odds, and this time, when I told father, he approved with great enthusiasm, brushing aside my mother's pleas. For the Soviets were in it now—to transform it magically into a people's war, he'd be proud and so on. Not about to give up, still seeking a safe berth for her son, mother came up with another name.

"This time it was a second cousin once removed, complete with Orange

Lodge credentials, who happened to be a captain in the Provost Corps. He saw me through the army chairs, to A-32 at Camp Borden where my already proven heroism under fire led quickly to a commission. In January '43, when I was over here at Farnham, down the road, I discovered a scam in an officers' mess, the usual stuff, funds diverted for personal amusements. My diligence was noted by CMHQ, who brought me into their Special Investigations Unit where I've been ever since. Then last year took over Six Company and promoted to captain."

"You had the nose for it." Bollock reddened at his reference to the other's most prominent feature. "Your service has been in England?"

"Not entirely. I've been out and about on various files, I may tell you about some time."

"Still, I wouldn't let it slip to our shadowy friends that you're an Irish Bolshevik. Hullo, what have we here?"

From the bar came the sound of splintering glass, splats of flesh upon flesh, shouts. Bollock bared the gaps in his teeth for what might pass as a grin.

"Same old tune. Your department."

15

How many times had he seen it—the debris of the rituals that were the handbook of barroom mayhem? First, an empty glass mug was tested on the edge of the bar, chipped off a sliver of oak but refused to shatter. Intact, was pegged at the mirror, then a chair followed to topple precious bottles. Four Englishmen on the far side of national service, the flesh of exemption absorbing crevices under white thatches, rallied in a corner, tankards awield, to snarl at these pretend Scots.

They're babies, nothing more than teenagers, Horobbins lamented as he shot out of the alcove, him an ancient at twenty-six. Forgot to don his jacket. The intruders paused to size up grandpops in shirt and suspenders, battledress trousers, khaki tie. Hey, an officer? A stocky man, cop written over him in black suit and take-charge manner, came out to hand the geezer his jacket. Jeez, a meathead with three pips. Headed for the door into two elderly constables who, with hope, caressed the bulge of their coshes under dark tunics.

Indecisive now, the soldiers backed up, gin and whisky bottles clamped to their chests. Horobbins leaped over the bar, found the phone intact, rang central exchange at the camp.

"Hold it," he called.

The young fellows dropped their spirits bottles, hoisted chairs and tried to clear a path out of the door; the two constables were struck aside, flopped over upended tables, chairs were tossed, the soldiers pushed out into two Jeep loads of four Canadian MPs. Game over, balloon deflated, they became sullen schoolboys, heads lowered awaiting punishment.

"You lot are off to the Mob Control Centre." Horobbins found his voice shaky with rage. "How in hell you get here?"

"Off back a truck."

"Where were you going?"

"Ewshot, they tole us." Repats who had dispersed themselves a little more widely than intended.

"You mixed up in the riots?"

"Nah, just got here. We figure we finish the job for the boys."

The corporal heading the provost detachment nodded to his men to squeeze the three into the Jeeps. "You won't be going home now. Detention, pack drill, no more pay, damages. Bloody idiots."

Bollock watched Horobbins step forward to peer at the prisoners' sleeves. On each one a vertical gold wound stripe, but only one red chevron marked a year's service, then he caught that look, the one he had seen too often, a foreknowledge of humanity's fate they could never share with anyone who had not been there.

"Wait a minute, corporal. You Pacific volunteers?"

"No, sir, we seen enough." The boy had a scar running from his hairline to his chin, the ridge snaking through the acne of a formative adult who should have been hanging out at his local soda fountain. "We didn't want Occupation, so they put us on ice. We're low point, see? The padre put in a good word, got us reboards; we limped around a lot, so they let us go."

"How old are you?"

"Nineteen, sir, same as them. We joined up last year, finished our infantry training at Debert, then they sent us over when we reached age."

Horobbins pointed to their unit flashes. "You from Windsor?" The

Ontario city across the river from Detroit.

"Nah, Canada."

"Very funny. You were reinforcements for the Essex Scottish?"

"Correct, sir. In March we was sent to the Essex Scottish in the Hochwald. Took one helluva pasting. The three of us, we got clipped for sure, ended up in hospital then rejoined the regiment for the run into Oldenburg at the last. That's about it, sir."

Horobbins took the corporal aside. "We'll follow you up there. I want to have a word with Major Clancy before anything's done about these men."

"Sir? They'll be . . ."

"I know. Leave it with me, eh?"

The corporal sized up this dark-visaged apparition, an alien of some sort, reluctantly conceded to rank and rounded up his entourage for the trek to the pokey. Horobbins went back into the pub to make abject offers of atonement and left word on how to claim damages from the panel already busy enough with the week's earlier tally. The innkeeper and remaining customers muttered incantations on Canucks and declined the offer of a round of drinks.

Bollock's car appeared by some Scotland Yard telepathy and, in the wake of the offenders, they set out for Ramillies barracks. Horobbins placed his scuffed briefcase on his lap as a makeshift desk on which he scribbled a note. Bollock waited until Horobbins had finished writing.

"You gone soft in the nut, Horobbins?"

"I'm writing to Dick Clancy. If I don't see him, I want this in the hopper. I'm recommending those boys be returned to billets for punishment by their commanding officer, or whoever's in charge. He can dole out field punishment, then send them home."

"So they get away scot-free after wreaking damage on our innocent civilians, same as most of your other mutineers."

"I wouldn't expect you to understand."

"Try me."

He had never tested mateship by calling the inspector "Timothy" or "Tim," let alone "Tiny Tim," thus began with, "Mr. Bollock, I suppose it doesn't matter now, except to pick up the pieces, like those three boys who'll have to be put back together again so they can rejoin civilization, if that's what we call it back home. Now, in a sense you broke your oath, or the Official Secrets Act, when you told me of the crisis here in May 1940 when the idea of giving up, conceding the game, floated about. In fair exchange I'll tell you about a situation that brought the Canadian army close to the edge of something similar. Just as your people were unaware that certain parties were about to open the gates to the Nazi barbarians, so too our folks at home have no idea of this and probably will not find out until the war is fading into distant memory. The fact is, by February and March this year, the Canadian army was on its last legs, thinned out, near collapse. The truth of over-commitment finally came home to roost and there was something akin to a panic that found its way from the Rhine to Ottawa. Those young fellows in the pub, I could see it. They knew. It was nothing short of mass battle exhaustion on a huge scale, a spent force that could no longer be called an "army" filled with its own citizens, one that became a kind of foreign legion reinforced by the British and almost every other contingent on the Allied side from the countries of Europe that had been overrun by the Germans. For one of the bloodiest campaigns of the war we will be hardly noticed. Of course, you've heard of the Ardennes, the Battle of the Bulge last December and January."

"Who hasn't? The Yanks, bless 'em, recovered, broke the Jerries' last big push, sent them packing back across the Rhine. In effect, won the war while we sat it out and did nothing."

"We can see it coming, the Hollywood factory in full swing. Come on, Mr. Bollock, you should know better. Our forces were on alert along the Maas, had reliable intelligence that General Kurt Student was massing troops for a second thrust. Would've struck if the Yanks hadn't finally got their act together. The objective was a pincer movement to cut off Antwerp, our main port for the buildup across the Rhine. Can you imagine? No, it wasn't over by a long shot, as we were to find out at heavy cost."

"The Americans were smashing into Germany further south. The Russkis were pouring through in the east. The Jerries were on their last legs, surely."

"If so, they had a funny way of showing it. What shook up our high command was to discover, after the Battle of the Bulge, that an entire German army was dug in on the west side of the Rhine to the left of the US forces. Not only that, it was the First Parachute Army—tough bastards, not your old men and kids, these guys were the best, adept with mines and booby traps, knew how to use ground and the old fortifications at the north end of the Siegfried line, the cover of the Reichswald and Hochwald forests, flooded lowland, you name any tricks of the trade. A nightmare waited. Montgomery somehow felt they had to be eliminated on the ground before the big offensive into northern Germany."

"Why didn't they bypass them, let 'em rot? Or bomb them into the mud?"

"Don't ask me. Whatever the reasons, it became yet another dirty job for the Canadian army, except it was so weakened that three-quarters of the troops were British and others. So, just a few weeks before the war ended came one last ballsup that I understand was worse than the Falaise Gap, the Arnhem drop, the Scheldt Estuary."

"At that stage of the war you'd think we'd learned."

"Not so you'd notice. Vast preparations were made, no shortage of material coming through Antwerp. Planning thorough and precise. What happened? First, the weather closed in with heavy downpours, sleet, even ice in places, turning the land into a quagmire, stalled vehicles and hindered air support. To add to the fun the Germans opened the floodgates. It was supposed to be a two-way vise closing in on them, but the American Ninth Army got bogged down to the south in floods from the Roer. Even so, that wasn't the major miscalculation: nobody, especially after the Battle of the Bulge, for one moment expected the Jerries to make a stand in an untenable swamp on the wrong side of the river. Much to the chagrin of our leaders they fed the last of their first class troops into the pocket instead of retreating across the Rhine to conserve the few fighting units they had left. It was beyond belief.

"It was attrition, the worst slogging match through mud and blasted forest, like World War One butchery. Incredibly, the British and Canadians finally pushed them out. Two of our guys, one from the Essex Scottish, won the Victoria Cross; everybody who went through it should've. Several of our top battalions rebuilt after the Scheldt were almost wiped out, notably the Essex Scottish. Those fellows in the pub were green replacements thrown into it. That's why I want Dick Clancy to cut them some slack. Not until March did outside pressures prompt the Jerries to pull their battered remnants across the river as the Ninth Army finally showed up, while to the south the Americans were mopping up and the Russians poured in from the east."

"Surely our lads took the same losses."

"No question. Your Highland, Scots, Welsh, Guards divisions took one helluva beating. Total casualties were in excess of fifteen thousand, but for us it was a drain of blood we'd have great difficulty replacing. The only major reinforcements in the pipeline were our two divisions coming up from Italy. They weren't up to full strength, anyway, and didn't arrive till mid-March. In Britain you could still call in more conscripts, such as they were. Ours, at last released for overseas duty, were only a trickle, while volunteers like those lads in the pub were few and far between. The army reeled. When reality came home to roost, feelers were put out suggesting that the Canadians should be placed in reserve and regrouped into a smaller force. In other words, we'd be leaving a big hole in the buildup for the last push across the northern Rhine. Now remember, I'm at CMHQ in London and pick up stuff that isn't necessarily down in writing, and it became well known around the shop that Montgomery had blown up, as much as called our generals 'yellow.' Signals went back and forth causing a near panic in Ottawa, a pall of disbelief that, if the public ever found out, would be an admission of the total manpower screwup. Under the 'loose lips sink ships' posters in the mess there was open talk that our own PM, Mr. King, earlier had written to Churchill whining for a reduced role for the weakened army. What the reply was I have no idea, or whether Montgomery was actually apprised of it, but it didn't matter in any case when he became stubborn and ordered the Canadians to take their share of the burden as part of the long standing plan for the final offensive. No doubt he was also worried about his own manpower situation—how he'd ever fill the gap if our army pulled out. The upshot was Montgomery prevailed, but our role had to be a lesser one than, say, it had been in Normandy. Perhaps he appreciated the qualities of our men better than our own leaders and, as far as I can make out, was completely satisfied with the performance of the Canadians—for the first time together in their own army when the units came up from Italy. So they crossed into Germany, cleaned up Holland, and saved people from starvation. The Dutch relief operation did more for morale than anything else, which makes it all more criminal that officers like Wellesley and Todder were diverting precious supplies for their own gain. And, as you described it, like May 1940, the stench of cowardice on the part of some of our leaders vanished in the euphoria of victory."

"Which leads us to what?"

"Not sure yet, but there's no question that our Montgomery—not the field-marshal—Nolan and even Helmers, seemingly unconnected, did have one thing they shared: a close proximity to Wellesley and even Todder, their contempt for those two palpable as a skunk at a garden party. And they played me for a sap. What they actually know we'll find out sooner or later, short of beating the shit out of them. Even under the gun, I doubt if our betters would approve. No, I don't see a pattern yet, but I'm beginning to wonder if it is possible that a collective mood of resentments, grievances, real and imagined, could lead to murder."

"Too deep for me, Horobbins. You'd have to consult the experts on that one."

"Experts?"

"Our late adversaries, the Nazis. They know how it's done."

Around 2100 hours Horobbins stood at the window of his newly-assigned room in the relative comfort of the spider hut to ponder if he had the energy to haul his bones to the ablution room to luxuriate in a good Canadian steamy shower. The invisible grime of the day needed to be scrubbed off.

On double daylight saving time the sky was spreading into a Turner salmon-pink with filmy tendrils like the dissolving contrails of the Flying Fortresses that had once flown high on their bombing runs. From lengthening shadows two figures appeared, walking very slowly towards the next hut, the CWAC quarters; one tall, willowy, as they said in those days, head down, shoulders caved forward, the other shorter, upright and gesturing. Kepis low, the peaks under diamond-shaped badges shielded their faces. Corporal Claire Evans and Captain Williams returning from their heart-to-heart.

Tomorrow, ladies. No church parade for you.

PART TWO

16

Charlene, the bookkeeper at work, said you don't want anything to do with that scruff—company of whores, lousy, dirty, the dregs. Worse than those ones, Charlene went on, pointing to the back of the shop where the pieceworkers cut and sewed the pelts amid obscene accented patter the bosses didn't mind as long as they made their quotas. Claire's mom nodded when she told her. Yes, there are some who say that, I've heard around. But her father intervened: trash is inside you. The uniform won't change you unless you let it, some fellas we had in the last one you wouldn't believe. You might want to think about it some more, but I'm betting you've made up your mind.

She had. She would join up to get away from them, not her parents or sisters, the ones at the furriers. At least, she hoped, among a bunch of other women there'd be safety in numbers, and among the trash she'd seek out decent confidants, somebody to share quiet girl talk to shield her or offer advice on how to handle them. Her own bitter self-appraisal would wait for years until she met Ambrose, the only one who had released her true nature, as if an old-fashioned corset had exploded, and now that he was gone she wanted more of it from another as yet to be found. Hidden scruff, all right.

"Great cans," those drips at school would call out as she navigated around them, her regal height, flushed skin, and jet-black hair arousing adolescent lust, not too difficult a task at any time. Which she outwardly ignored. Spurned clumsy advances, shuffling attempts to convoy her home; invites out to the show were rebuffed with blank disdain while her stomach churned at the pimply horde, leaping or slouching clowns—a mongrel zoo of Catholics, Polacks, Hebes, and a few others who weren't too bad when they weren't feigning menace in gangs. Thankfully she didn't have far to walk from Harbord Collegiate to home, a narrow three storey semi-detached house on a short street north of Dundas between Spadina and Bathurst in downtown Toronto. By the time she reached Fourth Form she found a way to escape the vile buzz of teenage boys. She decided to go to a private secretarial school; more than anything else to equip herself for survival in dire times within the company of other girls who wanted to better themselves, for it became evident to her that the rudimentary typing, sewing and cooking classes at school were not sufficient to compete for scarce jobs.

Claire's parents were quick to agree. They had a little put aside, her two sisters were younger, and James Evans had achieved a miracle—the actual ownership of the semi-detached house, a rare privilege during the Depression. Her father had pulled off the feat by his dignified social skills and prudence as the well-tipped doorman at the King Edward Hotel on King Street. She had never seen him in his black uniform with the brass buttons and his Great War service ribbons that he kept at the hotel. The house rule was never to drop by and wave while he was on duty. The girls could only imagine how imposing he must be: six foot three and pole straight. James, never Jim, did not venture beyond the hotel without his snapbrim grey fedora and brown suit. No bowing or scraping out on the street where equality prevailed.

The idea of secretarial school had grown slowly. When they weren't cutting up the jostling louts in the halls, her girlfriends of the moment, Wanda and Natalie, shared their thoughts as Depression kids who worried what fate might await them out there. Marriage and kids with one of those awful creeps? Until then, what? Job somewhere. How? You needed some kind of skill or trade. They kicked it around with the harsh realism absorbed from home, and agreed it's who you know not what you know in this dog-eat-dog world we're about to enter. Well, it occurred to her, she was acquainted with someone who had connections with the big shots—her own father, gatekeeper to the privileged.

One suppertime she asked her father if he could find her a job at the hotel.

James Evans laid down his knife and fork, fixed her with a frown the likes of which the hotel patrons had never seen. Her mother, in her way of a kind of placid fretting, her hair still as glossy black as that of her eldest daughter, flinched too at his reaction. He was not a tyrant at home, not bursting with anger as so many were in those days of fear and privation; nor did he talk much about his work, the discretion apparently bred within him, a pact of silence with his guests. When he did begin, as he did that spring evening when the kitchen windows were open to cool off the coal-fed oven, they listened in some wonderment at a glimpse into the life he must lead. An "asskisser" some of the boys on the street called him, but his own family knew it couldn't be true. Claire pictured him stately and grave, opening doors of the cars, a finger flick to bring forth a cab, no silver whistle for him, his white cotton gloves the only parts of his uniform he did bring to home to her mother to wash, the gloves perhaps raised in salute when someone of special importance came by.

Instead of directly answering his daughter's request, James Evans seemingly wandered off into the matter of the Liberal premier of the Province of Ontario, Mitch Hepburn, who lived in the hotel in a suite when he was in town. But it was more than a tale or anecdote. The girls and their mother around the table sensed that an object lesson was coming down the pike, perhaps a sermon or parable leading to rejection of his daughter's attempt to activate the who-you-know principle of job placement.

"Top drawer," James Evans told his family, the sarcasm passing over their heads at the time. "The premier, or prime minister, not of the country but of our province, as he likes to call himself. Where the elite meet to greet, eh? Every so often, you know, the preem asks me up to his rooms. I turn the door over to Whitey, the head bellman, for a few minutes. They get the word when I'm invited up.

"It's some layout, one of our best suites. There's a colour photo of our country's real prime minister, Mackenzie King, on a centre table, stacks of government documents heaped in a corner; but unlike King, our Mitch is a tad casual about such matters. On the wall there's a picture of the Dionne Quints' doctor, that Dafoe fella, and Ned Sparks, the comedian. Now Mitch himself—or the 'Chief' as everyone around there calls him—he always greets me like an old chum. Cheerful, dapper, round face, small chin, neatly brushed hair. Any time I see him he's wearing a double-breasted suit, which he must divest at other times. Radio dance music comes from the other room, girls' voices and drinks, anything you want. His bodyguard, Eddie, I know him well, he's always nice to me; in fact, he's the one who gives me the signal to come up, the girls, real lookers all over the place, call him 'Bruiser.' Eddie, when he comes downstairs to give me the high sign and take me up, he wears a camel-hair coat and a fedora with the front brim turned up. I'm always offered a drink or a girl and, Mattie," turning to his wife, "you can bet I don't take any of 'em."

"You better not."

"Can't have booze on my breath at the door."

"What about the other?"

"No time," a shy smile; "those gals and their ilk, we get plenty of them around the King Eddie. They dress smartly, always pretty, but not my type, if you get what I mean."

"I hope not."

"The routine goes like this. The Chief asks me how they're hanging. Have I seen any Tories skulking around? Then maybe he tells a joke, like this recent widow back in St. Thomas, his hometown, who's asked: 'Do you want him buried or cremated?' 'Both,' she says, 'just to make sure he ain't comin' back.'"

Mattie professed to be shocked.

"They don't expect me to hang around. Eddie gives the high sign to a fat bozo sitting at a kind of antique secretarial desk. When this guy opens the drawer I can see it's jammed to the gills with the green stuff, from which he peels off two tens, hands them to Eddie, who palms them off to me. As expected, I express my thanks and depart. That's how it's done. Nothing so crass as dropping a buck or two on me at the door. But," here James Evans turned his eyes onto the identical brown ones of his eldest daughter, "it's no place for you, chicken. I don't want any daughter of mine working in the hotel, even if you were on the desk."

"Some example he is," said Mattie.

"It'll catch up with him, that loose living, his temper getting shorter. He's never teed off on me, but I pick it up from the other staff. The people seem to like him for now—they don't know. But it'll come home to roost. So I don't want you or your sisters when they get older anywhere near that place."

The secretarial school ran classes year round. Claire began in July on a sweltering, musty floor in a 1908 building on Wellington Street, where the cage elevators were run by lecherous rheumies. The girls made sure they went in groups. Mrs. Laveston, who ran the school of two large rooms—one filled with the din of clacking Underwoods, the other a quiet place to struggle with Pitman shorthand and bookkeeping—also gave instruction on office decorum. After Labour Day, in September, they had to give up their light, colourful summer frocks and put on tailored black; stocking seams had to be straight, summer or winter. Those from untutored homes learned how to use deodorant and powder to be applied on strategic body parts.

What she didn't teach, as Claire found in a succession of temporary jobs in offices, often long streetcar rides away, was how to cope with the sticky paws, the leers, the offers of dinners, shows, and what-have-you from management, workers, and customers. It was thus with a sense of relief that she was interviewed and hired as receptionist, typist, and steno at the furriers on Spadina, walking distance from home. The owner, genial, fiftyish, crinkly eyes only for her skills, seemed to be a gentleman. Jack (formerly Jacob) McCloud presided over The McCloud Brothers, who had changed their name from one of too many consonants, Polish maybe, to something they thought would be more acceptable to Toronto's illiberal community; except their odd spelling of their new name brought only derision, for no Scot or Celt could recognize it as one of theirs. The McClouds were wholesalers to the retail trade and ran a sweatshop where the skins were designed and sewn, their speciality, much admired, being Hudson seal—actually not seal at all but sheared, dyed muskrat. Once again, though, with her height and good looks, Claire soon had to fend off the buyers and, worst of all, Jack's son, Marvin, who was squat and moistly horrible.

It was Marvin who suggested to his father that Claire should model garments for the buyers. The other two part-time models didn't seem to mind Marvin and found they could dampen his advances with jeering giggles. Claire hated the way he'd push aside the curtain when she was in her slip or less, sometimes wearing only her underthings under a long fur coat so she wouldn't show a bead of perspiration for the buyers, who sweated profusely themselves when they saw her and pressed their hands over and into the coat to feel its texture and hers. Marvin kept coming at her until she finally asked her mother what she should do. Mattie referred her to her father who was ready to go over a few blocks to Spadina to have a word—but she didn't want to lose her first job at sixteen dollars a week when few other prospects were in sight.

From gropes to utter degradation: pokes, prods, privacy out the window. If wartime rescued her from sticky paws, its mass repression was ugly in its own mindless way. No problem joining the newly formed Canadian Women's Army Corps in December 1941, down at the University Avenue Armouries where they hinted her secretarial training, her references from clergy and teachers, made her a prized recruit.

Not for long. Onto a shabby assembly line; male doctors snapped at them to strip to bras and panties. Depression styles were unveiled: droopy bloomers, some in flower sack knickers, others in stained cheap cottons. And the shapes: gouged bellies distended, lumpy red knees, stringy arms—in contrast to her own untouched flesh, noticed by some with curious grins she didn't much care for. TABT shots to make you woozy, then, squeaky clean as she was, the delousing bath, probes for head lice, the "cootie code" to measure live nits. Parades, when mannish sergeants raked your body for unpolished shoes, twisted stockings, or hair straggling below your collar. Was your skirt exactly sixteen inches from the ground? They brought out the tapes. All of this for ninety cents a day, compared to the dollar thirty bestowed upon male soldiers.

At first she worked in the quartermaster stores at Chorley Park military hospital until she became secretary to an MO, a nice elderly major. In those early days basic training was haphazard, held after hours at, of all places, back at Harbord Collegiate. Instead of far-away travel, she once again had to run the gauntlet of hooting gangs of her old pests, while on the street the neighbours clucked at her new getup. Mrs. Stein asked if she was a camp follower.

At last in February 1942, Claire Evans was shipped off to the first CWAC training centre in St. Anne de Bellevue in Quebec, where they were gawked at as an exotic hostile presence. From there to a temporary wooden building at Dow's Lake, Ottawa, an offshoot of a sprawling headquarters where nobody knew what they were doing and the men were worse than Marvin, if that was possible. Liberation came finally in December 1942 when she went off to the actual war, the second CWAC draft overseas.

From the train out of Greenock, Scotland, they had their first awakening. Images from the Blitz, plucky Londoners cheerfully carrying on in the fire storms, the nation united and implacable, gave way to hints of something else, disturbing enough to make some of the girls swallow hard, hold back tears. For there, coming into the city against a backdrop of gapped ruins and rubble, people were lined up beyond the wire fence like begging prisoners. Scraggly, grimy, pushing kids to the fore, they held out their hands, some with sacks. From the troop train and hundreds of others like it, mostly Yanks now, came a shower of candy bars, cigarettes, tins, packs of biscuits, and even toilet paper from K-rations. In their compartment, Claire's pals rummaged around for goodies to toss to the scrambling horde. How did they find out when the troop trains came through, or did they wait all day, their kids kept out of school as bait?

The medieval blackness of London matched a gradual sourness of mood, the exhilaration of the Blitz waning under deadly hit-and-run raids, the Luftwaffe otherwise engaged on the eastern steppes. Her next door bedmate, Jean Cullen, was a veteran of the first draft in November. They were in barracks in the west end, the ablution rooms shared with Auxiliary Territorial Service (ATS) types who were territorial indeed when it came to getting first dibs on the hot water. There were screaming matches with the condescending British ladies of the service. Jean Cullen, slow and lazy in manner, instructed Claire on wartime sex.

"A dirty fog everywhere," she said. "Everybody, I mean every last monkey with a pecker, will be after you, especially a pretty one like you. If you want to take a chance getting knocked up or a dose, up to you. One thing about us gals in uniform, we can fend off the unwelcome creeps. There's so much local talent they don't really need us. But be careful."

A fine one to talk. The next time she saw Jean Cullen she was hanging onto the arm of a Canadian lieutenant from the Regina Rifles. They asked her to join them at the Admiral pub off Lower Regent Street near where both women worked in a CMHQ office on Sackville Street. He, lean and dark with a devil's peak forehead, almost forgot Jean, as if she meant little to him, and focused on Claire with a sarcastic wit that entranced her. For the first time, long before she met Ambrose and his polished domination, she was taken with someone who affected the sophistication of the smart guys in the movies. His name was Doug Sayers and he was from the same western town as Jean, who he seemed to take for granted as a passage of familiar intimacy, a neighbour who was something more than an older sister. It didn't take long for Jean to catch the sparks between those two and haul her Dougie, as she called him, off somewhere on their own, saying, we have memories to discuss. Claire tried not to imagine the two of them together, doing it.

When Jean Cullen, possibly jealous of what she had sensed in the pub, gradually abandoned her role as soul mate and tutor, Claire was relieved to escape London for a posting to Beaumont barracks, Aldershot. There, she was to find her niche for the duration at the Canadian Reinforcement Unit, a hectic shuffle of paper and bodies until June 1944 when the little island tipped back to the horizontal, its southern counties drained of the weight of millions of troops. After D-Day the camp was a subdued ghost town of frightened replacements, rounded up and shipped away to fill graves across the Channel.

Not until March 1945 did a letter find its convoluted way to her from Doug Sayers, somewhere in a hospital in Holland. Had she heard that Jean Cullen had been killed by a V-2 rocket in Antwerp in December? No, she hadn't. "I wasn't too far away when it happened," Doug wrote, "got a bit racked up myself. They tell me the rescue workers at the Rex Theatre found most of them still in their seats, rows of the dead covered by dust and rubble staring at a non-existent screen. Jean was one of them." Then shyly: "hope you don't mind if I give this address in Edmonton, my parents' home. Maybe we could get together again when this is all over." She wrote back, also giving her home address, but his next letter was written in a shaky hand, on his way back to Canada for discharge, implying damage both to his psyche and body.

Once more she felt compelled to test the waters. Doug Sayers had never touched her, yet there was something unsaid between them. Not so when she allowed some fully clothed heavy petting with a staff sergeant, his scratchy battledress reeking with those peculiar barracks room smells: Heaven knows he tried, even snapped off his fly buttons in blacked out nooks. What was the matter with her? Nothing, as it turned out; she just had to find the right one with indefinable qualities she couldn't quite imagine. Doug Sayers had been nothing more than a nice idea from afar, now merely a memory from an unknown future. Not until June 1945 did the right one come along at last. And what did she do? She let herself fall into the one overriding, if that's the right word, taboo, her own commanding officer, Lieutenant Colonel Ambrose Wellesley, the Duke. Talk about smashing the code.

Earlier, James Evans had written to report that things finally had caught up to Mitch Hepburn. He had resigned as premier. "That bad bunch around him at the hotel and others. The trouble was you knew what Mitch was against— the big interests at times—but we never knew what he was for. His feud with Ottawa didn't help, never felt King was putting his all into the war effort, always appeasing Quebec."

To which Claire Evans added her own "amen," as day after day she listened to the repats when they came into the orderly room as if they could wheedle their way out of there. She wasn't surprised when the riots broke out, and worried when Ambrose seemed to take it personally. This he had confided to her before he was so horribly gunned down in his office. His devotion to send the boys home was unquestioned; he railed at sluggish indifference, the post-war lassitude of the upper brass, the almost deliberate sloppiness of his pick-up staff. Despite his long hours and cracking the whip, there were never enough ships. And for that, someone killed him? She tried to rein in her grief, at least not show it to the others, and stow it away into the file drawer of wartime loss.

How it came about happened so gradually and naturally she could hardly recall the moment. She brought in files, he talked to her, admired her intelligence, but was never obvious like Marvin or the others. The actual date was June 6, 1945, the first anniversary of D-day, a relatively modest celebration—this time no turning out the Quacks in their nightclothes, as they told her he had ordered back in Red Deer in '43 when Italy surrendered. Typical of him, he came back from the officers' mess early, relaxed and loose for a change, to find her slaving away on stacks of files in her cubicle down the hall. Almost shyly, a rare moment that entranced her, he asked if she would care to join him for a drink. He had a bottle of Scotch from the mess, and his car was outside, the driver Nolan released to head off to his own wet canteen. He took her arm, opened the front door of the car for her and, not the least bit sozzled, drove off into the late twilight, the post-war headlamps on, to a hill overlooking Aldershot, its dim rationed lights before them; and it was so ordained, no sweaty groping, no ripping at her or at his fly, only a gentle caress along her cheek with a soft finger, a slow almost pristine kiss—until London.

Now she sat nursing a shandy at the Queen's Hotel across from the camp. Captain Williams had suggested they walk on a fine sultry July evening across the deserted parade square. At the corner North Camp ended by the hump, the tumulus, Cockadobby Hill, supposedly an Anglo-Saxon burial mound where no artifacts were ever found. Nearby was a pillar and fountain, some obscure monument from the turn of the century.

At the guard post two British red cap MPs ogled, took their time to study the passes issued by Captain Horobbins. Their eyes hooded under peaked caps, they tried to chat them up and, daunted by stony response, finally raised the barrier to let them through. There was hardly any traffic. In the Queen's bar they were the only splash of khaki among a noisy gathering of blue-clad RAF types from the nearby airfield. More approaches were made, drinks were sent, but the two women froze them out, and at last settled down for the girl-to-girl chat and exchange of life stories that Corporal Claire Evans had been dreading all day.

17

When she first entered the flat she pictured the suite in the King Edward Hotel where the dissolute premier of Ontario once had held court, as her father had described it: a wireless playing British dance tunes—the tone not quite right here, missing the true American beat—tobacco smoke, spilt whisky, hints of perfume, another den of shabby hedonism. Let in by buzzer, she took the tiny cage lift to the third floor of the Georgian or Regency, or whatever it was supposed to be. A threadbare carpet led to the door where a man in khaki shirtsleeves and tie, the garb of an officer, his suspenders off his shoulders, let her in with a blank nod. Another man in sock feet and open shirt sat on a blue striped sofa with a young woman in a wrap, his arm around her shoulders. Claire asked for Lieutenant Colonel Wellesley.

"Be back in a sec. Gone to forage." The man who let her in was English. From a sideboard, the bottles in view, the custom here, he offered a drink. Her eyes widened at the array and she took a rare single malt, causing the man to shake his head when she added warm soda from a syphon. She stood uneasily by the once-white fireplace with its coin-operated gas heater. A woman dressed in a silk print, with a hat and partial veil worn now over her forehead, came out of a bedroom.

"I'm off, darling. See you tomorrow?"

"Fraid not, we have to go back. See you next week, I expect. I'll ring. We're leaving the place to Ambrose and her."

That was a relief, no orgies in the offing, unlike Mitch Hepburn and hangers-on.

"I should put meself together," said the woman on the chesterfield. Irish? She went into the second bedroom.

"Sit," honked the man who had let her in. From a chintz-covered armchair she glanced around the lounge at small cartons, like a collection of Christmas gifts, piled against one wall. The once-smart layout, now with stained beige Wilton carpets, chipped sideboards, split yellow lampshades askew, prompted her to reach over and straighten the lampshade by her chair.

"You a nursing sister?" asked the man on the divan.

Claire smiled, shook her head. Her dark blue dress with the buttons down the front and attached Eton (actually Eaton's department store back home) white collar must have seemed like a uniform. She had rolled it up in her kit-bag and brought it over here, but she didn't have a hat. In Aldershot she had slipped out of the spider hut, careful to wear her raincoat and issue kepi where, behind the orderly room, Stan Nolan, the colonel's driver, awaited, worried and twitchy, to take her to the station downtown. Once on the train she removed her kepi and put it into the valise she had bought in town. As agreed, Ambrose had gone on ahead.

Following his written instructions, from Waterloo she took the Bakerloo tube to Oxford Circus, the westbound Central line to Lancaster Gate, and up the lift to Bayswater. Across from the park where darting figures in various hues searched frantically for comfort, she found her way to Sussex Square, stubby Bathurst Street of all places, a reminder of home, then, unbelievably, an off-shoot named Augusta. Around her milled the surges of military drab or blue desperate to find someone, the Yanks as usual lounging, cool, cuds of gum, smoking, offers of Luckies to parading teenagers, both groups barely out of the cradle. Off the street the rooms where she found herself exuded assumptions, another hothouse of sex, though more relaxed with landed trophies. It was everywhere, and she tensed at the revival of the anxieties she had once felt when she worked in London. There were no groups of uniformed women pals to shield her now.

Thank goodness, to her relief, Ambrose came in carrying a valise that clanked glass, very much the dapper civilian in his navy blue serge, a subtle erasure of rank that made him even more endearing to her—the reality of who he actually was beyond the artificial and temporary harness of army command, a switch to his true self. Yet, the military life had left its mark for, one evening in the staff car, he had admitted he was not sure if he wanted to go back to the kind of life that went with his father's brokerage business on St. James Street. He never mentioned his wife and two young sons, forbidden territory, as she found when she had allowed she was anxious to see Montreal. A vague icy cloud passed over his eyes, the look everyone at his unit in Aldershot recognized as a time to get out of his way. The mixture of evasions and commitment puzzled her, but were forgotten in the pleasure of the moment when he came back from the kitchen, perched on the arm of her chair and put his arm around her. No one had asked her name.

"Everything in order?" he asked the others.

"Not to worry. It's in hand," said the taller British officer who was tightening his tie in front of a circular mirror.

"When're we moving this?" Ambrose nodded towards the row of cartons by the door.

"Tomorrow, there's a pickup. They'll ring."

"When?"

"Eleven hundred hours sharp. You'll be up by then?"

Lieutenant Colonel Ambrose Wellesley let loose another one of those bond salesman's grins she had never seen at the camp.

"We'll be here. What's it in?"

"American dollars. You make the deposit as usual."

The men now in uniform, she noticed, wore 21st Army Group shield patches, Northwest Europe gongs; one of them emerged as a major, the man who had been sitting on the chesterfield who seemed Canadian with a black and red regimental flash of some kind on his shoulders. The other officer, with a pip and crown, was a half-colonel like Ambrose. They left with the one remaining woman who had dressed in the bedroom. She never said a word to Claire.

"My God, how was I to know? You never told me," Ambrose said afterwards. They were in a lumpy bed with used scratchy linen sheets. It didn't matter.

"It's all right."

"My God," repeated Ambrose. He swung over the side of the bed, his moustache glistening with her juices, removed the thin bath towel she had placed under them. "You knew, didn't you?"

"Of course." Her voice throaty, serene, oddly disappointed, wait till the next one; soon, she hoped.

PART THREE

"I used the safe." He peeled it from a drooping flesh tube, rolled up the bloody towel to put into a canvas bag. "You okay?"

"Fine, darling, don't worry."

But he was. "I wouldn't have if I'd any idea. At your age. You must've led a sheltered life."

"You could say that."

"Claire, as much as we care for each other, I hope you understand that I have certain responsibilities, including a wife and two kids."

She remembered his other musings about a reluctance to return to a society that had remained only slightly affected by wartime privation while he had changed in more ways than one.

"You never know, do you?"

"What's that supposed to mean?"

"You've been over here a long time."

"Claire, I don't want to discuss it now. We'll have to see, won't we? Want to try it again?"

Dimly stirring, half comatose, she heard the buzzer, him going out in what seemed to be a frayed communal robe he took from a hook on the door. English voices of the lower class variety outside; a warning prod far back in her daze told her not to peek. Later, when she did wake up again to wander naked out to the silent lounge, the cartons were gone, and at the desk he was writing in a small notebook, saw her, and smiled his admiration.

"Have to pop out for a while. Will be back soon. We'll find a nice spot for lunch."

None of this she revealed to Captain Williams as they ate sausages and mash with several more shandys at the round table in the Queen's. She had a sudden yen for good rotgut rye whisky, which she had never cared for. Her efforts to postpone the inevitable with her stories of her own backgound and life back in Toronto had run out of purchase. The two of them lapsed into a silence that was no longer companionable. Her boss, Claire realized, had a job to do, a report to write.

"You're long service," Captain Williams said, her squarish highly roseate features giving intimations of impending blood pressure ailments. She touched the three pips on her epaulet. "Funny how it goes, eh? Just because I was a high school commerce teacher in Dartmouth I was in line for a commission. You should be more than a corporal."

"Them's the breaks."

"If you're not in any hurry to go home you could sign up for Occupation. B Echelon, the records office, is moving into Germany. It could mean another stripe. There's really nothing to keep you here, is there?"

"What do you mean by that?"

"Come on, Claire, it's all over. You and the Duke."

"I don't see what that has to do with anything. I had nothing to do with killing him. I have no idea who'd do that to such a fine man."

"Claire, we're not stupid. Your bunkmates saw you change into your dress, the car waiting to take you to the station. Listen, I'm trying to help you. We have that awful inspector from Scotland Yard and that slimy guy from the provost with the funny nose and name. Sooner or later they'll put two and two together or one and one. I don't want to see you in their hands. Why don't you own up?"

"They ordered you to do this, didn't they?"

"That Horobbins or whatever he is, was trying to be tactful. Assumes through gal talk I can persuade you to confide in me. They have to find out, Claire. I'm trying to make it easy for you. I'm sure they don't think for one minute you had anything to do with it, but they believe you can help with inside dope on the Duke's other doings, which I gather stink to high heaven.

"Whatever possessed him? Must've had a screw loose somewhere. They don't have a handle on it yet. That's the problem. And various persons on high are leaning on those two and their horde of dicks to come up with something pronto. So under the circs they're in a corner and running out of patience and time. You see the face of that chief inspector, or whatever he is? He'd love to have us turn you over to them to work over in some cell at the Yard. So how about it, Claire?"

"What on earth would they want from me?"

"I'll let you in on the lowdown Horobbins told me. They're after a couple of small notebooks the colonel kept. They also want the straight goods on what went on at his flat in London. No, not the two of you; who came and went and what they passed around. You give me that and I believe I can hold them off, for now, at least."

"They'll still want to interview me?"

"Of course, but it'd go a lot smoother if you tell me now where you and the Duke went in London, what you picked up on those little outings on the train to Waterloo. I'll make sure I'm there to back you up."

Claire pushed aside the glutinous pile of mashed potatoes and sawdust-laced sausages. What did it matter now? Soon his pretty wife in Westmount would have to wake up to the fact she was a widow. And so was she, in a way.

18

The incoming freight was getting to the acting commanding officer, his furniture van skills inadequate for the complexities of moving thousands of troops to the ports, let alone being cooped up on a Sunday. As if he needed it, an irate call from Cynthia in London, her usual nasal drawl clipped with anger. Two detectives had shown up at her Mayfair flat for routine inquiries about the movements of Major Philip Todder on the sixth of July and preceding visits.

"Not every movement, I hope," attempting a light tone.

"You're an absolute git, Philip. Anyhow, I was able to satisfy them we were together."

"I hope you're as satisfied as I am."

"Stuff it, Philip. What're they after you for this time? Anything to do with your departed colonel?"

"Afraid so. Hordes of flatfeet turning the place upside down. Thanks, luv, confirms I'm in the clear."

"Not quite. Geoffrey writes from Rome. He'll be back in mid-August. What are we to do?"

"Captain Williams is waiting, sir." Staff Sergeant Kelly peered around the door past the MP guard.

"Bit of a bad patch, luv. Don't know when I can get away. Massive brutes in white webbing are keeping an eye on me, even clump around outside my window at night."

"You'll have to find another way of letting in your poppets."

"Come on, darling. None of that. Try to hold on. Must go now."

Her face puffy with pink blotches, Captain Williams asked about attendance at the late colonel's memorial service.

"You have the screed. Thirteen hundred hours today."

"It says here restricted to selected officers."

"Not to worry, you're invited."

"Corporal Evans has requested if she could go."

"You might rethink that, captain. Do we want to set tongues wagging more than they already are? The decree is from upstairs. Not my doing." Next an ecstatic call from Liverpool from his transport officer who had lined up the *Samaria* for troops and war brides. "A lethal mix. Indent for rolls of concertina wire." Todder yelled for Helmers, the late colonel's secretary who he had inherited. "Where've you been?" He sniffed a sickly sweet emanation. "What in God's name are you wearing?"

"Cologne, sir. Bought if off one of the fellas. Has a carton from Brussels. You want me get some for you?"

"No thanks. I suppose it's an improvement. Where do you keep yourself?"

"That MP sergeant, sir, has the girls watching while I go through my notebooks for any personal stuff the CO might've given me. I think they want to talk to you about something."

The dark and faintly sinister Horrobins loomed over the meaty shoulders of the abject Helmers, who lumbered away, for him, at top speed.

"Hope you're satisfied, captain. Yard types have harassed my London squeeze into a cat fit."

Horobbins studied the haggard acting authority: the moustache trim showed signs of neglect, his jacket draped on the back of the chair, shirt armpits stained, a holstered sidearm pressing down a stack of requisitions on the cluttered desk, within reach as if he had bought the idea someone might come for him.

"You seem to check out for now. They report few witnesses, except at the restaurant."

"There weren't any witnesses in her boudoir—at least I hope not."

"There are gaps, sir, from the time you said you left her apartment on the night of the sixth and logged in your personal car at the compound. The mileage may not be out of line, but you could've arrived here earlier."

"Horobbins, you're getting more dippy by the minute. What's that you're waving at me?"

"My people found this stuck in the back of one of Helmers's notebooks.

Why, I don't know. He claims he put it there for no particular reason. It's dated third of June, the day after the colonel and you arrived to take command here. It's the flimsy of a message transmitted by Signals to a Major Frederick Lefebvre, Transport Liaison Section, HQ British Army of the Rhine, Bad Salzuften, Germany. Very cryptic. 'RV London as agreed.' End of message. He was setting up a meeting, probably at his flat."

"What was Helmers thinking of, holding on to it? Ambrose would never let anything like that get away from him, unless he was beginning to lose his marbles."

"This is the third copy, the pink one. Helmers says he returned the second carbon to the colonel who seemingly didn't notice the other one missing. Claims it fell off or something, so he put it in the back of his notebook."

"In shorthand, right? I mean his notes. Your people found anything of interest yet? No? If Ambrose had other business he'd probably find a phone somewhere."

"What other business might that be?" Horobbins thought of what the driver Nolan had told him about stopovers at assorted phone boxes on their daily tours around the area. That way, no logging of trunk calls through central exchange. "Do you know this Major Lefebvre?"

"Old Freddy? Of course, was with us at Canadian Section, 21st Group in Brussels before it was disbanded. School chum of Ambrose from Montreal, typical mix of both races, completely bilingual, big plus in Belgium. He'd been transport officer with one of those ghastly Quebec battalions, was wounded at Falaise, posted to Group as transport liaison with the Brits."

"What else? You're holding back, sir, I'm staying here until. . . ."

Company Sergeant Major Allen, a rangy Third Div. veteran stuck in demeaning dog work, made noises from the open doorway. "Sir, you want the men in Blenheim and Malplaquet in gym kit, after church parade?"

"You have trouble understanding the order? Shape 'em up, see to it they sweat. Far too lax around here. See me later about closing down the gambling dens."

"Lets off steam, sir; we don't need any more riots."

"There won't be any disturbances around here, Mr. Allen. Staff Kelly, for chrissake, can you find someone to take dictation? Your fault, Horobbins. Now what?"

The staff sergeant peered in from his cubicle. "Inspector Bollock is waiting for the captain. Says it's urgent."

Reluctantly, Horobbins abandoned his cross-examination of Todder and his Brussels connections. At 0815 hours the ever-resourceful army, disregarding Sunday torpor, had tea brewing, supported by scrounged buns and Peak Freen biscuits. On the way he snatched his breakfast. He was expecting Corporal Evans and her unwelcome guardian, Captain Williams, who stuck around as if expecting to earn litigation fees.

"We have the address yet?"

"Fisher." Bollock nodded to the detective sergeant who hobbled off, his arthritic knees creaking, to find out if the Met's awesome resources had produced anything on a weekend. Then Horobbins noticed a third man, a bald stenographer from the Hants police, a scribe supposedly immune to loose lips everywhere around the camp. Before he could ask why, Bollock upended a paper bag to dislodge a Luger pistol clattering onto the table, followed by its clip.

"Fast work from Hendon. Must've sounded like World War Three. Here it is, complete with tag. Ballistics match. The idiot wanted it back, didn't he?"

"Who'd be?" Horobbins sent an MP to extricate Pearly Gates, who gaped at the weapon with its small tag tied to the trigger guard. "Private G. S. Gilmore. You remember him, sergeant?"

"Vaguely, sir; I believe Corporal Barr did him." He pawed through the stack of papers on the desk. "Here he is."

Bollock added: "The clip was loaded except for one round missing, one up the spout, safety catch on. No prints worth a damn, smeared by the sticky fingers of thousands."

"Where is he?"

"Probably returned to duty, sir. He's in the shipping transport coordination section. Penpusher."

"Says here he admits he was at the craps game in Malplaquet that night. When was his pistol picked up?"

Gates peered at the tag. "Kit inspection the next day, the seventh; it was found under his palliase in his bunk. I'll bring him in."

The police steno unsheathed his notepad and dreamt of Sunday walks along the Basingstoke Canal.

Another sad sack, Horobbins groaned. Unlike Helmers, this low category mess was bone thin, bottle thick glasses magnified heavy eyelids as if he was struggling to stay awake, his face pitted with tiny white scars like chicken pox. A trick leg shot out when he was ordered to sit, drawing eyes to the splayed limb, then to a vertical gold wound stripe on his sleeve.

"Where'd you get that, Gilmore? Typewriter drop on your foot?"

"V-2 in January, sir."

Bollock started, his creased ruddiness sagging as though someone had walked over his grave. He went to a corner of the room and lit a cigarette.

"Your leg?"

"Yes, sir, among other things. I was coming back from CMHQ to my billet in South Kensington. Damn thing came down, blew out the whole block. My left leg, glass in the eyes, these," touching speckled cheeks. An MP dropped off the man's personnel file and paybook from which Horobbins read aloud, his eyes widening.

"'Private Gilmore is commended for his assistance to the authorities following a V-2 attack. Despite severe injuries he declined medical attention to rescue victims from the wreckage. Only when he had escorted a number of casualties to the ambulances did he allow himself to be transported to the hospital. MO's report (att.) states he had a section of iron railing protruding from his thigh. His face was bleeding from the blast, his glasses shattered, and his vision impaired. Initially he shook off attempts to provide assistance, though his leg was bleeding profusely. However, he did pull the spike from his thigh himself and permitted a medical orderly to apply a first field dressing. Then, according to witnesses, he hobbled off, almost frenzied in his determination to help the victims. This soldier, employed in a non-combat clerical position, is a fine example of courage and dedication worthy of the highest behaviour under battle conditions. Delicate eye surgery performed at Number One Neurological at Basingstoke. His reboard regrades him eligible for discharge. However, this soldier has applied to be returned to light duties. In view of his record his request has been approved on a temporary basis. He is assigned to clerical duties at Canadian Repatriation Units, Aldershot, eff. 25 May 45 until further assessment of his medical condition.' Signed by no less than the Deputy Adjutant General in London. Heavy duty endorsement, Gilmore."

Bollock growled from his corner. "Bloody hell, lad, why didn't they give you a medal?"

The ruined face emitted a cracked smile. "Nothing more than a civilian in uniform, I guess. Won't make no difference. The next one'll be rockets out of nowhere, you'll never see them or the enemy. Everybody'll be a target. Not a chance."

Horobbins, avoiding learned discussion about future wars, picked up on something. "It says here 'frenzied.' Just how frenzied can you get? Enough to pop off your CO? You resent the way you've been treated?"

"Don't have no complaints, sir. They fixed me up pretty good, and when I asked if I could stay on they sent me here, out of London. What saved me, I figure, was a christly cold day, sleet coming down, so I wore my greatcoat; you should of seen the holes, burns and junk stuck in it. Goddam right I was mad. My foot kicked an ear on the ground, a sleeve wrapped around my neck, a woman's blouse. They nailed Mrs. Hanley, my landlady—she was like a mother to me, flattened her place into matchwood. I only did what I could. Sorry, I didn't get what you said there about the CO."

"Gilmore, you may be some kind of hero, but ballistic tests confirm that one round from your weapon killed Lieutenant Colonel Wellesley. Is this yours?"

"Why yes, sir. I didn't knock him off."

"I want to be clear about your situation. Unless you have proof, witnesses, ironclad alibi, it's your balls in the wringer, assuming you have any. We can take you in right now as prime suspect."

"Holy shit. Me? Can I say something? First off, sir, they say it was one round that plugged him." He touched his thick glasses. "It'd take a whole clip for me to find him, even coupla feet away. You check my medical records, I shouldn't even be here, except they let me stay a spell. One lucky shot? Not possible, sir."

"Point taken, but not conclusive till new eye tests. Go on."

"Well, if was me, it ain't likely I'd leave my pistol around, even under the mattress—the first place they'd look. Anybody who done it'd figure out how to dump the gun somewhere it wouldn't be noticed. And I'm pretty sure I know how."

"Enlighten us."

"I won it, sir. That night at the craps game."

"You won it? Who from?"

"On my soul I did and don't have any idea whose it was. The boys have to do something, poker and blackjack at Blenheim, craps at Malplaquet. I don't see the cards too well, so I go watch the craps table there in the can. Goes on all night—blankets over the windows, lookouts at the doors. Like most, I hang round, the stakes are too high for penny ante. That day, though, I get a postal order from the folks back home. Dad's working extra shifts, has some to spare. It's fifty bucks Canadian. The boys drool. You promise to sign it over you're in. Most fellas are broke, bets are mostly in kind. Those guys oughta run a pawnshop, takes them no time to add up what items are worth, how they compare in value—like you got cartons of smokes, a bottle or two, tons of loot from over there, jewellery, ornaments, watches, cameras, perfume, colognes, Jerry military badges, and every type of souvenir pistol. I figure we must of cleaned out several countries. They let me stand next left to a guy trying to make his point, and he craps out on the seven, so I'm the shooter. My hands are shaking, fingers stiff from the injuries. Anyway, I breath life into the bones the way I seen 'em do. My money order's on the table, the others have faded stuff you wouldn't believe, anything to get their hands on fifty bucks. My eye catches a Luger down the way, always wanted one. The rest of it'd be nice to send home to the folks. Jeez, if I don't make a pass, I shoot an eleven. I clean up, including the gun. Well, I'm damn near lynched right on the spot. I say thanks fellas, leave 'em steaming, hightail back to my bunk where I stash the valuables under my blanket and the gun under my pillow in case some bozo gets ideas. I check out the pistol and, of course, I can't tell if the clip is fully loaded or not. I pull back the cocking slide, put one in the chamber to be on the safe side, but I make sure the safety is on, and don't get much sleep that night, I can tell you. Next day I lock the other winnings in my desk drawer here where I figure it's a bit more secure. You can go see, here's the key. I guess on the morning of the seventh I was moving my stuff over here to the office and forgot about the gun under my mattress where your guys found it. That night, though, when I checked out the pistol, I sniffed the muzzle and thought I could smell powder as if it had been fired not too long ago, but I took no notice at the time, just glad to have it. Those Lugers, they balance in your hand like they grow there."

"Glad you enjoyed it, Gilmore. Who faded the gun? You must've seen him."

"Can't recollect, sir. There was maybe twenty or more players and a bunch crowded around behind making side bets, mainly on future pay draws, I mean IOUs going back and forth. Same as the other guys, my eyes were glued on the action, and my vision ain't exactly in the eagle line. Most of those here are repats, not known to us on staff. Whoever rubbed out the colonel may've come in, put the gun on the table, then left or stood around with the others, kinda fading into the woodwork, so to speak."

"Did you recognize anybody from your own bunch at the office?"

"Nope, don't recall any."

Ranks had closed once again, the code of the jail house. Horobbins frowned at Gates to imply deficiency in the grilling of the elusive gamblers. "So what time was it when you cleaned up?"

"Dunno, sir. Blankets on the windows, never look at my watch."

"If there were strangers around you'd have noticed, wouldn't you?"

"As I say, most of 'em are strangers."

"I mean civilians, anyone out of uniform."

"That I would've noticed. Nope."

"Any women?"

"You're kidding, sir."

The olive visage of Horobbins grew darker. "Your story's full of holes, you've got to have some idea who bet the gun."

Gilmore's strange voice faltered as though debris from the V-2 rocket still rattled around in his gullet. "Come to think of it, when I reached over to pick up my winnings I did ask who belonged to the Luger. Nobody'd own up. Somebody says: 'Tough shit. His loss, take it.' And I did."

Horobbins glanced at the pay book.

"Tell me, where'd you take your training?"

"Basic at Camrose, Alberta, driver training at Red Deer, clerk course in Edmonton."

"This whole goddam place is an A-20 reunion. You and Helmers, you know him there?"

"Never met him till I came here. I came over in August before him, was posted to London. The deal was us low category types would replace the ones in soft jobs who were fit enough to fill in for the slaughter over in Normandy. Poor fellas never had a chance."

"When you were in Red Deer, did you ever come into contact with Colonel Wellesley, Major Todder, or Captain Williams?"

"Only here. Never seen 'em up close back there, not much here either."

"Ever run into a Corporal Timchuk at Red Deer?"

"Doesn't ring a bell. What're you getting at, sir?"

"Did you take a respirator from the storeroom?"

"No way, sir. That's a funny one, ain't it?"

"Side-splitting. Gas drills were held at Red Deer. Any problem with that?"

"Only with my glasses—had to go on gas parade without them, bumped into a few guys, messed up the line, got chewed out for that by the sarge. Gas, the CO was keen on it."

"Did Colonel Wellesley ever notice, come over and find out what the hell was going on? Make you mad enough to nurse a grievance, maybe he orders extra fatigues in the kitchen or the gravel pit, then, when you're posted here, who shows up but him, and you figure to square accounts?"

"Jesus, sir, you're not going to hang that on me."

Horobbins invoked the interrogator's silence. Gilmore's thin frame shrank into a smaller pile of bones, if that was possible, while the captain ignored him, made notes until the time came to make a decision. "Private Gilmore, you appreciate the situation you're in."

"I get the drift, sir, I'm the fall guy."

"Whether you get off the hook is going to depend a lot on your cooperation and assistance. You're not owning up to everything you know. Therefore, under the circumstances I can't allow you to resume your duties. We're holding you in custody and will likely charge you under Section Forty, conduct to the prejudice of good order and discipline in that you had an unauthorized weapon in your possession."

"Holy shit, sir, how about half the camp?"

"You're our special favourite, Gilmore. You'll undergo detention for now at the Mob Control Centre. From time to time you will be brought back to assist us in our inquiries. While you're in the cooler, you do some cool thinking about what really went on the night of the sixth. It's up to you now. Questions? Dismissed."

A splayed foot caught the MP escort on his shin as Gilmore found the door, somehow navigated through it. The military cop was about to wreak havoc on the gimpy clerk until Gates waved him off, then poked his head around the door.

"Captain Williams and Corporal Evans are waiting, sir."

"Send Captain Williams in first." The police steno stood up to leave. "You better stay. I want a verbatim transcript of this one."

There was no body, no coffin while the powers-that-be pondered breaking the mould to ship the late colonel's remains home to Montreal. Perhaps the words of the memorial service held in the Marlborough lines Garrison Church on Evelyn Woods Road would drift to the stiff in the freezer at the Cambridge Hospital morgue. Those who gathered did note that the church itself had a hospital aspect to it and, in fact, had been one before conversion to worship. Its wooden exterior and pillars under an overhanging roof seemed more like a transplant from a small town in Canada. Coke stoves along the sidewalls, a small altar below a round stained-glass window, added to the pioneer look.

A clump of officers dragged out for the occasion sat around General Spry, their whispers rising in the cavernous space for over two hundred worshippers. Major Todder and a couple of his juniors turned to glare at the provost captain and the Yard chief detective inspector in a pew apart from the others. When the senior padre for the base, his Church of England garb concealing a major's crowns, intoned prayers in a parade ground basso, the khaki torsos slumped forward to kneel. Captain Williams, a Methodist anyway, did not bend her knees or didn't want to pop her stockings. A lieutenant colonel from Spry's entourage read a massaged tribute, dreamt up by the information staff, to the late Lieutenant Colonel Wellesley, so tragically destined to meet his Maker after having survived the perils of war. Horobbins noted the general had avoided straining himself to deliver the eulogy. Perhaps London, at last, had provided him with a background briefing on the suspicions that had never been proven.

Outside in the July sun, the general at his staff car crooked a finger at Horobbins and Bollock. "You really believe that poor sod Gilmore could've done it? A rocket's coming in from your Colonel Cameron and your own superiors, inspector; it'll be waiting for you when you get back to work, which I urge you to do smartly. I've spoken to them. They want the two of you on deck to attend a joint 'O' group at Cockspur Street tomorrow, Monday, 1500 hours. When you return I want a briefing from you both. This isn't going to wash, you know."

"We're not satisfied, either, sir. The investigation will continue."

"We devoutly hope so, captain." While the general paused outside his car to hold an impromptu prayer meeting with his own staff, Bollock took Horobbins aside.

"Off to London tomorrow, are we? Bloody waste of time. Still." He lit a much-needed Sweet Cap, no longer of use to its former owner. "Horobbins, why don't we do something useful? The Met has located the colonel's flat. We could. . . ."

Major Todder, smirking, interrupted. "Not getting anywhere, are you? Private Gilmore? You have to do better than that. What in heaven's name?"

The hovering brass gaped and pointed at running figures bursting out onto Evelyn Woods Road—geese flapping, knees up, scattering before a posse of provost and a wildly careering Jeep. Bare white legs flashing, faded blue gym shorts, yellowed singlets, in PT kit, they snickered, panted, and ran on in unspoken mobocracy, a dash for freedom from the parade square outside the barracks where NCOs, under Major Todder's attempt to emulate his former boss, had ordered them to do pushups and the like after church parade. Except they hadn't dreamt for a moment that post-war lassitude would give way to yet another round of protest. Nothing more than a few sly grins along the line, not a word needed for them to break ranks and sprint off, to dash God-knows-where, to seek an instant of something freely done, as they streamed past the khaki mourners at the garrison church.

"This your idea of keeping 'em fit? You take command of this place, or by God I'll find somebody who will."

General Spry had turned on a stricken Major Todder.

19

Would they ever leave her alone? Claire Evans smoothed down the hem of her khaki skirt, the left hand of the driver having strayed from the gear shift lever to brush her knee. As the car crept out of Aldershot behind an army convoy a despatch rider on his Norton entertained her with perilous wheelies. Fumes from the lorries drifted into half-open windows to add to streams of cigarette smoke from the back seat where Karen Williams was squeezed midships between Bollock and Horobbins. Their silver-haired driver should have known better, a shabby Met holdover in his shiny black suit and frayed cuffs daubed with ink. Was the Yard short of ration coupons? Near retirement or retrieved to fill in for fitter cops off in the forces, grandpops out for a quick feel.

Those two policemen in the back seat of the black Wolseley saloon were hardly prizes, either. Across a sullen, quiet Williams, as if she was not there, they chortled over some shenanigans with the upper brass, apparently a game of some kind that had led to this eccentric side trip to London. Only the Monday after Ambrose's death and the two point men on the case were abandoning the crime scene to their minions to grind away at alibi and motive among the staff and repats. Why? She tried to piece together snippets of chatter, at times coded to disarm their two passengers. Then, out of nowhere, one of them would come at her with a question, just to let her know they were still in business.

"You're still convinced this Gilmore didn't do it?" the provost captain shot at the back of her head.

"It's ridiculous, sir. George isn't capable, should've been discharged long ago. He couldn't hold a gun straight. What possible motive would he have? A harmless soul."

"Your whole flaming outfit is made up of harmless souls, except for one," said the inspector.

"What do you think, Captain Williams?"

"Not a clue. Why would I?"

Claire turned her head sharply to scowl ahead out of the windscreen, avoiding eye contact with her leech, her permanent chaperone or guardian, and her betrayer who had squealed to them the confidences she had poured out at the Queen's hotel. What had she been thinking of? She had weighed the odds against her commander's official duties and her genuine concern for her welfare. Guess what won out. Now here she was, her substantial hips in the vise of the two seated captors on either side, supposedly her protector who had insisted on personally escorting her to Ambrose's London apartment;

anyone of lesser rank would not be suitable for such a delicate task. The provost captain, in feigned gallantry, had opened the front door of the car for Claire, as if he too was anxious to safeguard her from further shocks. Well, if they were so damned worried, why did they demand her presence? She had told them all she knew, which wasn't much. And they had condemned her to more tension as she shoved away the prying hands of the old duffer at the wheel.

Now, having been barred from yesterday's service, she would transform the visit to his flat into her only farewell to him and the memories of being awakened by gentle and considerate love.

Yesterday morning, when they had made her wait while Captain Williams was ushered in for a private séance, she watched Private George Gilmore being led away. Her remaining guardian, a ribbon-less young MP whose compassion for her—at least she hoped that was all it was—suggesting his place was more properly in the chaplain service, brought her a chair and tea, informed her of Gilmore's arrest as the owner of the fatal weapon. She gaped, then realized voices could be made out behind the flimsy cubicle wall. Claire pushed the chair against the wall, simulated fragility by closing her eyes, and rested her head against the wall, one ear pressed against the green plasterboard.

You want to *what*? Captain Williams raised her parade square tones a notch. Claire heard the level voice of the provost captain say something about a CMHQ meeting Monday afternoon that they had to attend in London. They'd use their time in the morning to conduct their own search of the colonel's flat, now sealed tighter than a drum, and they wanted Corporal Evans on deck to act as an inside source who knows a helluva lot more than she's letting on. Not much really to let on, Claire told them silently. It's not on, Captain Williams was heard to say, can't put the poor thing through that. From the other side of the wall the poor thing agreed: you said it, sister.

Then it seemed the private chat with her captain took another tack and, in effect, became a snap grilling. She picked up questions about familiarity with firearms, ever used a Luger? You kidding? Only the required pistol practice with those damn Smith and Wessons, not designed for women, for sure, and I didn't plug him if that's what you're getting at. That night I was on patrol, witnesses will confirm; we didn't know if those thugs would turn their depraved attention onto our helpless girls. Horobbins turned to the night of Italy's surrender in 1943 when, back in Red Deer, Williams had complained about the gala laid on by Lieutenant Colonel Wellesley. Nothing was ever done, so you wanted to get even, right? The exasperated Quack officer treated the query with due contempt: big surprise she was suddenly desperately needed overseas. Who blabbed to you about it, that creep Todder? Yet, Horobbins went on, it must've been a shock when they found you in Aldershot under their command again. No big deal, I was here before them. And, he persisted, what do you know of their illicit activities on the Continent, the colonel obviously mixed up in something run out of his London flat? Search me, snapped her own officer commanding who, after a brief pause, caught the drift.

All right, you win, she was heard to growl at the two policemen, you be goddam careful when you take her with you. In fact, I want to be there. Now why would that be? asked the Yard man. She needs protection from the likes of you, was the answer. Horobbins spoke: there's one more thing, we'll need to stay overnight and return first thing Tuesday. What in heaven's name for? Claire could picture her superior's heavy jaw dropping. Our meeting, said the police inspector, may well extend into the evening, our masters may wish to personally interview Corporal Evans, and, depending what we uncover at the flat, we could well require her for further assistance. And, added Horobbins, we can't recommend you return to Aldershot by a late train, the situation there is a bit dicey for two service women to be wandering about alone at night. Williams responded with a jibe at the vaunted provost corps who supposedly had everything under control. You saying it ain't so? Never mind, Horobbins said, at the end of his patience; go get someone on your staff to find you two a hostel near the flat, say around Lancaster Gate and Bayswater. You should take advantage of the break, get away from this foul place for a while, but no carousing, make sure she's tucked safely in bed good and early and sober.

Mystified and angry at being treated as an exhibit to be packed around here and there, Claire Evans at first refused to cooperate. When they brought her into the cubicle, the first thing placed under her nose was the Yard man's hand. The key to the flat, if you please, missy. She yielded it up and, in the hope they might abandon her trip to London, did her best to explain she really didn't have any idea what went on there. Yes, flash women came and went, two officers from the Continent showed up on occasion; no, she never learned their names—one was a Canadian major (Horobbins asked her to describe him, made a quick note) and a half-colonel, British, with 21st Army Group patches; the cartons appearing and disappearing; Ambrose in civvies off on vague business. Nothing more she could offer.

"We'll see," said Bollock, with the cynicism of one who had accompanied legions of suspects to the scene of the crime.

Now on their way to London, another agenda began to emerge. Bollock, apparently oblivious to the curiosity of the two women, was saying, "Assuming the meeting doesn't go into the wee small hours, I shall look in on Florence. Don't care to be away from her for long."

"I should drop in on my digs, then I'm off to . . ." Horobbins stopped.

"You're an odd lot. Some of you trash Aldershot to hurry up your return to the other side of the pond. Others linger on, reluctant to leave. What's the attraction, as if I didn't know?"

"The weather and the food."

"Where exactly is our meeting again?"

"Cockspur Street, the old Sun Life building, the firm that shipped your gold bullion to Montreal."

"Now that'd be good pickings for the Duke and his ilk. I hope we get it back."

"You'll need it."

"Too true. Britain's broke. Fine slogan, eh? Once Labour takes over we'll be in the glue. Look at their posters: 'Let Us Face the Future.' I'm afraid Churchill is about to take the high jump."

"Hard to believe, after everything he's done."

"You watch. The troops are restless, as we've seen, not just yours."

Breaking away from the interminable convoy they made better time through Hounslow. Except for reminders from gaping bombed out ruins and the boarded windows of abandoned buildings, the war seemed long gone. On the pavements, at last free of death from above, women wore bright summer frocks.

"The meat ration's on the street," Horobbins said.

"Over there." They turned at the catch in Bollock's voice. "Chiswick. My home's a few streets over. I realize I shouldn't take the time, but I have to watch over her when I can. My son's away at school—too young, thank God, for service. My daughter's at BSA, Birmingham."

Claire Evans, a recently qualified expert on human anguish, picked up the inspector's sudden transformation into a grieving human soul, and swiveled around to meet his smoke-shrouded eyes.

"Sir, did something happen?"

"Corporal Evans." Horobbins shook his head.

"No, no." Bollock waved his cigarette. "It's all right. That poor lad, Gilmore, he knows."

"Last September it was, the eighth, a few rows over from us on Stavely Road an enormous explosion. The first I heard about it I was up in Hampstead on a dig for the body of a woman. Someone heard on the wireless. Gas explosion in Chiswick. I commandeered one of our drivers and he turned on the bells until we came through the barriers of rescue teams and police. One of the worst I'd ever seen, and remember I'd been through the Blitz. Crater some twenty feet deep, at least a dozen houses demolished, whole area shredded. They were already hauling out the dead and maimed, our neighbours. When I arrived at our home there wasn't a window left, and there I came upon her, Florence standing outside, her clothing covered in grey dust, and my heart almost stopped when I saw her face and glassy stare, as if she didn't recognize me, this fine lady who had led singsongs through the Blitz. I just picked her up, never went into the house, placed her on the rear bench of the police vehicle and took her to the hospital. Except for some nasty cuts from the shattering glass she was unhurt, except in her mind—a form of shock, they told me. Well, she's a pretty game bird is Florence, and she has struggled to find her balance, so to speak, but there are lapses when she rolls up under the bed and her vibrations pass through the house like a minor earth tremor. You know what it was."

"The first V-2 rocket," said Horobbins.

"Too true. The authorities were unusually thick about it, stunned is more like it, as if they couldn't grasp what had happened. First thing they did was to impose a news blackout. As more of the V-2s came down, people began to call them 'Chiswick gas mains' until the powers-that-be finally saw the light and admitted we were under attack from a horrible new weapon. You were here. Over a thousand of the buggers, huge casualties; some of our chaps went off their heads at the mortuaries trying to piece together body fragments, dealing with relatives and destruction on a vast scale. The war was won, in its final stages, then they plastered us with Hitler's parting shot, a last gasp. No one could believe it. Morale was never lower. If it had kept up we might indeed have cracked. We were saved by our lads who finally overran the launching sites, but think of what might have happened if the Nazis had started sooner, maybe even used airbursts of gas, or went on to develop a trans-Atlantic model that'd smash into the skyscrapers of New York. It was a near-run thing, all right. And your Private Gilmore has earned a medal, not the gallows or a firing squad."

Shaken tones, a guttural flutter, startled them. Captain Williams reached over to place her hand onto Bollock's knee.

"I think we understand now, inspector. It's okay."

She left her open palm there, moist and warm enough for him to feel it through the serge, until their car reached Bayswater and they were joined by a traffic warden who led them to the flat.

20

Pried out of a cellar dungeon, the man's name was given as Wilson, but he had a foreign cast like Horobbins, plus a vague accent. The constable handed Bollock Egyptian papers and apparently genuine temporary residency documents denoting Wilson had been in Britain since 1941, hardly a tourist.

"Let me advise you, Mister Wilson, if you don't cooperate you're on the next slow boat back to the Cairo slums. You own this place?"

"No, sir, just the custodian."

"Then who does?"

"A numbered unit trust of some sort. I have the names of my contacts in my room."

"Constable, go with him and find out. I want a list of all tenants. Who leased the flat?"

"No lease, sir. They pay in sterling. Six months ago they took it, but they're never here for any long stay. For their leaves in London, they told me. Officers, perhaps a bit noisy at times."

The constable turned to Horobbins. "Perhaps you'd speak to the custodian, sir."

"Mr. Bollock already has."

"I mean in his own lingo, maybe he'd talk more to one of his own." Before Horobbins could strangle him, the policeman took the hint and led Mr. Wilson away. The tiny lift took Bollock and Horobbins up, then they returned it for the two women. While forensic types dusted and probed the rooms, a CID detective sergeant in an armchair smoked his pipe and marked up the football pools. Bollock greeted him as Jimmy.

"Find anything?"

"Not yet. Signs of multiple occupancy. Telephone is a private listing, name of R. Smith. They give cash to the custodian to pay for it. Bleeding waste of time."

"Among other things we're trying to find two small pocket notebooks, probably taped to the underside of something and a ring or chain with keys on it. Don't miss the loo." Bollock took Claire Evans by the arm. "Now, corporal, let's have our walkabout."

She went over it again, trying to be helpful. She pointed out where the cartons had been stacked along the wall and how they tended to vanish, presumably collected at odd hours when she had been out with Lieutenant Colonel Wellesley or (shyly) in bed. A week ago Thursday, Ambrose had been particularly anxious to make the trip to London, necessitating her plea for a rare seventy-two hour pass. Looking back on it, she surmised that his timing could have been his need to get to a bank during business hours on Friday. No, she didn't keep belongings here, nor did the others except for towels, sheets, two communal bathrobes, utensils in the kitchenette. With no batman at beck and call, the officers had been amazingly tidy. On occasion she'd do the wash up or run the sweeper over the carpets. Don't remember seeing guns, documents, notebooks, or money floating around. Extremely careful. The searchers had created the mess in the kitchen. Tins and non-perishables littered the sideboard, some of them already opened, their contents overflowing the basin.

"Canadians or Yanks," said Bollock as he opened the door of the small electric fridge. "Iced beer."

"Never saw any Yanks," Claire said.

After they had torn the place apart, Bollock sat down with a bottle of cold

Amstel across from the detective who had not moved. "Corporal, you must have a better notion of who these people are, what was going on. Did you ever see his notebooks or the other keys?"

"She's told you all she knows," Williams said.

"You ever been here, captain?"

"Heaven forbid."

"You never went with him when he went out on so-called business?"

"No, sir," said Claire. "I seem to remember some talk about deposits, currency, a bank in Westminster was mentioned, I think."

Bollock sighed. "Likely a security box under some code name. We can begin inquiries on the off-chance, see what the Met can do." Mr. Wilson returned with the constable. "They pay you cash, you say? Let me see your receipts, who they were made out to. No receipts? They never asked? Very trusting lot. You must keep a ledger. Only shows the rental by flat number? Constable, confiscate the books. Did you see deliveries coming or going?"

"Only going, sir. I believe they brought various size boxes with them, carried them in themselves, then I would see an unmarked lorry, dark brown, I believe. Civilians."

"You didn't mind if they used the flat as a warehouse?"

"Not for me to say. They never had more than a few boxes at a time, not left here for long. It wasn't a storage depot."

"They must bring low bulk, high value contraband over by aircraft. What do you know of our air space surveillance, Horobbins?"

"Difficult, as you can imagine. Perhaps they could slip in under the radar. But where? We can raise it at our meeting. Let's grab a bite to eat."

Bollock winced at the last swallow of cold beer, stood and bowed slightly to the women. "You ladies set for tonight? We shall drop you off at the hostel, pick you up tomorrow 0700 sharp. You have any plans?"

"I think I'll look up some of my old friends," Claire said.

"Whatever you do, don't come back here."

"We can take care of ourselves," said Williams.

After they had left the two women at a Salvation Army hostel nearby, they stopped at a pub for a quick bite before Bollock took Horobbins to Cockspur Street, then himself on to the Yard. Both men were to report separately to their own superiors to clear the underbrush before the afternoon's conference. Over lunch Bollock's curiosity got the better of him.

"What exactly are you up to later on?"

"I'm heading out to Putney, Manor Fields."

"Manor Fields? Rather posh, innit?"

"When her man went into the army in '40 they sold their house in Wimbleton, took a flat there in Bede House. Very nice, overlooks a verdant courtyard. We're awaiting word on his return from Burma. Then we'll see."

"It's an epidemic. Well, good luck."

"Are they going to buy Gilmore any more than we have?"

"Not on your nelly. My guv Rossiter is there to stiffen spines, has his marching orders from on high. Conspiracies needed. Churchill's in a bind. Labour wouldn't stick with him for the final effort to finish off the Japs, they've read the public mood. So the old warrior rants on about Labour setting up a Gestapo, while he condones a roundup of unlikely suspects. Your mindless buggers played into their hands with their little Aldershot uprising. Now someone has handed them a dead colonel complete with dire warnings. Gilmore is nowhere near the starting gate. On that score, I agree."

Sugar plums in the shape of Mavis, her rather thick English ankles no deterrent, keep intruding as he sits through the inquisition in the conference room in the former Sun Life building on Cockspur Street. Can hardly wait to break free. Almost three weeks since he has seen her, an eternity forced by the shoot-up in Chester and discovery of the gang of deserters in Liverpool.

Perks up when the signal from the British Army of the Rhine is read out. Yes, Major F. Lefebvre is on TOE (Table of Establishment), transport liaison, absent on four-day pass UK. A second officer, UK, Lieutenant Colonel Samuel Yates, logistics coordinator same office, also took leave. Horobbins tells the group they hadn't shown up at the flat, yet. Around the table, a collection of headquarters brass, familiar faces, beams at his discomfort.

"If there's any basis to suspicions of Wellesley's illicit dealings in precious goods and cash, I suggest the Mounties in Montreal be asked to check on any unusual deposits or deliveries traced to him through his family or the brokerage firm. But how do we get a handle on loot stashed here or banks offshore?" Horobbins shoots a meaningful look at the Scotland Yard contingent.

Bollock's guv Rossiter, in uniform perhaps to impress the military, is flanked by a delegation of three in nice suits. Rossiter has a narrow skull, bushy foliage under his nose, and speaks in convolutions that betray his legal training. He labels the detention of Gilmore as "pitiful," and paints the big picture he has no doubt been instructed to do.

"Here we have a nation teetering on incipient anarchy while you thrash about with petty criminals." Glances as "Nigel," the senior spook first seen at General Spry's confab, who has nothing to add at the moment, having failed so far to unearth the dire plots so badly needed by Whitehall.

Colonel Cameron is quick to protect Horobbins. "We intend to pursue the paper trail to the Continent, whatever it takes to track down black market proceeds. If someone wanted our colonel out of the way, the scope of the problem is enormous. Deserters, gangsters over there with outlets here in Britain. Captain Horobbins and crew have recently uncovered such an operation in Liverpool. There's always the possibility that a party in Aldershot set up the victim."

For the moment back in control of the meeting, Cameron lays out three steps. "One, SIU officers who investigated Wellesley and Todder in May have been located at Bad Zwischenahn, Canadian headquarters, Germany. They're out on duties; we've put out word for them to come in. Second, the two officers described by Corporal Evans are likely here now. Keep your eyes peeled and bring 'em in. Third, liaison is under way with RAF re tracing of flight plans, unofficial drops, location of unused airstrips around London." He turns to Nigel. "You were special operations for undergrounds, the Maquis and such. What aircraft are we looking for?"

Suddenly awake, Nigel's droopy eyelids raise a curtain to flaunt his wartime expertise, no longer classified.

"Piece of cake to come and go by air, avoid RAF and USAF stations. No problem to find a plane and hire an unemployed pilot over there. But lax as it is, you don't leave a kite out in the open on an old airstrip or field; you need a shed or abandoned hangar. They fly in black market goods, are met by local villains, offload, lift off smartly. Rendezvous times at dusk or nightfall. They'd set out flares, as we did."

"Bit risky, isn't it?"

"Not now. No Gestapo about, perhaps curious or venal locals. Radar stations are at half-mast or asleep, not expecting hit and run by Japs, no Pearl Harbor in the offing. They'd need aircraft with short landing and take off capability. Any hard field will do. Their best choice is the old Westmoreland Lysander. We used 'em a lot. Ungainly crates, high wing, up and down in no time. Only problem is they can't take bulky cargo. We used 'em to drop or pick up bodies, weapons, explosives, that kind of thing. One must assume jewellery, gold, diamonds, currency, narcotics, anything of low bulk, high value garnered from God-knows-where."

Cameron to Rossiter: "We shall need your resources at the Met to track down local gangs with contacts over there."

"We have some interesting files in the hopper, right, Freddy?" Nods to the suit beside him, who makes a note. "We'll see to it. Now what about this Todder chap? Seems like a prime witness or participant. You aren't getting anywhere with him, are you? Turn him over to us. We'll open him up."

Outraged, Cameron says we can handle our own interrogations, thank you very much. "One thing we do agree on: Private Gilmore is an unlikely suspect, but how he came into possession of the weapon doesn't wash. Has to be more to it. Pressure continues on the hooligans in custody and those confined to barracks. We're dangling carrots of a quick exit home if they'll give us info. So far, no joy. We're pursuing all avenues, but frankly, sir, we aren't convinced yet of mass mutiny, revolution, or subversion."

"Then what do you make of the note and threat implied in the gas mask left at the scene? The assassin makes a point of taking the victim's notebooks and keys. Why? Are you telling us none of those things mean anything? You'll have to convince us otherwise. The policymakers are quite properly concerned that a larger game is afoot. There is still a war on, in case you haven't noticed."

And it was when Horobbins finally got back to his own flat, and rushed to answer his ringing phone, that he found out exactly what game was afoot.

21

The two-tone bleat of the phone, the only one on his floor, brought him running—elated—along the dark stope that passed as a hallway, its ceiling fixtures long expired, and, as he did so often, cracked his hip against a discarded electric trousers press, which the landlady once told him had been there since 1939 and never reclaimed. Exalted provost status had equipped him with the phone in his attic digs in the Regency house on Inverness Terrace, to the envy of other deprived officers billeted in better rooms, who forever wheedled its use. Had Mavis changed her mind, after all? No such luck. Captain Karen Williams from the Sally Ann hostel a couple of streets over. He had left his number with her, if needed. Now it was.

"Where've you been? Claire's gone. Picked up in a car around 1800 hours. Two men in civvies and a driver. They weren't police."

Over two hours ago? Williams struggled to make amends: she had located Bollock in Chiswick and he was already at the flat. Also took initiative to reach the duty officer at Six Provost who set about to organize the search. He sprinted through bemused strollers, found Williams at the door of the soot-streaked building with its black door and iron railing stubs left from wartime scrap drives.

"What were you doing? You're supposed to stick with her."

Usually for female other ranks only, the Salvation Army had bent its holy rules to accommodate an officer who presented herself as guardian of a special case. A small bedroom on the ground floor had been found for her, while Evans had gone upstairs to share a dorm with three snickering WAAFs from a base in East Anglia.

"Thought she was up in her room waiting for her gals to meet her here. Seemed safe enough, so I went around the corner to eat at a pub, took a walk. When I came back her two girlfriends were waiting in the lounge. She's not upstairs, they said. The old duck on the desk told them she had already left with two smartly dressed civilians."

"Nice work, Williams. You'll get a medal for this. That her?" He pointed to a dumpy woman with stringy grey hair and a moth-eaten cardigan in the summer heat. "Ma'am, tell me what happened here."

As the conference at Cockspur Street began to drift off into late afternoon recriminations, Colonel Cameron had declared adjournment. Actions were noted, fires lit under investigators, reconvene next week for sitreps. Rossiter spirited Bollock off for more inspiration. The officers from the upper floors smiled their skepticism, as much as ordered Horobbins, for chrissake, to shape up and get on with it, somebody there in Aldershot, go find him. Or her, smirked an army lawyer in tailored gabardine. At the post-mortem in his office, Colonel Cameron invoked basic police work, just in case his chief investigator had forgotten: follow the money, follow the weapon.

At last escaping, he took the tube back to Bayswater, off at the Queensway and, toting his overnight bag and briefcase, walked to his subsistence quarters where he changed into clean duds, the place musty with his absence and July heat. Mavis also had inherited a precious telephone. He savoured the evening ahead. He would go over to Notting Hill Gate, take the District Line to East Putney and walk up the hill to the portal where a petrol station once had served the residents of Manor Fields. Across the spacious green courtyard to Bede House, and there she'd be, having divested the stylish pullover she wore for her volunteer canteen work, naked under a filmy silk wrap. On the way he would stop at an off-licence to pick up a couple of quarts of Scotch ale, her favourite. Later, perhaps, a meander on the Heath to step smugly around bodies thrashing in the underbrush.

It was not to be. Mavis's high reedy tensions conveyed repatriation show-down, the "epidemic," as Bollock had called it—an infection that had reached Horobbins. Word from Burma: David was to be invalided home with malaria after his long ordeal with Slim's Fourteenth Army through the landings at Arakan, the muddy plod to Mandalay, everything, but it had caught up to him. Horobbins pictured a gaunt, stubbled wraith tottering through foul muck. Mavis once had read out a phrase from one of his letters: "the butterflies are gorgeous." Now the fancier of beauty amid humid squalor was about to show up expecting care and understanding. Mavis didn't want to see "her Hugh" tonight. She had to work it out in her own way, whether to wait for David, find out if they could start over. What with the war there had been no children. Weeks before he's home, Horobbins argued lamely. No, she had to go into seclusion to ponder their future. "Depending how it works out, darling, we'll come to a decision." "I can't say how much longer I'll be here. Sorry I couldn't tell you. Assignment in Aldershot. You've read in *News of the World* about the colonel shot dead at his desk? That's the one. Very difficult case." "Have you decided to go to the Pacific?" "Pass David in the night? No, not if I can help it. I want to wait for you here." "That's sweet, darling, I love you."

Ruined. But hungry, shuffled to a pub off Porchester Gardens for greasy rabbit stew and Scotch ale in remembrance. Servicemen at the bar glowered at his shoulder patches. He tried to make himself invisible in a corner and contemplated going over to Whiteleys to find a gift for Mavis. Forget it. Across Bayswater the park teemed with blobs of khaki and blue and summer prints: one enemy down, the one remaining so far away it defied imagination, until the grey survivors, like David, began to return.

Back at his rooms the phone was ringing.

The hostel lounge was a tableau of female guests in varied uniforms who sat or stood around, gathered up by the police, while a detective pawed through the contents of Claire's overnight bag laid out on a table. Williams had acted quickly, had taken over the hostel's primitive switchboard and had made a trunk call to Aldershot.

"She made me pay for it," Williams said, pointing to the grumpy Sally Ann concierge, who reluctantly allowed Horobbins to call Bollock at the flat.

"They were here, all right, in and out like a shot. Rear door was locked, but they had a key."

"There wasn't a guard at the back?"

"Afraid not, a balls up, our men had left the flat, leaving the constable at the front door of the building. How soon can you be here?"

"Give me a few minutes. I want to check out a couple of things." Horobbins faced the concierge.

"The two gents asked for her by name, perfectly polite and respectable. I went up to the dorm, didn't I? 'Two civilians,' she asks, 'not an army captain and a civilian?' When she came down to the lounge she seemed to recognize them, sort of stood there not sure what to do. They greeted her friendly-like, and from what I could hear, offered sympathies on the death of somebody, all the time easing her towards the door, holding her by an arm on either side, and escorted her to a motor. No force I could see. The motor sped off."

"Did you notice anything unusual? She try to signal you in any way?"

"No, sir, but she seemed puzzled. I began to wonder and thought I'd watch from the entrance. It's a black Vauxhall saloon. What I did notice was a third man, the driver, also in a lounge suit. He stood on the pavement as if to make sure she didn't make a bolt for it. Didn't much care for the looks of him. The other two seemed like gents, one was darkish with moustache, had a Yank accent like you, the taller one blonde, English, military types, weren't they? The driver was a sturdy bloke, odd hair, blonde tufts standing up."

"What direction did they take?"

"I wouldn't know, would I? They drove away in a hurry. Last I saw of them. Something wrong, innit?"

"Indeed there is." Glared at a chagrined Williams, turned to the two CWACs she had ordered to wait. "Tell me what happened."

"We came to meet her and go out for a bite," said the younger, dark-haired one. "She'd already gone."

They gave their names, old friends from 42 Company, and explained how Corporal Evans, accompanied by her captain, had arrived at the Canadian Wives' Bureau on Sackville Street where they worked. "We found it strange she had an officer with her. 'My keeper,' Claire whispered to us. We were busting with curiosity, but couldn't ask her, so we arranged to meet at the hostel and go out. Her captain ordered us to travel in a pack and return directly to the hostel, she wouldn't spoil our outing by hanging around. That's about it. Claire didn't mention anything about others coming to pick her up. She in some kind of trouble? We'd sure like to find out what this is all about."

"Some day," Horobbins said. Two more calls before he left for the flat. His subordinate, one Lieutenant Stevens, duty officer at Six Provost, confirmed they were following up on the mayday from Captain Williams who had described the four persons to be traced. Somewhat stretched, sir, what with most personnel with you in Aldershot. It would be a slow grind. Six Company carried out joint patrols with the Met police, and runners in Jeeps—some equipped with notoriously unreliable Number 38 wireless sets—would seek out detachments at railway stations and other key spots across London. Yes, confirmed Stevens, trying to calm his usually unflappable boss, we've alerted RAF and USAF to track any unauthorized flights, coming or going. Then, lump in throat, Horobbins bared his soul to Colonel Cameron, ensconced in his office after Stevens had rousted him out of a club on Jermyn Street.

"You lost her, for chrissake. You find that gal in one piece. And bring in those kidnappers, Wellesley's goons. I'll be here till you find 'em."

"We were had." A shaken Bollock was devastated they had missed the obvious. "Probably after the keys or something else entirely. Whatever it is, they've taken your corporal to lead them to it, her being Wellesley's poppet and all. Secrets of pillow talk to be extracted from her." Bollock pointed where the tape on the apartment door had been peeled off, replaced loosely. "Came up the rear stairs. Our man at the entrance did call in from the post at the end of the mews, about 1830 he's logged, to report an attempt by the service-woman he remembered and a civilian gent with an American accent to talk him into letting them in. The constable had not followed them when he turned them away. His orders were to secure the front entrance. Seems they went in the direction of Westbourne, possibly had a vehicle waiting—if so he didn't see it."

"How'd they get in?"

"Must've crawled over fences. Obviously had a key to the rear entrance. Let's take a dekko. Odd, though; if they had actually done him in or arranged it, they wouldn't be here now to search the place for whatever it is they're try-ing to find. Probably flew over from Germany or Holland, anxious to get here before we found it. Too late. Rattled to see the place already under police guard. I should have ordered a more discreet watch. Wasn't thinking ahead. So they espy a copper at the door, more going inside, then we hand it to them. Crikey, they see us leave with Corporal Evans. Instant recognition. They tail her, wait for the opportunity to nab her at the hostel. We, the experts, have been shadowed all day. Nice work, wouldn't you say, Horobbins?"

"What're they after, anyway?" Horobbins went to the kitchenette, studied the piled tins and boxes, sniffed at the stench from the basin where contents had been dumped, but it appeared the police had not finished their search that day or hadn't bothered. A number of containers were still unopened. In fingerprint dust on a counter he found two rings left by tins that had been removed. No others stacked nearby had been opened. He called Bollock over.

"After your men were here. Two tins picked up. Good way to hide valu-ables from snoops or burglars. Opener right there. Dusting needed."

"Constable, you find another tin opener and empty every one of 'em. Bring the fingerprint boffins back in here. And you," turning to another, "find the custodian, he may've let them in."

Downstairs the back door was unlocked. Bollock lugging his own murder bag hopped like a black toad across the patch of yard with its overgrown Anderson shelter. A policeman who crawled in to look around emerged with cobweb lace on his helmet and shook his head. On sparse grass baked by summer the footprints were faint, but Bollock found a narrow heel mark from a female shoe and light brown threads dangling from the top of the fence. From the murder bag Bollock took out tweezers and a paper bag to lift them off, grunted over the wooden fence to find more threads atop the masonry wall one building over, abutting the street.

"They came in here over the wall and the wooden fence to the rear door." Mr. Wilson, the custodian, vowed he saw or heard nothing. "Would they have a key to this door? Right. No time. We have to do this ourselves."

The building was a warren of tiny flats, some with nameplates. Bollock, Horobbins, a detective constable and one uniform used the stairs and ran down empty corridors to pound on unresponsive doors. From a top floor bed-sitter the only living soul at home was an elderly woman, humped by osteoporosis, cane in hand more as a weapon than for support, peered at warrant cards and welcomed the entertainment. Yes, from her open window she had heard voices and went to look. Two men, civilians, assisted a woman in a brown uniform over the fence. The morals these days, a terrible breakdown, but none of my business, is it?

"Can you describe them?"

"One was stocky, dark moustache. The other was large, possibly fifteen stone, black lounge suit. Cropped blonde hair with bits sticking up."

"I'm sure we'll have him, the coiffure rings a bell," Bollock said outside. "I'll stir up Criminal Records. If they can do a matchup we'll bring in the old party here and the woman from the hostel to confirm. Then I need to see my chums on the Special Duty Squad working the black market operators. We'll no doubt end up on my old turf in the East End. I still have a few of my own snouts on the string."

"Mr. Bollock, we're in your hands."

"You might bring in a few of your men to work with our Information Room crew. I'll arrange it. It'll be our central command post where you might wish to park your weary bones. I can't very well take you with me and the Special Duty Squad—uniforms not welcome. Frankly, I don't see any point in you dashing around in Jeeps or whatnot, unless you want to work off your spleen. Be careful, you're a copper not a vigilante. As to your two prize officers, your chaps in Germany should be onto them by now and have some idea what they've been up to over there. Well," an unusual pat on the shoulder, "it seems your line to the Continent begins to make sense. There's only one basic flaw."

"And that is?"

"If your colonel's demise was to be arranged by his partners in crime or a rival mob, why in his office in Aldershot? Take him down here in London, remove his keys or notebooks, make sure he disappears without a trace under a pile of rubble or such like. Mark you, the timing was spot on: confusion after the riots, the note, the gas mask to point the way to subversive plots. But the taking of the notebooks and keys still stumps me. This afternoon I rang Hendon to do another examination of the colonel's jacket, spoke to Dixon who, you may remember, removed personal items from the corpse and handed them over to us. I asked him if the outside upper pockets where he'd keep the notebooks were buttoned before he, Dixon, opened them to root about. Consulted his notes—very meticulous is he—reported, yes, the two pockets were buttoned before he opened them. Nothing inside, the other items were taken from other pockets. Definitely no keys anywhere on his person. It doesn't seem likely he'd hand over the notebooks to the killer or his accomplice—there may be two of them involved—and, tidy as he was, rebutton his pockets."

"You're saying someone already had the notebooks."

"And still does. One of your pitiful witnesses told you the colonel even took his notebooks and keys in a pouch into the shower. Never let them out of his sight. Unless the killer instructed him to button up his jacket after handing over the notebooks and the keys. Rather a stretch."

"A pickpocket? Hardly your typical street dips in that lot."

"You might ponder that while I'm off to lean on various unsavoury types, but there's little doubt in my mind that our two villains who came over from the Continent don't have the keys or notebooks and they are in a flap to find whatever they need to lay their hands on the lolly. I'll put odds on a key to a security box at a London bank. Corporal Evans intimated as much when she described her dear Ambrose leaving her at the flat while he went out and about on business. Very much the gang boss, he kept control of the stash, didn't completely trust his partners, although they must've relied entirely on his well-proven executive abilities to set up the operations and divvy up fairly when they were ready to close up shop. Now, with his demise, they've probably decided to take the money and run, not to mention his share. They didn't trust your fine Major Todder enough to cut him in on their latest rackets, or he'd made enough and dropped out. Very tight, well organized with connections to our own gangs here. Well, that's the way crooks work, innit?"

"Even if they did find what they wanted here in the flat, the fact is Claire Evans can identify them. The odds of her making it to a ripe old age. . . ."

"Rather dim, I'm afraid. Why would they let her go? A ticking time bomb, another type of disposal squad at work here."

22

It is said that 274 years after the second great fire of London—lit by thousands of silvery tubes—the incendiary bombs dropped by German Heinkels, Dorniers, and Junkers let loose a grotesque flood of boiling sludge. On two freezing nights of the 29th and 30th of December 1940, a white heat turned the East End into an inferno that dwarfed the ruin of the past four months of the Blitz.

Out of the warehouses, shops, and docks from St. Katherine to Surrey and the Indias, both banks of the Thames flowed lava—a fine blend of human and animal fat, tar, oils and petrol, spiced with brine, melted cheese, margarine, bread-stuffed pork for vile sausages, gamy horseflesh, mixed with scorched rice and grains. And swimming, drowning with singed fur, the rats surfed on the streams around flaming debris, smoking bricks and stone, to plunge to sizzling immolation into the river. Scuffles or scrambling overhead, you wouldn't notice unless you were in the blind, silent dark, were testimony to their ultimate survival. They had returned, bred again, generations of rats going on five years.

On the reeking mattress she reached into her bag, thoughtfully left with her or overlooked. Touched the edge of a box of wooden matches. Non-smoker, why did she carry them? Feeling the emery band, she managed to strike a match and blinked in the acrid flare. No beady eyes were caught. The dank room, sealed tight, bred other vermin to prickle her legs, crawl ever higher, burning down below. Vermin, for sure. Or something else? That sweaty night when he awakened her again. What a sap she'd been. Prize chump.

With a second match she crept to the steel door, debating whether to pound or not. Could hear nothing outside. Not too smart to draw attention.

Might stir them to—what? Her bladder sent her to a stinking bucket revealed in a corner. She squatted, holding another match until it burnt her shaking fingers. The cell was a hideout or a prison, well used, the airless fug of dead sweat.

Where they had ended up she had no idea. Blindfolded, she heard one of them tell the driver to pass well clear of Stepney, still in disarray from the last V-2 in March. The car jostled and weaved, creaked over potholes until she caught a whiff of tide or mudflats.

Curled up in foetal ball, shivering from dread and fury, she realized how she had been taken in by her abductors and, worst of all, by Ambrose himself. The last she couldn't bear, for they had broken her spirit as surely as the Gestapo, the spunk that had kept her defiant blown away. Why they had postponed her disposal she couldn't fathom. Was it a lingering reluctance to commit another crime, or had she bought time with her last try at bait? She had drawn upon her reserves by at first going along with them, for the sake of Ambrose too. A futile loyalty, God rot his soul. When at last it dawned on her the options they were mulling over, she took a stab at the lure of the missing notebooks, so vital to them, it appeared. So she held out the prospect that only she could find the notebooks hidden in Aldershot. A lie, but at least sufficient for a postponement, but now that they had found a key in the tin at the flat, what if they didn't need the notebooks after all? If the key was not the right one, then what? They would have to find the notebooks and hope that Ambrose had left a clue.

At first they had acted as though it didn't matter that she had recognized them from those weekends at the flat, but the logic now became obvious. Loaded with their ill-gotten loot, sooner than they had planned when Ambrose was still in charge, they intended to disappear for good and make sure she did too. For the first time she could feel she was about to become a kindred soul in the last moments of so many: that "oh, no, not me" instant when the ME110 night fighter raked the belly of the Lancaster, or the 88 airburst puffed over the open slit trench, or her friend Jean Cullen sitting upright, her dead eyes fixed on the movie screen in the Rex Theatre in Antwerp, as the rocket dropped.

The fact was, even in London or Aldershot, the so-called "cushy" jobs had not been without danger. On the fringes of the war zone, yes, but V-1s and V-2s tumbled out of the sky; hit and run air raids by solitary Huns out of nowhere. Hit and run, too, by speeding vans in the blackout, the medieval darkness always a menace for a woman in uniform, let alone groping hands and subtle threats of unwanted sex—until he taught her. Vulnerable, but not afraid. Even experienced a strange detachment from the riotous mob in Aldershot, secure in her faith that the tide would not reach their billets. And what did others do amid the carnage? They went on, young enough to block out the reality of early death, say, like her father at Vimy Ridge. It was the only way to keep sane, day after day, a fleeting privilege of youth. But it didn't matter now. Her spirit was flattened: what they had jeered at her about Ambrose. Fatalism is fatal, her father said, but now it had become her only refuge.

Away from the hostel, pinned between the two men in the back seat, she could feel her armpits ooze, her breasts shedding talc. They hadn't blindfolded her yet. So polite, familiar old pals coming to call, the Canadian especially effusive in apology. It's something Ambrose would've wanted us to do in remembrance of him; thus her help was needed, as I'm sure she would agree it'd be his last wish from beyond the grave. Come along just for a short while and we'll return you to the hostel. In broad daylight, the throngs on the street somehow reassuring, she was at that moment trusting enough to share her grief with the hangers-on from the flat.

It didn't take long for doubts to creep in. For one thing, the thuggish driver with his bulging neck, shorn head and its blonde tufts. At her right hip the half-colonel she remembered from the apartment was stiff, remote or reverting to English toffism in a navy blue lounge suit. The charm of the Canadian at her other side began to unravel when she insisted she had had no information that would help them. As he spoke she recalled him in a uniform with the red shield and its blue cross, the 21st Army Group insignia and the Fusiliers Mont-Royal shoulder patch. Like Ambrose, he was from Montreal—so bilingual he seemed Anglo with no trace of accent. They must have known each other back there. With growing unease she sensed his exasperation, his affability fading into his soft post-war jowls, black moustache, and heavy eyebrows intimating the menace of a cheap spiv. The two of them were a lot more scary in their civvies than the raffish indolence of underemployed army officers on weekend furlough.

"We saw you come out of the flat. What did you tell them?"

"You know I was with Ambrose, nothing more. I haven't a clue what went on."

"What do you suppose went on?"

"Search me, any more than those other girls you had up there. You going to pick them up too?"

"We can see to that, guv," the driver's voice like Bollock's. She began to realize.

"Can it, Spike." (Spike? Laughable otherwise). "Why'd they take the trouble to come up to London to search our flat? You must've spilt the beans."

"What beans? They found out from others that Ambrose had the flat and I'd been there. They're leaning on everybody. From what little I can gather there's a file somewhere about things he's supposed to have been mixed up in on the Continent. With nothing else to go on for now, they're following that line of inquiry. They were called in for a meeting at CMHQ and decided to do the flat as well." No tremor in her voice yet.

"How did your name get into it?"

"No secrets around that place. Others ratted about my weekend trips to London, and I wanted to help them find whoever killed Ambrose."

"Good little girl scout. What'd they expect to find at the flat that had anything to do with his death?"

"They don't let me in on that." Claire managed to draw on wells of sarcasm. "Something to do with a couple of small notebooks and a set of keys that weren't found on him after he was shot. Somebody has them, but not me."

"Who has them?"

"The killer presumably. Why, the police don't know."

"Come on, Claire, he entrusted them to you, didn't he?"

"No, sir. Why would he? He didn't expect his own death, and nobody gave them to me after."

"Good Lord," said the Englishman, "at this moment someone may be on his way to the bank, beat us to it."

"Take it easy, Sammy. All he'd have is the key and the coded stuff the Duke wrote in his notebook. He showed it to us and how to read it if push came to shove. It'd take him or them forever to figure it out."

"Then why take 'em?"

"Good question. You have an answer to that, corporal ?"

"Never ought to have left it in his hands." The Englishman's plummy tones were chilled. "Once when he was a bit knackered he hinted a spare key was somewhere in the flat, but was sober enough to say he'd show us at an appropriate time, never expecting of course . . ."

"Spike, wheel around and go back."

"The place is crawling, guv."

"We'll recce it. So you don't think they found the spare key at the flat?"

"Not that I'm aware of."

The Vauxhall turned on Edgeware Road, came down to Oxford onto Bayswater, cruised slowly onto Augusta Mews. Outside the portico stood a lone uniformed bobby. They circled.

"Say again, Claire. Nobody has a line on who popped off the Duke?"

"That's my impression. The British government has sent in teams of agents to beat the bushes for subversives based on the threatening note and respirator left on his desk. You don't know about that?"

"That's rich." When the two officers laughed with an anxiety that didn't escape her, she realized her captors were strangely at sea about the details of the murder, almost as though they had made a quick, panicky trip across the Channel. And—putting two and two together—if they had ordered his death, wouldn't they have been prepared to follow up? Or, were they afraid those who had bumped him off would be seeking them out to locate the same thing they were after, probably a stash of money and loot? So, she concluded with a clarity that amazed her, these two were frightened or apprehensive. Then the purpose of this expedition must be to pick up their marbles and take it on the lam. Was that it?

Spike had strolled past the constable on duty, had gone along the side street, up the masonry wall to peer over and make sure no one was at the rear door. The major took her elbow in a vise grip.

"You and I will approach the copper. You'll find out if anyone is up there and, if not, persuade him to let us in. I am a member of the investigation team. You stick with us for a short while and you're free to go. Understood?"

The copper was adamant, recognized the CWAC corporal, but not him, and denied entrance, but let it slip there was no one in the flat at the moment.

They retreated back to the car where it was revealed the English officer did have a key to the back door. Now in command, he ordered them to make their way over the wall and inner fence and, in clipped authority, urged them to "look lively." No stomach for climbing, he remained in the car to ensure his lounge suit remained unsullied. At the masonry wall on the side street, the major swore while Spike jibed at him about obstacle course exercises. A few spectators paused. The major heaved the driver to the top with cupped hands, rusty battle school tricks.

"Locked out," he smiled to the interested watchers. "Lost the key to our flat." Maybe Spike had been in the forces. Having already tested the wall on his first reconnaissance, the recce, he locked his legs onto the top of the masonry, apparently oblivious to embedded glass, stretched down to haul Claire up by her elbows, then the major. Amused onlookers drifted away. Next a wooden fence, easily scaled. Claire wondered why she hadn't broken loose then, screamed and ran. Curiosity killed the Quack?

The hallway was tiled in that peculiar green, as if the British had their own Eaton's catalogue. With no police at the back door, they went up the back stairs where the major, too anxious to worry about fingerprints, peeled off the police tape on the door. The place was littered, surfaces white with fingerprint dust and rows of tape marks. Spent flashbulbs crunched under foot. While Spike kept watch at the door the major studied the upended cushions and open drawers, shook his head and ended up in the kitchenette with its jumble of tins and boxes on the sideboard.

"Bogged off without finishing the job, probably tea time. Never latched onto these, here look at this." He had rummaged through the tins until he plucked two unopened ones with Spam labels, and pointed in triumph to finely soldered ridges. "Not as thorough as you'd think." He found an opener, reached into pink muck to emerge with a flat key, the type common to bank security boxes. Exclaimed, opened the second one to pluck, one by one, a dozen or so cut diamonds, their facets glinting in blobs of meat. "Kept these for himself, didn't he?" The major wrapped up that tin in a paper sack and stuffed it into a side pocket of his now dusty lounge suit. In the car he handed the washed key to the colonel. It was then, as if reading her thoughts, the major rolled up a handkerchief, tied it over her eyes. Angry now, Claire tested honour among thieves.

"Ambrose told me those diamonds were kept for me."

"What diamonds?"

She could hear the paper bag rustle out of the major's pocket. "Found these. I was about to show you." On her right the colonel must have taken the tin, judging by distasteful sniffs. "Freddy, I am a bit disappointed. We've always operated on trust. I shudder to think how Sal would carry on at the shop. Well, yes, it was Ambrose who kept them back, and I doubt very much he did so for you, missy. Too late now to go to the bank. We shall have to stay over till tomorrow. Spike."

"What about her?"

"She'll have to remain with us. Spike, you have the lads cancel tonight's flight, if it's not too late. Restage the exercise for tomorrow after dark. You can reach them at the kiosk. Right."

So there was an aircraft somewhere. They spoke as though she was one of them; more likely it didn't matter, she wasn't going anywhere—ever.

Her blindfold was removed in a creaking goods lift, and she was marched along a corridor in a warehouse of some kind to a gloomy lounge of sorts with greasy divans and cartons of whisky. A hideout.

"Spike, shake a leg, ring your chaps at the airstrip, then go find a takeaway, fish and chips." The colonel, taking over, led Claire to a grungy chesterfield. "Corporal, you've been less than open with us. What else can you tell us?"

"My stockings are ruined. You have a loo around here?" Nobody laughed. "The notebooks—you will need them if the key isn't the right one."

"Clever girl. Go on."

"Supposing I can find them. I'm sure I know where to look in Aldershot. No, I don't have them, but I can search out some places they've overlooked. I can't promise, but it's your best bet, isn't it?"

"If you think for one minute we're taking you back there, you're nuts," said the major.

"We shall have to consider your offer." The English colonel was thinking ahead. "I have to ring Sal anyway to pack up and stand by, but I'll ask her what she thinks in the off chance the key isn't the right one."

When she bent over to roll down her torn stockings, the major stared at her white legs.

"You guys know she was a cherry before Ambrose got at her?"

Spike, coming back with fish and chips in newspaper and bottles of ale, winked. "We'd get good lolly for this piece in Amsterdam."

Resistance crumbled, utter betrayal drained her brief attempts at spunk. Ambrose had blabbed their secret, a story to pass around among his pals, nothing more than another quick lay to brag about: boys, this one was something special, a lulu, played out in the smirks of the three men. Cramps doubled her up, her head down for a dab at the tears she could no longer hold in. The smell of greasy chips waved thoughtfully in front of her brought about dry heaves, but nothing came up.

When she raised her head again it was to the icy blue stare of the English colonel. At his nod Spike lifted her up and walked her along a corridor lined with cartons. He breathed heavily in anticipation, but tried nothing. He could wait. The windowless cell had a light bulb dangling from a long cord. The heavy door squealed shut, a key turned and the light bulb flickered out. It was then she began to hear faint scratches above the ceiling.

23

Unless the Japs had a nasty surprise up their kimonos, the map of wartime London was an historical artefact. Horobbins peered down at four large-scale maps of the Metropolitan Police District in glass-topped tables. Around him the Information Room, ground floor, North Extension, The Yard, crackled with incoming traffic from the telephone posts, radios, and district police stations. Four of his own provost manned phones and radios to their command centre at Cockspur Street to track the searchers out on the prowl for Corporal Evans, a metro-wide net of civilian and military police, including British red caps, Special Police from other services, even American white helmets. Bollock, back to touch base after a run at his old haunts, chuffed and voluble to be in action again, gave a guided tour of the maps.

"The red stars are the Blitz period from September '40 to May '41; the green ones are after that. The blue markers are V-1s, the yellow ones V-2s. The red lines designate areas severely damaged or in ruins. You've seen 'em overgrown with thistle, weeds, willows. Tag ends of a civilization perhaps. You'd have to conjure up those nights, the entire East End burning two miles into the sky. Factories, warehouses, gasworks going up; on the river blazing ships and barges cut adrift; fireboats pissing into the inferno from low tide. Poor sods in the East End. You've seen Anderson shelters, but to dig up your garden means you must have one. Down there no one has a patch—cheek by jowl, no shelters for them. Had to be evacuated by water, or most went into the tube stations. And today," his crooked teeth bared, "there are crocodile tears about Dresden. Come off it."

"And you, what were you doing then?"

"Back in uniform to show the flag. No need for a CID sergeant when the city was in flames. Did everything: traffic, rescue, crowd control, helping them to the tube stations. Mum and dad, they had a green grocers off Cable Street, near St. George-in-the-East, landmark bombed out in '41. They were doing poorly. With a copper son they couldn't very well tap into the wares offered by the spivs or fiddle ration coupons. Anyhow, they got out alive, the shop flattened, no insurance. Went down to Poole where my brother is a chemist. As for the missus, she saw it through in fine fettle until that first V-2 I told you about."

Captain Karen Williams paced, smoked, head lowered in disgrace. She had been hauled along when Horobbins didn't know what to do with her. She poked at the glass-covered maps, her sympathy for Bollock's wartime ordeals on the back burner.

"Very touching. Now how're you going to find her?"

Bollock seemed amused, unhurried to deliver the sermon during the long vigil ahead.

"Some buildings have survived, or, if damaged, fixed up inside, a good many of them to serve the black markets, bane of our existence. Gangs pilfer everything in sight, aided and abetted by a populace fed up with the shortages. You ever been to Rumford, the markets down the river? The trouble is the authorities send us mixed signals. There are those who believe the black markets, from ration coupons to chickens, provide a way for people to let off steam, helps to prevent more social unrest than we already have now that our war, here at least, is over. Your blokes, your fine colonel and cohorts would have no difficulty linking up with the gangs here to dispose of ill-gotten gains from the Continent, crawling as it is with deserters and other villains only too eager to oblige. Possibly as many as twenty thousand of them rampaging around the liberated countries and the occupied zone. You follow me, captain?"

She nodded, a guilty skeptic to the last.

"What we're trying to do here is ferret out the snouts, grassers—informants to you—to lead us to their local connections. In May we formed the Special Duty Squad. The press, bless 'em, dub it 'The Ghost Squad.' The chief is my old chum Johnny Gosling, East End bloke like me. He works the 'Crooks' Dormitory' out Aldgate way and beyond. Has a network of snouts you wouldn't believe, gutter rats with exotic street names like Tommy the Talker, Slicer Fred, Bacon Sam, and so on. As you may gather, I've been spending time with Gosling. He and his men are our best hope. Johnny is of the opinion the black Vauxhall was driven by one Straw Spike with the tufted blonde hair, as described by the ladies from the hostel and the flat. They've been interviewed separately, seen his photo, and agree it's probably him. Straw Spike is a heavy operator linked to a chain of deserters and evil-doers on the Continent. Feeds high-class loot such as diamonds, jewellery, gold, furs, wines, brandy, and drugs to the middle men. They in turn connect with wartime affluent *nouveau*, anyone who's awash in pound notes nowhere to spend. The cross-Channel traffic has burgeoned since the Yanks left and their supplies dried up here."

"So where is he?"

"We don't know yet."

"Fat lot of good that is," said Williams.

"A start has been made." Bollock, having smoked the late colonel's supply, was forced to revert to a Senior Service fag, and couldn't resist showing off snippets of underworld lingo, as if he missed the fun of the old days. "Johnny sent a crew to tumble Spike's rat and mouse up in Hampstead. Restored cottage backing onto the Heath, sited no doubt where he can put the skates on, bog off in a hurry if needed. Keeps nothing incriminating at the house except his cheese and kisses, his latest from the Windmill. Very careful to blend in with the good burghers. Fittingly, not far from the bombed out ruins of Jack Straw's Castle. His caches are a movable feast, shifting anywhere from Brick Lane to the Surrey and India docks, semi-derelict houses, flats, warehouses, in and out. The problem is our Straw Spike, born as one Ronald Mayberry, is off the radar. Done a bunk. We've alerted county constabulary to the north. Gosling believes his Hampstead digs give him quick access to abandoned airstrips and fields to drop off goods to and from the Continent. There's been an official crackdown on planeloads of leather goods, champagne and the like trundled in by our brave lads in various air forces. The two officers who picked up Corporal Evans, your bailiwick." He handed over a manila envelope. "Fingerprints from the flat, Spike's included. Your mates over there can have a go at them. And, captain," turning to Williams, "we need her photo immediately if not sooner, top priority messenger. If you'd write out her physicals we'll print up posters."

While she, stirred by a task, was on the phone to Aldershot, Horobbins asked, "What are the odds on her now?"

"Our gangs are violent enough, but not inclined to slaughter unless absolutely necessary. Your two officers were mixed up with the more bloody-minded villains over yon with their guns and bazookas. The fact is she can identify them and Spike. You appreciate they aren't thinking straight or they never would've picked her up. They are or were latching on to her to help them locate what must be a horrendous pile of loot converted to cash or diamonds the good colonel had put on ice somewhere in London or possibly other locations in Belgium or Holland. An unexpected and premature bunk, most likely. Who can say? I must report we've ordered Thames Division to start dragging for her. Sorry."

"Jesus."

"By God I'll have your guts for gaiters." On the blower Major Todder launched a preemptive strike at Horobbins.

"I think you mean garters, sir."

"Any of the above. You and that idiot flatfoot swan off to London, leave the scene and place one of my staff in mortal peril. You'll answer for this."

"Sir, I think you can assist us with information about the two officers who abducted her. We have little to go on except descriptions from witnesses and a signal from the British Army of the Rhine (you've heard of it?) that your chum Lefebvre took leave to the UK with one Lieutenant Colonel Samuel Yates, a Brit. You know them both, right?"

"I told you about Freddy. Yes, Sammy Yates was in Brussels with us; tall, blondish chap. You sure it's them?"

"Little doubt. It appears those two flew in from Germany, probably to collect something they'd entrusted to Colonel Wellesley. Whether they had anything to do with his murder we can't say. If you come clean on what they're after it could make the difference. Maybe save her life."

"Haven't a clue. The file is closed and forgotten. We were cleared. If Ambrose set up something with his old cronies from Brussels, I wasn't in on it."

"I want your best guess on where they might've taken her—a hideout, a drop, anything."

"What does it take, Horobbins? I never went near his flat. He never told me anything. We were a bit distant on personal matters."

"Distant? He was quick to bring you back here as his Two IC. What's so special about your expertise, organize moving vans to haul the loot? He wanted to keep an eye on you. And you might as well cough up his notebooks and keys. You're the only one in Aldershot who could make use of them, know what they mean. So don't lecture me about putting Corporal Evans in danger. If you're so concerned about her, you tell us now."

"You're sick, Horobbins, should be sent home as a nutcase. Wasting my time and yours when you ought to be out finding her. You bring her back safe and sound."

"Duly noted, sir, subject declines to assist us. We'll see about that. You be sure and let us know if they contact their old crony Todder in any way. Who else would they think of?"

As part of his burden that awful night, Horobbins found himself fending off an invasion of red tabs from the front office, including a delegation of irate CWAC officers and even the top man General Montague himself. Colonel Cameron seemed to be the only one who grasped that the Information Room did not welcome the clutter, that the Met's tentacles far outclassed anything the military could do. They were, Horobbins was informed, keeping vigil in a conference room, extension number noted and, by God, they wanted results soonest. Wearily, Horobbins tried to divert them by counter requests to track the two missing officers and their shenanigans from Canadian and British headquarters in Germany. As there was nothing coming in from Bollock and the Ghost Squad, he had nothing much to pass along, until from the other end he could hear sounds of heavy breathing and faint snores. Horobbins and Williams caught twitchy naps, heads down on desks. The subsiding babble of the Information Room in glaring light tinged with the blue-green of stark walls faded into a troubled dawn.

Then around noon the next day, the police having contacted banks in Westminster, an assistant manager from a branch twigged to something and reported in by phone.

"This morning when we opened, two gentlemen in smart suits went down to our vaults. One signed in as a Colonel Weston. We have the signature card. The custodian of the vaults used his master key while one of the gents employed a key to withdraw one of our larger security boxes, took it to a cubicle, evidently emptied its contents into two cases. The custodian observed several thick envelopes drop onto the floor, the box overflowing. One gentleman was heard to say: 'Good old Ambrose. Looks like it's all here.' He spoke with an American accent. 'Not till we count it,' says the other. 'Not here,' says the first.

"The reason our custodian recalls the details so minutely is the two gentlemen, having packed the contents into the cases, placed the security box back into its slot, but our chap noted as they departed they left the key in the lock as though there was no further need for it. Didn't bother signing out, either. When our man rushed to point this out to them, they told him to 'sod off,' or unseemly words to that effect, and bounded up the staircase to the entry level, their haste remarked upon by members of our staff. Our doorkeeper, also on the alert, observed the two men enter a black saloon waiting outside.

"Now, sir, we assume they have no further need of our security service. It has been paid for in advance for one year. As we have a substantial demand for the larger boxes we need to know if we may lease it. Yes, you may interview the custodian for descriptions and bring in your fingerprint experts; no one has touched anything. Our custodian wears white cotton gloves. How long would that be? We shall have to close that section of the vaults until they've finished, won't we? Some of our clients won't be too pleased, will they? You say the authorized lessee, Colonel Weston, is probably deceased? We assume then that the gent falsified the signature. Of course we shall surrender the card. Could the army authorities provide us with verification of Colonel Weston's identity and demise so that we may lease the box again? Thank you."

"Colonel Weston, was he?" Horobbins said. "We need your handwriting experts. So they've found their stash, and they have no further use for Claire Evans, Philip Todder, or anyone else. They'll be gone before we know it."

In the airless sea-green cavern the clipped voices trailed off. A couple of Met coppers pulled off their earphones and exchanged stricken shrugs. The traffic was drying up except for one fling. A tall, dark-haired CWAC corporal had been found vomiting in Covent Garden, doubled up on the cobblestones. Not her. That was it. Nothing left but to wait for the Ghost Squad hammering away at snouts for a line on Straw Spike to lead them to the two officers and her. Bollock had left again to lean on his somewhat decayed network of touts in Limehouse and Whitechapel. Horobbins held a long sitrep on the phone with Pearly Gates in Aldershot, who reported the civilian gentlemen from other agencies were properly pissed that the whole caper might be an offshoot of lowlife black market scum, not subversives, but this didn't deter them from their roundups. Gates said he had taken Private Gilmore on a walkabout to identify players and hangers-on at the craps game. We worked out signals so they won't catch on they're being fingered, so we've corralled a few of them for more intensive interviews.

"Listen, there's something I want you to do. It concerns the missing notebooks and keys. They may not need them any more, but we do." Horobbins gave Gates his briefing and what was required. The provost sergeant whistled.

"We'll have a shot at it, sir. Our prayers are with Corporal Evans."

On the same wavelength to Aldershot, Captain Williams ordered Claire's comrades in the Quack detachment to attend a prayers parade to be led by the same chaplain who had conducted the memorial service for Colonel Wellesley.

Another day passed in the police bunker, the constant diet of Argentine corned beef sandwiches bringing forth only staccato belches to break the low murmur of despair. The Ghost Squad was their only hope now.

24

Enter Terence the Stamp (no relation), king of the ration coupons rackets. The word was he was the brains behind the theft of some 600,000 clothing coupons from the employment exchange in Moorgate. Terence was to become the bubble that burst same.

The sociable ferrets of the Ghost Squad winkled him out somehow to follow up on a tip that he harboured a grudge against Straw Spike, allegedly for blagged monies owing among other things. Found Terence in a "social club," an after hours watering hole off Old Quebec Street where he was given assurances they weren't after him for the moment. If he cooperated on a possible murder inquiry as a dutiful British subject, it would be duly noted should any future occasion arise, which was not beyond the realm of possibility. He was primed with illicit ninety proof vodka as an educational aid that finally brought him to see the dawn, perceptive enough to realize who they were after, not him for now, if he went along and grassed. Nothing to lose, they assured him, just a word or two and we're on our way. Nor are we suggesting that Spike is a prime suspect in our murder inquiry. We need to speak to him because we believe he has information that can assist us. That's it. After much befogged second thoughts, Terence asked if they were aware of Spike's Hampstead digs. Been there, they had to admit, but he wasn't. Long pause. Well, he does have a hole in the wall off King's Road in Chelsea where he keeps a bint from Theatre Royal, Drury Lane. Her stage name is Loretta Oberon, a mix and match of the more famous film stars, an improvement on her birth name of Winifred Hansack. Terence allowed he had actually lost her to Spike who had more to offer in the way of furs, jewels and the like, an added value grievance he, Terence, could not forgive.

Whereupon the detectives enlisted the help of the duty sergeant at the Chelsea district station to provide uniforms to cover the exits. Outwardly, Spike's safe house was nondescript in a dingy row of mews with garages handily on the lane. About one AM they found its interior coziness somewhat in disarray. The raiding party crunched in through broken glass and china on the floor, wall mirrors shattered, chairs upended, the front door partly open. A screeching Loretta Oberon flung herself, startled, into the grasp of burly gentlemen in the front lounge. She appeared to be fleeing from an enraged Ronald Mayberry, a.k.a. Straw Spike. Both occupants were scantily attired in what passed for bedtime wear. When he saw his abode crammed with CID busies his first impulse was to dash for the rear door in a futile hopping gait on bare feet bleeding from the shard-littered floor. When he was tackled and sat upon, they retrieved from his tight claw a thick envelope found to be stuffed with five thousand quid. The black Vauxhall was in the garage.

In the small hours of a new day, Spike and Loretta were transported to the bladder, the Yard, to be greeted by Bollock, Gosling, and other hard nuts. Horobbins was invited to observe skilled interplay that shifted between separate rooms along the hall from the nerve centre. Dabbing at fingernail scratches on his cheeks and slashed bare feet, Spike, true to form, had nothing to offer. But the still furious performer from Drury Lane made plain her outrage at what had turned out to be a receding meal ticket. Horobbins did his best to follow without the aid of a translator.

"His cut was to be ten thousand quid he'd use to set me up." In what she didn't say, but they could guess. Without her stage makeup she was a tiny but angry wraith so blonde in every respect she could have been a doxy for a Viking invader. Along with most of her clothing, Loretta also had shed the pearl tones of the stage performer and had reverted to her East End roots. "He handled everything (everfin) for 'em, they couldn't have brought the stuff in and flogged it without him. The big bloke, the Canadian mucky-muck, the colonel wot was bumped off—Spike didn't top him by the way, why would he?—kept his promises. Spike says he was an honest man. Then his mates, them two from over there, fly in to clean out the stash, close it down now that the brains of the outfit was gone. They found the key to the box there inna bonkers and take off to divvy it up, pay off Spike his share and blow."

"Did Spike indicate to you in any way that the two officers had arranged for the colonel's death, maybe cream off more for themselves?"

"Nawn. So Spike drives them up to the field near Chelmsford where the split is supposed to be done. Spike, he leases the farm, been using it for his drops among others. Inna van Spike's two mates meet 'em there. They're ex-RAF, same as him, see the crate's watched over, set out flares for it to land and take off. Spike, he says the plane is a 'Lizzie.' Can land onna tanner. Field's just a bit of pasture they're packed smooth with rollers. Tonight it's all pizzle and drizzle up there. Black as a copper's arsehole, pardon me, gents. The plane's already there, innit? His mates pull in the flares so as not to rouse local clods or busies snooping about.

"Them two toffs, they're off to somewhere over there with the swag. No posh colonel to take his share. They're loaded with sterling, Yank dollars, Swiss francs, and diamonds from the box at the bank, the last split. But Spike, he's canny as a Scot. Before they get outa the motor he takes the trouble to count up his take in the envelope they hand him. Bloody hell, he says, it's a fiver here, not ten. Where's the rest? That's it, sport, they say, we're off. Spike tells 'em in no uncertain terms this innt a Jack and Jill caper, they owe him five. Whereupon the Canadian pulls a Luger, aims it at Spike's loaf. No grief, you got plenty, they say, snotty like. Spike scratches his nut, wondering how to handle this. His two blokes are in the van jawing with the pilot. And they don't carry pieces. Guns aren't used much in their circle, leave that to the Yanks and Canucks from the Wild West, like inna pictures.

"What's he do? Spike shrugs. Do well in Drury Lane, wouldn't he? All the time using his noggin till he gets an idea. Seems to go along, takes his split five thousand short and says, can't argue with you gents, not wif that in yer hands. Right, I'll send my mates to set out the flares. Crate's turned round ready to go. The pilot can warm her up. You gents wait here outa the rain. We'll see you on your way, nice doing business with you bastards, the colonel, he'd of played it straight. Listen, says the Canadian, you made plenty out of our deals, this was just a bonus. New game, sport, bets off. And don't get ideas. You'll never find us. So get cracking.

"The pilot goes to do his check, him being solo he has to set it up himself. Spike wanders over and has a word with the lads. They go out in their macs and place the flares. He goes back to the saloon, bows his lackey act and waves 'em to the plane, wishes 'em a bong voyage. His lads take out them wedges under the wheels as they always do. Spike tells me it's one thing when they come in to land, wing slats bring her down quiet-like inna steep dive, but taking off, its big engine makes one helluva racket. So's not to wake every bleeding village inna county, they lift her off fast as they can. Off it goes, but not for long."

"Something went wrong."

"Too true. The plan was, see, they'd move the flares, aim the plane at this big ditch onna edge of the field. It'd nosedive inna mud, Spike and his boys they'd pick up the swag and disappear like greased monkeys. He reckons they'd be wracked up pretty bad, easy marks. Spike and crew would lift the cases and disappear. Them officers, wot'd they do, if still alive? They'd be up against the whole damn underworld, as you call it, wouldn't they? Odds on they'd be in for a lotta grief trying to explain to you lot how come they're over here inna old crate up nowhere in a field. And Spike has other landing spots around he can use again. Too bad about the pilot, RAF bloke like they was. Well, if he wanted to earn a few shekels doin that kinda work, up to him, innit? Anyway, Spike calculates he's in the clear no matter wot happens, those chaps were outa the picture one way or t'other. He'd have the whole bleeding stash. We'd be in clover, maybe Spain."

"We? You're in dreamland, Loretta. What makes you think Spike'd ever take you? His number one is up in Hampstead. You owe him nothing. Come on, what happened?"

"Hampstead? Yer leading me on, aincha? Dirty double—Awright, the way he tells it, the pilot tries to clear the ditch and trees, but the old crate has fixed wheels, see? It clears the ditch, not enough lift, bloody thing goes crashing into stands of big fat oaks. Wing shears off, damn thing blows up, no survivors, too hot to get anywhere near, and anyways nothing in those cases would be coming outa that wreck except maybe, Spike allows, some diamonds, but there's no way he can wait till it cools off what with a ball of fire seen for miles even in the rain and dark. All that's left is the five he has in his pocket."

A sergeant from the map room was summoned to raise the Essex county police, probably already on the scene of a strange fireball down a country lane. Contact Northholt RAF, surely with their ten-centimetre radar they must've picked up something, maybe not if the Lysander had hedgehopped in. Find out if the Essex police have IDs on the bodies, send a CID team up there.

"Spike arrives back here with his five, not ten, let alone thousands more burnt up inna crash. When he told me I lost my nut."

"The girl," interrupted Horobbins. "Where is she?"

"Wot girl?"

Down the hall they confronted Straw Spike, baggy-eyed and in raspy menace hinting that Loretta Oberon might expect a truncated life span if he ever got his hands on her again.

"Not on. You're up for murder, three blokes in the plane, committed with malice and intent to kill, let alone possession of ill-gotten gains. Then we have the Canadian army girl. If she's dead you're up to four counts. If she's alive, abduction and involuntary confinement. Number five: you topped the Canadian colonel, the brains of the outfit, set him up in Aldershot. You paid somebody there to do it, didn't you? Feel that rope yet? They make it quick, Spike, the way they put weights on the feet, you drop through the trap like a stone."

"I want my wig. You can't fit me up for the colonel bloke."

"In good time. Why not save expense before you ring him? Now let's review the facts, then we'll take a statement."

"That bint in there, she's lakes, barmy. Don't believe nuffin she blabbed."

"Suppose we begin again."

No stranger to interrogation, Horobbins chafed at the slow unfolding gavotte, every moment a death sentence for Claire Evans, if she wasn't already. A cooling of the earlier rhetoric, the English voices dropped into softer, deeper tones as though both accusers and accused were having an earnest discussion about the finer points of a cricket match. He wanted to yell: where is she? But he became reconciled to the long convoluted ritual that would force Spike into concessions that might lead both parties to an accommodation of sorts. One thing that stuck with Horobbins was Spike's defiant, puzzled denial of having topped that colonel chap in Aldershot, part of his litany of innocence, including the charred Lysander now confirmed by the Essex police. Yet oddly, when it came to the killing of the Duke, he was more vehement, swearing absolutely no connection. Why would I? He was my bread and butter.

Bollock circled, threw out temptation in the form of emergent mercy. If the girl is still alive, it might help to save your skin, Spike, the other charges could be reduced to manslaughter or ferocious wounding, the aftermath of thieves falling out. The pilot of the Lysander is another matter. We'd have to think about that one. Any idea who he was or where he came from? Then there's receiving stolen property and currency. You understand there could be alternatives to be explored? If we work together on it and you also fit up your associates for us, we may be able to spare you from the rope. I can't promise, but you think about it.

And, bless him, Horobbins realized as the cards fell into place, Spike sized up the odds of swinging, how it could, just possibly, be converted to a bird, a prison sentence with the prospects of ultimate escape or leniency from the soppy wets who would soon be running the next Labour government. He took a deep breath, possibly exhaling dubious remorse about her, and told them, as far as he knew, the girl would be still alive if they moved smartly. He would show them. Horobbins grabbed a phone to ring Colonel Cameron who promised an ambulance, medics, and outriders, and perhaps himself. The latter possibly not a good idea under the circumstances, Horobbins at his tactful best—suggest you wait until she's in hospital, assuming she is still alive.

The light outside in the hallway of the warehouse was dim, nothing more than one yellow bulb, but to Claire Evans it was blinding. The iron door groaned open and the electric torches beamed around the dark nooks until they formed a halo around her white face. Her arms twitched as she scratched. For the first time she reached out to her tormentors, the provost captain, the Scotland Yard inspector, and her own Captain Williams looming in the doorway. She was lifted gently off the palette and taken across the hall into the room where her captors had jeered at her naivety, and in so doing had buried Lieutenant Colonel Ambrose Wellesley forever with her misplaced love for him. She started and had to be supported when she saw one of her abductors was still there, the beefy Englishman with the spiked blonde hair. He seemed strangely relieved to find her alive. Now her captain took her into her arms, her solid embrace somehow unwelcome. They seated her once again on the greasy chesterfield, and it was the provost captain who held the cup of water to her lips. He seemed so pleased to see her, his swarthy features so lit up; his brown eyes moist, she almost felt a pang of affection for him. But not for long.

25

"Coming up in the world, are we?"

"Todder's staff car. Drove it myself, too many big ears around. Colonel Cameron has summoned him to London for a working over in the Sun Life vaults."

"About time. Wheels of justice grind slow, eh? At least they took care of that dumb bastard in Italy. Took long enough."

A hefty cargo for the Dakota that flew them into RAF Farnborough, the two provost officers, massive in breadth and matching cynicism, exuded unaccustomed warmth to Horobbins. On a short leash after the London debacle, he had been ordered to remain in Aldershot while the two mountains would be sent to him from Germany, both of them eager to unload their frustrations onto one of their own in an official capacity sanctioned by the front office. At last they could fill in the blanks in the stripped dossier, their accusations buried by the reluctance of upper echelons to besmirch those fine officers. Now their findings were welcomed in the context of unsolved murder, three others thought to be solved, and a squalid abduction.

Here they were: Captain Jeff Hagstrom of fabled Number One Provost Company, the originals drawn from the Mounties back in 1939. A former RCMP sergeant, he had endured two years in Sicily and Italy with First Div, then to Holland where he became witness to a strange convoy and who, upset and suspicious, had conveyed his worries to Captain Alfred (Alf) Murphy, currently in the Special Investigations Unit in the newly formed Occupation Force HQ near Oldenburg. Following up on Hagstrom's sighting, Murphy had dogged the case against the Duke, Todder, and two others, until ordered to channel his energies to escorting German prisoners, from whence he had at last been extracted by London entreaties to follow up on two officers unexpectedly cremated in England, their fireproof ID discs intact in the smouldering wreckage of the Lysander amid a blizzard of strewn diamonds.

When Horobbins contacted him on the phone, Murphy spoke in a low rasp as if he was being watched, and filled him in on the stir the news had made around the new headquarters in its tongue-twister location of Bad Zwischenahn. His boss, Colonel Tyrell, had marched him in to make the report to Major General Chris Vokes, recently arrived to take command of the Canadian Army Occupation Force.

"Vokes snarls he's losing more officers after the war than during. Had no recollection of Major Lefebvre. 'Get his personnel records from Second Echelon in Lemgo. Who'll write to the bereaved, if any? Me? Not bloody likely. The man was up to no good.' Sent us off to the British Army of the Rhine HQ where we attended on Brigadier Charles who'd received word about Colonel Yates. 'Sammy? Mixed up in what?' Hauled in his senior red cap, a full colonel, who clucked and tutted and allowed a certain Captain Affleck had pursued inquiries in Antwerp and Brussels that might have relevance. 'Then who popped off your colonel in Aldershot?' Had to admit we didn't know yet, but likely there was a connection. I told them I had worked with Affleck in May when we investigated the suspicious death of a Corporal Timchuk and related matters. Where was Affleck now? In Austria, it turned out, big game hunting for art treasures and missing gold around Linz and Salzburg. We're trying to reach him, I was assured."

Hagstrom was over six feet, as cop-like as Bollock, fleshy jowls, bulbous nose, and opaque eyes that have seen everything. Murphy, in his late thirties, came from the Canadian Pacific Railway police in Montreal, hence his rapid posting into SIU work. Wider than the ex-Mountie, puffy cheeks, dense eyebrows, he would be at home tossing hobos from a boxcar.

They drove to Ramillies barracks, site of the Mob Control Centre now being dismantled as the miscreants were shuffled off to awaiting fates. Horobbins didn't want them anywhere near the scene of the crime. Major (Spotted Dick) Clancy, senior provost officer on deck, had been ordered to drop his paperwork to attend the meeting. He was joined by Major Balfour, a natty member of the Assistant Deputy Judge Advocate General's staff from downtown. Detective Sergeant Fisher represented Bollock who was still embroiled in paperwork and recriminations in London. As much as he would have wished him there, Horobbins had other followup priorities for Pearly Gates. Jugs of lukewarm mild and bitter, the inevitable Spam sandwiches, and a tea urn supported the effort. Clancy greeted his two old pals from the Continent.

"How're things over there?"

Hagstrom pointed. "The Dutch beer's better than that swill."

"Welcome to the victors. England's blown the wad. Rations cut again, no poop or good beer left."

"You oughta see the Jerries," Murphy said. "In the ruins, stinking scarecrows, empty bellies, you know what they're doing? Cleaning bricks and numbering them. Don't kid yourself, they'll be back sooner than anyone thinks."

"Not for another war, surely."

"No way, you know them: at your feet or at your throat. It'll be the Russkis. You oughta see what they're up to. Brutal."

"Okay, for the benefit of everyone here, Hugh here will recap events to date. Then why don't you enlighten us, Jeff?"

Hagstrom sizes up his suspects and finds them wanting when it comes to the inside dope on the Dutch relief exercise in the spring. His audience, eager enough it seems, consists of one aged civilian, a spiffy major with no campaign ribbons, and his two provost colleagues from Britain who hadn't been there. He picks up the nod from Murphy.

"How much time we got? Start-line okay with you guys?"

Waves of assent spur him on, at least for now.

It begins, Hagstrom tells them, with the old sweats, First and Fifth Divs up from Italy. "D-Day Dodgers," they call us, as if it was a picnic down there. Back with the Canadian army at last, First Corps, we're ordered to clear Fortress Holland in the west. By mid-April, when we take Apeldoorn, we get some idea what's happening to the Dutch people. We don't even shell the town, it's full of some 80,000 starving refugees and locals. Terrible sight those weak, trembling kids, eyes popping out of their heads, bellies distended. We feed them everything we can, but I'll never forget them begging while we gobble our rations. We finally move our cookhouse far out of town.

What it goes back to is the botched Arnhem airdrop last September. "Market Garden" they called it. Only harvest was those sitting duck paratroops. Now the Dutch, they're stubborn if not suicidal. Seeing the sky filled with parachutes, they figure the war'd soon be over. To nudge it along they go out on a railroad strike. This Kraut governor, Reichskommisar Seyss-Inquart, one of their prize thugs, an Austrian waltz king no less, decides to teach them a lesson on real power. He lays down an embargo on food for the western cities, Amsterdam, The Hague, Utrecht, Rotterdam. The farms are in the east, you see.

The Dutch government in exile in London gets the wind up. Over three and a half million people face starvation. We hear they're eating tulip bulbs, cats, dogs, and horses, and looting, selling off precious belongings, jewels and such for food. Twenty-first Army Group is handed the problem. They stockpile supplies in Antwerp, but there's no way of getting them in.

Despite the hungry civilians, we had mixed feelings about the Dutch. They had made a great resistance effort, but we took casualties out of Omersfoot up against the 34th ss Division Nederland and their collaborators. Tough going. Some of those bastards never made it to POW cages.

By the end of April we've pushed on past Nijkerk to the Grebbe line, old Dutch fortifications the Germans reinforced. We caught our breath and waited. On our left under command was the Brits' 49th Division, West Riding—the Westies. Tough little buggers you don't want to take on in a pub. We'd worked with them through Holland, at Nijmegan bridge and so forth. So the Brits and us sit there waiting on the rumours flying around. The Jerries were about to flood the entire area, blow up the huge sluice gates. They're rounding up Dutch resistance in the cities and killing them off. Eisenhower dithered. Despite pressure from the Dutch in London, he didn't want to divert resources from the buildup for the north Rhine crossing. Then word came down the Jerries were ready to deal. By 19 April we were told to stand down, stay on alert, don't move. We tried to dry out our socks.

Finally realizing the human tragedy about to unfold, Eisenhower changed his mind. He agreed to respond to Seyss-Inquart's overtures, contrary to Allied policy—as you well know, no truck or trade with the enemy, unconditional surrender only.

By 28 April we heard contact had been made with the Germans, a shaky agreement reached for a ceasefire on our front, a temporary truce. A corridor was mapped out north of the Waal. The Jerries agreed to food and fuel convoys and airdrops, and in return they'd stop opening the dykes. First Canadian Corps was geared up to deliver over a thousand tons of food a day to be supplied by 21st Army Group in Antwerp. You can guess how stretched we were, running traffic control and such.

Never before had I seen such pride, the feeling we were doing something good for a change, mixed with churning guts that the Jerries might renege. Virtually unarmed Service Corps lorries, loaded with food, while the Jerries at their guns in those coal scuttle helmets, watching, their fingers on the trigger for any treachery on our part. Strict orders came down not to show weapons or make any gestures, like giving them the finger.

On the second of May the first convoy moved into enemy lines: thirty vehicles every half hour, twelve transport platoons of three hundred and sixty lorries stretched out to the food depots set up near the towns and cities. There were basically three columns heading towards Utrecht, Amsterdam, and The Hague. Canal boats and railways delivered to Rotterdam from Antwerp. Aircraft dropped supplies. It was magnificent, the lives we saved; I think we won the hearts of the suffering Dutch forever.

Now we come to it. I'd taken myself up in an Air OP Auster, usually spotters for the guns. We had sporadic radio contact with the lead Jeeps and our own provost. The pilot, an artillery captain, was a trifle edgy, didn't trust the Jerries. We'd be cold meat. Registering enemy targets since Falaise, he didn't relish some damn fool on the ground bringing him down now. In fact, he admitted, his most perilous flight was last August over the Falaise road when the RAF dropped its load onto our own troops. He went up and flew right into their formations, waggling his wings, pointing, firing off Verey flares, to no avail. Damn near got myself chopped up in their props, he says.

As we flew over the sodden land it reminded me of the flooded plains of the Po Valley, blinding reflections when the sun came out. The convoys were strings of toys on narrow bands of asphalt. When we caught a balls-up down there, the pilot would cut the engine and glide over while I tried to sort out the blockages or breakdown. If no radio contact, I'd make hand signals, yell at them, or drop messages wrapped in shell casings I had the foresight to bring along. Generally, though, it went smartly. Those drivers, they were real pros, kept it moving. The way it worked, depots had been agreed to at various locations where the civil authorities would collect and record the deliveries, then on trucks fuelled and supplied by us, civilians hauled the goods to the towns and cities and handled distribution.

Late in the day on the second of May we flew over the Brits, the 49th

Westies. On the river we saw tugs and barges bringing supplies to Rotterdam. Then I noticed something not quite right. On the Rotterdam highway out of Wageningen I picked up a small convoy of just eight vehicles, seemingly apart from the others and nowhere near one of the approved transfer depots. In fact, it was way beyond the zone where our convoys stopped and the Dutch authorities took over. Instead of a Jeep, a staff car led them, one of ours with a white star on the roof.

My pilot cut the motor to come in silently over them. I went through my roster and couldn't find ID for this group. We turned around towards a battalion HQ strip behind the Westies. I fired off a Verey, and they cleared off vehicles to let us land. We saw running figures. Apparently the descent of an Auster, engine off, has the same whistling sound as an incoming mortar bomb. The Tommies assumed the Jerries had opened up. I took my maps and lists in to the adjutant in a tent and described what we had seen.

"Yes, I believe they passed through. Small party, what, only eight or so vehicles." He tapped the map with a malacca cane. "Something amiss?"

"They could be free-lance; don't fit into any authorized ops. You recall anything about them?"

"Not really. Don't remember seeing them myself. Hold on." He went over to the signaler at his radio set to give him instructions. Shortly, a provost lieutenant, one of their red caps, drove up in a Jeep.

"Thought they were ours," he reported. "Our Service Corps vehicles, staff car from 21st Group. The johnny in charge was one of yours, a half colonel, a major with him. Rather high-priced help, I thought, for such a small party, but then it could've been a recce of some sort."

"He give his name?"

"Didn't ask, I'm afraid. Very self-assured, tall, pointed nose. His major seemed Sandhurst; well turned out for one of your lot."

"Did he say where they were going?"

"No, we assumed they were off to the nearest transfer point."

"We spotted them far beyond the authorized sector. Seems they're into forbidden territory on the way to Rotterdam."

"You want us to chase them up?"

"No, too dicey. We'll track them, but if they do come back anywhere along your lines, would you hold them till we get in touch?"

"Sir, we're up to our eyeballs moving the convoys back and forth."

"How many are led by a staff car from Group wandering out of bounds?"

"You have the screed, Quinn. Assist when you can," said the adjutant.

"Very well, sir. You have a wireless in your kite? Right, leave your call sign with the signaler here, net in with us if you can. I'll be in touch if they show up. Whether I can hold a senior officer, I'm not sure on what grounds."

"Neither am I. Use your imagination."

At that moment we almost blew the truce. Back at the plane the pilot was glumly fingering two holes in the single wing.

"Goddam Krauts, small arms fire."

The adjutant swore and ran back to issue a stand-to alert. Troops who'd been lounging around headed for slit trenches. I tried to cool down the adjutant and his CO, a lieutenant colonel, when they made noises about calling in their company commanders to set things in motion.

"Sir, we must be careful not to over-react," I said. "I'm going up to have another look-see. Maybe it wasn't the Jerries."

"What d'you mean?"

"It's just possible someone from the convoy took a pot shot at us when we glided over them."

"Good God, what for? If you see anything come back and report."

At the plane I asked the pilot if we could fly.

"Sure. Had much worse."

We caught up to the small convoy and kept well behind it. Below we could see a clump of enemy on the road watching us, perhaps wondering what to do about military vehicles beyond the point of no return. Or, on the alert themselves, someone may have heard the shots. I couldn't make out if any of their weapons were aimed at us. So far the ceasefire was holding. But for how much longer?

At a crossroads east of Rotterdam, the city clearly visible, the vehicles turned off onto a road leading north, where they stopped outside what appeared to be a one-storey factory or warehouse. Once again I checked the coordinates on the Ordnance map and the overlay of grease-pencil markings for the authorized drops. Not there. Several trucks were parked nearby, obviously waiting. Men in coveralls rushed out to unload cartons, but instead of taking them into the building to be duly inventoried, they passed them along to be loaded into the vehicles. No enemy in evidence, yet. Their curiosity must have been stirred. Instead, a couple of armed men kept a few salivating locals at bay. What was this caper?

In full view we circled. The two officers outside the staff car bared white faces at us and tried to wave us off. By that time we were low on fuel and had to turn back. At First Div outside of Nijkerk I got on the blower to the SIU at Army in Eindhoven. Fortunately I patched into Alf here who heard me out and, I guess knowing who I was—that is, not apt to get my balls in a knot over some trivial snafu—said he'd make inquiries. I told him I couldn't hang around, had to return to my herding tasks over the main convoys. He asked me to call him back when I could.

The fact we had two bullet holes in our aircraft spurred you on. Right, Alf?

26

Prompted by tales of the starving Dutch, the assembly refueled on Spam sandwiches, ignored the tea for the mild and bitter at approximately the same temperature. Except for Horobbins, they lit cigarettes and waited for the enormous Murphy to clear his mouth and memory. When he began it seemed he had lost his bookmark, but with curiosity outgunning impatience, they slowly came to see where he was leading them. He began with diamonds.

Yes, diamonds, says Captain Alf Murphy with a nod to Horobbins. Your poor Quack gal tells of cut diamonds in a Spam tin at the colonel's love nest. Swine before pearls, eh? And a security deposit key. And diamonds glittering in the mud and wreckage of the Lizzie in Essex, little fortunes for the locals or the constabulary. What's that point to? Only one place: Antwerp. The story begins and ends in Antwerp, which today is restored as the leading diamond centre in Europe, the wartime hoards disgorged, the South Africa pipeline up and running, the surviving Jews trickling back since last fall. Now Van Eycklei Street and the exchange on Pelikaanstraat are going full tilt. Curious business—deals for millions sealed with a handshake. And there's a link there with our dearly departed racketeers, if you'll bear with me.

So last September when we take Antwerp, near normalcy prevails: booze, women, dances at the hotels, even ice cream in plentiful supply. No evidence of starvation. The Jerries sulk over in Merzem. The White Brigade, the Belgian Resistance in their strange white butchers' coats, clear the docks. There it is, the one big port we need for the buildup into Germany—miles of slips, warehouses, cranes, dry docks, the whole shooting match captured intact. But, as you know, there's one big catch. Antwerp is some fifty miles inland on the Scheldt. Instead of attending to his knitting, Montgomery gets wet dreams of a carpet of airborne opening the way to Germany. Result: Arnhem. Our failure to clear the banks of the Scheldt Estuary when the enemy was in disarray is one of the worst crimes perpetuated on our boys. When the brass finally woke up after the airdrop disaster, big surprise: the Jerries once again had recovered, flooded, and fortified both banks of the Scheldt and Walcheren Island. That little lapse in concentration cost us over 6,500 men, not counting British or others.

The Germans weren't slow to latch onto the strategic value of Antwerp. The objective of their Ardennes offensive in December was Antwerp, and God help us if they had broken through. By October the nice civilized place we had liberated in September was blasted into a shambles by some four thousand flying bombs and V-2 rockets pouring into the area until the end of March this year. I've seen estimates of over three thousand civilians killed, countless wounded. More crucial, many dockworkers were killed or wounded. And, no doubt, you've heard about the Rex Theatre. The city was declared out of bounds except for units employed there, such as Second Echelon, which eventually moved out. All of this is the backdrop to the Wellesley-Todder extravaganza as it unfolded in the grip of temptations only a fool would ignore, at least to their way of thinking.

Anyway, enemy resistance ends on Walcheren by the eighth of November after terrible cost to both sides. But it takes three weeks for the navy to clear the mines planted in the estuary. Not until the 28th of November does the first convoy enter the port. We're rightly pissed off. No Canadians who made it possible are invited to the ceremony. Despite the rockets, tons of stores are landed. We can see the end of the war is within our grasp, but having seen the ability of the Germans to bounce back, we fear it'll be longer than the bloody optimists at Allied high command predict.

Then we come to April and the other big buildup for Dutch relief. As Jeff says, the truce is worked out and the army turns into a humane agency.

Where's the base for all this? Brigadier Smith, Deputy Director Supply and Transport, sets up his HQ in Antwerp. And who comes into the picture? None other than our two friends Wellesley and Todder. Major General Burns, commanding Canadian Section, First Echelon, 21st Army Group in Brussels, sends the two to Antwerp allegedly to help coordinate the supply drop. Later, when we're tracking them down, we find Todder spends most of his time at the Excelsior Hotel imbibing Advocat and chatting up the local talent. Wellesley, as befits his rank, is ensconced in the Century Hotel. They operate out of a warehouse on the docks. Once the rocket attacks stop at the end of March, it's clover for them. And, as I found out, they work closely, if that's the right way to describe their crimes, with one Lieutenant Colonel Yates, a Brit, and his aide, a Canadian major named Lefebvre. Ring a bell? Instead of an abiding compassion for the Dutch, they have other things on their little minds, as we were to find out.

When Jeff here briefed me on the suspicious convoy outside Rotterdam I had visions of the whole damn ceasefire coming apart. First thing I did was report to the Deputy Provost Marshal to warn him one of our spotter planes had been fired on and the Westies were standing to. After some delay I managed to scare up Major Bigelow, in charge of our transport for the "Faust" relief operation, as it was called. Taken aback, he wasn't too receptive to any more aggro, yet his curiosity was sufficient for him to take time to check his own rosters and maps, and soon was back on the line.

"Haven't the foggiest what you're talking about. Yes, we have Brit vehicles, but I can't trace this lot. Why in hell would a staff car from Group be leading a string of vehicles beyond the designated drop line? Why don't you go ahead and track it down? Whatever you do, don't stir up the Krauts. This thing's dodgy enough."

Right. The obvious way to find out in a hurry was to invoke the NBS, Nederlanse Binnenlandse Strijdkrackten, Dutch internal fighting forces with their orange armbands. I sought out their chief liaison officer, one self-styled Colonel van Rijn, obviously a *nom de guerre*, a huge blonde with an eye patch. I had worked with him before on the touchy matter of sorting out collaborators. Finding he had relocated to Apeldoorn, I signaled ahead, laid on a Jeep and took hours to cover the short distance. Those European countries are peanuts compared to home, but with the traffic I began to wish I'd taken a Triumph motorbike. Found him in a fine whitewashed house he described as once the abode of an "evacuated" Nazi sympathizer. His English, with its glottal shadings, was colloquial. Several of his menacing aides stood around in the pastel living room with its Vermeer prints while I outlined the problem. They became very angry, muttered to themselves. I told them I needed intelligence soonest, but could not myself venture beyond the truce line.

"Righto," says Colonel van Rijn, his English that of the mother tongue, as he agreed to send some people up there. I gave the map coordinates, and left them to their planning while I went to find a billet in Apeldoorn, and waited overnight listening to the gears of the convoys moving through. The next morning, the third of May, I went back to the house.

What the underground could lay on was truly amazing. The previous day, two of their number from Rotterdam donned Grun Polizie uniforms, the Green Police, Nazi stooges, and in a purloined official car drove to the site. By the time they got there the factory was deserted, except for one lone truck along the road, a breakdown apparently. Two men in coveralls who were fiddling with the motor quickly put up their hands under the guns of the bogus police. Inside the lorry they found cartons, opened a couple to find sulfa drugs, morphine ampoules, and the like. The two men were known to the Resistance as petty criminals involved in the black market. What happened to them, I didn't ask. The NBS men fixed the lorry and drove it to one of their safe houses near the city.

Before taking care of the two criminals they interrogated them, rather harshly I suspect. It appears the staff car and empty army vehicles had long since departed, wouldn't be back. Yes, there had been two Canadian officers and their driver. The Tommies in the lorries seemed to have no idea what was going on, assumed it was part of the act of mercy. No, the enemy had not stopped them.

Then I remembered what Jeff had told me about alerting the British provost. When I managed to reach Jeff on the ground in front of the Loyal Edmontons, he gave me instructions on how to net in with the red caps down the line. Finally raised the lieutenant he had talked to. Yes, the lieutenant confirmed, the staff car and empty lorries had passed back through their lines late the previous day. He had stopped the car for a supposedly routine check. The two officers in the back seat were shirty, refused to show their credentials and, outranking him, told him they were headed back to Antwerp, urgent mission of mercy, had to pick up another load. The young lieutenant relented, but before letting them go, he ordered their driver to step out while he checked his Standing Orders. Much grumbling from the back seat, but they really couldn't stop him. The driver was a corporal in our Service Corps assigned to the colonel. Obviously intimidated by the growls from behind him inside the car, he refused to divulge names, but we do have his, one Corporal Orest Timchuk, and the vehicle's registration. I thanked the red cap for his diligence, who added, considering the turnaround time every half hour, he did note that particular convoy never returned. Made only the one drop, apparently.

Now I realized I was in over my head and would need some heavy backing to follow up on this one. Like Jeff, I've kept carbons of my reports; be my guest if you want to transcribe them. In sum I wrote down every detail, including verification from the Dutch resistance, and requested assistance to identify the two officers from Group. Needless to say, harried as they were with other more pressing matters, our superiors, if that's the right way to describe 'em, were not too pleased with my allegations. No big deal, I was told, go do something useful. My report was swallowed up in the maw. I went back to more routine tasks, and nothing more was heard.

Until the body of Corporal Orest Timchuk was hauled out of the Neder Rijn.

27

So there I am, Murphy continues, babysitter at a POW cage in a demeaning argument about rations with a jeezly SS officer, nine foot tall maybe, right out of the movies, eye patch and scar, him in snazzy grey duds groomed for a Nazi rally. Outside of Amersfoot, we were, a fitting name for the long shanks' mare the Germans would face to plod their way, escorted by Three Provost, back to a devastated Third Reich. They had surrendered in Holland on the fifth of May, and I don't know if you've heard this before, but we had to allow some Jerry units to keep their weapons as protection from Dutch revenge. Anyway, this ss officer, he can't believe they'd lost the war to a bunch of amateurs. Nor can we, I says to meself. In good English he made the pitch that we were now allies, soon to fight side by side against the Red hordes. I remembered only too well what the ss had done to our guys over Caen way, and kicked him out.

The messenger from Colonel van Rijn grinned and came in. Could I come to Rotterdam immediately? Not a prayer, I answered, until I saw the colonel's note. The body of a bludgeoned Canadian soldier had been found floating in the harbour. Our MPs on the scene found no ID tags, but had located inside his battledress blouse a soggy letter from home addressed to a Corporal Orest Timchuk.

At length I managed to raise Major Clark in Eindhoven and read him the riot act as best as I could to my straw boss. Yes, he could confirm the body had been found, an officer from Eleven Provost, in Rotterdam to assist civil affairs, was on the scene.

"Why wasn't I told? It's the corporal in my report."

"Hadn't made the connection," he admitted. Had anyone read my report? "Stand by till I get back to you." Before he signed off I could hear him yelling for the file. The Dutch messenger went off to the mess to stoke up on our rations. Much to my surprise, Major Clark was back to me inside an hour.

"Sorry about that, Alf, we weren't on top of it. It appears the corporal had severe trauma to his head and went into the drink upstream. ID tags missing, he floated down, got snagged on some wreck, was found by the Dutch. An ambulance has been sent to remove the body to the nearest field hospital for autopsy. I've cleared with the Deputy Provost Marshal it's an SIU case. Very suspicious. You're in charge of the investigation. We've asked Second Echelon for the corporal's records. You are to report to British military police in Antwerp. Your contact is a Captain Affleck, your counterpart on the scene. May be a bit chaotic, but do what you can. Turn over to your Two IC and be on your way."

On the way to Antwerp with two of my NCOs, we crept along behind, beside, within convoys, up and down Maple Leaf route. Almost dark by the time we made our way through the suburbs to the waterfront where the "Faust" relief exercise was still under way. That's where I first met Reg Affleck.

The British provost captain had cleared our entry and laid on billets, my two men in makeshift quarters in a warehouse, me upstairs over a nearby café on the Flemish-speaking side of the street. Obviously a former cop, Affleck was burdened with a Midland accent, had button eyes, and seemed out of shape with flab acquired in the fleshpots. Was not looking forward to the imminent move to Bad Salzuflen in occupied Germany. The two of us repaired to the café on the ground floor.

"Your findings concur with my own," Affleck told me. "A pattern emerges. We were already investigating leakage of medical supplies and other stores. The Belgian resistance informed us of diversions organized by local spivs with inside-army contacts, not all of lower rank by any means. Diamond smuggling is back in full flower. I turned my lads, few as they are, onto tracking the transport and stores manifests. Over protests from the pooh-bahs I confiscated some requisitions that caught our eye—little anomalies, such as no precise points of delivery, small numbers of transport, senior officers often the escort. Most related to medical stores. Boffins at the storage depots maintained the work orders were kosher, but the penny dropped when we noted it was the same four senior officers who appeared in person or signed for the loadings. My sergeant obtained descriptions we then matched with the requisitions and work orders for vehicles from the motor pool. Same signatures, they were apparently too careful or too arrogant to indulge in forgeries that might have aroused suspicion. Four of them: three of yours, Lieutenant Colonel Wellesley, Major Todder, both from your Service Corps, liaison types at Canadian Section from Brussels, plus Major Lefebvre attached to one of ours, and Lieutenant Colonel Yates, liaison on stores allocations. Beautifully placed, weren't they?

"Then I'm afraid we were shuffled off on more urgent matters, such as traffic control. I suspect our famous four got wind of our snooping and complained upstairs. Until your corporal, Colonel Wellesley's driver, turns up dead—snuffed it seems—and your people seek our assistance pending your arrival.

"All I've managed to accomplish today was to interview the blokes at the motor pool. On the day he bogged off, Corporal Timchuk signed out a Jeep, the log shows authorizing officer as Major Todder. The vehicle has not been found. I sent off some of my chaps on a quick recce, but no trace. We don't have the time or gear to drag for it in the drink. We have made contact with the Belgian police, criminal investigation types, who're also trying to close down their racketeers. They speculate our four suspects must have set up contact with certain gangs, but again the *gendarmerie* is too stretched to lurk about and trace the movements of Allied officers. That's our job, we were told in no uncertain terms. However, some of their own villains under surveillance have been noted coming and going from the Excelsior and Century hotels. At the moment, local law enforcement is fully occupied with the robbery of one of the diamond merchants, a major haul, they tell me. Don't you have authority to search the quarters of your own officers? I didn't admit to him, no we don't, and in any case probably wouldn't find incriminating souvenirs stowed away in their kit bags."

The next morning, Murphy goes on, Captain Affleck and I attended on a major on Brigadier Smith's staff to receive our briefing. Stunned at our allegations, he kept us on ice while he conferred with the brigadier, the august personage himself apparently too busy or reluctant to become involved, enough on his plate without this. At length the major ushered us into a makeshift office where Wellesley and Todder had been ordered to wait.

What do you call him? The Duke? For sure majestic, glittering eyes and contemptuous air that made us feel guilty of something. Todder tried to look impressive, without result. As you'd imagine, we got nowhere. Everything in order, duly authorized as a special mercy mission to send in urgently needed medical supplies. A rush job, turned it over to the proper Dutch authorities. You can't trust those self-styled resistance fighters with the orange armbands. Don't be naïve, captain, without question it was the enemy who fired on the spotter plane. Its presence almost blew the entire truce. Your man and the pilot are the ones who should be on the mat, not us. On he went. You can guess the rest of it. I've been up against some tough customers, but this colonel, he was different, there was a kind of chill about him, not just class or upbringing looking down his nose at the lower elements; more of an outside presence beyond human intelligence that reduced the rest of us to moron or idiot level as we struggled to decipher the mockery of his eyes. He ragged us unmercifully. Yes, Corporal Timchuk was a loyal soldier, I have no idea what might've caused him to end his own life.

Reg Affleck, despite his humble Midlands origins, was not so easily intimidated by colonials with pretensions. "He was coshed, thrown into the river."

When Wellesley smirked and shrugged, Reg blew up. "You bloody well get around a lot for a chair warmer, sir. Regular whirlwind, aren't you, the major here and your two chums Yates and Lefebvre. Your Group records show an amazing series of jaunts to London on RAF transport. How did you obtain permission to justify your absence at a time of intense activity? What exactly were you doing?"

"Short breaks to recharge the batteries. Personal, not your concern."

"The many diversions of Brussels couldn't top up your batteries? Then, Major Todder, even more strangely, you apply for leave to Dublin in the Irish Republic, not aware apparently such travel was banned in 1944. Permission denied. For what purpose?"

"Stuff it up your—" Todder was cowed by a flick from his master, who informed us the interview was terminated. He would lodge complaints up the chain of command. Dismissed. Get lost. We did.

Outside the brigadier's office, Murphy tells them, his major handed me a signal just in from the personnel records section of Second Echelon.

"Corporal Timchuk's next of kin. Parents reside on a farm outside of Vegreville, Alberta. His brother, Sergeant Metro Timchuk, is with the Strathconas, Fifth Div, probably up in Delfzijl on the north coast of Holland. At least that's where they ended up. They're trying to reach him."

I took down the brother's details, while Reg Affleck went off to corner Yates and Lefebvre. It didn't take long for him to come back, stonewalled again, then, ever hopeful, he sent his men to interrogate the drivers and batmen attached to those two, without result, as it turned out. We speculated they had been paid off, perhaps indicating a miserly lapse on the part of the Duke when it came to Corporal Timchuk.

"How does this damn thing work, anyway?" I asked Affleck.

"Infinite variations. Their run up near Rotterdam must've been worth thousands, but no money would change hands on the site. There'd be dollars, sterling, or diamonds at a prearranged drop back here; they'd divvy up and one of them would look after safekeeping, false names, coded tallies, London, Brussels, even Dublin. And the sad truth is that we don't have the manpower for the round-the-clock surveillance you must have in cases like this. I'm sure you don't either."

Too true. We did manage, however, to interview some of the British lorry drivers who didn't have a clue there was anything crooked about their trek, just relieved to escape with skins intact. We located a bunkmate of Timchuk's when we picked up his kit, and he told us his pal had seemed down in the mouth on his return. Timchuk had signed out a Jeep around 2000 hours, never to be seen again or noticed in the traffic passing the checkpoints beyond Wagingen. Major Todder had insisted his own signature was a forgery. Sure. Was Timchuk about to blow the whistle? Was he chased along the riverside highway? By whom? Or, as we mused, was he angry at no share in the loot, or wanted a bigger cut?

We were never to find out.

What finally sank me, Murphy tells them, was the medical examiner who did the autopsy. Overloaded, exhausted, sloppy, who can say? His report was ambiguous. Yes, the man had severe head injuries sufficient to render him unconscious, but they could be equally consistent with him driving the Jeep full throttle into the river. He could have removed his ID tags if he had planned suicide, equally, he could have been struck on his forehead, breaking his nose with resultant frontal fractures. There was water in his lungs. No alcohol in evidence. Unless we retrieve the vehicle for forensic examination the cause of death must remain inconclusive.

Still, I soldiered on, sent in my report calling for a Court of Inquiry. Guess what? With everything else going on—many more bodies, military and civilian to be accounted for—my request was buried somewhere and hasn't surfaced since. Wellesley must've had unbelievable contacts up the line. Interesting, though, they were quick to remove him and Todder from the scene. Foisted them onto Dan Spry at Aldershot. Lucky Dan.

"Steady on," said the dapper major from downtown. "General Spry is not 'Dan' to you. He had the highest regard for Colonel Wellesley. The whole screed is completely out of character."

"Somebody did him in, sir. For a reason."

"You're trying to tell us that a fine officer from a good, wealthy family in Montreal society, someone who didn't need to dabble in black markets for the money personally, among other things led an illegal shipment of drugs to Dutch racketeers?"

"Must've had a screw loose." Of equal rank, Dick Clancy could get away with it. "It may be circumstantial in a courtroom, but we've got enough to know he was up to his eyeballs."

"Still doesn't add up," said Major Balfour.

"Doesn't have to, sir." The ex-Mountie Hagstrom rumbled experience. "The fact he's from a privileged background, that he carried out his duties efficiently, has nothing to do with it. I've seen it before. Rich kids out for the thrills, consorting with underworld types for kicks. Not for them the prospect of battle with risk of personal injury. Another kind of gamble, more fun than cowering in the mud. Take those pampered bucks on their motorbikes tearing around Montreal sporting German helmets. In their own way it's a test of courage to defy those who are suckers enough to support the real war. Yeah, same thing."

"You have more to tell us Alf," Horobbins said.

"For sure. When I was briefed on the fry-up in Essex, we tried to track their movements, abandoned airstrips and the like from Germany or Holland. When I attempted to contact Reg Affleck with the good news, I was told he was away off in Austria investigating the disappearance of art treasures and gold—tons of it apparently purloined by senior Yank and Limey officers. In Werfen, south of Salzburg, a 'gold express' loaded with treasure was seized by the US Army. Found to be Nazi loot taken from the Jews. The leakage is stupendous, much of the stuff ending up in the sticky hands of at least five American generals and God knows how many other senior officers from the Allied forces. Made our guys seem like small beer. Still, they had obviously coined in enough swag to shoot the bundle, probably planned their own disappearance, but not the way it happened to three of them, anyway.

"Finally reached him in Vienna, occupied by Russians, Yanks, Brits, French, a snake pit of crime and intrigue. Despite his workload, the worst being forcible repatriation of Soviet POWs, Affleck found time to call for the personnel file of Colonel Yates. When I told him they'd found diamonds scattered through the Lizzie's wreckage, Affleck laughed. All set to do a bunk and assume a new identity somewhere, then send for his family. Family? I ask. Yes, his wife runs the Yates Jewellers shop on the north side of Lynchford Road, South Farnborough, a long-established row of shops to entice the troops. And he says, with some mischief, handy to your late Colonel Wellesley in North

Camp. Just pop over with a case full of diamonds or currency or whatever for Mrs. Yates to process, in addition to the deposits in London. The amount of loot must be staggering." Murphy pointed to Detective Sergeant Fisher. "Perhaps you might have a word with the Hants police and get warrants for banks in Aldershot. Bet they're cleaned out, already."

"Shop's probably intact," said Clancy. "The rioters did their damage in Aldershot."

On the departure of Fisher, Murphy waved a folder. "Before getting on the plane I was handed the personnel file of our late Major Lefebvre. And here, gentlemen, we find our own little diamond among the muck. A lady, no less."

Murphy paused to wet his whistle with mild and bitter, now almost at boiling point in the stuffy room, while the others gaped.

"Frederick Lefebvre, Les Fusiliers Mont-Royal, was divorced. His ex is one Elspeth Wellesley, sister of the late colonel. Freddy had no remaining ties to Montreal, was about to reinvent himself somewhere else, possibly Switzerland, in high style now that he had his brother-in-law's share. What does that tell us?"

"Unless he went for the whole kit and kaboodle, greed beyond belief, it's most unlikely he'd be involved in bumping off the Duke, his partner in crime." The others made noises of agreement.

Horobbins leafed through his own dossier. "She isn't listed as a next-of-kin. Todder must've known all along. We'll ask Canada House to send us the obits from the Montreal papers. How do you get a divorce in Quebec, anyway? Wasn't Lefebvre Catholic?"

Major Balfour was pleased to offer his legal expertise; after all, it is what he was paid for. "Divorce is within the jurisdiction of Parliament enacted by private bills that originate in the Senate, then to the Commons, and usually rubber stamped. We can find out the status of the Lefebvres, the grounds for divorce, who initiated it. Committee procedures are public record."

"Doesn't much matter now," said Clancy. "The only one left is Todder."

"He'll be replaced as acting CO immediately," said Balfour. "We'll send in one of ours."

"He's being worked over in London. What if he doesn't talk?"

"Probably won't," said Murphy. "But you may not need him."

"How come?"

Okay, stymied at every turn, Murphy tells them, I had decided to follow up on one last lead about Corporal Timchuk. I turned up at Goesbeek Cemetery in Holland for the corporal's burial, delayed by the botched autopsy, in the hope his brother would be brought in. He was. In his black beret and shabby Fifth Div garb he was tall, dark-featured, and steaming for vengeance, didn't believe for one minute it was any accident or suicide. I took him into town, sat him down for a beer or three, and frustrated and angry myself, I fear I told him more about what we thought had happened than I should've.

"Listen, I have to ask you. Did your brother ever send you money, or money and valuables home to your parents? Did he ever indicate to you anything about what was going on as he drove the colonel around?"

"Who, Orest? A straight arrow, if ever. No way. We never met over here; he was down in Brussels and Antwerp, I was up there. We didn't write much. He was dog's body for that goddam colonel. He did him in. Set him up with his gangster pals. I bet Orest, he was going to blow the whistle. That's what."

I backed up in a hurry. "We're not absolutely sure. It's circumstantial, if you get what I mean."

"What're you doing about it?"

"We're tracking down every possible lead, but with everything going on I can't promise we'll crack anything soon. That's the best I can do. Personally, I won't give up."

"Me neither," says Sergeant Timchuk. "Never thought I'd see the day I'd shake the hand of a cop, but I appreciate what you told me and what you've done."

That was my one and only meeting with the brother.

Horobbins asked: "Where is he now?"

"Far as I know, probably back in Canada. He may well've passed through here."

"You realize how many T-Ones are floating around? Thousands of 'em, coming and going since the disturbances."

"Tell me about it," groaned Dick Clancy, his floorwalker starch wilting.

The major from downtown fixed on Horobbins.

"Captain, get cracking."

Seasoned as he was as a former prison guard, Pearly Gates was perplexed by

190

the code of silence he couldn't shake loose in the interviews Horobbins had assigned.

"They seem resigned to old age in Aldershot," Gates said.

"Drop it for now. We've got another one. Put the entire clerical staff on it. We want to find out when a Sergeant Metro Timchuk, Strathconas, most likely passed through here or is still around. Go find him."

28

It was a snap to get in, up the steps through the Victorian portico with its tall pillars, into the entrance hall of the Connaught Military Hospital. Cinch, this far. Show fake pass to meatheads at checkpoints, walk along Duke of Connaughts Road. Guys tossing a ball around outside Blenheim, sunbathers flaked out near Malplaquet while sweltering MPs gawk enviously. Then Ramillies, their so-called Mob Control Centre, scene of yesterday's bull session, staff cars parked, offsite, secret, as if we wouldn't find out. Over there the mean, ugly walls of the Limey detention barracks, the Glass House, to be avoided at any cost. Brits drilling for the Far East outside Tournay barracks, poor dopes off to another war, lot worse than the one just over. On the hill over on the right the Garrison Church where they held that joke of a memorial service for our beloved CO. They haven't decided what to do with his corpse, maybe still on ice at the Cambridge. Good.

Old duffer in navy blue, First War ribbons, at reception desk. Half asleep, sees familiar uniform, falls for it that X-ray plates are inside large envelope, and gives directions to the lab. Casually: have mail for Sergeant Metro Timchuk. Leave it with nursing sister on second floor, end of corridor, take lift over there. High ceilings, long halls, broad windows, spacious, unhurried care of the afflicted. Canadians often here till D-Day last year when the whole shebang crossed the Channel as Number Eight Canadian General Hospital. Spooky, except for muffled coughs and hacks from the wards.

Jackpot. Nobody at nursing station. He's in an almost empty ward, the others spread well apart behind drawn curtains. How contagious is this jaundice anyway? What'd they call it: hepatitis? There isn't any mail for Timchuk. Yellow papery skin, caved in cheeks, opens eyes with glint of frail hostility, but not for long. Have to whisper into a jug ear, even though the other inmates seem out of hearing, can't take any more chances. Once he grasps what's been going on, he manages a split in his jawbone that might be mistaken for a smile. His voice is a low croak, which he seems liable to do any moment. Wouldn't mind, actually. Prime witness out of the picture before they find him.

This big envelope, see, with X-ray marked? Thought you'd want to see the London papers. Having a field day. "Black Market Ring in Fiery Crash." Stuff like that. You have the strength to hold 'em up you'll get a kick out of it. And here's a souvenir, more like a trophy, thought you'd want to see. His keys there on a ring, made him throw 'em on the floor before you-know-what. Poor dope figured it'd get him off the hook. Speaking of hooks, you know where they were hid? In the stores on the board where they hang keys. Nobody noticed. Now don't get your balls in an uproar, I'm going to do the same here, put the old devil's keys on the board there behind the nurse. Bet she'll never notice them. So, to finish off the works, there's a way your pal Major Todder's going to be fixed, if those dummy harness bulls running around ever smarten up. How're them apples?

More display of teeth, maybe whiter now that he can't smoke no more, when I relate how that numskull Gilmore has been arrested because he has the gun. What a chump, could be on his way home instead of hanging around here, useless. How long he'll be the fall guy is hard to predict, not much longer, maybe. Then those rust-coloured eyes of Metro's, they take on moisture when I recount the fiasco in London, the buddies of the Duke duly consigned to hell in a Lizzie. The cavalry on deck to rescue our innocent doll, with whom, of course, he is acquainted. Nods in faint drools when my finger sketches her dimensions in the air. Goddam jerks almost got her killed. He gasps and sputters. Should a sister be summoned? Not yet. Wheezes a question: how come you got this inside info? Ve haf our vays—my takeoff on Nazis in stupid war films.

More gagging, chuckles, until the purpose of the visit is dumped on him. The arrival of two meatheads from Holland and Germany, provost heavies, officers, the ones who tried to nail the Duke and Todder for doing in your brother. At Ramillies yesterday, closeted with Clancy, a major from downtown, a Limey dick and that dark one who claims he's Irish. About as Irish as my ass, never seen a Paddy like him, half-breed, more like it. Over in Holland you recall a big fella taking you aside after your brother's funeral? Well, that's one of 'em who came over. Get it? They'll soon track you down, even if some sheets of the posting have been lost accidentally on purpose. Seen to that. Any time now they'll be in here to give

you the once over, jaundice or no. Look, the job was done for you, for her, and all
of us. Now it comes down to you, Metro. You squeal, the whole goddam thing goes
up the spout, right? Swear on a stack of Bibles or that jaundice is going to take a
turn for the worse, right now.

Sergeant Metro Timchuk manages to whisper: "Okay."

"What're you doing here?"

The nursing sister crackles in through the door. She wears a white apron over
a blue tunic, cinched by a belt, and a watch pinned to her ample tits. Like a nun
with that flying head dress.

"No visitors. Can't you read?"

Sure, ma'am. Just here on another errand, dropped in for a sec to see an old
pal and drop off some things for him. No need to make a fuss or report it. Not try-
ing to make trouble for you or anyone else.

She escorts me to the lift to make sure.

Photos in black frames already on the walls, one of family on a cleared desk
where the "Out" tray outweighs the incoming for a change. The wall pictures
are of guys in coveralls fixing things: the workshops and light aid detachments
at work on tanks, anti-aircraft guns and assorted ordnance. They are the
"Reemees," Royal Canadian Electrical and Mechanical Engineers. Ordinary
troops, unskilled in anything except survival, have dubbed them "wire-
pullers," double meaning intended. The new CO, Lieutenant Colonel T. S.
Capson, a neatness nut, long pale face, horn-rimmed glasses, not army issue
steel frames, he was already in training for civvy street. Remembered him as a
note-taker at General Spry's conference. No, didn't want to touch the late
colonel's office with a ten-foot pole. He'd stay here.

"Thank you for your briefing, Captain—ah—"

"Horobbins, sir."

"What kind of name is that? So Major Todder is now confined to quarters
under guard, pending charges to be mulled over by the front office. He won't
be in this chair again. What a shambles this place is. What can I do for you?"

"We need your assistance, sir. The chances are that Sergeant Timchuk
passed through here. A search of the files turns up some missing pages, we
believe the ones we need. If we can find the pages and the person who took
them out, we're on our way."

"To be devoutly wished. How can I help?"

"I need your approval to use the expertise of the one person on your staff who knows the records inside out."

"No sweat. Who's that?"

"Corporal Claire Evans."

"Ah, I see. Poor gal. You have my authorization subject to her clearance by the officer commanding the Quacks, Captain Williams, is it?"

Williams in shirtsleeves leaned back in her chair, her face shiny, and a glazed stare as if oxygen had hit a wall outside the open window.

"You'll gum up the works again."

"Can't be helped. Sergeant Gates reports the missing entries. Now I need the assistance of the one person around here with the smarts and the memory of an elephant."

"No you don't."

"She's back on duty, isn't she?"

"At her request. I think it's premature, but she wants to keep busy."

"Why don't we ask her?"

"We'd have to watch her closely. She was under observation in the Cambridge, treated for dehydration, menstrual cramps, various infections, but insisted she was fit enough for work on an out-patient basis. Okay, say the docs, but don't push it. She's alone next door doing light duties for me, and I'm not sure how she might react. With justification she holds you to blame for what happened. As much my fault, too, and that Bollock person, haven't seen him around. Hope he's on the mat with his superiors. We should never have exposed her to such danger."

"Amen. Now, tell me, did you ever come across a Sergeant Metro Timchuk? No? Stuff is missing and so is he. If her brains weren't too shook up by her ordeal, we need them."

Karen Williams wrapped her arms on top of her grizzled hair, exposing stained armpits, and without another word rapped on the thin wall of the cubicle.

She was thinner, her neck shrunken, her collar loose, the skin white; her head weaved as if in an internal breeze, but snapped into place once she saw the provost captain. She sat down, refusing to raise her eyes to meet his. Betrayed again? Well, not exactly. Seemed she was now indispensable. Not that she cared any more if the killer of Ambrose was ever found, good riddance and thanks for the initiation, buster.

For such strong personalities the two officers were strangely diffident, almost hesitant to lay on an order. More of a plea for help. That she could grasp, and she found herself straightening up, her true self-worth showing a twinge of revival in the context of a complex problem that must be solved. They caught her reaction and allowed themselves to exchange glances that could be omens of relief. She was, in effect, welcomed back.

Out in the orderly room the thuggish Pearly Gates handed her two thick wads of legal-size paper marked with tabs. She glanced around the room at scattered papers and teetering files. Should've been on deck sooner. How'd she ever restore order to the system, her system? The other clerks, her bunkmates from the spider hut, and the fat slug Helmers and the twitchy driver Nolan and the former batman, Montgomery, all dragooned for paper shuffling, broke into applause. Claire whipped through the sheets, beginning with the typed rosters of the repats, name, rank, number, unit, from where to where, on which dates. A good many ruled through with fine red lines, the lucky ones sent to the ports. The work gang peered around the stacks in front of them in a state of suspended animation, frozen by curiosity, anticipation, and maybe something else. At last she gathered up two thick files and marched into the makeshift office where Horobbins had his own strewn debris from endless interviews.

"Sir, it comes back to me now." She nodded towards the paper-thin walls. "Can we go somewhere else?"

Pearly Gates brought around a Jeep and drove them over to the near empty Ramillies, its only prize inmate Private Gilmore. The duty sergeant found a cubicle that still had traces of sweat and fear from the riot interrogations.

"The day before Amb—Colonel Wellesley was killed, I was on duty in the records office, as usual. Two of your provost, Nine Company I think they said, came in to report they'd picked up an NCO the previous night, the first night of the disturbances, propped up by two pals. They thought he was drunk till they had a close look at him and decided he was sick as a dog. Took the three to the Connaught, saw that he was duly signed in, got the names of his two buddies, made sure they were signed in for observation. That evening the MPs came back to see me, busy as they were with the troubles going on downtown. They were doing a favour for the sisters at the hospital and had come to collect his file. As you know, personnel files often don't catch up, what with Second Echelon on the move and general confusion. But his did. He'd been here since 28 May. Then I remembered he had shown up in the orderly room and spoke to me first as if I could do anything about it. How would he go about applying for compassionate leave and discharge? His brother had been killed in Holland and he wanted to be home with his parents in Alberta. Fair enough. I personally typed up the forms and sent them down the hall. At that time we were just setting up here, and expecting Colonel Wellesley and Major Todder momentarily to take command of the unit. A few days after they had arrived—this had to be first week of June—Sergeant Timchuk, for that was him, all right, came back to me and asked me to withdraw his request. For Heaven's sake, why? I asked him. He stared at me with those eyes of his, and said something about not wanting *them*—whoever they were, but I suspected he meant the CO and Todder—ever to see his name. And, he added, I guess I have some business to attend to, so take my name off the list for now. The carbons have been torn out of the files. See? But the originals that were picked by your two MPs must still be at the Connaught. Presumably he's still there. But one thing's for sure."

"What's that?"

"He's not back in Canada."

The MO didn't want them anywhere near Sergeant Timchuk. "Condition deteriorating, severe jaundice from hepatitis, yellowish hue brought on by excess of bile pigments, liver inflammation acute, tests for bilirubin. Very weak. Trying to prevent complete liver failure. We've examined his two friends who brought him in. They're clear, discharged, were sent back to their barracks; by now probably in other camps. Names here on record."

"I want their names and medical reports," Horobbins said. "Need to talk to them if they can be found."

"How Sergeant Timchuk acquired hepatitis we can't tell, has to be direct physical contact of some sort—contaminated food or possibly a streetwalker, of which we have not a few in the area," the doctor went on.

"Is there a rash of cases, sir?" Gates asked.

"No, actually. Merely another four from various camps. There's no epidemic."

Horobbins put on his best cop stare, his dark visage adding menace, he hoped. The British major in white smock was not cowed, had his fill of Canadians, especially their staggering VD rate, for the duration and beyond.

"Sir, you are aware of the murder of our Colonel Wellesley the night following the disturbances."

"Who isn't?"

"This man Timchuk is more than likely our key witness, even if it now seems unlikely he committed the deed himself. We must speak to him for a couple of minutes. That's all we ask."

"Some cheek, captain. I don't give a damn what you're about, he can't be disturbed."

"If I have to I'll go to the area commandant or right to the top in your own branch. Don't think I won't."

"How charming." The MO seemed about to make knots in the stethoscope on his desk. "Very well, come with me."

On the second floor at the end of the hall, the duty nurse rustled to her feet.

"Anything to report on Sergeant Timchuk?"

"No, sir, unchanged. Here's his chart."

The MO glanced at the clipboard, beckoned, finger on lips for silence, led them to a curtained bed. Crumpled newspapers with headlines about the fiery crash in Essex, were on the floor, untouched by the cleaning staff. The yellow mummy that was once Sergeant Timchuk opened eyes at the rattle of curtain rings. Beyond the doctor he seemed to focus on the provost contingent for a brief moment, then he actually winked, as though they were in a conspiracy together, a giant hoax he assumed had now been unraveled, and fell back into sleep or perhaps coma.

"There goes our last hope, sir," said Pearly Gates out in the hall.

"I warned you," said the doctor.

"Say again, his chances of recovery?"

"About eighty-twenty against. We shall do our best for the poor chap."

"I'm sure you will, but it doesn't help us now."

"Sorry."

The nurse frowned at them. "I must say, Major Hilton, I'm rather surprised you permitted this. Absolutely no visitors."

"It will not happen again, sister."

"I trust not. How that other one got past us, I'll never know."

"What other one?" Horobbins turned.

"Yesterday, crept in when I was away from the station. Had to see that pneumonia case in Ward 3B. When I returned I found to my horror that Sergeant Timchuk had a visitor, and left those ghastly papers with him. No wonder he's so depleted today."

"The papers are still there on the floor," the MO said.

"Not my job, the orderlies haven't been by yet. And," she took a set of keys off the hooks behind her desk, "are these yours, by any remote possibility? Certainly not ours."

"This visitor yesterday," said Horobbins. As he took the ring and fingered the long flat security deposit key, he and Gates held their breath. "Sister, could you provide us with a description?"

29

The shame of their commander meant that the carpet, if there actually had been one onto which they were called, was threadbare, as thin as the reprimand Horobbins felt obliged to deliver. His facial colouring was a sepia drainage, the funk and self-recrimination to be shared with Pearly Gates and Lance Corporal Fielding, a beanpole who tried not to allow the slightest lip twitch. The three of them had conducted the interviews, poked the entrails, and had missed the obvious. Their only unspoken excuse was the rush to thumb through stacks of service books and personnel files.

"By a mile. Okay, dismissed. Let's go."

That was it. Fielding went outside with Pearly Gates who issued orders to a section of MPs rounded up to secure Ramillies barracks, the site of the defunct Mob Control Centre where only one inmate remained—Private Gilmore, whose status as prime suspect was about to change. Gates sent a wrecking party to take apart the wing of the spider hut in question. Brooding over yet another screw-up, Horobbins was interrupted by DS

Fisher, accompanied by a police steno and his report from the Hants constabulary. They awaited the arrival of Bollock, at last pried loose from bureaucratic harassment at the Yard.

"Yates Jewellers is closed, sir," Fisher said. "They've done a bunk. Our locals are obtaining warrants to search the premises and get access to the banks. Their home near the Abbey is unoccupied, neighbours say that Sally, Mrs. Yates and two youngsters, packed a Humber and left yesterday. No idea where. Inquiries reveal no funeral establishment has been contacted to perform a burial service, at least locally. The colonel's remains, such as they are, rest in a morgue in London awaiting autopsy. Ports and airfields alerted. They're trying to locate any relatives, but I think we can assume she has absconded for parts unknown. Not likely to return for interment of the remains, I'd wager. We conjecture it was a prearranged departure when she intended to join the late Colonel Yates somewhere. We assume an adequate amount of wherewithal has been amassed to finance a comfortable exile."

"Swell. Bring Mr. Bollock here as soon as he arrives."

Horobbins shook himself, turned his attention to the matter at hand. The pocket-sized brown booklet, "Canadian Army Soldier's Service and Pay Book," was still clipped inside the file cover. He riffled through the pages with their tiny scrawls and indecipherable signatures in blue ink.

Page seven: "Certificate applicable to all Arms to be completed and signed by CO Bn etc. before a Soldier proceeds Overseas." Then: "Forty-eight days basic completed. Qualified in addition: Part I and II Advanced Trg RCASC."

Page eight: "Particulars of training: gas chamber. Driver Class Three. Clerk steno (11 VTS) qual. Clerk C, then B."

Pay dirt came in Section VIII, page nine: "Rifle Range Course completed SMLE .303, LMG Bren, Sten. Rifle and LMG practices fired on 30 yd, 100 yd range. PIAT 5 rds, 36 grenade 6 rds." Here it was: a more advanced rifle course. "Practice fired on 200, 300 yd range. Completed." Then a hook. "Pistol range, 30 yds. Completed." Marksman material, for sure. But why had they moved on to a weapon that a lowly clerk would never use? Hadn't anyone noticed?

The rest he skipped through, pausing at Section XII to confirm eyesight category as an E-3, very low, although a prescription for glasses raised it correctible to E-1, as noted on page fourteen. Stuck in the back were two small booklets: "Clothing and Equipment Statement," nothing more than standard issue kit. Then Part II, "Soldier's Pay Book" recorded an increase from $1.50 a day to $1.75 trades pay, half assigned to parents.

Horobbins sat back and sighed. Not enough yet. A puzzle. Until Pearly Gates steamed back, his ridged oyster shell of a face showing rare signs of circulating blood. He held up a fairly neat uniform, the hooked collar pressed open for the black tie that soldiers were now allowed to wear for walking out. Hadn't done much of it the last few days. Gates pointed to the small pocket on the right front of the battledress trousers, its purpose a mystery to everyone except the fashion designers. From his other hand he passed over a folded up square of yellowing paper, opened it out carefully for his captain. And there it was, jagged on one edge as if torn from a personnel file, a souvenir, validation or removal of evidence, likely all three. In handwriting an unreadable Captain Smudge had offered his assessment.

"On initial SMLE range tests at 100 yds, this soldier fired a perfect score, every round in the bull. I ordered Sgt. Carter to test him further. Range extended, the soldier's groupings continued to perfection. I asked for a pistol range test. Same results at 30 yds.

"When interviewed, the soldier stated he had hunted gophers and rabbits, small targets requiring skill. Had been brought up on firearms from a very young age. He does wear glasses (E-3) but not a handicap to his skills. Could be a sniper, but physical condition not suitable for Infantry. Recommend he be reassigned and trained as a small arms instructor."

A note at the bottom of the creased letter poured out his superior's scorn. "This soldier isn't fit for anything other than a clerk. Not suitable as an instructor, poor appearance and attitude. Post him to clerical duties as qualified." Signature blurred. Could it be A. Wellesley? COs did have the final word. Horobbins swore.

"Blind as a bat. Overweight slob. Can't hit the broad side of a barn door with a typewriter. Dead Eye Dick we've got. Bring him in."

No matter how discreetly he tried, Sergeant Pearly Gates could not extract Private Glen Helmers from his desk in the orderly room without causing another ripple among the page-turners.

"A word of assistance," he had said to the staff sergeant in charge. "Need to talk to him."

Once again eyes shifted, expressions clouded as Gates took Helmers by an arm and led him out to the Jeep. The indoors crew remarked on two MPs upright in the back seat, like liveried escorts in a royal carriage, and it didn't help that Helmers waved to them, an unmistakable farewell, leaving only faint traces of his recent obsession with looted cologne. The abandoned Mob Control Centre at Ramillies was about to welcome its second guest.

Roughly strip-searched in an empty medical inspection room redolent with disinfectant, the ribald insults of the Gestapo all too familiar, Helmers was given back his reeking battledress, taken along to the star chamber, a duplicate of Lieutenant Colonel Ambrose Wellesley's office, except for the lack of furniture. The quick march up to a long trestle table was a clatter of hobnails on the uneven wooden floor. There, four men watched his arrival: the provost captain with the permanent tan, the major with pitted face, an elderly civilian with a peeling red pate and white hair fringes, probably a detective or funeral director, and a man in police uniform with a notebook.

"Private Glen Helmers," began the dark captain, "we want to talk to you about the murder of Lieutenant Colonel Ambrose Wellesley on the evening of the sixth of July. You may sit. How can you enlighten us?"

The pale blue eyes, magnified behind thick glasses, were steady; his heavy jaw and sagging neck flesh showed not the slightest tremor. Meaty shoulders pushed back on the wooden chair.

"I don't know what you mean, sir."

"It has puzzled us from the beginning who among the odds and sods that populate the admin staff, or even those confined to barracks, could produce someone who could take a Luger, stand several feet away from the victim at his desk and drill him neatly between the eyes. One round, no need for a second. It had to be someone the colonel would not be surprised to see in his office. Instead of passing through the orderly room where he'd be recognized, the killer went to the end door outside the CO's office, knocked, and was admitted by Colonel Wellesley himself. Perhaps waved a file or papers to make it legit, then the colonel went back to his desk, looked up and asked what was so urgent at that hour. Around 2130 hours he stared for the last time into the muzzle of the Luger. He was ordered to throw his key ring onto the floor in front of the desk, but this didn't save him. The prewritten note was placed on his desk. Nice diversion to arouse panic of a wider conspiracy in the wake of the disturbances. The gas respirator; perhaps you can explain what it's supposed to mean. You follow me?"

"Don't know what you're talking about, sir."

"Helmers, we got you cold. You're just a lowly clerk, rotten category, a menial paper pusher, right? How about this found in your belongings?" The creased sheet of paper extolling his marksmanship was placed on the table and his pay book was waved in front of his myopic glaze.

"Speaks for itself, sir, but there must be dozens of prairie boys who'd show the same. We grew up shooting. You checked out their records?"

"You're the only one who dazzled everybody on the pistol range."

"Perhaps some of the officers, sir?"

"Here's a sworn statement taken from Nursing Sister Candice Lowell from Connaught Hospital. She describes you as the visitor who broke the rules to see Sergeant Timchuk. She will be here in due course to confirm her identification. She also found this set of keys on her board that weren't there before your visit. How come you had them?"

"Okay, sir, I own up to seeing him. Don't know nothing about keys. I met the sarge when he was at Malplaquet; we struck up a friendship. When I heard he was sick I took him some London papers. Just went to buck up a pal."

"How'd you know he was sick and in the Connaught?"

"His name was struck out on the repat list with a note he'd been laid up at the hospital. Anybody in the orderly room could've seen it."

"Not so fast. That sheet is missing, probably torn out so that no one would know where he was. Why? You didn't want anyone near him after the murder because it was Timchuk who sold or gave you the Luger."

"You can't prove that, sir."

"We already have. After the sister gave us your description we visited Timchuk at the hospital. The MO allowed us in and, weak as he was, Timchuk understood what we said to him. We told him we knew about his brother and how he must feel, but if he did recover he'd face court martial as an accessory to murder. However, for the sake of his parents and what happened in Holland, we'd recommend clemency, home on medical discharge. All he had to do was cooperate and admit he'd provided you with the gun."

"Sir, do you have a sworn statement to that effect? When I saw him he wasn't capable of nothing like that."

"He heard us clearly and, after some thought, nodded his agreement, duly noted in our report. Don't kid yourself, we'll have it nailed down. While Timchuk is quite weak now, the MO says his prospects for recovery are good, and with proper care will be in a position not only to sign a statement, but also to appear as a live witness. And don't get any more ideas. We've posted security at the ward."

The impassive blob remained skeptical.

"As a peace officer with powers of arrest, I intend to charge you with the murder of Lieutenant Colonel Ambrose Wellesley. We'll prove you did it. No sweat. We'll resume this session later. You will be confined to temporary detention here. You have anything to say at this point?"

"No, sir."

Horobbins stood up. "Think again. You any idea what we've got in mind for you? Over there in the Glass House they have a cell waiting for you. We've instructed them to bestow upon your carcass very special treatment; you'll be lucky to survive for your court martial. Don't kid yourself. In case you haven't heard, on the fifth of July in Italy a private soldier, one of ours, was shot by firing squad. For murder, see? Two months after the war. I can tell you the top brass is out for blood. On the other hand, if you cooperate and own up, we could see what can be done to return you to Canada in one piece. You might even avoid the firing squad or the noose. But, by God, Helmers, you've got to meet us halfway."

The moon face assumed the pallor of the doomed, the flesh crammed inside the wrinkled uniform quaked; no matter which way he turned, unspeakable horrors awaited. Helmers managed a sickly nod and turned himself over to his escorts.

Spotted Dick Clancy shook his head. "Hugh, for chrissake, you made that up about Timchuk. You told me he never uttered a word or that you'd even spoken to him. The doc never said he'd recover, did he? His defending officer will take you apart. Our best bet is for Helmers to crack before they find out."

"We'll get him," grinned Horobbins. "Not bad, eh?" The risks were obvious, but he'd break the Kiska Kid and, as for interrogation methods, everybody upstairs would want a quick court martial and conviction to clear the decks of another blot on the army's honour, a pressing necessity to signal that military justice was not to be trifled with or convey any hint of slackness before the horrible prospect of excruciating stress and breakdown during the attack on Japan.

"I'm still wondering how Timchuk was able to persuade that poor slob to plug his CO. It's one long stretch from bellyaching to murder. Here we are, already assuming he acted alone without some kind of backup. At the time of the murder, Timchuk was out of the picture. So who was there to help Helmers dispose of the weapon and take those notebooks? We don't have it, yet, Hugh; more work needed. What'll we do about Gilmore?"

"Don't spring him yet, he's got more to tell us."

"Listen, Hugh, don't take this too far without checking with Colonel Cameron and the Judge Advocate General's crew. They'll have to prosecute and they'll want a clear run."

"If I deliver, they won't worry."

"Still."

Clancy turned as Sergeant Pearly Gates hustled in a fragile bespectacled Pay Corps private who peered around anxiously as though an overpayment had been discovered. "Colonel Capson wishes to see you both, sir," the Pay Corps runner said, fresh off a wobbling bicycle. "It seems two of his staff have driven off in his staff car to parts unknown. They are assumed AWL."

"Who—?"

"My information is it's Private Nolan and Sapper Montgomery, sir. The CO wants you soonest."

30

If Lieutenant Colonel Capson hadn't summoned his staff car, the two probably wouldn't have been missed until the next tea break. When the CO sent the Pay Corps runner to find Nolan and bring his car around, the driver was not to be found. Sent again on an unaccustomed sprint, the clerk reported that Nolan, accompanied by a large Engineers sapper, had signed out the vehicle an hour ago and were seen driving off towards the Farnborough Road. The orderly room staff sergeant denied any errand, and when he made a quick check it was discovered that blank pass and transportation warrant forms had been torn from their moorings in the day book. The Fixer, as he had been named, sighed as Horobbins and Clancy briefed him on Helmers.

"Once they saw Helmers picked up, they decided to make themselves scarce. They've got to be in on it."

"I am about to recommend that we close down this whole flipping office and start it up elsewhere, preferably Scotland. An utter balls-up. No wonder the troops are restless. Who're you?" He peered through his horn-rimmed glasses at a stocky civilian in a black suit who bustled in as if he owned the place. A relieved Horobbins introduced Bollock.

"Can't you stay put? Finally located Fisher who gave me a quick runup. You won't need me much longer. Big operation under way, Straw Spike needs more tender care before we roll up his network. We'll hunt down the remaining Yates clan."

"What's in that case, Inspector?" asked Capson.

"My murder bag, sir. Pack it everywhere."

"You keep murderers in there? Now listen, I want my car back pronto and those two consigned to the nearest rock pile."

At this crucial stage, Horobbins was worried about any sudden loss of the Yard's backup. "I hope you'll stick around a bit longer. We'll need forensic experts to testify. Right away we want your assistance to alert local police on two soldiers who liberated the CO's staff car. I think I know why."

The colonel called after them as they left. "The tappets. Bring in those chaps with the echo sounders. Damn thing can be heard for miles."

Off the buzzing orderly room, back in his cubicle, Horobbins, from a shuddering pile, plucked the interview reports of the two men on the run.

"Guildford. Montgomery told me he wasn't ready to go home. Married lady, as usual." Skipped a beat. When would he ever find time to ring Mavis? "Dick, can you send out a posse? Alert the red caps. Don't have an address, but Montgomery ain't exactly invisible. Where Nolan might head for, who knows? At some point, he'll abandon the car."

"I'd hazard," said Bollock, "he'd follow A31 through Farnham, along the Hog's Back to Guildford. Give us the plate number. The Met will get the word out in London and the counties."

Horobbins blanched like an old Africa hand trapped in an English winter. "Leave it with me, Dick. I'll pass on the good news to Colonel Cameron. I gather they didn't get anywhere with Todder."

"You still believe in miracles? Better you than me. Catch you later."

The catching did not take long. A vast apparatus in a small country peeled its eyes, so to speak, a demo of how easily the Nazis could have kept the lid on had they triumphed. It seemed the two AWLs, for such were they now stigmatized, had inclined easterly then south, the latter by Nolan solo. Not far from the cathedral on Stag Hill, westerly Guildford, they unearthed Montgomery. While the local police were well inured to Canadian and Yank absentees, deserters, and run-of-the-mill troublemakers, since D-Day the great tide of soldiery had receded to wavelets of spreemakers, easily spotted and subdued. Especially when disapproving neighbours once again had noticed the massive Canadian paying another clandestine visit to Pamela, her expecting the hubby home any day. Drove up large as life in a brown saloon. Perhaps, they told the inquiring constable who had received a tip and came around on his bicycle, it was a "ta-ta ducks" stop in, but then possibly not. Wouldn't want to be in their boots if Charlie pops in unexpectedly, would I? When the neighbours described the visitor, the constable retreated to a call box to summon the local equivalent of the Flying Squad, no more than six reinforcements to block off the street, the rear of Pamela's house, and to gather apprehensively at the front door.

Like any good burgher about to take a post-coital bath, Montgomery was in a somewhat ecstatic daze, his trousers hastily pulled up, suspenders looped below hips, badly laundered vest with top buttons undone pulled over tousled head. The woman, Pamela, in a silk wrapper sent home from India by her other half, shrank against the brown patterned hallway wall. The sated Montgomery was hauled off with unexpected ease. The absence of resistance astonished Horobbins who speculated that the ex-miner could have demolished the entire crew of constabulary, enfeebled by skimpy rations, and made good his escape. It was almost as though he had felt the need for a last farewell before meeting his fate, perhaps, Horobbins mused—a screw of the turn.

Equally puzzling was the behaviour of the battle exhaustion case, Stan Nolan, whose actions, as revealed later, were a bizarre mixture of scientific curiosity and a naïve belief in church sanctuary. As a former high school teacher, was he gathering lore in the hope he might somehow regain his spiritual balance in the classroom? Foolhardy, all right, but still Horobbins seemed to understand why. Nolan's first sighting came from an eagle-eyed Limey red cap at Brighton railway station. Two hours after he had dropped off Montgomery in Guildford, Nolan apparently parked the staff car at the station and disappeared. Horobbins, awaiting the arrival of Montgomery and an escort not a little spooked at the prospect of transporting King Kong, went through Nolan's file again. He appeared to be one of those rare birds who kept up the flagging morale of the itinerant education officers by attending their sparse lectures. In Nolan's kit, brought in from the spider hut, there were personal letters on blue onion skin neatly arranged by date in a nice green folder, no doubt sent from home. Then a typed letter from the curate of the church of St. Mary's Rye, one of the silted-in Cinque Ports east of Brighton.

"Yes," the curate assured Nolan, "we do have a pendulum in the worship area of the type you describe. I shall be pleased to show it to you the next time you have some leave. I can provide you with a full account of its history. In any event, it is a freely suspended, long, heavy pendulum, its tip barely above the floor. You are no doubt familiar with the concept. Suffice it to say, it swings according to the diurnal motion of the earth by rotation of its plane of oscillation. I suspect you will also be interested in our notable sixteenth century quarter-boy clock. There is a Georgian reservoir in the churchyard."

"I can see him going for a pint at the New Mermaid, but a chunk of swinging iron?" said Bollock. "We'll be on to the county police, coaches easterly from Brighton stopped and searched. Is someone going to collect the staff car?"

When he was grilling the captured Nolan, Horobbins was curious about his flight to an obscure little Norman church in a small town.

"We had a lecture on gravity when I was at Number One Nuts. The prof described various methods of measuring gravity, including work by Kater in 1818 and Foucault in 1851, and mentioned the pendulum at St. Mary's. You have the reply there from the curate, Father Watson. Sorry I never made it; the cops picked me up when I had to switch buses."

"If you had, then what?"

"Sanctuary, sir."

"Sanctuary?"

"Why not? I'd throw myself on the mercy of the church. You guys couldn't touch me."

"And you'd stay there for how long, the rest of your life?"

"Sure, in a moth-eaten cassock, snuffing out candles."

"Hold on." Horobbins spent ten minutes on the phone, an interrogator's diversion to encourage a suspect's reflection upon his own sins, until someone from the chaplain's office produced a snippet of erudition. "Father Vincent says there hasn't been church sanctuary in England, as far as crime was concerned, since the seventeenth century James One, to be exact, in 1623. How about them apples?"

"But I'm not a criminal, sir."

While they had been awaiting apprehension of the fugitives, Clancy, Horobbins, and Bollock had mulled over their options. Clancy was not happy with the manpower he'd need to keep the suspects, four of them now, in isolation and secure. Ramillies, a sieve with no bars on the windows, he'd have to place guards outside the windows and doors, and how to make sure there was absolutely no communication among them? Are we to administer field punishment on those two? The CO's out for blood, yet we need them along with Timchuk to build our case against Helmers.

"If I may," said Bollock. "At this moment we're on rather thin ice. Helmers has admitted to nothing, his identification by the nursing sister doesn't link him to the murder. Anybody could have placed the keys on the board. Your star witness, the sergeant, is incapable of testifying, and I have no doubt you are fully aware you might jeopardize your case by inventing his statement. Even if he did recover, he could well refute it. Now if I've learned anything in this business, it's to go after the prime suspect's mates and, nine times out of ten, if you want them to grass, you have to work out a deal with them. What with your CO about to heave the book at them, you won't be in any position to negotiate the testimony that'll put Helmers into the box."

Instead of resentment, the two provost officers grinned as if he was indeed reflecting their own unspoken thoughts. They waved him on.

"I don't pretend to be familiar with your military justice system, but obviously Nolan and Montgomery will have to undergo some form of punishment for theft of the staff car and putting on the skates. Supposing, though, that it could be made minimal, offer them quick removal to Canada and honourable discharge, conduct blemishes duly noted. In other words, they don't take the fall as accomplices to murder if they cooperate."

"Is that the kind of deal you're working out with Straw Spike?"

"Not too different. And I, too, have to bypass the more bloody-minded of my superiors for the sake of the longer game—that is, to close down his entire network. The question, then, you might pose to your vengeful commander, is this. Which is more important: punishment of the two soldiers or solving the murder of Wellesley? If he goes along, the odds are so will your higher-ups. If they testify to what I suspect happened, even the poor sod Helmers might escape the rope. You want him convicted, all right, but I'm not sure either one of you truly want to see him executed for topping a criminal like Wellesley. And I must say, I'm just as curious as you are as to who and how this lad Helmers was persuaded to actually commit murder. Seems bit of a stretch, doesn't it?"

"Because he could shoot straight."

They laughed and turned to Pearly Gates who announced the arrival of the first prisoner, Joe Montgomery.

Lieutenant Colonel Capson regarded the delegation before him as akin to wartime bellyaches from his artificers, or "tiffies," about, say, those goddam Bofors guns and their bulging or exploding barrels. His mantra to his disgruntled craftsmen was, "We fix the impossible. Go do it." As it turned out, the only remedy for the reviled ack-ack gun was complete replacement of its barrel. Life, however, became more complicated for The Fixer when he had to reconcile the misdeeds of his inept temporary staff with the big picture of resolving the murder. Horobbins laboured to spell it out.

"Sir, we must have an airtight case to take to court martial. If that means we have to bend the King's Regulations to get two key participants or witnesses to testify, then we'll do it. We need the cooperation of Nolan, Montgomery, and Timchuk to nail Helmers once and for all. To do that, we can threaten them with dire punishment as accessories and dishonourable discharge. Or we can offer them inducements, namely, fairly light stints for their misdemeanors and passage home for demob at the appropriate time. Our view is the latter will be more productive."

"Not on, captain. I want those two paraded at the crack of dawn to take my punishment. I'll march up and down their spines—they won't soon forget."

Bollock, the gap-toothed diplomat: "Sir, what the captain suggests is well within the bounds of our practices at the Yard. We're offering much the same to the prime suspect in the Lysander fry-up."

"You are?"

Capson pondered, ordered them to step outside for a moment. He phoned General Spry's office where a senior aide provided a lecture on major objectives to be gained *versus* routine army chickenshit. He summoned them back from the corridor.

"All right, gentlemen. Done. But those two ain't off the hook. Not by a long shot."

31

The air of mistrust that permeated the leftovers of the Canadian section of North Camp was, in Nolan's mind, symbolized by the middle-aged Hants constable who sat in a corner, notebook on lap, his uniform so shiny and worn it seemed polished. He, too, had heard Captain Williams ranting at the provost captain about his lack of faith in her own girls who were perfectly capable of making transcripts and keeping their mouths shut. To no avail. As round two of his interrogation began, Nolan lodged his own grievance.

"Honest to God, sir, I expected the CO to pull a gun out of a drawer and let us have it right on the spot. He fixes on me. 'Nolan, you never did anything about the tappets. My car sounds like a threshing machine.' Felt like saying you're the Reemee, do your own tune-ups. Thought better of it."

"A wise move."

"Then he throws us for a loop. Hands out only twenty-eight days to be served here, not the Glass House or Headley Downs, during and after the court martial. What court martial, sir?"

"We're your friends, Nolan, put in a good word with Colonel Capson. Even an honourable discharge. Means you collect your veteran's credits. How about a degree in gravity and pendulums?"

"What's the catch, sir?"

"You assist us in our inquiries and you're on the next boat after your stint on Blueberry Hill. Simple as that."

"I don't have beans to spill, sir."

"The CO went easy on you, against his better judgment, for one reason only. We asked him. You any idea what's really hanging over your head? We can charge you, Montgomery, and Timchuk as accessories to murder. You clear up a few things for us, and there's a fair chance we won't go ahead. Follow me?"

"Not entirely. Why'd we be involved at all?"

"You tell me."

"Sir, I'm not about to incriminate myself or others."

"You take a law course at the booby hatch? I'm trying to help you save your own skin."

"Why'd you want to do that, sir?"

"Good question. I guess I see you as a decent guy who's been through far too much in this war. You deserve to come out of it with a clean slate and I'll do my best to see that you do. Fair enough? I'm going out on a limb here to fill you in on some confidential stuff you have to keep to yourself. Then maybe you'll see the light."

"I'm not exactly running loose, sir. Okay."

"What you've picked up around, I don't know, but this is the official situation. We have interviewed Sergeant Timchuk: on his last legs, nothing to lose, he's admitted he gave Helmers the Luger to do the job. Gilmore picked it up off the craps table and owns up he can identify who put it there. His pay book and other papers show that Helmers is Dead Eye Dick. Confronted with the evidence he has confessed."

"Before I say anything, I'd like to see his confession."

"It's being typed up, then Helmers himself has to sign it. I assure you we've got him cold."

"In that case you won't need me."

"Hold on. There're a couple of things we're curious about where you can help fill in the picture. Timchuk has told us how he met up with Helmers, you, and Montgomery. The four of you went on from there. What's puzzling me, personally, is how come Helmers could be conned into taking the gun and, cool as a cucumber, shoot down his commanding officer?"

"You on the level, sir? I cooperate, you drop the other charges and I go home?"

"You got it, Nolan."

While he waited for Nolan to quit twitching as his rusty mental gears clanked, Horobbins reviewed his script for flaws. In the long silence, a squib, a filler from *Stars and Stripes*, the paper for American GIs, came to mind: "Salesman: Here's a house without a flaw. Customer: What do you stand on?" Quicksand, all right, the risk of being savaged by defence counsel at the court martial, a mistrial, case dismissed. What else could he use? Too bad Number One Neurological had folded its tents, the staff packed off home or to other hospitals. Must be another loony bin he could invoke, Bramshott maybe, if he had to. Nolan, he could discern, was properly suspicious, this Normandy survivor who had scrambled under the staff car when a defanged Heinkel went over, this teacher who wanted to become a student. "Harmless souls," Claire Evans had insisted, skeptical that any one of them could perform such an outrageous deed. Well, corporal, how about four of them? The question still hung out there: why?

He waited.

Nolan, ever the teacher, edged into it. "There isn't much good to be said for the army, but given enough time in one place, it brings guys from every part of the country together. We learn who to trust. In action it's unit solidarity. You can smell it when they're going to send you into the meat grinder long before it actually happens and the fear is like a measles outbreak. I hope I'm not making a mistake if I decide to trust you, even though you're an officer and a cop."

"My word stands."

"If I do tell you, I want two guarantees. One, you won't use it against the others or let on I was the one who ratted. Second, you won't get a word out of me if I have to testify before a court martial."

"Not a problem. We have everything nailed down. The brass wants a quick trial for Helmers, no complications. It's the 'why' question I want to settle in my own mind, that's all."

"What'll they do to Glen?"

"An officer will be assigned to defend him. I'm betting he'll go for mitigation on the grounds of temporary insanity or some such. Whether it'll stick, who can say?"

"If it doesn't?"

"You understand that military law requires a firing squad. Within these walls, I'm letting you in on something. While Aldershot was being torn apart, one of our lads in Italy was executed by firing squad. Convicted murderer, member of a gang of deserters in Rome. Not unlike you guys, eh?"

"Jesus-H, sir."

"That's why I need your help. If you can clarify what actually happened, how it took shape, maybe we can work it into our reports in a way that'll at least give Helmers some kind of a break. Personally, I'm hoping they'll agree to a prison term to be served in Canada. Murder's an unforgiving rap, as I told you, but Helmers isn't exactly your standard criminal type or garden variety hit man. I recognize he does have qualities, and that's what mystifies me. So it's up to you."

The way Nolan told it, a whirlwind arrived in June carrying Wellesley and Todder in on a tide that impressed HQ and led to the vast apparatus set up in North Camp, swollen with staff, a D-Day in reverse to put the troops ashore in their own homeland. The three, Helmers, Montgomery, and Nolan, at first were pleased to be shifted from old barracks downtown to the luxury of the spider huts. Their attachments to the colonel's needs became a kind of bond among them, gossip flowing from close contact with their boss, as it does anywhere, leading to growing suspicions of another game afoot. Old army hands, they had the acumen to read the trail signs of skullduggery. Little things, Nolan said, like when I'd drive him around the camps and he'd stop at those call boxes. The other fellas told me to keep track. Your guys found my notes in my kit on those calls, times, and places; maybe the cops can trace them. Then Montgomery was caught up in the way he kept things close to his chest, I mean for real, as if he had top secret papers—the notebooks and keys he took with him everywhere, even in the shower. As I'm not as conspicuous as the others they tag me to trail him when he strolls across the way to South Farnborough, always to the same place, Yates Jewellers shop, where we conjecture maybe he's buying presents for his wife back home. But once a week, or more often? And always carrying several thick envelopes in his briefcase that Joe sees him slip out of the tin trunk he keeps in his closet. You find anything in his case or the trunk? I gather nothing like that, just some goodies in the trunk anybody could've ordered. That was small time stuff. Anyway, we wonder if his walks along the Lynchford Road are nothing more than a quick lay with the stacked blonde lady who always greets him at the door. But only five minutes? No, we figure, unless he offloads awful fast right there in the shop in front of the customers, there's got to be more cooking than that. What the hell's in those envelopes? He seems to have them every time he returns from weekends in London. Major Todder doesn't seem to be in this picture.

Speaking of which, we become more disturbed when the colonel latches onto our favourite Corporal Claire Evans. She puts on an aloof act, but virgin territory—we agree from long experience among two of us, anyway. At first he'd take her out in the car on evenings, then he started sending me to drop off Corporal Evans at the station when he went up to London. We were sick about that, especially Helmers, who moped around like an ailing moose. In the meantime, Sergeant Timchuk arrives on the scene, and one thing leads to another.

Helmers runs across Timchuk over in the orderly room, Nolan said, where at first he goes in to agitate for return home on compassionate grounds to his bereaved parents in Alberta. Timchuk had taken to pestering Corporal Evans about it. A sympathetic soul, and rescuing our Claire from attentions he might—in his heated jealous state—misinterpret, Helmers sees how upset the sergeant is, takes him over to the NAAFI canteen for a heart-to-heart over one of those teas that would inspire revolt, not calm. But it isn't that he's after the gal at all, it has to do with the death—Timchuk says "murder,"—of his brother, and he asks Helmers what he does in the office. When he finds he's the secretary to Lieutenant Colonel Wellesley, the sarge does a doubletake. There could be only one with that name. On the muster parades and so on, he hadn't given a damn who the officers were, didn't recognize Wellesley by sight. And when Glen tells him the Two IC had come with him, a Major Todder, well, sir, Timchuk shits a brick. He relates the sad demise of his brother and how this Captain Murphy, one of your guys, had given him the straight goods at the funeral in Holland. Helmers, he can't believe his ears. That evening has Timchuk over to our billet where we fill him in on things going on we don't much care for, but we have no proof. This Metro, he says he has a Luger and he's about to head over there and drill both of them, he didn't fight in the war for the likes of those two, doesn't care what happens to him. He owes it to Orest, his brother. We try to talk him out of it, but Helmers, his eyes light up, and he says maybe there's a way. And that's when it dawns on us there's a fifth person in the picture.

Fifth person, that's right, sir, Nolan said slowly and hesitant, wary with good reason, I guess we have to come back to Helmers. You have to understand him if you want to find what this is all about.

Now you're familiar with barracks life. Take a guy like Helmers, what he goes through. Sure he'd been up in Kiska with the Zombies, but that didn't cut any ice around here. Glen, he's a tub of lard, gets a lot of ribbing for that, but he also has an affliction or ailment of some kind, something wrong with his innards, I dunno. The fact is he stinks to high heaven. Nobody'd take an upper bunk over him, saying they'd be gassed to death by morning. He was forced to take a bunk by himself in a far corner while others moved theirs far away as they could. He was a freak, see? Then his appearance. Can you imagine the razzing he took in the showers? When he did take a shower—we had lots of hot water in the spider hut—you have this glob of pink jelly, sagging belly, little bits of equipment hanging down there out of his sight. The boys are merciless. Catcalls about his "titties," "butter beam," "dinkytoy set" and so on. Nobody tries to cornhole him or anything. Whoever had any such ideas would get his own nuts cut off. You know the fellas in barracks, sir, none of that stuff. Just to make sure, Montgomery, our Charles Atlas, yells at them to knock it off and leave Glen in peace. I guess the two of us have human feelings left over from somewhere. We become his defenders. Not that anyone actually came at him physically, but just to make sure the message was out.

The problem is, even after taking a shower—Glen, he stinks like a honey wagon. In the spider hut there's one closed room with a bathtub where you can soak and whack off in privacy. We dumped Helmers in the big tub, but when he came out he still had this overpowering smell. He bought some cologne off one of the guys, but that didn't do much for the air quality. Funny thing, sir, almost by collective agreement we didn't jibe him about it on duty in front of others. Nobody called him "stinky" or "shitpen" or "pig sty;" kept that to themselves for the billet. Almost restores your faith in mankind.

Glen, he was one sad sack of flab. He told us how he'd been picked on and jeered at back home. Lots of cousins doubled up in their house during the bad times. Gave him a hard time, and it never stopped when he went into the army to escape. Now you can imagine this poor guy has about zero attraction for the gals or anyone else. He was a pathetic loner until Montgomery and I kind of befriended him. I don't mean we were drinking pals, but we got used to the smell. Montgomery had been in the mines and I'd inhaled a few barnyards. So we'd gab about things and found something in common trying to figure out what game Wellesley and Todder were up to. Then Helmers goes off the deep end.

The poor dope, Nolan continued, he goes apeshit over Corporal Evans. Yes, she's the fifth person. Don't get me wrong. She doesn't have a clue, at least I don't believe she does, about Glen or the torch he carries for her. When I told them the colonel was squiring her around at night in the car, then other times I'd drive her to the station for the train to Waterloo, Jesus, poor old Helmers, his eyes bug out, he shakes everywhere, a hula of lard and rage. I made a point never to tell him about the gamy smells in the car afterwards, and how I'd open the windows or find a used safe under the front seat. Glen moons around, outraged.

Now this Metro Timchuk who'd started hanging out with us, as I said, he catches Glen's fury about Claire Evans and I guess a light goes on, especially after we'd talked him out of going over and plugging those two officers, screw the consequences. He brings over his Luger, shows it to Helmers.

"You ever seen one of these before?"

Helmers shakes his head. "They're a snap compared to the Smith and Wessons."

Our jaws drop. So one Saturday afternoon, this was before the riots, we hitch down Farnborough Road south of the canal to Long Valley where, along there down into Caesar's Camp, you can find a sandy draw out of the way to do pistol practice. We can't believe it. The Kiska Kid, he lifts the pistol in his fat fingers, squints through his thick glasses, and at thirty yards knocks down a row of empty bottles: bing, bing, bing. Then Metro, he's brought paper bags he fills with sand, takes a grease pencil to draw in pretty good likenesses of the colonel and Major Todder. Big nose—sorry, sir—those Wellesley eyes, and Todder's toothbrush moustache. You recognize them, Glen? Then let's see you do your stuff. At thirty yards, without a wobble except maybe a quiver of rage, he blasts the paper bags. I know 'em, all right, he says.

Metro's careful and smart; he's simmered down from the idea of doing it himself, yet had asked Corporal Evans to hold his request for compassionate discharge for now, unfinished business to work out. He hadn't realized, of course, that Helmers was a marksman; anyway, it wouldn't matter much at short range. Metro must've kicked it around in his noggin, but didn't know how to trigger it, so to speak, if ever. Maybe inadvertently, I set it off.

One Friday afternoon after His Nibs has gone up to London, on his orders I wait for Corporal Evans down the road a ways, supposedly camouflaged under the trees at Queen's Parade. She comes along slowly, kind of dragging anchor, I think, as I watch her in the mirror. Naturally, I get out and open the door for this fine lady who had no idea every man in the camp has the hots for her. She never showed it, had no sense of the rays she sent out. The colonel, he didn't hesitate for one sec. Once he saw her, he moved in. Anyway, that day, coupla weeks ago I'd reckon, our Claire seemed pale and shaky, almost reluctant to make the trip to the station. Although she wore her issue raincoat and hat, I'd see her onto the train. Before it left the station she'd shuck the outer gear and there she'd be in a blue dress with white trim. Our Lady of Aldershot, for sure, she'd look fresh out of a nunnery. Still, that day I was truly concerned about her. At the risk of going out of line, I turned to her.
"You okay, corporal?"
"Why wouldn't I be?"
Her drop dead glare puts me in my place. In the mirror on our way to the station, I pick up glimpses of her dabbing at her eyes, then repowdering and slapping on fresh lipstick. Sir, I grew up with two sisters, and I'd have said our Claire was either having her monthlies and didn't feel up to going to the colonel's little orgies in his flat, or the other explanation is she's lost her virginity and is scared stiff of getting knocked up. I think of the more recent manifestations of screwing in the staff car, and begin to wonder.

I shouldn't of, I realize now, Nolan went on. Even then we had this kind of pact, we'd brief ourselves every day on any new dope we had on Wellesley and Todder. As it happened, Metro was with us that evening, came out of the shower, the shrapnel scars like chickenpox on his back, finds Helmers red-faced and about to explode. Timchuk decides he has him where he wants him. He's got his hit man. And if we cooked up his warrant to go home, Metro would be out of here before anyone makes the connection. Helmers, the least likely killer among the lot of us—he who'd never shot at anyone in his life the way some of us had—he was the one who could pull it off and get away with it. Rubber gloves, natch. Pass the gun to Montgomery who'd drop it on the craps table at Malplaquet. It's Metro's brainwave to dream up the threatening note, which he prints out himself. This is before the riots when he took sick. And that respirator, we had no idea those souvenirs would bring in such an influx of heavies who needed something to do; we'd thought they'd merely sidetrack the investigation, not cause a national uproar. Yeah, the respirator was Glen's little quirk, his alone.

There's no doubt the CO respected his speed and accuracy for steno work, but he couldn't help riding him about his smell. Yet, he kept him; the sad thing is he trusted Glen, and maybe thought he was joshing with him the way you'd handle a servant. "Chrissake, Helmers," he'd say, half joking, but no gag for the fella on the other side of the desk, "don't you ever take a shower? Have a good notion to order a bath parade for you alone, hose you down." On it went like that, day after day.

Now do you get it, sir? Helmers tells us he pinches the respirator from stores, puts it on the colonel's desk and says to him, even if he's already dead: "Fry in hell, put this on and you won't have to sniff at me no more."

On the spur of the moment, Helmers had ordered the colonel to throw out his keys onto the floor, because Joe Montgomery had suggested it, if possible, so that he could run over and open up the trunk in the closet, which he wasn't able to do when your guys were quick to seal off the room.

I'm getting ahead of myself. We had to figure out how and when, if ever, and set it up before Helmers cooled down. Once again I guess I tripped the whole thing. On the sixth, the day after the riots, I told them the colonel asked me to bring around his staff car that evening, park it by his office back door, leave the keys in and go back to my quarters, not the orderly room. He'd let me know when to collect it. Right away, I twigged. He couldn't wait to have another go at Claire, the horny bastard. With everything going on, that's what he had on his mind. The others jump. Helmers goes bananas.

Joe Montgomery has an idea, says he can lift the notebooks out of the colonel's breast pocket, knows how to do it. If they contain what we think they do, we'd plant them in Todder's little puddle jumper, your fellas would find them, and it'd fix him as the culprit. Falling out among thieves. Now Joe, he's working late at his ironing board in the ablution room to catch up on the last two days of neglect. Then, taking the laundry to the colonel's digs, he'd ask him to remove his jacket while he hands him a clean shirt and he'd touch up his brass pips and crowns. Wellesley's got only one thing on his mind and, believe it or not, doesn't see Joe slip the notebooks out of his pocket to hand to Helmers waiting outside. Doesn't even bother to pat his pockets as he buckles on his web belt and pistol and steams out to his office, maybe a hard on already.

That night of the sixth, when the colonel went back to his office, Helmers would knock on the locked door at the end of the hall and through the window the colonel would see him waving the two little notebooks. He could've just lifted them gratefully from Helmers and closed the door in his face, but Colonel Wellesley, he doesn't—didn't—leave anything to chance. He makes the fatal mistake of ordering Helmers to come in to find out where the hell he found his precious notebooks and also to make sure his clerk hasn't snooped into them or understands anything written down there. We'd taken a gander, and, except for numbers with a lot of zeroes, they were in some kind of code or a shorthand Glen couldn't make out. Demands to know. Bingo. End of discussion. Helmers takes the notebooks and keys, hands them to Joe with the gun and returns unseen to the spider hut.

What went wrong? Well, our plan to ship Timchuk out on forged warrants, the dumb bastard takes sick on us. Holed up in Connaught, a sitting duck if any of your guys make the connection and go after him. Which I guess you have.

"Too true, Nolan. But Helmers?"

"What I told you, I hope it'll help him. You know, he holds his head high and smiles at Claire Evans in a way she'll never understand, maybe she still mourns that bastard after all he and his pals put her through. The fact is, sir, Glen is a decent fella, and it should be taken into account."

"Has a funny way of showing it." Horobbins kept his skepticism under wraps for now. Very smart, Nolan, you've made Timchuk the fall guy, taken you and Montgomery out of the picture as nothing more than good bunkmates who went along for the ride. We'll see about that. "The notebooks, where are they?"

"Guess you'd have to ask Joe Montgomery, sir."

And, as if relegated by the director of a summer stock play in a sweltering tent, in came Sergeant Pearly Gates, his role now enshrined as a bearer of dire tidings, the entrance of the flustered messenger, his facial crevices in deep embarrassment. He tapped on the flimsy door to crook his finger, summoning a reluctant Horobbins to abandon his prize snout.

"Sir, it's Major Todder. He's escaped, disappeared, and on the way we're pretty sure he tried to finish off Timchuk."

32

He was an unlikely victim of an ambush, Lance Corporal Campbell, six footer, spic and span with immaculate white webbing, the shine on his boots blinding to the eye, ribbons from Normandy and beyond. One of those legendary MPs, source of much folklore. In mid-August 1944, amid the dust and heat of the final drive into Falaise, a member of Number Two Provost Company, he took his Jeep into a town that was rife with enemy snipers, and in front of a shattered bistro placed his "Out of Bounds" placard, away ahead of the advance elements cringing up the road. Now sent down from Six Company, in the old Henrietta Hospital site near Covent Garden, his task merely was to attend on this major, who, after all, had given his word as an officer and gentleman that he would observe banishment to his quarters pending charges to be dreamt up by the big brains in London stymied by his buttoned lip. Campbell had escorted the gentleman to the ablution room in the spider hut, he had personally brought in the meals sent over from the officers' mess, and had watched carefully when the major's batman picked up his laundry and performed other grooming tasks. Piece of cake.

Until that afternoon when Major Philip Todder called him in. The first thing Campbell noticed was the major had promoted himself to a half-colonel, apparently by stitching a skewed pip onto each epaulet beside the crown. And was pointing the three-inch barrel of a Belgian Browning automatic at his forehead. Humiliated to stretch out face down on the floor, mouth expertly taped, feet and arms tied, sidearm plucked from holster. With much grunting and curses, Todder, well muscled as he was from his moving van days, rolled the MP under the bed, wrapped his legs in blankets, removed his boots so he couldn't thump for help, looped a rope around his neck to prevent head movement. Then, valise in hand, out the window. Campbell reported afterwards he was certain he heard a car drive away and, to this day, wonders how Todder obtained the gun.

Lance Corporal McDonald had been mentioned in despatches for unbelievable coolness under fire, also in Normandy, Number Thirteen Provost Company. It was during the Quesnay Wood disaster when, amid falling bombs from the RAF—the same inferno that had crazed Nolan and so many others—he directed traffic through an anthill of panic with the aplomb of a cop in his hometown of Fredericton, New Brunswick, where a mild form of chaos happened only on Saturday nights after a pay day. He too had been detached from Six Company to toss Aldershot rioters into lorries on those two nights that had caused him shame to wear the Canada patch. After the gunning down of that colonel, he had been running picket duty to keep the confined repats under wraps while the search went on for suspects.

Now he was teetering on a chair outside a ward in the Connaught Hospital, guarding a very sick soldier who was supposed to be connected with the crime. Sat reading the London papers and drinking tea the nice nursing sister had brought him when a tall blonde officer in a somewhat wrinkled uniform, the knees scuffed as if he had been at prayer, strode towards him. The rheumy commissionaire from the front desk following him at a distance, made hand signals to McDonald who, veteran that he was, divining trouble, took the precaution to unsnap the holster on his hip and remove his Webley, muzzle down at his side.

"Put that thing away, corporal. No need. I am Lieutenant Colonel Hamilton sent here directly on the orders of General Spry. I am authorized to speak to the patient, Sergeant Timchuk."

"He's not well enough, sir. Strict instructions not to be disturbed."

"Only a minute or two. Highly secret. Vital link to the murder of Colonel Wellesley, must have a word, or General Spry himself will be here."

Quick at the eye frisk, McDonald picked out oddities. The uniform had dusty traces of a scrabble of some sort, no red tabs on collar, no swagger stick, dubious shifting of eyes. And, in the side pocket of battle dress trousers, the faint bulge of a pistol. He gave a slight nod to the commissionaire who retreated back down the corridor to summon backup.

"Sorry, sir, I need a written order."

The bogus half-colonel put his hand into his right pocket to finger the pistol. McDonald used his thumb to cock the revolver. Philip Todder must have pondered the risk of having a shootout to finish off Timchuk once and for all, his escape plan in place, this a minor diversion his escorts had tried to dissuade. His batman, Blain, had equipped him for the task and now had fifty quid in his pocket for taking the parcel from Kevin at the pub downtown and bringing it to him buried in his laundry. By the time they latched onto Blain, he'd be long gone, yet he was grateful to his man servant for keeping him informed of what was going on. Admittedly, it was a high wire act, but another Timchuk less, here or there, was of no consequence, except to him. This one had to be closed down. God knows what he could tell them about the death of his brother, and how it had been arranged, from the investigators in Holland. And, for the sake of good old Ambrose, finish him off for setting up the assassination of his closest friend and mentor who had made it possible for him, as well, to be set up for life. Why Ambrose couldn't stop, or maybe couldn't get out of the game, remained a puzzle. He had gone too far with his post-war dealings with the black market gangs here and in Europe, but was amenable enough when he, Todder, declined to join in on the dodgy excitement of dealing with the real underworld. Well, after Timchuk, one more score to be settled, Ambrose, then we'd both be free. When he was in London to undergo that pitiful third degree at CMHQ, he had sneaked in a quick phone call, and now they waited outside in the Vauxhall. He'd soon be away to a new identity, a life of ease and riches in the Irish Republic as one Seamus O'Reilly, the American expatriate veteran returning to his roots, a safe house in Dublin until a suitable property could be found in an obscure town. He realized he had to move fast before the army's punishment machinery groaned into motion and they finally put together a case against him, but now he began to regret his impulsive foray. What had he been thinking of, maybe lousing it up at the last minute?

So what to do now? This lunkhead wasn't about to fall for it. From the corner of his eye he'd glimpsed the dark-uniformed custodian slipping away. What were the odds of Timchuk packing it in, anyway? Only a moment or two and he'd have smothered the fragile mummy. Time to back off.

"Corporal, I am returning to telephone HQ and inform them of your lack of cooperation and outright insubordination. You'll regret this."

"Very well, sir."

Todder marched out, erect as ever, to the lift and out of the rotunda where he could see the old fart babbling into the phone. The two bodyguards from Dublin were there in the Vauxhall, waiting for him and their cut. They seemed relieved he had returned intact.

"No joy there, lads," said the temporary half-colonel, already loosening his belt, unbuttoning his jacket. A navy blue lounge suit was draped on the back seat. "Plan B, let's go."

Curiosity got the better of Horobbins. After reaching Bollock, he went back into the cubicle.

"Nolan, perhaps I shouldn't tell you this, but Major Todder has escaped from his billet. Apparently he went to the hospital to finish off Timchuk, couldn't bring it off, thanks to one of my men, and has slipped away, for the moment. Took off in a black Vauxhall, two civilians seen in the front seat; they'll no doubt change cars and head out of the country somewhere. So what about Todder?"

"I don't get what you're driving at, sir." Nolan, stunned at the thought of Todder on the loose, crunched at a thumbnail.

"Where does he fit? Doesn't Timchuk blame him as much as the colonel?"

"Sure, but first things first, eh? It was a tough call."

"Just tell me, no charges on this one."

"You swear, sir? Well, Timchuk calculated it'd be too much to do both at the same time. Too obvious. As it turned out, Major Todder wasn't around the evening of the sixth, and Joe couldn't put the notebooks into his little roadster. It was always the idea to incriminate him for the killing."

"Todder always insisted he was clean, had nothing to do with the colonel's off-base doings."

"Best as we can figure, he didn't need to. Metro, he's convinced Todder made his pile on the Continent, has big bucks banked away somewhere. Didn't want any part of the Duke's more risky capers with the gangs, probably thought he'd gone over the edge seeking out cheap thrills. I bet Todder's already got a new identity in some place nobody'd look. You'll never find him now."

"You can stop biting your nails. Somehow I don't think he'll be back to finish you guys off, at least for now."

When Bollock stirred up the Met once again the first report came in that Major Todder's lady, Cynthia, was still in residence in her Mayfair flat. Furious at his desertion, forever she realized, not a prayer where he might have gone. Never discussed it with me. Good riddance. Just the same, she was placed under surveillance, but he never called or showed up. A recap of his personnel records confirmed what he had earlier told Horobbins, no known relatives or next of kin listed. If anything happened to him, please contact William McClintock of the moving van company in Toronto.

Montgomery, confronted with Nolan's statement as distilled by Horobbins oral account, careful to keep at least part of his pact of no incrimination of others, finally was brought around by the same promises of repatriation after field punishment, and no charges of being an accessory to murder.

"Don't wanna go home," moped the giant. Horobbins, reminded of Mavis and the imminent return of her sickly husband, nodded in a sympathy that Montgomery realized was genuine.

"What does your lady in Guildford have to say?"

"She says wait and see. I want to wait."

"Then suppose we arrange for you to be posted to one of the depots outside Aldershot and you keep your mouth shut and your nose clean."

"Jeez, you'd do that for me, sir?"

"Depends. One, you have to give me a statement that you were handed the smoking gun by Helmers and put it into play on the craps table. Second, I want the colonel's notebooks."

A huge bass laugh from away down in the hardrock drifts. "In the map compartment in Todder's MG. I'd planned to put 'em there right after the colonel was nailed, but when I went over to the vehicle park after dropping the gun on the craps table, his car wasn't there and soon enough the place was swarming with those guys in green smocks. I waited for a day or two before I could sneak back, remove the tapes and plant the notebooks. Course it never struck me for a moment that nobody'd be back to check out his car again. The major would've taken the rap for the murder for sure. Kinda sloppy work, wouldn't you say?"

An escort of four MPs confirmed his story and brought back the small notebooks. Scribbled in the Duke's cipher, except for astronomical sums of money in pounds and US dollars, zeroes marching out to the margins, then coded names and, manna for the Yard, a series of contact telephone numbers.

"Deal, sir?"

"Done. Whether or not you'll have to testify at the court martial, I can't say at this point. If you do, I'm counting on you to stick by your statement." He nodded to the police steno.

Private Gilmore was duly released from custody after his deposition that, yes, he was quite sure now that he had seen Montgomery at the craps game, but couldn't swear he'd actually seen him place the gun on the table. A frayed code of silence, however, failed to produce any other repat who could remember anything. With the transcripts being typed up in the safety of the Hants nick, Horobbins felt he had enough to proceed with the arrest of Helmers the next day and to extract from him the confession he so desperately needed.

Horobbins got on the phone to Captain Alf Murphy in Germany to ask for a memory refreshment. Hadn't that British captain found evidence in the 21 Group files that Todder inexplicably had taken leave to make his way to Dublin some time in May? On Murphy's affirmative, he was able to help Bollock narrow down the search to air space over the Republic and to the Irish Sea, probably all too late. Undercover spooks over there would have to try and ferret him out.

When he finally mustered the courage to approach Colonel Cameron, already briefed by Clancy on Todder's escape, Horobbins outlined the deals he had made with Nolan and Montgomery, at least on that score pleased with himself, and hoped his boss would agree to the slightly underhanded tactics to bring the culprit around to confession and trial, no fuss, no muss, which was what the upper echelons want, isn't it, sir? Those fellows were on to Wellesley and his involvement in the rackets and, in a way, it was their own version of rough justice in memory of our valiant lads who had fallen in the higher cause. A long silence from his boss, followed by a sigh of resignation, not at all what Horobbins had expected, which could have been a reprimand for stepping out of line and making the decision to let accomplices to murder off the hook in exchange for vital information. Horobbins was ready to invoke precedents, including Bollock's arrangements with Straw Spike and company. Common practice for police anywhere. But that wasn't it.

"Sorry, you'll have to put everything on hold."

"On hold, sir? But we . . ."

"I know. You are not to take any statement from Helmers, yet. Understood? I'll be there tomorrow morning, a meeting at General Spry's office, 1000 hours. You and Clancy, but not the Yard inspector. Something has come up."

Then Colonel Cameron unloaded the really bad news.

PART FOUR

33

Amid the clutter of dun workhorses, the Chevvies and Jeeps, were a black Buick with righthand drive, Canada House car pool, and a Rolls Royce Silver Cloud, no doubt out of wartime storage and immune to petrol rationing. Brand new tires possibly furnished by Straw Spike or like associates. Horobbins, alist with the heavy briefcase, walked down to the headquarters building and paused to contemplate the Buick; he hoped his father's spot welds had been done in his post-sabotage phase when the Soviets had made it a people's war.

Smaller cast this time in General Spry's conference room. Red tabs as usual, worn by the general himself, Colonel Cameron and two legal beagles in uniform who were from the Judge Advocate General's staff, one from London, the other from Aldershot, the same Major Balfour who had sat in on the meeting with the two provost officers from the Continent. Dick Clancy and Horobbins were the lowliest, without much visible adornment. Two civilians were the objects of attention from white-coated mess attendants. Florid hued, the visitors did not seem undernourished as the army servants plied them with cakes, real jam, and buttered scones. Beside the urn were bags of genuine Nabob coffee, as if everyone on staff had been ordered to donate a luxury item from the Canada food parcels.

Roland Falkirk, KC wore the dark striped uniform of the Inns, his white moustache and deepset blue eyes a deceptive Colonel Blimp cover. The other civilian, a James Rowell, third secretary or some such from the Canadian High Commissioner's office, had the puffy weariness of one burdened with paperwork and problems like this.

General Spry, trying with some difficulty to stay judicial in tone, asked for a situation report on the Wellesley case. The three provost officers each offered their piece. Thankful at the foresight of the Hants police stenos, Horobbins distributed the statements he had taken from Nolan, Montgomery, and Gilmore, plus his brief account of his first meeting with Helmers. Knowing their onions, the clerks had cut stencils directly to mimeograph copies that were now perused, the civilians making lip noises at the typos or revelations. Colonel Cameron raised shaggy eyebrows at Horobbins for allowing unedited transcripts out of their care, replete as they were with the seductive tradeoffs proposed by the investigating officer. General (Lucky Dan) Spry glared at the provost contingent for baring its soul. Mucking around with his Water Rats on flooded polder was a cinch compared to this.

"My intention is to convene a Field General Court Martial soonest. I have no doubts about the outcome. Perhaps, Mr. Falkirk, you'd inform us of your interest in what is strictly an internal military affair." As if he didn't know.

"Sir, I am the solicitor representing Mr. Andrew Wellesley, the bereaved father in Montreal, and indirectly on behalf of Mrs. Frederick Lefebvre."

"Who the hell is she?"

"Her maiden name is Elspeth Wellesley. She was at one time married to the late Major Lefebvre who perished in the crash of the aircraft in Essex."

"Good Lord, those Wellesleys do get around. Why her?"

"To merely point out that the lady also has an interest in the family reputation and that of her late ex-husband. I should point out that their solicitors in Montreal are attempting to obtain an injunction against warrants issued by the RCM Police to gain access to their bank accounts and security deposit boxes." He frowned at the grins from the provost. "Sir, the transcripts you have been good enough to share with us today confirm information that has come to our attention from various sources. We submit these documents are most inappropriate to be used as the basis for the charges against Private Helmers. That the texts purporting to record the testimony of soldiers involved in a conspiracy would be aired in court would be highly detrimental to the excellent reputation of the Wellesley family and its commercial interests, if not survival of the latter."

"We won't make it into a circus, Mr. Falkirk. By invitation only. The press will not be admitted and all ranks will be warned of any contact with same. A communiqué will be issued stating the verdict in its barest form."

"I draw your attention to the plethora of copies on this table. The potential for leakage. . . ."

"Obviously, the testimony of the witnesses is essential to secure a conviction. One of them, as you are aware, is seriously ill and unable as yet to make a statement." Meaningful eye contact with Horobbins for indicating otherwise to the suspects. "What would you propose as an alternative?"

"Allow me to reiterate, sir. The allegations that prompted this gang of soldiers to take such drastic action are based on unsubstantiated supposition and flimsy evidence. To use such unreliable material as the basis for prosecution could have far-reaching consequences for the Wellesley family and their business in Montreal. I remind you that a brokerage firm depends entirely on probity and reputation, intangible qualities that can be seriously damaged on the slightest hint or rumour of scandal or dishonesty."

"Mr. Falkirk, as a solicitor who prepares many briefs, I am sure you appreciate that the police, in this case our own provost, offer inducements to encourage witnesses to testify against an accused. I understand it is common practice in police work."

"You misunderstand me, sir. What is offered to witnesses or associates of the accused is of no concern. I might question the wisdom in view of their alleged involvement in the murder, but I am not suggesting that they be arraigned as accessories to murder or the equivalent in military law. On the contrary, our concern for the Wellesley reputation depends in large measure on their *not* testifying, or at least not in the form of their statements we have just read."

"Good God, man, you're suggesting that we drop the whole bloody case?"

"I think, sir," said the Canada House man, a bomb removal expert if ever there was one, "that Mr. Falkirk is here to assist you and your colleagues to explore alternatives to these statements which impugn the Wellesleys' good name."

"The late member of the Wellesley clan might've thought of that beforehand. We can't change the facts."

"With respect, sir," none intended in Falkirk's rolling vowels, "they are subject to dispute to the extent they could muddy the waters at trial." The Canadian legal contingent twitched. "Allow me to pose this question. Is the intent of the accused established?"

"If I am correct, he has not yet signed a statement. We postponed his final interview as a courtesy to you gentlemen."

"Which is soundly appreciated."

Horobbins jumped in. "His intent, no doubt about it, was to kill his CO. It was carried out deliberately."

"Then the question remains: why?"

"From the evidence we have gathered so far, he was prepared to act as a surrogate for Sergeant Timchuk who believed his own brother was . . ."

"Never mind that one, captain. What else?"

"This isn't a bloody courtroom," said Colonel Cameron, who was waved down by the general.

"Private Helmers harboured a deep hatred for Lieutenant Colonel Wellesley based on jealousy and anger. Helmers was also infatuated with a CWAC corporal, one Claire Evans, who later suffered a terrible ordeal at the hands of Colonel Wellesley's brother-in-law and associates. Anyway, Helmers was convinced the colonel had debauched her, taking her out in his car, then to his London flat where his unsavoury cohorts hung out, the two who perished in the Lysander incident."

"Has this wretched soldier been examined by a psychiatrist?"

"Not yet. He will be."

"Then is it not within the realm of possibility that he might be diagnosed as temporarily or even totally insane, based on his obsession with this woman member of your services?"

"It's possible. There's little doubt he was able to detach himself from normal human feelings to commit such a dire act. On the other hand, it does appear that others, notably Sergeant Timchuk, took advantage of his unsettled mental state and were able to prod him into it. His decision was a calculated risk implemented with deliberation and a steady hand. How a psychiatrist might analyze his mental state, we can't predict at this stage."

"Do you believe any such assessment could mitigate the severity of punishment?"

"Not likely," said the JAG man from London. "The intent was clear."

The Canada House official, Rowell, tried to extricate the Wellesley solicitor. "I think we're moving off point here. Let me ask the legal and provost gentlemen this. In your opinion, was the primary motivation of Helmers based on sexual jealousy and rage?"

The khaki jury huddled in whispers; the lawyer from CMHQ was elected as foreman.

"It's the considered opinion of my colleagues, in all probability, yes. But he was goaded into it by Sergeant Timchuk for different motives, and the others went along."

"Against whom you are recommending leniency. What is unusual is your willingness to accept at face value their rather fantastic tales of black markets and a murder on the Continent. You appear to accept their word for everything."

"Not just theirs." Horobbins was furious. "We have full reports from two senior provost officers on the Continent and their British counterparts who investigated Colonel Wellesley's illicit activities. A civilian now in the custody of Scotland Yard has direct knowledge of the whole setup. We have also recovered notebooks in which the colonel detailed his transactions and with whom. Then there's Major Todder."

"Ah, this Todder, he has slipped through your hands, has he not? Suppose he is located and brought back. What might we expect from him?"

"Difficult to say. His flight confirms what we have always suspected, that he made a pile of ill-gotten gains over there, as did the colonel, who cut him in on a good piece of the action. We suspect Todder has a planned escape route complete with a new identity. We have evidence he attempted to dispose of Sergeant Timchuk at the hospital before he took off. We have information his likely destination is the Republic of Ireland, and we are planning to ask the British to put their agents on it."

"Actually," said Mr. Falkirk, too late to recover from the gaffe, "it'd be better for all concerned if Major Todder is never placed in a position where he could wreak further damage. If there is a villain in this piece, it's him, and we are of the opinion he is the one who led Lieutenant Colonel Wellesley astray, not the other way round."

In the stunned silence, the Canada House man trotted out his diplomatic armoury. "In view of the controversial and unsubstantiated nature of the allegations against Lieutenant Colonel Wellesley, would it not be prudent to construct your prosecution solely on the basis of the culprit's sexual fury? Temporary insanity it may be, but as Captain—ah—has explained, the deed was carefully thought out and executed. Whether or not he had assistance, tacit or otherwise, doesn't detract from the man's resolve and ability to carry it out. In other words, everything else is extraneous to the successful completion of the case. What I am suggesting is that sexual infatuation and jealousy could become the basis for the prosecution. The other witnesses, with their tales of illicit activities, could be dispensed with."

General Spry was aghast. "You're suggesting the Wellesley family could live with a sexual scandal, but not one involving criminal behaviour?"

"They reside in Montreal, sir, not Toronto."

The conference grinned. The climate thawed slightly.

"If you could see your way clear to pursuing the course of action suggested by my friend here, my clients would be chagrined but not disgraced. With long absence in the war, there is a certain tolerance in society for such peccadillos," said Mr. Falkirk.

The general pointed to the mimeographed sheets. "Are you proposing that we not introduce these statements or we alter them?"

"Surely it would not be untoward to conduct followup interviews with them to confirm the motivation of the accused," said Falkirk.

Colonel Cameron clamped a hand onto Horobbins's shoulder to hold him down.

"Given the direction of this discussion, perhaps I should now introduce this," said Rowell, reaching into a briefcase. "I have here copies of a letter from our prime minister, the Right Honourable Mackenzie King. It is an expression of sympathy to Andrew Wellesley on the dastardly and untimely death of his son in the aftermath of the Aldershot disturbances. He promises his old friend, and I may say financial supporter, that he will personally ensure that every resource is directed to the arrest and punishment of the perpetrator. The High Commissioner, too, is well acquainted with Andrew Wellesley."

"I don't recall receiving a copy," said the general.

"It arrived only yesterday in cipher from Ottawa, sir. Mr. Massey has seen it and commends it to your attention."

Falkirk seemed to veer off course again. "May I ask, assuming this soldier is found guilty, will he face the firing squad, same as that chap in Italy?"

Spry, pretending to be shocked, waved a finger. "Mr. Rowell?" The diplomat blushed. "Yes, a much-delayed execution at our depot in Avellino, east of Naples. One of those gangs of deserters in Rome, he apparently knocked off his pal, another Canadian, also on the loose. Thoroughly bad bunch. The sentence by court martial was referred to Ottawa, as is required, and finally approved after a certain political event in June. It's the only case I'm aware of in this war. In the First War a couple of dozen Canadians were executed for sins we no longer regard as capital offences. Also, a number of rioters were shot in an outbreak similar to the one we've just endured, in Wales in 1919.

But at no time in this war has a senior officer been shot down in cold blood."

"And there are the hangings."

"Yes, six of our men were duly convicted for murder here in the UK, tried by British courts and hanged."

"And did His Majesty's government not take a close interest in this case, agreeing to the secondment of manpower from Scotland Yard and other agencies?"

"Quite right. The threatening note and the gas respirator left at the scene aroused concerns of wider implications. We have cooperated fully with them. As it turns out there was no political or revolutionary conspiracy. Except for the Yard men who are still assisting us, I believe the other investigators have stood down."

"If I am correct, sir, it still could be possible for Whitehall to express an interest in the case under the Visiting Forces Act."

"As I'm sure you know, the Act applies to civil offences."

"Murder was considered a civil offence when your six soldiers were executed."

"No civilians involved here. When a soldier shoots an officer at a Canadian base it is strictly a matter for disposal by military law. I assume the High Commissioner's office will make that clear to the British authorities. Mr. Rowell?"

"No argument there from our standpoint. Of course, with the British election we can't predict what the policy of a new government might be."

Mr. Falkirk wouldn't let go. "In all likelihood, then, this soldier will also face a firing squad?"

"Until I am instructed otherwise, that's the drill."

The Canada House man now ventured into deeper waters. "Sir, you're well aware of the Order-in-Council in May 1944 to the effect that where a sentence of death has been passed by a court martial under Canadian military law, the Governor-in-Council has the exclusive power to confirm both the finding and the sentence of the court martial."

"Of course. The cabinet approved the sentence to be carried out in Italy."

"Is it not within the realm of possibility that considerations of higher policy objectives could enter into this case with wider implications than the straight forward case in Italy? I need not remind anyone in this room that we are still engaged in a mighty conflict with Japan. If the savage battles for Saipan and Okinawa are any indication—in the latter over twelve thousand American deaths, let alone Japanese military and civilians in human wave attacks and suicide—we are in for a lengthy and difficult time. We must assume that Kyushu and Honshu will be far worse even than those campaigns. Our forces will face extremely high casualties, possibly leading to another reinforcement crisis even more acute than the last one."

Spry was contemptuous. "Mr. Rowell, Canada is committing only one division and supporting arms, a miserable token effort. If we can't maintain one division in the field what kind of country are we supposed to be? Our allies will laugh at us."

"We well remember what happened, sir, when on the outbreak of war in 1939 it was thought that a relatively risk-free, low casualty effort would suffice. The exigencies of the struggle dictated otherwise. It could occur again, is all I'm saying. We can't predict, but there are concerns arising now about the problem of maintaining morale once the invasion begins. Mr. King's unwavering devotion to national unity and support for the war effort will, I suggest, supersede anything else, including the warmth of his affection and sympathy for the Wellesley family.

"Therefore, should such policy considerations prevail, it is conceivable that the cabinet could instruct the army to return the convicted man to Canada for ultimate decision as to execution. I am not in any way contradicting what you said, sir, but they could conclude that this is no time to stir up public debate over the firing squad death of a hapless, mentally disturbed soldier who until now, I believe, has a conscientious record of service. Especially so when the conviction of enemy ss officers responsible for the cold-blooded slaughter of over a hundred Canadian prisoners in Normandy seems to be bogged down in technicalities. The comparison might well prove to be odious. A half-hearted effort to arrest and convict mass murderers, but severe justice for a poor demented soul who, unlike the other one, is not a deserter or gangster. It's entirely within these considerations that the cabinet might conclude that the convicted man should be sent back to Canada and his execution postponed until a more suitable time or even indefinitely if he was to be confined to a psychiatric institution."

"Mr. Rowell, what's your rank at Canada House? What gives you the authority to spout forth on high policy matters?"

"Of course, sir, these are not my own. The High Commissioner has given his usual careful thought to the question. I am merely conveying his preliminary views. Mr. Massey summoned us after Mr. Falkirk had seen him. He then asked me to communicate his thoughts to this meeting. Naturally he will explore the implications with Ottawa and your superiors."

"Good Christ, man, couldn't you have given me some prior warning? Frankly, I'm amazed. You realize what you're proposing? That we pervert the due process of military justice? I'll get on the blower to General Montague. None of us here," meaningful glower around the table, "is in any position to comment on this outlandish proposal."

"If I may continue, sir. If this possibility was indeed to be held out to the accused, he might prove to be willing to sign a statement along the lines we put forward."

"The Wellesleys and the government both off the hook, eh? Very ingenious, gentlemen, but it won't wash. Yes?" Spry swung around to a staff captain who tiptoed in with a piece of paper he held out to the general. "Gentlemen, I have to report that the prime witness for the prosecution, Sergeant Timchuk, passed away at 0800 hours today. Liver failure."

The Canada House man bowed his head, not in prayer.

"A shame, poor man."

34

On a soft damp morning the soldiers confined to barracks since the murder awakened to find the siege had been lifted. In vests and baggy shorts they gathered outside to wonder at the empty square, the absence of MPs and Hants police who had vanished overnight. Their unknown sergeant loped over from the orderly room to read out the names of those who, as Pacific volunteers, were granted first dibs on transport, to be moved out to Liverpool the next day from North Station. Their elation was muted by thoughts of what might await them once they had passed through Canada to the US army base in the South, probably Fort Bragg, to be armed with Garands and bazookas, and packed off to the unwelcoming shores of Japan.

At that time they knew nothing of the Jornada del Meurto Valley near Alamogordo, New Mexico, where the radiant sands had risen to the sky in the first A-bomb test. Nor did they have an inkling by Tuesday, 31 July 1945 that the end of the war was nigh. Agreements and understandings had been made, and on 21 July Churchill and Truman reluctantly decreed the A-bomb must be used, bearing in mind that the fire bombing of Japan's cities, with the loss of some 280,000 lives, had failed to bring forth pleas for surrender from a stubborn island folk like the Brits, plus military estimates of upwards of one million casualties in a land invasion. When he was informed of their decision, Joseph Stalin didn't raise an eyebrow; certain scientists on the Manhattan Project already had told him. On 26 July the US Strategic Air Forces were ordered to deliver the first "special" bomb on or about the third of August. Four target cities were selected, but the Americans told no one they had only two bombs ready. Even after Hiroshima, Japanese resolve and belief remained firm that there was only one workable bomb—until the second one dropped on Nagasaki.

And equally in the dark, as it were—those shut into the card room of the officers' mess of the old cavalry barracks in downtown Aldershot—awaited the trial of Private Glen Helmers. Whispers of dire retribution were rampant. You believe it? They shot that poor guy after the war, for chrissake.

Actually, the court martial of Private Helmers could have been held earlier, but there were British expert witnesses, Bollock, his forensics and others, who might wish to cast their ballots in the election of Thursday, 26 July. It was more than mere courtesy, a cautionary pause to wait and see and, as it unfolded, to be shaken as were so many others at the defeat of Churchill by that grey mouse Attlee. Bollock was in a foul mood on the following Tuesday morning. His approach to the central officers' mess building on Wellington Avenue had added to his gloom. The past greeted him with its nineteenth-century façade, the pilasters, the Royal Arms carved above the portal. The future was hinted at in the garden where little green men, Italian prisoners with amused lassitude and drooping fags, dabbed at imaginary weeds. Bollock flipped his passage at the sentries and went in along a hall of glass hutches filled with obscure silver trophies.

"Ruin. Utter ruin. And when they've finished, the workers will wake up to the old class system still in place," he told Horobbins who became distracted by Bollock's slump. "Maybe I should migrate to Canada."

"Think again. A great future, but you realize there are no pubs?"

"Where do you go for a pint?"

"Beer parlours. Awful places. You have to get a government permit to buy spirits." Bollock shook his head in disbelief.

Uniforms milled about in the tiled foyer while striped and pipped wranglers with clipboards sorted them out under the anxious eye of Colonel (The Fixer) Capson who was charged with overseeing the exercise, a comedown from the days of hauling in burnt out hulks of Sherman tanks. Witnesses, hived off to separate rooms to brood at muskets and spears on the walls, were watched lest they get any ideas. So installed were Nolan, wobbly from pack drill at Maida, and unsweaty Montgomery, having enjoyed the mild workout; Claire Evans, the forensics, medical officers, and so forth.

Bollock and Horobbins, not on call, took their seats behind the prosecutor's table and made their professional scan of the trial scene as the much-restricted spectators were allowed in, a contingent small enough to fit into an English country house library, as in the finale of an Agatha Christie mystery. The Press was kept far off limits by a barrier of military police.

Lancers in tight breeches once had sprawled here to "haw and by George" at the day's riding school, their iron-shod friends, the mounts, evaluated with the same snide critique as the fillies at the last squadron quadrille. As if the windows had never been opened, the faint imprint of stale cigars, port and brandy remained. Cracked leather divans had been pushed to the crested walls to make room for a few rows of antique wooden chairs. At right angles a line of elegant card tables of tropical woods denoted where the court martial panel would sit, beyond the blackened stone fireplace under its display of sabres and lances.

Karen Williams behind him tapped Horobbins on the shoulder.

"They won't let me stay with her."

"Not to worry. We'll see if the court accepts her written statement. I've persuaded the prosecutor and defence to lay off."

"She's in no shape to."

"One thing we agree on."

"This is terrible," Claire had said to Horobbins. "I can't go. It has nothing to do with me."

"It had everything to do with you." Horobbins, having been given his orders after the session in General Spry's office, hoped his distaste for the revised scenario didn't show. "Helmers would never have shot Colonel Wellesley but for his obsession. There are other factors, yes, but we aren't pursuing the vengeance question. In any event it was secondary, nothing more than the little push that sent Helmers on his rampage."

"Fat, smelly Glen? I can't believe it. You mean he was mooning after me all this time?"

"I'm afraid so, as confirmed by Nolan and Montgomery. Unfortunately, we no longer have Sergeant Timchuk to testify. You can read the confession I've obtained from Helmers. No doubt about it, he was convinced he was saving you from a fate worse than death."

"Can we show a bit more sensitivity here?" said Karen Williams. "You realize what you're saying to her, that she was the direct cause of murder?"

Horobbins sat back and allowed his more kindly instincts to soften his olive face. He pulled at his hooked nose, came down from the Gestapo role-playing he had needed to return to the witnesses and persuade them, actually order them, to review their original testimony, that is, if they entertained any hope the mercies he had promised would go through. He could not reveal, of course, the whole deal was a scheme to save Wellesley face, as in a kind of Oriental ritual. The revised statements were then presented to Helmers with the bait of return to Canada, possibly even escape from execution over the course of time, if he could face up to a stretch in the loony bin to plumb his twisted motivation. As well, his loyal pals depended on him coming through; his last good deed to save them from dire fates as accessories to murder. You wouldn't want them to be fingered for that, would you? Helmers, having brooded alone in his cell, wondering why there was an absence of the third degree, appeared to accept the glimmer of daylight. At length, without much more push from Horobbins, he went along, agreed to admit guilt, and to subject himself to interview by a psychiatrist. More hesitantly, as part of the deal, he allowed he would subject himself to the attentions of an Anglican padre who was anxious to examine the accused's spiritual depths, or lack of same. His family, Helmers told the provost captain, belonged to some Calvary or Nazarene congregation and had no use for the Church of England, but okay, he'd go along.

"Should I babble or something?" he had asked Horobbins with amazing resilience.

"It might help."

"What if I say I thought he was the devil?"

"Good idea."

The problem was the authorities wanted Claire Evans on the stand to confirm that she had no knowledge of Helmers's unwelcome yearnings, nor had she given him encouragement in any way. This was what she was resisting.

"You mean he actually thought that Ambrose had forced me to go with him, that I was his victim? What's the matter with him? He saw me in the office every day. Couldn't he see that I was happy, in love or infatuated? At least before I found out what he was really like, but that happened after Ambrose was shot. Glen had no reason to believe I was doing anything else but following my own emotions of my own free will."

"Say that to the panel. You may not even be asked. I'll do what I can."

"I appreciate you'll do your best for me."

"We've had enough of his best," said Williams.

"I'll try to persuade the prosecutor and the defending officer that nothing is to be gained by subjecting you to this ordeal. You've been through enough. But one thing I can't do, I can't prevent the court from ordering you to appear as a witness. We'll just have to take it from there. If you will come with me, we'll take your statement."

"I guess I'm in your hands."

With an army melting away, a scramble for the cast of characters required for a Field General Court Martial on General Spry's convening order threw out a wide and tattered net. Eventually rounded up, cajoled, threatened, a motley group of officers straggled to Aldershot. Most leaned upon was a young lieutenant, Edgar Maxwell, who was fished out of the repat pond, pounced on for his year at Osgoode Law School in Toronto. Age twenty-one, fresh out of officer training in Brockville to arrive in Holland in mid-May, he had volunteered for the Pacific Force, bereft of campaign ribbons but sporting a Royal Winnipeg Rifles flash, a place he had never been to and never hoped to see. A press gang of white webs had lifted him from a lorry out of Ewshot repat depot on the way to a troopship.

"Splendid dry run for a dazzling career on Bay Street," said Balfour from Spry's entourage. "You are to defend the evil slob who popped off the colonel."

"That one? Jeez, sir, I'd rather be on my way to Japan."

"Plenty of time for that. The first waves will be mowed down. Here's the bumf. Better go see the guilty bastard."

It began with a petition submitted by Lieutenant Edgar Maxwell who showed alarming signs of taking his job seriously. Colonel Capson, as chief mechanic, had denied his request. Now the indulgence of the court was craved. Horobbins frowned, annoyed at Bollock for being transfixed by the mimeographed copy he now passed along with a resigned shrug. It seemed Maxwell had consulted a number of press cuttings from the *News of the World.* The document was a request to summon a key civilian witness, one Ronald Mayberry, AKA Straw Spike, in police custody relating to the deaths of Lt. Col. Samuel Yates, Maj. Frederick Lefebvre, and an as yet unidentified pilot. As Mr. Mayberry, the petition avowed, had an intimate relationship with the late Lt. Col. Ambrose Wellesley, his testimony as to the alleged illegal activities of the primary murder victim, viz. Lt. Col. Wellesley, is essential to clarify the character of same and what could be interpreted by the perpetrators as justification for their actions in persuading a naïve and innocent soldier to execute the deed for them.

"Denied," said the court martial president. "The person you would bring before this court is a criminal, a liar, and could add nothing to the procedures on hand. Irrelevant."

"Sir, the question that must be decided here is who exactly is the criminal."

"Sit down, Mr. Maxwell."

The president, turning a baleful eye onto the prosecutor, ordered him to call his case. The battered major assigned to what should be a snap, handed over what he termed "undisputed statements," the forensic, ballistics, autopsy reports and the like. The panel skipped through them, pausing only to hover over the romance of Corporal Evans, to cluck and smack lips and, eager to view her in person, gave a collective nod to admit her written statement. They watched avidly as Karen Williams brought her into the courtroom from a witness room and, despite her nun-like paleness, silently agreed she was a dish. No wonder good old Ambrose. . . .

"Seems to have recovered," Bollock said on the afternoon of the first day. "A budding barrister, no less."

Young Maxwell clearly was showing signs of an aptitude for litigation, rather than the corporate law practiced by his father's firm in Toronto. A forerunner, twenty years before it became fashionable, he had discovered the exhilaration of a subversive tweaking of authority and its rigged trial. Some vague sense of principle had stirred him. Justice? A fluid goal not to be defined solely by those who sought revenge to protect the reputation of one of their own. For that was the brief here. No other.

In a manner he would later hone to a fine art of cross examination, he appeared to stammer, hesitate, a lock of blonde hair a pendulum brushing his concerned brow and, as he went on, he began to affect a stoop, leaning towards the witnesses who were unshakable in their perjury. With no Sergeant Timchuk to contradict them, both Nolan and Montgomery said their piece, obviously programmed by inducements from Horobbins and company. Marching orders had been issued. Both men denied complicity, even though Montgomery admitted to taking the murder weapon from Helmers to the craps game. From the same hymn book they swore Helmers had purchased the Luger for a quid or two from Sergeant Timchuk. They invoked social work. Concerned with their fat pal's infatuation over the delectable Corporal Evans, they had tried to dissuade him. A glamour puss, all right, Montgomery had put on his best leer, causing heads to swivel again in her direction while the object of this attention gave every signal of wishing she could drop through the floor. Maxwell regretted he had gone along with the provost captain's request on humanitarian grounds not to call her and allow her written statement to suffice. Even with the rejection of his petition for Straw Spike and the rigged testimony, he soldiered on.

The rubbing of khaki derrieres on antique card chairs was, Maxwell realized, not entirely the impatience of a lynching party, but a bunch of mostly red tabs who wanted it over with so they could pack their bags for the next troopship. The senior officer, the "president" of the court martial, was a full colonel in more ways than one. Seemingly a holdover, stout with grog blossoms, he had been extracted from some back office on Cockspur Street as if he had gone into hiding when the old army sots were weeded out and sent home early on, before the war turned serious. Two half-colonels and two majors from God-knows-where rounded out the five-man panel of judges who, instead of judicial robes, wore black and red armbands.

The one he kept his eyes on was not an actual member of the panel, but an alert and pushy half-colonel who sat at the elbow of the president. In effect the ringmaster, he was the Judge Advocate out of the JAG staff in London, with the implied authority of *de facto* judge and jury. Thin in face, steel-rimmed glasses, razor jaw line, the very stereotype of Puritan justice, he whispered constantly into the president's purple ear to dictate spot rulings on the admissibility of evidence and to hand him scribbled cues. His hostility to Maxwell almost shook the young lieutenant from his appointed role, the buzz of the Italy execution now seen as precedent. But with Japan on the horizon he decided to try out his fledgling litigation wings with the knowledge he would soon be infantry fodder with the usual lifespan of three weeks, if that.

What could he do?

As he pondered his shrinking armoury of options, only one seemed to have any hope of uncovering the truth, and he would have to use a third party to do it. Before the trial, a brief meeting had been held with the examining psychiatrist, Major Solomon. The prosecutor and Maxwell had attended together to settle the fundamental question: Was the accused fit to stand trial? Yes, he was, the psychiatrist assured them, but with the provisos in my preliminary report. The prosecutor, Maxwell thought with the trepidation of an untried subaltern, is one tough cookie: Major Hazlet, with gongs on his chest to suggest more than one war, including a Military Cross, enough wound stripes on his sleeve to attract gold speculators, and a reconstructed face with white skin grafts, the badges of so many true warriors. A top gun from General Spry's staff sent in to nail it down. Whatever his legal training, he was totally confident and dedicated to a guilty verdict, hence his quick dismissal of the psychiatric evaluation of the accused.

"That's all we need to know." Hazlet scanned the report and put it away into his briefcase. "Mr. Maxwell?"

"Agreed he's fit enough to stand, but I want to read the report very carefully."

"Won't cut the mustard. Don't waste your time."

Now Maxwell watched uneasily as the accused was marched in with an escort, a private from the orderly room where he had worked, possibly his only friend, at least for now; the latter duly saluted, reported in and sat with Helmers who was hatless and still as a bowl of vanilla pudding. After failing to create any rapport or much response in his interviews with Helmers, his defence counsel decided not to call him to the stand. Military protocol gave the prosecutor, Hazlet, first crack at burying the accused with expert proof of guilt. After the devastating attack, Maxwell desperately called upon one last card, a faint hope, to be sure: the psychiatrist who had also tried to get under the fat clerk's hide and, judging from his report, with somewhat more success. The prisoner apparently had enjoyed the exercise and played along obligingly to provide the profile of one temporarily demented, his only hope to elude the firing squad or noose.

Okay, Maxwell told himself, we'll ambush the bastards. Worth a shot.

"Fuckin' A, sir," as the scabrous members of the platoon he had briefly shepherded in Germany would put it.

"What so amuses you, Mr. Maxwell?" the president wanted to know.

35

"Doctor, or should I say 'Major' Solomon, could you describe your qualifications and background in treating soldiers with mental or emotional disorders?"

Major Solomon had a slight flutter of his left eyelid, a winking effect that might lead one to bromides such as "physician, heal thyself." Whatever the distraction, the repose of his gaunt countenance and deep bass voice soon overrode the tic to the extent that several in the room wondered if he was open to private consultations.

"I am currently a consultant neurologist and psychiatrist at CMHQ, London, and am an adviser to the Judge Advocate General's department. Prior to that I was at Number One Neurological, Basingstoke, before it closed earlier this month. It was a unique facility, combining neurology, neurosurgery, and psychiatry under one roof. None of our allies had such a fine service. I was also involved in establishing forward treatment units in Northwest Europe from July 1944 to January this year. Relevant to the matter before this court, I carried out examinations of soldiers under sentence in English penitentiaries for offences under the Visiting Forces Act."

"Including the six unfortunates who were hanged by the British?"

"Three of them, yes. I also did a special assessment of soldiers in detention centres with attention to the psychopathic personality. However, this work was interrupted by the D-Day landings and my duties on the Continent."

"I believe you are a recognized authority on battle exhaustion or shell shock, as it used to be called. Correct? Then do you have any observations in that area that would be helpful to the court?"

"Frankly, I don't see the relevance here."

"But you have articulated certain conclusions."

"My views are well known and committed to paper. The slowness and reluctance of senior army commanders in Northwest Europe to learn from the earlier lessons of battle exhaustion in our forces in Italy had dire results. . . ."

"Lieutenant Maxwell, have him stick to the matter at hand," the president said, prompted by a note passed by an irate Judge Advocate.

"If I may rephrase, sir, do you have views on psychoneuroses that encompass more than battle exhaustion?"

"Yes, I do. Again my reports are duly on file. As I examined the psychiatric problems of the army in England and after it went into action, I came to certain conclusions, namely, that the conditions of war itself affect everyone in the forces to some degree. The impact of actual battle is a specialized field of study and treatment. Battle exhaustion cases are only a small part of the overall pressures of being in the army in wartime."

"If I'm not misinterpreting this, Major Solomon, you are implying that even those in non-combatant roles may be vulnerable to various forms of mental dislocation."

"Correct. For instance, during the rocket attacks on London we did see, for the first time, symptoms similar to battle exhaustion among clerical staff and drivers at CMHQ and other units."

"That's understandable, but thinking of the long period of inaction in England, entirely aside from bombing raids or rockets, what would be typical symptoms?"

"Military culture itself creates its own social pressures: irresponsibility, alienation, boredom, resentment of discipline, to name a few, often resulting in anxiety neuroses and reactive depression."

"Yet, until very recently, our entire army overseas was made up of volunteers, unlike the British or Americans. Did you find any difference in behaviour?"

"I haven't examined that question. I suspect the overriding tensions of military life under wartime conditions would be basically the same. Whether volunteer or conscript, the citizen soldier must contend with a conflict of values."

"Values?"

"Yes, the values of individuals as civilians *versus* the duties of soldiers imposed upon them by impersonal and demanding mass conditioning. Essentially, training to do the unnatural; that is, to destroy the enemy."

The president shook off jabs from the nemesis at his elbow. "Absolute balderdash. It's a slur against the gallant record of Canadian troops. Our boys joined up for a high purpose, to defeat the Nazis and their foul assault on those civilized values you speak of. Next, the beastly Japs. Most of our soldiers come from good Christian families. Are you trying to tell us that dedication and religion don't matter?"

"Sir, I didn't intend to leave that impression. Of course there was an underlying purpose, a nasty job to be done. Few illusions there. And I agree, we found that soldiers with religious beliefs tended to be better equipped for recovery than some others. What we learned, despite resistance from some senior commanders, is that prompt front-line treatment could turn around most battle exhaustion cases in a few days. As well as the factors you mention, sir, the prime motivation of the soldier in the field is not to let down his comrades in his unit. New replacements were particularly vulnerable, lacking, as it were, the unit bonding so essential to physical and mental survival. I'm afraid it is true that, over and over again, our troops were committed to highly dangerous tasks by their senior commanders who tended to ignore the thinning of ranks, the replacement crisis, and extreme hardship on those remaining. One general I won't name accused our worn out soldiers of a 'lack of gumption.' Battalion commanders who objected were removed. Based on our recent work, my colleagues and I estimate that modern warfare generates a very high cost in what we might term 'invisible' wounds. The trends we have observed and dealt with can be projected into a rate of at least thirty percent of all casualties invalided out of the army in the future will be on the basis of psychiatric disabilities."

"If your witness persists in inflicting an academic lecture, Mr. Maxwell, I shall ask you to stand him down. We haven't touched on the mental state of the accused, which I presume is why he's here, nothing else."

Maxwell showed courage under fire. "Sir, I hope you and the distinguished members of the panel will bear with us. To understand the mental state and motivation of the accused, we need in all fairness to examine the underlying conditions of service that Major Solomon has so ably described. We still need his assessment of the accused himself."

Whereupon the panel huddled in whispered argument and sent their president back to the cat-bird seat to allow Maxwell to continue, but for God's sake remain on target.

"Major Solomon, your account of recovery from battle exhaustion emphasizes unit or team loyalty as a key factor. You depend on your comrades; they depend on you. Then, sir, what kind of ethic sustains those who are not in such close, mutually-supportive situations? Do they have the same sense of responsibility to one another?"

"It's much more complicated. Barracks life, by its nature, brings forth friendships, alliances, and enmities. Discipline exists; duties are performed. The intensity of bonding, however, is not the same where actual danger has to be confronted."

"Is it possible, though, that a few men might find a common cause or carry out certain actions based on shared concerns?"

"Are you referring to the recent disturbances in Aldershot?"

"Could they not be interpreted as a spontaneous outburst against the conditions of military life you have outlined, prompted by delay in their repatriation?"

"The psychopathology of crowd behaviour or mobs is another branch of study."

"I'm not referring to the riots. The question here is one of a few soldiers who sincerely believed they were carrying out an action to redress a grievance and injustice, and so persuaded one of their number to do it."

The president didn't need a note to intervene. "Mr. Maxwell, I'm calling this line of examination to a halt, right now. Major Solomon is giving evidence, not you. Witness, please turn your mind to your own assessment of the accused, his mental state, and motivation. Let's move along."

A quick student of military behaviour, the psychiatrist now tiptoed through the minefield.

248

"My time with the subject was limited to about forty-eight hours, not continuously. I hope the court appreciates that my observations must be preliminary. A number of tests I would usually administer were not made. The subject, however, was cooperative and attempted in his own way to be helpful, a rational decision on his part that I suspect was in response to some inducements offered by the investigators. That, of course, is beyond my purview. In short, sir, I concluded that the accused is mentally competent to stand trial and so conveyed my findings to the prosecutor and defending officer. He was quite forthcoming about his background, which may have had a cumulative effect among other factors to allow him to undertake the extreme action he did. The court should realize that he does not deny he pulled the trigger. However, he has not come to terms with the prospect of execution as a consequence of his crime. He does have certain protective traits, including dissociation, as if someone else had carried out the act."

"Sir," interrupted Maxwell, "you've done research on military criminals and psychopaths. Would you describe the accused as a psychopath?"

"In my limited time I can't offer you a firm opinion. Some of the characteristics are there, especially the inability to foresee the consequences of certain behaviour; on the other hand, he does not conform to the traditional patterns of the psychopath. Such personality types are totally refractive to any form of discipline and are incapable of group allegiance or bonding of the type essential to cooperative survival in battle. They are egocentric, follow their own instinctive drives, and never learn from past experience. Impulsive, immature, they cannot accept collective motivation. In fact, there was an experiment with the assumption that strict discipline and rigid rules could modify the behaviour of repeated offenders discharged from detention. A Number Ten Canadian Training Company was formed. Frankly, the experiment was an utter failure. Working together, teamwork, discipline had absolutely no meaning to them. On those criteria I cannot classify the accused as a psychopath. His record of service, his relationships with this superiors and bunkmates, showed no typical behaviour patterns of the psychopath."

"Then in God's name, what was he? How could a supposedly normal person commit such a heinous crime?" The president again broke step to confront the witness directly.

"The victim was the psychopath," Maxwell was heard to mutter.

"I didn't mean to imply that he was completely normal, a subjective concept that can't be quantified precisely. He does have the symptoms of a personality disorder within a rather narrow range of stimuli. It is quite possible that pressures of familial and institutional socialization may have led him to act out his perceptions of reality. I draw your attention to his army service record, including the Kiska expedition, where his performance was rated highly. Only belatedly did the investigators discover he was an expert marksman. With your permission, I'd like to review some of the salient points brought out in my interviews."

Permission granted.

"From an early age Glen Helmers sensed he was an unwelcome addition to an already small, crowded household with two older brothers and two sisters who called him 'an accident.' He was reluctant to say how his parents treated him, but he did refer to being 'belted' for slowness in performing chores and resistance to church attendance. Perhaps subconsciously in rebellion, Glen became a fat child, physically unattractive in a family that, from his accounts, prided itself on appearance. Then in 1931, when drought and disaster ruined the Prairie farmers, their little home east of Saskatoon became overcrowded with other children sent by relatives who could no longer support them. As many as five cousins slept on floor mattresses or in the basement. They, too, subjected Glen Helmers to merciless teasing and, he claims, physical abuse. When I raised the matter of sexual abuse, he became uncommunicative and shook his head.

"Under these conditions, it is not surprising that the accused took steps to isolate himself from what he felt was an intolerable home environment. Around the age of ten, like most boys in the west, he had access to a twenty-two rifle. Firearms and ammunition were kept carelessly for general use. He found ways of sneaking away with a rifle wrapped in a blanket. Open fields were nearby where he took flour sacks, filled them with earth, and drew faces of his tormentors on them. Despite being myopic he became an expert shot. In the household armoury was a twenty-two long-barrelled revolver, which he also mastered. The shooting of dummy replicas was a form of catharsis and enabled him to cope with constant harassment. He admits a repressed desire to actually shoot his cousins, but never followed through. 'They weren't worth it,' he told me. 'But Colonel Wellesley was?' I asked. 'Damn right, he had it coming,' he exclaimed. When I went on to ask him why, he stared at me in a pitying kind of way and merely said: 'You haven't figured that out, yet?'

"As soon as he was eighteen in 1943, he joined the army. Unlike his brothers, of course, he didn't meet the physical standards of the navy where they now serve, or the air force. Not surprisingly, military life was not an escape from torment—if anything worse, because of the ribbing he took from conscripts, in his estimation a bunch of lowlife cowards. His uniforms never fit properly; he's described in his personnel reports as 'untidy, sloppy, with a poor attitude.' I suggest this may be more attributable to his physical appearance and personal withdrawal. Yet, as we see from his records, nobody complained about his abilities as an intelligent, efficient clerk."

"Major Solomon, sorry to break your train of thought, but I believe there's some reference to a pervasive body odor that further isolated him. Can you comment?"

"You'll appreciate, Mr. Maxwell, there wasn't time to conduct clinical tests along those lines. Yes, it's the first thing you notice if you arrive in his vicinity."

The panel of officers and spectators guffawed, snorted and nudged, bringing forth for the first time a reaction from the defendant. Helmers raised his head, his grey eyes scorched the room until it fell silent. It didn't help him, Horobbins noted, when the panel sat up and took notice, as if realizing that this bulging sack of jelly indeed could commit mayhem.

"Yes, a sensitive matter to raise with him," Solomon resumed. "It appears the condition did not develop fully until he arrived overseas. Emotional stress can stimulate overactivity in the apocrine or eccrine sweat-producing glands. The former, located under arms and in the anal-genital areas, can produce strong body odor. As the clerical tasks at the repatriation unit were not especially onerous, we must look to other factors. It seems emotionally he became enamoured of the CWAC corporal who he idealized. While he made no overtures to her, in fact, he may have intensified the body odor syndrome subconsciously to signal his own unattractiveness and hopeless prospects. In passing, I am of the opinion that Private Helmers is heterosexual in orientation."

"I should hope so," said the president.

"When it became evident the woman was becoming romantically involved with Lieutenant Colonel Wellesley, he was devastated, disappointed in her and blamed his CO for exploiting her innocence. In his duties as the colonel's clerk-typist, his resentment was exacerbated by his superior's derogatory jibes at his personal hygiene.

"However, it is a giant step from sublimating one's emotions and ideals to committing murder. How he arrived at that state of mind is difficult to reconstruct with exactitude. Much more time would be needed. It is apparent, though, that a number of factors occurred. One came from his friends and protectors in billets, where both Private Nolan and Sapper Montgomery shared views that their CO was involved in illegal activities of some sort. Then along came one Sergeant Timchuk, a repat who was startled then enraged to discover Colonel Wellesley in command of the unit. Timchuk had been briefed by an investigating provost officer at the time of his brother's funeral in Holland in May. Corporal Timchuk, the brother, who as it turns out was Colonel Wellesley's driver, was the drowning victim of a suspicious accident. The investigators believed the corporal had been murdered when he was apparently about to expose the colonel and his aide, one Major Todder, for alleged black market activities, notably diversions of badly-needed medications intended for the weakened and ill Dutch population.

"Sergeant Timchuk attached himself to the three men, in particular Private Helmers who he found was increasingly receptive to suggestions of just retribution for the colonel and his associate. Helmers, I would postulate, began to envision an opportunity to create a sense of self-worth he had never felt before. And remember, he never had the opportunity to test his courage in battle. It is quite feasible to assume he began to think along these lines: If so little value was placed on his own worth, him blameless without sin or crime, why should someone, even if he was in high authority, get away with it? This one who debauched virgins, who stole away the lives of the sick and needy people in Holland, who set up the murder of his own driver. It was a stain on his rank, an insult to the boys who had fought and died in good faith. From there, it was a short leap to the evening of the sixth of July . . ."

"How did Private Helmers refer to his late commanding officer when he described him?"

"Several times he did refer to him as the 'devil' and as an 'evil bastard.' One can conjecture that internalized anger over a long period of time, from childhood and adolescence, could lead to paranoia or a delusional state."

"Then would you classify him as insane, if only temporarily, brought on by the extreme intensity of his feelings at the time?"

"That is one possible interpretation of his mental state at the time, yes."

"That's sufficient, Mr. Maxwell. The witness may stand down."

The president's eyes bulged; the Judge Advocate and the panel members seethed over revelations that had not hitherto surfaced in the admitted written statements or witness testimony. The prosecutor, Hazlet, not deterred, readied his demolition of the psychiatrist's findings as "cursory, speculative, and irrelevant."

"An unexpected loose cannon," grinned Bollock. "Do I see your hand in this? Solomon didn't pick up that stuff about the goings-on over there from Helmers. Not part of his program."

"Might've had a word or two," said Horobbins. "But it won't make any difference."

36

Queen Victoria had decreed that the grounds of her Aldershot residence, the Royal Pavilion, should be abandoned to the whims of nature. Off Farnborough Road, inside iron gates, shade trees, pine and fir amid wild bracken, purple foxglove, heather, and the inevitable rhododendrons did their best to camouflage what was now the officers' mess of Aldershot District headquarters, most Canadians long gone, to the relief of all.

"Great place for jungle warfare," said Horobbins from the back seat of Spotted Dick Clancy's Jeep.

"Or lumberjacks."

The other occupant of the back seat, Lieutenant Edgar Maxwell, managed a wan smile. Followed by Bollock in his black saloon, they took the carriage drive around to the goldfish pond that marked the north entrance of the sprawling bungalow with its white pinewood walls and green shutters. They had scooped up Maxwell temporarily to adopt him.

"He looks a right Charlie," Bollock had said as he smoked a Buckingham donated by Clancy, and noticed the officer standing alone on the steps of the calvary barracks, shunned by everyone else, disgusted with him for his last ditch defence of the hapless accused and his impugning of the reputation of the victim.

"Contrary to appearances," Maxwell had summed up, "this is not a simple open-and-shut case. I won't take the time of the court to review the testimony of witnesses whose statements must be taken with a grain of salt. It is obvious they have been offered inducements to be selective in memory. Such blandishments extend even to the accused, whose confession must be regarded with skepticism. Indeed, possession of the murder weapon has never been definitively traced to him. So suspicious is his convenient admission of guilt that we must ask ourselves: is he covering up for someone else? This seminal question has never been pursued.

"It still remains for the prosecution to prove beyond reasonable doubt, beyond a dubious confession, that Private Helmers actually pulled the trigger. Moreover, it still remains to be proven that if he did so he possessed the necessary *mens rea*, that is, guilty intent. This is an essential element missing in his conviction. Reasonable doubt remains here on those grounds alone, entirely aside from the accused's mental capacity or state of mind. The psychiatrist, granted he had little time for thorough analysis, has performed for us a fine service by explaining the pressures of wartime military life, even for non-combatants. He has described how a fragile personality prone to fantasy, self-delusion, and dissociation, might be moved to commit deeds he would not normally consider. Or, in fact, be led into confessing to a crime he didn't commit. I submit, gentlemen, that the court must remain open to reasonable doubt on two grounds: one, the unreliability of the witnesses and evidence, compounded by the untimely death of a potentially key witness; two, the mental condition of the accused.

"The basis for a proper judicial decision on reasonable doubt cries out for further investigation of the facts and obvious perjury committed here today by witnesses. There is a larger story here, one of corruption and betrayal of trust that points not to Private Helmers, who in all respects is an honest, exemplary soldier, but to the victim himself who must be seen as the true criminal. The only course open, given the unreliable testimony we have endured today, is to bring in the verdict of 'not guilty because of insanity.'"

The court was aghast. The Judge Advocate was furious. "Guilty act, guilty mind. Simple as that," he instructed them, a couple of whom showed vague discomfort.

Helmers was marched out. The five members of the court martial panel, without the JA to keep them honest, retired to the billiards room where they remained, surprisingly, for over forty-five minutes. But the few seeds of doubt sown by Maxwell and Solomon were not sufficient to derail the inevitable.

Guilty as charged: capital murder. Whereupon the prosecutor was asked to inform the court of the service record of the accused. Helmers tilted his head, the clerk checking out the file that listed his own service of drudgery. Maxwell's final plea for mercy was received in stony silence and not a few snorts from the spectators. Then the JA gathered up the court again for the billiards room where the sentence would be decided, and this time he went with them to ensure they understood there was no option on punishment. Not a squalid dispute among criminals, as in Rome, but premeditated murder of a senior office carried out with deadly efficiency.

The president read from the note prepared for him. "It is the verdict of this court that the death sentence be carried out. However, in accordance with instructions issued by the order-in-council of May 1944, the sentence will be referred to the cabinet in Ottawa for confirmation."

Witnesses and hangers-on spilled forth from the games room. Senior officers puffed to staff cars and sped off before the newshounds, lurking beyond the security barriers, could reach them. Dick Clancy hovered as Nolan and Montgomery were bundled into a fifteen hundred weight for return to Maida punishment. Helmers was given the luxury of a staff car, complete with an anxious padre, for the drive to Headley Downs and a solitary cell among the army's more flamboyant misfits. Gallantly, Clancy found a provost Jeep to take Corporal Evans and Captain Williams back to North Camp. Afterwards he told Horobbins of Claire's anger let loose on him, the nearest available target, and that in so doing she had implied a changed opinion of her slain lover.

"It's not fair. The poor soul doesn't deserve that."

As for Horobbins, he never had any occasion to see Claire Evans again. They were to go their separate ways on the roulette wheel of military whim. With Mavis fading from the scene, he probably daydreamed about the fragile beauty and courage of the corporal, her snappy brown eyes forever lodged in his memory, and, on that day, no doubt mused on her final words to Clancy who now switched to notions of comfort, the quick refuge of soldiers anywhere.

"Got signing privileges at the Pavilion. You're billeted there, Maxwell. Come along then, I'll stand drinks and dinner. Food over in the east wing tends to be a bit dicey, comes in from the kitchen by underground tunnel, then up in a lift. They do offer beef, even if somewhat congealed. Before D-Day Canadians were in profusion, still we managed to leave the place reasonably intact."

After quickly inhaled whiskies in the chintz-striped lounge, the group began to unwind. Maxwell, his lank blonde hair awry again, realized he had been abducted for a postmortem. At the moment the court was about to rise they had watched a courier deliver an envelope to the Judge Advocate who handed the only carbon copy to Maxwell. The prosecutor read the original, shook his head and silently returned the message to be passed around the panel. The president seemed about to rip it up until the JA handed him a paperclip for attachment to the written verdict. The paper was not read into the record.

"Let's have it, lad," said Bollock, too curious to rush back to London and his ailing wife.

"Your hospitality overwhelms me."

"That won't be all that overwhelms you if you don't cough up," said Clancy, his acne pits aglow as he regarded the young officer with the ferocity he had once applied to shoplifters in the department store.

Maxwell, loosened up by a second whisky without the benefit of a splash, grinned and brought forth the paper from his briefcase. "From the High Commissioner in London. Cable begging commutation of sentence for Helmers to life and his return to Canada. It's from one Diefenbaker of Saskatchewan."

"Red Indian palaver?" asked Bollock.

"Member of our parliament, noted for quixotic causes. The western province where Helmers comes from. Copies to Prime Minister, Minister of National Defence, and so on."

"Why would they back off?" Clancy asked. "They didn't before."

"Nazis go free, but we shoot a poor benighted soldier who believed he was committing an act of justice."

"You did your job," said Clancy. "Now come on, here in the lodge, do you truly hold that Helmers didn't knock off Colonel Wellesley? Forget about client privilege and that crap."

"Of course he did. The question is who really pulled the trigger. Who actually persuaded him to carry out his mission?"

"We know that."

"You sure?"

"We're just poor dumb cops here. What'd we miss, wiseguy?"

Edgar Maxwell, warming to a half-potted audience of three, resumed his apprentice courtroom manner.

"Hey, I'm not faulting your work. The fact your extensive investigations into Colonel Wellesley and associates were never revealed in court tells me you were leaned upon from on high. Am I wrong? The evidence presented against Helmers was a crock, and you know it. Solomon did open up Helmers to some extent, got him meandering off the screed he was supposed to follow, and I picked up a few things from my interviews with Nolan and Montgomery. They, too, wandered off the script at times."

"What script?"

"Come on, Captain Horobbins, you're a party to it. Limited as my time was, I began to wonder about Glen's good pals. I can't believe that Nolan and Montgomery, aided and abetted by the late Sergeant Timchuk, could persuade the passive, decent Helmers to actually go ahead and plug his CO. Think of the enormity. Sure they thought they had a foolproof plan, and it almost worked, but maybe, just maybe, that's not the answer."

"You're implying we did a rum job?" said Bollock.

"I say again, sir, not at all. Captain Horobbins dogged the trail to the Continent and followed up. Frankly, I'm amazed that your colleagues over there weren't called in to testify. That tells us something. In my humble opinion, gentlemen, you still haven't answered the question: Who gave Helmers the final shove?"

"He didn't need one. He was in cloud cuckoo land, the knight errant out to avenge injustice and do something useful for once."

"You accept that?"

"What else is there?"

"Well, as I pondered the whole setup, I began to zero in on two people who could've actually prodded Helmers into murder, who had the ability to persuade him it was not merely another living soul at the end of his Luger, but the personification of evil."

"He managed to arrive at that state himself."

"Let's have another round here," said Clancy. "Illuminate our abysmal ignorance, Maxwell."

"Look, the object of the whole exercise was to turn it into an act committed to save the honour of this Corporal Evans. Bit of a stretch, isn't it? I bet you were given your marching orders from on high to preserve the reputation of the Wellesleys and make sure none of his crimes ever came into the picture. I was hoping the psychiatrist would blow the whole thing wide open, but I was closed down. Now why don't we take another reading on the lovely Evans? Could she be one person who could've persuaded Helmers to do the deed?"

"Won't wash, Maxwell. At the time of the murder she was still nuts about the colonel."

"Tell me, Captain Horobbins, did you check out her medical records?"

"Why would we? She was under care for stress and exhaustion after her ordeal in London."

"I mean for VD." They gaped. "Suppose she'd picked up a dose from the colonel who wasn't exactly a monk. I bet she knew, despite her denials, that the pathetic Helmers mooned after her, and she must've seen Timchuk hanging around with Helmers and the other two. She could've picked up on their hatred for the colonel. No secrets around here, eh? So she finds she has the clap, goes to Helmers, and plants the idea of retribution against the colonel and maybe she'd bring herself to be nice to him. Enough to stiffen up Helmers, one might say, with an added reason to carry out Timchuk's plan. A hero on both counts."

"Farfetched, Maxwell. Knock it off."

"Is it? Pure as the driven snow but, oh, how she drifted."

"You don't know her the way we do, unless we've made a monumental misjudgment of character."

"It's a possibility."

"Leave the poor bint alone, she's been through enough," said Bollock. "Who's the second?"

"Captain Horobbins, remember at our first meeting I asked you about the colonel's Two IC, this Major Todder, and where he fit into the picture. You told me he took off after trying to do in Timchuk. You also repeated Todder's claim that he was clean, that Wellesley had cut him out of any more deals over here. Two things occurred to me. Todder must've resented being thrown off the gravy train, or he didn't care. He'd amassed enough ill-gotten loot from Holland and Belgium to keep him in clover for the rest of his natural, but there was one fly in the soup. Both he and the colonel had assumed the investigations on the Continent had been deep-sixed. The colonel had awesome connections. Todder didn't. Mistrust between the two must've been a factor, otherwise Wellesley wouldn't have insisted Todder be posted here as his Two IC, to keep an eye on him. Supposing Todder sees his boss's greed or craze for thrills running rampant again, dangerous stuff with the bigtime black market operators. It's only a matter of time till he gets snared again, this time with no second chance, so Todder decides to take off with his loot, yet if he is to disappear safely without a trace he has to do something about Wellesley. Can't have him spilling the beans. He sees the need to eliminate Wellesley. But how?"

"You're blowing smoke, Maxwell."

"Bright lad, even if somewhat daft," said Bollock.

"You won't deny Todder's a smart cookie. Your description of his cover as the fool upper crust dragoon is worthy of the Light Brigade idiots so revered here in Aldershot. Latches onto Helmers who does some steno work for him too. Senses something bothering the fat boy, probes quietly and picks up hints of deep grievances against the colonel—at first about Corporal Evans. Or he bribes his batman or another chairwarmer to find out more. You didn't winkle out that informer, did you?"

"Sure we did. This Blain, his batman, he smuggled the gun to Todder. We got him under wraps."

"After the fact, eh? Todder figures he's on to something, takes the trouble to call up fat boy's personnel records and finds the notation about his marksmanship. You sleuths check out the docket, who'd last drawn his file? Do I see a show of hands? No? Anyway, when Todder realizes this blind-as-a-bat tub of lard would make the perfect assassin, he puts on a big show of relating to Helmers in all confidence how it was Wellesley who arranged to bump off Timchuk's brother, not him. Feeds Helmers gin in his office. Your subjects ever comment on Helmers showing signs of drinking on the job? Maybe his bodily aura kept everyone beyond sniffing range. So given everything, Todder plants the idea it'd be a service to mankind if the colonel were to be on the receiving end of an act of true justice. If someone didn't, he'd get clean away with a fortune, even the murder of his driver over there, and for sure he'd drop the Evans woman like a hot potato, maybe even knock her up or leave her with a dose. Helmers goes away in a frenzy, broods, talks it out with his pals and this Sergeant Timchuk who's egging him on anyway. Helmers interprets Todder's musings as an order to do the job, and no doubt has been assured of full protection from prosecution. There'd be a foolproof plan, his pals could see to it. Who do you think opened up the back door for Helmers?"

"Todder was away in London. The colonel himself opened the door when he saw Helmers waving his notebooks."

"That's his story. All you have is when Todder logged in at the vehicle compound. He could've been here earlier."

"When I get home I'm thinking of going into law. Wouldn't want to run up against you in court," Horobbins said.

"You are? You're from Toronto? Here, I'll give you my father's name, senior partner in an illustrious firm of Bay Street sharpies. When you're ready for articles, get in touch, I'll drop him a note now. In the unlikely event I survive Japan, I'll be there ahead of you."

"Now see who's on the tit," said Bollock.

Horobbins blushed, a purplish tint emerging on his olive skin. "Back to earth, Maxwell. What's next?"

"I intend to lodge an appeal with the Court Martial Appeal Board and follow up on that MP Diefensomething's pleas."

"They'll put you on the next boat home, toot sweet," said Clancy.

"Better still, I'll have my thirty days leave, Dad can open doors in Ottawa. We'll go for commutation of the death sentence, get him sent home, do his stretch in a loony bin. If enough time passes on every appeal we can dream up, he may yet avoid the noose."

"It won't be the noose here. Firing squad," said Clancy.

"You're kidding."

"I can see Home Office having a bird," Bollock said. "Now that we have the wets in Labour, can you imagine the outcry if Canadians shoot one of your own on British soil after the war is over?"

"Shouldn't bother them. You've already wiped out six of ours," Clancy said.

"By hanging, duly convicted by jury, sentenced by judge. No, you'll have to spirit him over to the Continent where executions of collaborators and the like is an everyday occurrence."

"I hope we never get to that," Horobbins said, his blush replaced by a muddy sheen. The indigestion pangs had returned.

Maxwell glanced up when he recognized another officer from the Winnipegs standing with kit in the doorway.

"Bob, what brings you here?"

The two-pipper squinted around, his battledress bereft of campaign ribbons, his beret rolled under a shoulder strap, its badge polished once again when there were no lurking snipers, and his slicked blonde hair, with no low lank cowlick, leaving the impression that junior officers were chosen for Hollywood box office appeal. Another latecomer doomed to Occupation or quick demise on the coasts of Japan.

"Hullo, Edgar, what's up? Beached at Eindhoven air base for God knows how long. The CO had orders sent down from Occupation HQ who got them from here. Guess whose turn it was in the barrel. Brought along ten badly trained bodies and one ancient sergeant. Signal came in this morning from a Colonel Capson (is it?) to be here by One August, start our range work. God knows they need it. Doubt if any of 'em can aim straight. The exercise, I gather, a forgone conclusion. Nasty business."

"What is?"

"The court martial over yet? Guy who brought me here says he's big enough even my bunch can't miss. That dumb-ass who plugged the colonel. Firing squad. We're here for rehearsal."

37

In January 1946 Horobbins, back home taking pre-law at the University of Toronto in special classes with free tuition for vets based on time served, plus sixty dollars a month, was on St. George walking south from Bloor when he saw someone he knew. Like himself sporting veterans' chic, an issue greatcoat with unpolished buttons, the only civilian item a fur hat with earflaps against the cold. The overcoat was worn over a once-detested battledress blouse shorn of insignia, the dark outline of patches fraternity signs the initiated could decipher. The kids who, fresh out of high school, had to cram up near the vets in huge classes, often in an amphitheatre, sniffed distastefully at lingering barracks room smells, or worse.

It was his sergeant, Pearly Gates, his creases lifted in a grin. They went for a coffee in Hart House. Gates was in first year commerce and finance, a good fit with his eye for fine details and nits to pick, the one-time penitentiary guard turned embryo auditor. Gates told him he didn't get back until November, a tight squeeze to enroll for the January term.

"How come you stayed on?"

"One thing after another. Problems moving prisoners out of detention for transport back here. You left in a helluva hurry."

"I applied for discharge in September. Simple enough—she finally decided to stay with her returned mate. Maternal instincts or loyalty, perhaps. He was Fourteenth Army, in terrible shape, but there was family money apparently."

"Wins out every time. Listen, glad I ran into you. Did you hear about the *Cadiz*?"

"I don't keep in touch. What's the *Cadiz*?"

One of the last duties for Sergeant Pearly Gates was to be senior NCO on the provost escort for a group of Canadian soldiers under sentence for major crimes, the worst elements to be shipped home where jails awaited the hard cases. In due course, no doubt, they would be released to resume their criminal ways. Over three hundred, 317 to be exact, from Number One Canadian Detention Barracks would be herded aboard a stripped down Royal Navy escort carrier, the *Cadiz*, out of Southampton on the tenth of November, 1945. Five officers and eighteen NCOs shepherded the gang from Headley Downs near Grayshott, Sussex, on the shortest journey possible to prevent any more mass escapes, and did so with few problems. Yet they were edgy, apprehensive at handling the prisoners on a ship about to set forth on wintry seas. It cast a pall on thoughts of going home at last for discharge.

"And," Gates grinned, "guess who was among them? Glen Helmers. You saw the stuff coming through after the trial. Had the decision been made before you left? At any rate, this Diefenbaker and the Maxwells, who really did have connections in Ottawa, got through to the PM and cabinet. He was to be spared execution in Britain or on the Continent; instead to be sent home for disposition, maybe hanging, but maybe not. Once further appeals get under way he might well end up with life in the nut house and, I'd bet, a prime subject for parole—supposedly a harmless soul, as our Claire Evans would have put it—other than his one deadeye shot. He'd be the very model of sanity amid the afflicted."

"Did you know what happened to Claire?"

"Heard somewhere she went home for discharge in late August with the intention of looking up some fella out west. You were . . ."

"Yeah, I know. Go on."

Scrunched up in a corner of the railway carriage compartment, a handcuffed Glen Helmers had shrunk, his face pasty with sagging dewlaps. He didn't seem to recognize Gates. Just as well. The prisoners around him never spoke and instead nudged each other, practiced death stares, or glowered out of the windows at the lush countryside, once so ripe for plunder and mayhem.

In Southampton the carrier was alongside a pier overlooking the Ocean Dock, a huge tidal basin of more than fifteen acres where liners and troopships once had dropped anchor. Wartime bomb damage, remaining in heaps of rubble shiny in a cold drizzle, added to the gloom of the occasion. Then, on some pretext or arcane grievance, the dockworkers walked off to the local pubs, leaving the provost, sailors, and troops to load cartons, sacks of vegetables, slabs of meat onto cranes for the ship's hold. A bedraggled group of MPs, their usual spit and polish tarnished from unseemly labour, and some Service Corps types, sloppy anyway, were on hand to meet the train when it arrived. The prisoners were assembled on the dock ready to be marched aboard to improvised quarters on the hangar deck. Once it cleared the Isle of Wight the vessel hit rough seas, the swells heaved the bow up and crashed it down, sending squeals and shudders through the jerry-built Liberty ship, top heavy as a makeshift carrier. Bucket of bolts, Gates said, we feared the rivets would pop. Foul weather meant everyone stayed cooped up inside except for two smoke breaks a day on deck, passed up by retching addicts, Gates included.

Two days out of Halifax: a bombshell. The head count revealed one missing prisoner. Muster parade again confirmed 316 shorn skulls. What to do? The ship was ransacked. Where was he?

"'Jesus,' says Captain Stone, our senior provost officer sent from CMHQ, your replacement. Remember him? 'There'll be a Court of Inquiry in Halifax. We'll be tied up till the next war. Everybody wants to get home and we want to offload this lot, no fuss, no muss, right?'"

Gates, searching for a known face, finally overcame his lurching stomach, woke up, and personally inspected each prisoner. As he dreaded, the missing one was Glen Helmers.

"This one's special," Gates informed the ship's captain and Stone, in private. "Be hell to pay, he's the one who shot that colonel in Aldershot."

"Wasn't there a head count when we embarked?"

"Yes, sir, but something may have happened between the head count and actual boarding, what with the problems of loading, confusion, pickup gangs milling around. Or he did make it on board and someone pushed him over the side. Or he jumped himself. Any of the above."

"You sure he isn't hiding somewhere on board? We can't find him we're in deep shit. Let me see the nominal roll."

Captain Stone contemplated the sheets, flipped them over several times, sighed. "Sergeant, there's no hope of finding him aboard?" He took out a fountain pen and was about to strike a line through the name of Helmers, and initial and date the six copies, when some inner caution prevailed. "We have to assume that somehow there was an error in the first count. The men you've interviewed deny ever seeing him on board, right? We'll signal Six Company detachment in Southampton to make a search and enlist the local police. He might've jumped ship on the docks. For all practical purposes we must assume he was never on this tub. You knew him by sight, I need your confirmation that you never did see him here."

"Correct, sir, but I've been somewhat under the weather, not up to scratch, I guess."

"Understood. We've all been tossed about." Captain Stone himself had a greenish tinge, not from gathering moss. "You're absolutely positive?"

"Had no reason to, sir. The ones I've talked to on the hangar deck have done little else but groan and whine in their hammocks. Nobody owns up to seeing him."

"Most extraordinary," said the Royal Navy skipper. "Before you go about striking him off the roster, I'll turn every rating loose on another search."

The battered carrier finally docked in Halifax where the officer commanding 33 Provost Company, not noticing anything amiss, duly signed for 316 prisoners and packed them off under escort to assorted detention centres. The ship's provost contingent, including Pearly Gates, quickly made themselves scarce as they headed off to their home depots for discharge.

Not until the member of parliament, John Diefenbaker, made inquiries of the Department of National Defence did the pennies begin to drop. The killer of Colonel Wellesley could not be located. Where is he? demanded the politician, wagging a finger at the puzzled front bench. Not a clue, stunned brass in the offices of the Provost Marshall and Judge Advocate General had to confess.

Myself and Captain Stone were tracked down and summoned to Ottawa, Pearly Gates told Horobbins. This was mid-December. The Southampton detachment of Six Company, since returned to London, reported having received a signal from the *Cadiz* requesting a search for Helmers. With scanty manpower, low motivation, and zero interest on the part of local police, the unit reported no results. The prisoner wouldn't exactly have been invisible unless he had outside assistance, the duty officer suggested on the message pad. Stone was duly reprimanded for striking out the missing soldier's name from the nominal roll. Such was the general unwinding, a climate of forgetting and the hell with it, that no further effort was made to find the answer. Mr. Diefenbaker tried to arouse the Press and, given that investigative journalism on that side of the pond was still in its infancy and wartime constraints lingered, he did manage to instigate a "Where is colonel's slayer?" wire story out of the Canadian Press bureau in Ottawa. So prompted, National Defence eventually issued a statement admitting that Private Glen Helmers was missing, presumably at sea. An information officer at the department let it drop they assumed the prisoner had jumped off the troopship, either to commit suicide in remorse for his heinous crime, or was taken care of by other inmates. To trace every man of the more than three hundred on the ship was a task beyond the limited post-war resources of the department, even if so inclined. No further inquiries would be made. Ottawa's agitation over the gaffe was soon overcome by an abiding sense of relief that they would not have to deal with the ultimate fate of Private Glen Helmers.

"And," resumed Gates, while Horobbins pondered if he should call him "Pearly" or something more fitting for a civilian, "I am, I have to admit, consumed with guilt."

"What in heaven's name for?"

"Well, I kept my mouth shut when maybe I should've told Captain Stone what I saw that day, or rather, who I saw. You can picture the shambles, the dockworkers off the job, bodies everywhere milling or hanging about, and, okay, it was nothing more than a quick impression, but the more I think about it I'm sure my hunch was right. We do get 'em in our line of work, eh? The fact is, one fellow caught my eye and struck a note somehow. I remember him, tall, in a tweed cloth cap and green jacket; seemed to be a foreman or someone in management. At that time the SUS, the soldiers under sentence, were in wavering clumps, groups watched over by our men, then I saw this gent in tweeds point his finger. Two navvies in coveralls went up to one of the prisoners, but before I could make out who he was, my attention was taken with a scuffle between two detainees nearby. The escorts converged to break up the disturbance. When I looked up again the tall guy in tweeds was gone as were the two guys in coveralls, whoever they were. Occupied by the dust-up under our noses, we didn't take roll call again. Captain Stone ordered us to march the SUS onto the ship soonest, keep that lot under control, which we did.

"Yet, as I recalled the incident, sick as a dog as I was on that damned ship, I began to get shivers. The moustache was missing, his hair was black, the bearing not so straight, his clothing no longer spiffy, but I knew down here in my gut who it was. The major."

"You mean Todder?"

"It was him, all right. Why he was down in Southampton or how he found out about the transfer of prisoners, I have no idea. Must've had some kind of network he could plug into, maybe bribed guards at Headley Downs. Who knows? You thinking what I'm thinking?"

"That's the moment Helmers went missing, before he ever got on the carrier. He must've pointed out Helmers to his goons, paid a couple of guys to make the disturbance, whipped him away, right under your nose. But why go to all that trouble, come over from Ireland or wherever he is, even with changed appearance? Crazy stunt if I've ever heard of one."

"Maybe it makes sense to him. You told me about the go-round you had after the court martial with young Maxwell who had this idea that Todder may've set up Helmers to dispose of his boss. Thieves falling out, the Duke with the inside dope on Todder might blab if he was ever picked up and worked over. Helmers was the only one left who could actually finger Todder, and it was a short jump for our fine major to conclude that he had to be taken out, just in case he was persuaded to spill the whole story with promises of clemency and the like. He might even have picked up some clues about Todder's escape plan."

"Good try, but Todder covered himself, took off when he realized things were about to close in on him after his grilling in London. Nobody's ever tracked him down. The British agents in the Republic were called off. And suddenly he turns up on the docks, large as life in plain daylight. Well, your good work as usual. . . ." Horobbins still couldn't decide what to call his former sergeant and hoped he hadn't reverted to officer-speak.

"Yeah, but I missed it. Too much going on, I guess."

"Don't blame yourself. Doesn't matter now. Still."

"All we can hope for is that they finished him off fast. He was a nice young fella, despite what he did. Compared to the others. . . ."

Horobbins sat back and visualized a weighted globule of pale suet dropping to the floor of the Irish Sea, perhaps to be snagged on the mast of a sunken freighter, a similar fate to the one that had befallen Corporal Orest Timchuk in Holland. The gilled residents would stir. And he imagined the parents, alone now in the small empty bungalow near the CPR tracks in Sutherland. The Depression refugees, the unwanted relatives who had so tormented Glen Helmers would be long gone, having driven him out to the dubious haven of the army; the other siblings would be away to parlay their good looks into a post-war prosperity their fat brother would never see. At the end of the street the blood-darkened grain elevator would be a barrier to views of endless prairie stubble, or perhaps a monument, and the white birches in the front yard would be brittle with ice over powdery snow covering the yellow medallions of small leaves on the ground.

Acknowledgments

This is historical fiction based on events in the summer of 1945 when Canadian troops actually did lay waste to downtown Aldershot. The murder of a Canadian senior office is fiction, as are most of the characters, including Wellesley, Todder, Horobbins, Bollock, Evans, and many others. Some of the higher echelons, Spry and Cameron, to name two, are based on real people, and I hope by inventing their dialogue for the sake of the story it reflects properly the views and decisions they would have been likely to take. The details of military "culture" are mostly based on my own army service.

Many acknowledgments are due to individuals, working in libraries and archives, who made the novel possible by providing facts and historical perspective to the author's own experiences and memories. Any errors, of course, are mine. From Ottawa: The Canadian War Museum, Historical Research and Development Branch; The National Archives of Canada, Government Archives and Records Disposition (Military Archives, Record Group 24); Department of National Defence, Directorate of History and Heritage. From Toronto: The Royal Canadian Military Institute Library; The Ontario Ministry of the Solicitor General, The Centre of Forensic Sciences; the Toronto Reference Library and various lending branches.

Of the many individuals who went out of their way to help, I want to express special thanks to J. L. Granatstein (then Director & CEO), Dean Oliver and Serge Durflinger, The Canadian War Museum; Ann Skene Melvin (d. Apr. 2003) and Arthur G. Manvell, librarians of the fine collection at the Royal Canadian Military Institute, Toronto, and Jean Portugal whose Vol. III of the *We Were There* series, published by the RCMI, provided details about the CWAC; Captain (N) C. Fred Blair, Canadian Forces (ret'd) formerly of the office of The Judge Advocate General, Canada, who provided invaluable guidance on military law; Finn Nielsen (ret'd 2001) Firearms Examiner, Ontario Centre of Forensic Sciences; Andrew Horrall, Military Archivist, National Archives of Canada, Ottawa; Major Irvine Scarlett, Canadian Forces (ret'd) formerly RCEME. And, of course, my family, notably my wife, Alys, and Paul Earley, who reviewed earlier drafts. Warm thanks to my literary agent, Beverley Slopen, to Ruth Linka and crew at NeWest Press, and to my editor, Harry Vandervlist, University of Calgary, whose hometown is Aldershot—Ontario.

As to published sources, the official histories published by the Department of National Defence, Ottawa, especially the volumes by the late Colonel C. P. Stacey, formed the basis for much of the book. Many other histories and memoirs of the war were consulted and are listed below.

Despite the above, I must mention the following histories that I relied upon to verify facts, events, descriptive material, and to straighten out my own memories.

Watchdog, A History of the Canadian Provost Corps, by Colonel Andrew R. Ritchie (d. Feb. 2002) The Canadian Provost Corps Association, Canada, 1995 (the Association disbanded in June 2000), along with documents from the National Archives, provided details on locations of provost units and their actions during the war. The last chapter of this novel is a fictionalized account of an actual episode described by Col. Ritchie, the time and place changed for the sake of the story. In reality, the missing soldier on the transport was never found.

In addition to general works about southern England, two histories provided specific information on the Aldershot area. *The Story of Aldershot, A History of the Civil and Military Towns*, by Howard N. Cole, Southern Books, UK, 1980, updated from the 1951 edition, oddly enough never refers to the July 1945 riots. They are mentioned in *Aldershot's Canadians in Love and War, 1939–45* by Mark Maclay, APPIN Publications, UK, 1997, an excellent account of our times in the area.

As to background on crime and police in Britain, three histories in particular have provided background material which has been fictionalized for this story: *Crime in Wartime, A Social History of Crime in World War Two*, by Edward Smithies, Allen and Unwin, UK, 1982; *Strictly Murder, Famous Cases of the Scotland Yard Murder Squad*, by Tom Tullet, Bodiley Head, UK, 1979, and *Famous Stories of the Murder Squad*, by Leonard Gribble, Arthur Barker, Ltd., UK, 1974.

When I was involved in Ontario Liberal Party politics there were still old-timers around who regaled us with tales of the "Hepburn Era" of the 1930s and 1940s. However, for accuracy's sake I have consulted one biography of the premier: *Mitch Hepburn*, by Neil McKenty, McClelland & Stewart, Canada, 1967. The description of the premier's hotel suite is adapted from the book, in turn quoted from an article in *Saturday Night* magazine.

Winston Churchill's outrage at the Aldershot riots, as recorded in Arthur Bryant's *Triumph in the West,* Collins, UK, 1959, has been embellished. The subsequent "entry" in Brooke's diary is fiction.

Battle exhaustion and related issues are adapted from *Official History of the Canadian Medical Services,* Vol.II, by W. R. Feasby, DND, 1953, Can., and *Battle Exhaustion: Soldiers and Psychiatrists in the Canadian Army, 1939–1945* by Terry Copp and Bill McAndrew, McGill-Queen's University Press, 1990, Can.

A latecomer to my research appeared in the fall of 2002. *A Keen Soldier, The Execution of Second World War Private Harold Pringle,* by Andrew Clark, Alfred A. Knopf, Toronto, has provided more background on the soldier shot by firing squad in Italy, in July 1945.

A complete list of sources is available on the NeWest Press website, WWW.NEWESTPRESS.COM

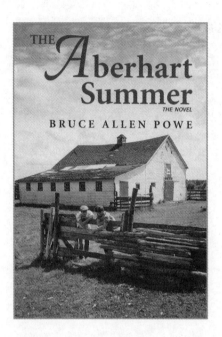

The Aberhart Summer: The Novel
Bruce Allen Powe

It is the summer of 1935, and while young Doug Sayers is spending the summer going to the movies and sneaking cigarettes, and his friend Babe Roothe is discovering women, William Aberhart and the Social Credit Party are promising twenty-five dollars a month for everyone in Alberta. Babe's mysterious death is the first in a chain of bizarre events, freak thunderstorms, and political intrigue.

"A sweetly nostalgic comedy and a cracking-good murder mystery, all rolled up into one big, bright ball of theatrical energy and verve."

—*Calgary Herald*

Books by Bruce Allen Powe

The Aberhart Summer
The Ice Eaters
The Last Days of the American Empire
Killing Ground: The Canadian Civil War
Expresso '67

Born in Edmonton, Alberta in 1925, **B r u c e   A l l e n   P o w e** dropped out of high school to serve in the Canadian Army from 1943-45. In *Aldershot 1945*, Powe draws on his experiences as a young soldier in World War II. On veteran's credits he earned both his BA and MA in Economics from the University of Alberta. During his career Powe worked for the federal government and held jobs in public relations and advertising until 1990 when he started his own corporate writing company. Despite a hectic working life, Powe has published five novels including *The Aberhart Summer: The Novel* and *The Ice Eaters*. A proud father and grandfather, Powe now makes his home in Toronto, Ontario.